"WE'RE NOT HIGH ENOUGH!"

Quint spoke so calmly that Hannah lifted her head to look forward quite slowly. When she saw the cliffs this time, she gasped. He was right. If they kept going as they were they would be dashed into that solid white face with the same deadly force as the breakers crashing against the cliffs.

Hannah glanced up at the balloon's silver silk above and saw the flags on the ropes flapping wildly in the wind. From what she could guess, they would reach the cliff in fifteen minutes or less, and they needed a lift of at least another three feet to clear the summit.

"Hannah." Quint's voice was still calm. "We don't have anything else to send over."

Hannah narrowed her eyes at the approaching wall. This was no way to die, no way for an adventure like this to end.

"We have our clothes," she said.

SKYLARK

ELANE OSBORN

CHARTER/DIAMOND BOOKS, NEW YORK

SKYLARK

A Charter/Diamond Book/published by arrangement with the
author

PRINTING HISTORY
Charter/Diamond edition/November 1990

ISBN: 1-55773-410-0

Charter/Diamond Books are published by The Berkley Publishing
Group, 200 Madison Avenue, New York, New York 10016.
The name ''CHARTER/DIAMOND'' and its logo are trademarks
belonging to Charter Communications, Inc.

PRINTED IN THE UNITED STATES OF AMERICA

10 9 8 7 6 5 4 3 2 1

Chapter 1

Quinton Blackthorne signed his name to the bottom of the document with a determined flourish. Setting his lips in a firm line, he dipped his pen into the ink and added the numeral III behind his name, followed by "Sixth Earl of Chadwick, St. Albanswood, June 23, 1895."

Quint's lean fingers tightened on the barrel of the pen as he stared down at the piece of paper that would ensure the future of the Blackthorne name, and seal his fate. With a sigh, he placed the pen in its holder, got slowly to his feet, and crossed to the large mullioned window to his left.

His gaze skimmed over the sloping green lawn to watch the pale light of dawn seep through the fog hanging over the forest separating his land from that of Squire Summerfield. His dark green eyes narrowed as he gazed at the outermost trees, less than a hundred yards from Blackthorne Hall, then shifted to study the draperies that hung on either side of the long window.

The green velvet sagged on the rods, and large patches of nap had been worn away, leaving paler patches to stain the once rich fabric. Quint tightened his jaw and returned his gaze to the blurred lines of the forest as he raked impatient fingers through the unruly black waves falling onto his forehead.

"You've signed the agreement?" a crisp feminine voice asked.

Quint nodded without turning.

"And now you're weighing the worth of the trade, are you, my boy?"

The barest hint of hesitation in his grandmother's low voice made Quint turn slowly. Lady Evelyn, the Countess of Chadwick, stood between the open door and his massive mahogany desk. She was dressed in the stark black she had worn ever since her husband's death twenty-four years earlier. The severe line of her dress was broken by a narrow belt that accentuated the still small waist separating her full hips and ample bust. Her granite-gray hair was drawn back from a square face that the pull of time had softened slightly.

Lady Evelyn possessed a starched, noble bearing despite her seventy-one years and the silver-tipped black cane she grasped in her left hand. Deep vertical lines framed the woman's pursed lips as her gray-green eyes peered through oval spectacles at Quint.

After examining her grandson's shabby brown jacket and the tan breeches tucked into worn leather boots, Lady Evelyn looked back up to meet Quint's dark green gaze. His black brows were lowered in their habitual frown, but she could see no regret in their depths.

I've done well by him, she thought. Succeeded where I failed with his father.

Even as this thought crossed her mind, she saw Quint glance over his shoulder to look once more at the forest. His lean features softened into the look of a lost young boy, an expression that made her want to comfort him the way she had her son.

Guilt pierced her breast as she studied her dark-haired grandson. Tall, lean, and broad-shouldered with the handsome aristocratic features his father had lacked, he looked every bit his title. But at what cost? Lady Evelyn let her eyes shift past Quint to stare at the mist-enshrouded woods. She knew all about the fanciful stories Quint's empty-headed mother had told him, was aware of the solitary games he'd played beneath those shadowy branches before he was forced, far too young, into the position of earl.

As the twisting ache in her chest deepened, Lady Evelyn straightened her shoulders and tightened her jaw. The past was unimportant. It was the future she was concerned about, and she needed to know how Quint felt about this betrothal. She suspected that if he'd had any choice at all in the matter, he would never have agreed to the contract.

And if there had been any other way, she'd never have suggested it, but both of them had learned to put personal considerations aside in their battle to restore what his father had gambled away. It was best to leave things as they stood.

"I see you are dressed for the outdoors," she said as she tapped her way across the threadbare Oriental carpet to his side. "Are you going to examine your acquisition before the pact is sealed?"

The countess's voice was low, her tone even. Quint turned slowly to face her. His grandmother's eyes held his with calm determination, and Quint felt the muscles in his stomach tighten as he replied, "The *pact,* as you so delicately put it, was binding the moment I signed it, as you well know, Grandmother."

Lady Evelyn blinked once behind her glasses. Instantly regretting the sharpness of his tone, Quint forced his lips to curve into a half-smile as he spoke. "And none too soon. The old place is falling apart before our eyes."

He watched his grandmother's gaze shift to the very curtains Quint had been examining, and he saw an expression of pain tighten her features. Then, just as quickly, her face softened. The faraway look in her eyes was one with which

Quint was most familiar, a sign that she had been transported mentally to the past, when her husband kept Blackthorne Hall in the manner worthy of his beloved wife, the daughter of a marquess, before their only son came along to dissipate a fortune that had taken four generations to build.

The burden of obligation deepened within Quint's chest. He reached over to take his grandmother's dry, wrinkled hand in his long fingers as he spoke quietly, "With Cicely's dowry we'll have the Hall completely restored within the year, just as you remember it."

The countess blinked, then looked up to the man towering above her. Her lips tightened slightly as she frowned and nodded briskly. "You'll be thirty-one next October. It's time you took another wife. All the pains we've taken to restore the Hall will be for naught if you don't sire an heir."

Quint's brows quirked up slightly. "There's always Parker, you know."

"I hardly consider your brother a suitable heir to Blackthorne Hall. He displays far too many of your father's traits." Her gray-green eyes narrowed. "I'm afraid I haven't been any more successful in instilling a sense of responsibility in him than I was with my son. And I never will be, as long as he continues to spend so much time with Hartley Summerfield, drinking in the pub, running around London, and racing balloons and horses."

"Grandmother, we've hardly given Parker a chance to do anything else." Quint spoke softly, his brows dropping to a deep scowl. "Parker was too young when Father died to have any real memory of what the man's drinking and gaming had brought us to."

Lady Evelyn glanced sharply at the draperies. "I should think that would have been obvious."

Quint shook his head. "Oh, he sees the result, but he has little memory of the cause. He only remembers the pain of losing the man he loved." Quint paused and sighed.

"And I'm afraid Parker's association with Hartley can be laid directly at my feet. If I'd made more time for my brother, he wouldn't have had to turn to Summerfield for companionship."

"Don't." Lady Evelyn laid a hand on Quint's arm. "You've done what needed to be done, and you've done it well. And Parker's friendship with Hartley is really of no consequence. What *is* important is that Cicely is nothing like her brother." She paused and went on in a soft voice. "She'll make a good wife for you, quiet and reserved. She loves children, and I think she'll come to care for the Hall as we do."

Quint gazed into his grandmother's eyes. He could almost hear her unspoken assurance that Cicely wouldn't be like his first wife or like his mother. On the tail of that thought, the sound of whimsical, lighthearted laughter echoed through time to tease his memory. He took his hand from between his grandmother's and turned to gaze out the window as the older woman spoke again.

"And of course your marriage to Cicely will return the forest to us." His grandmother's voice quavered uncertainly. When Quint turned around, he saw her lips ease into a tight smile. "Once the papers are delivered to the squire, he will arrange for half the girl's dowry to be transferred to you immediately. Perhaps we can restore the master suite before the wedding."

Quint met his grandmother's level gaze, understanding her perfectly. They were partners, had been ever since Quint's sixteenth birthday, when his father's death left the family in near poverty.

Together he and Lady Evelyn had faced a huge estate that cried out in need of repair wherever he turned, and they had been forced to make one difficult decision after another. Blackthorne Hall was stripped of the best of its furnishings. These items were then transported to the town house in

London, to enable the family to realize some profit from renting it out each Season. Quint had reluctantly sold off his father's stable of prize horses and given up all hope of attending Oxford. Being the Sixth Earl of Chadwick was going to take all of his attention and energy.

By the time he was twenty-one Quint had managed to improve the output of his tenant farmers so that both they and the Blackthornes were realizing profits. Still, the land and Blackthorne Hall cried out for repairs and improvements. Only with a large sum of money could he return Blackthorne Hall to its former glory and provide for future generations.

"Actually, nothing official has been announced." The countess's voice broke into Quint's thoughts. "You can destroy the contract and call this off yet today if you so choose. I know you aren't in love with the girl."

Quint turned to stare into his grandmother's eyes for a moment, then shook his head. "Cicely's father has asked half of London down to the betrothal party. To back out now would for no good reason destroy our place in society completely. Besides, it will be just as you said. Cicely will fill the position of my wife admirably. She isn't silly, like so many young women, or ambitious, and she certainly is not frivolous. She'll take well to the quiet life we lead."

Again a look passed between grandmother and grandson, along with unspoken memories of two women who had been too merry and too undisciplined to embrace life in the country for long.

The countess nodded slowly, then gestured toward the window. "Well, unless I've misread your clothing, I think you were planning to visit *our* forest before you set about your duties today. Why don't you take your rifle? It's been fifteen long years since your father signed the woods over to Squire Summerfield. I would very much enjoy tasting one of our pheasants again."

* * *

Once Quint was inside the woods, the gray mist closed about him like the welcoming arms of an old friend. The musty scent of moss and the acrid smell of rotting wood teased his memory as the forest played a familiar refrain. Quint held his breath, listening to the trill of a warbler followed by the sharp popping sound of a nuthatch cracking open a meal, underscored by the soft song of the small brook murmuring over rocks at his feet.

Quint glanced down to see that lacy ferns still grew along the banks of the narrow stream, providing homes for creatures like the buff-colored rabbit that gazed up at him with chocolate eyes before turning in a flash of white to disappear behind the curtain of green.

In a clear spot on the other side of the brook, between the twisted roots of an old beech tree, a circle of mushrooms grew out of the loamy earth. A fairy ring, his mother would have said. And he would have believed her.

Quint frowned, as against his will he recalled the stories his mother had filled his young head with, tales of fairies meeting in the mists, holding banquets, dancing and cavorting over roots and around bushes. He shut his eyes and fought down the old pain. His mother had been full of fanciful stories, accenting them with her tinkling laughter and smiling eyes. And he'd believed everything she told him, especially when she said she loved him.

Quint's eyes flew open. Lies, only lies. A mother who cared wouldn't have run off to France with another man. He didn't believe that she had loved him any more than he believed fairies danced in a circle beneath that beech tree.

Tension knit Quint's brow as he began to walk again. As he stepped forward he let his gray-green surroundings soothe him. His stained leather boots trod silently on the soft ground as his tall, lean form bent forward to duck beneath the overhanging branches of a willow.

To his right stood two huge elms. Their limbs twisted upward to disappear into the mist, bearing leaves heavy with dew that fell in a constant, almost imperceptible patter. Above the sound of the dripping water, Quint heard a scraping sound, followed by the soft echo of lilting laughter.

Quint stopped and listened to the early-morning whispers, straining to hear the sounds again. His rifle rode easily in the crook of his left arm, barrel pointed downward. His dark green eyes narrowed in concentration as he held his breath. When the soft rustling sound reached Quint's ears once more, he stepped forward slowly, ducking to keep his brown plaid cap from being brushed off by another low limb. He hesitated for a moment when he reached a tall hedge. He studied it a moment, then reached forward to the almost hidden opening, parted the tiny intertwined twigs with one hand, and passed through the narrow, prickly gap.

Quint tugged his left sleeve free of the grasping branches, stepped into a clearing, took two long strides, then came to a stop before a small pond that spread out within an enclosure of bushes that were tinged a soft gray-green by the engulfing haze.

An ancient stone bridge arched over the misty surface of the water not ten feet from where Quint stood. It was there that his gaze was drawn, for sitting in the very center of the bridge was a wood nymph, busy with her early morning toilet.

Quint Blackthorne was no longer given to flights of fancy. His well-developed sense of logic made him scoff at this impression of the slender female form, arrayed in a cloak of misty gray, features hidden by the honey-gold hair that fell in a rippling mass as she bent forward over the water.

But Quint resisted the clamor of reason for the moment, as his mother's voice echoed softly out of the past, whispering of elves and fairy princesses. More than once as a lad he had made secret early morning forays into these woods, hoping to see just such a sight as this one. Now his heart beat quickly as he stared at the figure on the bridge. He stood, bemused, as the creature before him lifted her hands. He watched silently as her slender fingers began to gather the thick golden waves, twist them slowly, then knot them into a gilded rope atop her head.

Quint could see her face now. Her skin was pale, almost translucent. Her profile revealed a small, straight nose, high cheekbones, and a sharply angled jaw. Quint watched her silently, hardly breathing. She held the glittering mass atop her head with one hand as the other took a silver comb from the folds of gray in her lap and lifted it to the twisted crown.

A second later the coiled mass escaped her grasp and tumbled down to her waist again, falling once more like a curtain over her features.

"Blast!"

The oath, uttered in a soft, feminine voice, echoed across the water. The corners of Quint's mouth lifted in a slight smile as the rational part of his mind claimed its victory. This is what you get for thinking about shirking your responsibilities, the voice of logic mocked. Fanciful illusions and phantom mirages.

Quint frowned at the quiet voice. Yes, it was true that he'd stared at the betrothal contract long and hard before signing his name. He had no desire to marry anyone, for he knew the promise of love and security that came with marriage to be the cruelest of illusions. But he'd been reared with a sense of duty, and marry Cicely Summerfield he would.

However, for these few moments that the mists swirled about him to shut out the rest of the world, Quint wanted to forget responsibility, ignore the voice of logic, and enjoy the fantasy that he was viewing something magical and otherworldly.

The figure on the stone bridge tossed her head, and the

silken curtain of hair drifted over her shoulder. Once more her slender fingers captured the threads that glimmered dark gold within the silver mist. Again she twisted her hair into a thick rope, coiled it into a loose knot atop her head, and forced the silver comb into the thick, burnished roll. Slowly her hands moved away from her head. Quint saw her lips curve, then watched as the coil loosened and the wavy locks tumbled rapidly to her slender waist.

"Blast again!"

Quint smiled widely at her impatience, then spoke before it occurred to him how much this might startle her. "Excuse me, miss," he said. "Might I be of assistance?"

Hannah Bradley jumped as Quint's deep tones shattered the morning silence. She swiveled around, her heart racing. Her gaze skimmed the misty surface of the pond, stopped at the sight of mud-spattered brown boots, then moved upward past tan breeches that fit snugly over long, leanly muscled thighs to the brown tweed jacket and waistcoat.

It was then that she saw the rifle the man held cradled in one arm. Hannah caught her breath, then lifted her eyes more slowly, staring at the dark blue tie knotted in the center of his high white collar for a moment before finally raising her gaze farther to study the man's face.

Thick black hair framed features that were sharply drawn. The man's jaw was lean and firm; his blunt chin showed the hint of a cleft, and his nose was short and narrow. The slender black brows that arched over his eyes like the wings of a gull were lowered in a scowl over dark green eyes that stared openly at Hannah, while his full, well-formed lips were twisted into a bemused smile.

The smile made Hannah breathe a little more easily, relax her numb fingers from the small fists that had formed as she continued to stare at the man. With the wisps of fog swirling around his lean form, he appeared to have stepped out of the film of gray behind him, like some prince stepping out of enchanted mists in a childhood tale. For one brief moment she entertained the thought that he was just such a figure, come to whisk her away from her wicked uncle.

Just then a magpie called to its mate in the trees behind her, and Hannah blinked away her fantasy. There was nothing cruel or wicked about her uncle, she told herself. Squire Summerfield was simply overbearing and pompous. And the man before her could not possibly be a prince. Although his features were decidedly aristocratic, his worn brown jacket, faded plaid cap, muddied boots, and rifle told her he was not a member of the gentry. Most likely he was employed by her uncle, his gamekeeper perhaps. He was probably looking for poachers.

That is, she thought, unless *he* is a poacher.

Hannah stared again at the man's lopsided smile, her heart pounding with renewed fear. Yet she saw no threat in the way one corner of his mouth tilted up and the other down. When she lifted her eyes to his, she saw only amusement beneath his half-frown. She felt compelled to stare into those dark green eyes and for several moments did just that, conscious only of their warm expression and the continued pounding of her heart.

A bird fluttering in the branches overhead made Hannah blink and force her bemused mind to think. The man had asked her a question, had wanted to know if she needed his help. And since she'd managed to get herself lost, she certainly did need that. Slowly she let her lips curve as she nodded. "Yes, sir. I could very definitely use some assistance."

Quint had been studying the young woman's face as she sat staring silently at him with large violet-blue eyes that reminded him of the wood hyacinths that grew along the path in the forest. Her finely boned face was angular, with high, wide cheekbones that narrowed down to a pointed

chin, the sharp lines softened by the roundness of her eyes
and the full curve of her pink-tinged lips.

Now that she had spoken, Quint could smile at his fanciful
thoughts. She was most definitely real, though very different
from any other woman he'd ever met. Even her speech
carried an unusual accent. As he continued to gaze at her,
he saw her dusky eyes widen. Remembering his offer to
help, he began walking toward the bridge, stepping carefully
along the mossy shore of the pond.

Hannah's eyes were drawn to the power in his well-
formed legs as he moved forward with strong, smooth
strides. She lifted her head and noted how tall the man was,
how broad were his shoulders, and her muscles tightened
as she began to doubt the wisdom of accepting aid from
this stranger. More than once she'd been cautioned against
being impulsive in her judgment of other people, and now
with the mist wrapping itself around the man's ankles as he
neared the edge of the bridge where she sat, a cold flame
of fear flickered to life within her stomach.

The heel of his boot echoed loudly as he stepped onto
the stone surface, and the icy fire blazed to life, sending
chills skittering through Hannah's slight form. When his
second heel struck the gray flint, bringing him to within a
foot of her, Hannah's heart thudded to a stop and she was
gripped by a sudden need to escape. She stood with such
swiftness that her shoulder caught him under the elbow
cradling the rifle, forcing his arm upward and sending the
gun arcing out over the water.

It fell with a loud splash that was scarcely noticed by
either Hannah or Quint. The force of their clash had thrown
both of them off balance, and now they rocked wildly on
the narrow bridge, battling to keep from plunging into the
cold water below.

After a few moments Quint gained control over his swaying form and managed to draw himself up to his full height

as he steadied himself. When he glanced at the girl, he saw that her arms were still flailing wildly as she tottered on the edge of the bridge. Her gray cape fluttered about her, parting down the middle to reveal a simple lavender frock that skimmed over her small form as she fought to keep from falling.

In one swift motion Quint gathered her into his arms and drew her to him. Within seconds he knew that this was no child he held. Though the top of her head was several inches beneath his chin and the form pressed to his was slender, he could feel the swell of firm breasts pressing against his lower ribs, and the soft curve of her hips beneath his hands spoke of the maturity of womanhood.

His sensitive fingers encountered neither boning nor the stiff buckram of a corset, only the titillating heat of soft skin beneath the thin cotton. Quint took a quick breath, drawing in the soft scent of lilac, and for one moment he grew dizzy and had to fight to keep from losing his equilibrium once again.

Hannah clung to the man's shirtfront as a drowning person might grasp at the relative safety of a floating log. Though she was still tense with fear, a portion of her mind registered the feel of firm thighs brushing against hers and the hard contours of his chest beneath the crisp fabric she clung to. She was aware, too, of the heat seeping from his body into hers as the cold, numbing mist chilled her back.

Hannah forced herself to take a deep, steadying breath. Her senses were filled with the clean scent of the starched shirt and the musty smell of the forest blended with a deeper, musky essence she couldn't place. The warmth radiating from this man started a strange sensation churning in her stomach even as her mind warned her of danger. As her head stopped spinning, Hannah's earlier fears of the man once more invaded her mind. She opened her hands to press them against the solid wall of chest.

The chill of her small hands passed through the fabric of Quint's shirt. He glanced down to see the fey creature gazing up at him, her violet-blue eyes wide with terror. He felt a moment's trepidation himself, still only half certain that the form he held truly belonged to a human being, that he hadn't actually managed to capture the fairy princess he'd once hunted. But the second this thought flitted through his mind, Quint recognized its folly. A self-deprecating smile curved his lips and he spoke softly. "Easy, little one. I'm not going to hurt you. I'm here to help, remember?"

Hannah stared at the gleaming white smile that altered the man's previously scowling features, as his deep voice settled her nerves. She directed her gaze to his dark green eyes and saw only concern. Slowly she nodded.

"I'm sorry," she said. "I shouldn't have been so skittish. I'm afraid I've ruined your rifle." Noting that his head was now bare, she added, "And your hat as well."

Quint glanced briefly at the gently rippling surface of the pond, then shrugged. "The water isn't deep. The gun can be retrieved and cleaned up as good as new. And as for the hat"—his grin widened—"I should have discarded it years ago."

Quinton still held Hannah in his arms, though not as close as before. His deep voice echoed pleasantly in the stillness, and she found herself smiling in reply as the mist swirled about them in tattered shreds. For the first time in months she felt safe, warm, and cared for and amazed that a perfect stranger could conjure up these feelings.

Hannah blinked as this thought sifted through her mind. A stranger—he was most definitely that. Yet here she stood, allowing him to hold her in his arms far beyond whatever time was proper. Hannah's smile wavered, and she caught her lower lip between her teeth as she quickly stepped back from his loose grasp.

Quinton resisted the spontaneous reflex that made him

reach forward to pull her back to him, allowing his suddenly empty arms to fall to his sides. His brows lowered to their habitual half-frown as a small voice in the deep recesses of his mind mentally berated him for the mixture of disappointment and longing that rushed through him. But the blood pounding in his ears had reduced those rational words to a mere whisper, barely more audible than the hum of a gnat, which he mentally brushed away.

Quint stared down into her large eyes for another long moment, then shifted his gaze to the thick web of golden hair falling about her fair face. His hands tingled with a desire to smooth the disheveled waves back from her angular features. Instead he cleared his throat and forced what he hoped would be reasonable words to his tongue. "I believe you were having trouble securing your hair. Do you still wish my assistance?"

His words puzzled Hannah for a moment. Hadn't he offered to help her find her way out of the woods? No, she remembered, he'd simply offered his help; he'd never stipulated the sort of assistance he was volunteering. A small smile tugged at the corners of her mouth as she realized that he would have had no way of knowing she was lost, whereas her struggles with her wayward tresses must have been most obvious.

Hannah's smile widened as she replied, "Yes, of course. I only hope my comb didn't follow your cap and rifle into the pond. I dropped it as I stood."

As Hannah finished speaking she glanced down to the stone surface beneath her feet. Her eyes caught the glint of something silver resting dangerously near the edge of the bridge.

"Is that it?" The man's deep voice echoed in the mist. Hannah nodded as she bent to retrieve her comb. Quint leaned forward at the same moment, and again they collided. The impact of Quint's shoulder against Hannah's sent her reeling backward. Her eyes widened as she heard something plop into the pond. As she fell hopelessly backward, she became certain that the next sound would be a loud splash as the cold water closed over her.

Chapter 2

A strong hand closed hard over Hannah's wrist, halting her fall. Hannah hung out over the water, her heels slipping on the stone bridge for a long moment until she was drawn slowly up and forward, and once more found herself enfolded in a warm embrace.

Hannah stood perfectly still, numb with the aftereffects of this latest scare, listening to the rushing of blood in her ears. She frowned as she heard the echo of an answering beat, then blinked as she realized that her cheek rested against the man's firm chest, that it was his heart that raced in rhythm with hers.

She knew she should move, at least release her arms from around his lean waist, but she felt so wonderfully secure that she simply stood where she was for several more beats of her heart, soaking in the heat from his hard form, letting her breathing ease, and waiting for her heartbeat to slow.

Quint felt his body respond to the soft, willowy form in his arms. He was completely conscious of each rise and fall of her firm breasts against his ribs, of the slender arms encircling his waist, and of her shapely legs pressing against his thighs. His blood pounded through his veins, and his

ragged breathing echoed in the quietness of the morning.
His mind was a tangle of conflicting emotions as the heat
of desire for this mysterious young woman battled with cold
reason, while a breathtaking sense of wonder held him motionless.

The voice of logic at last won out. Reluctantly Quint
relaxed his tight hold on the young woman and stepped back
from temptation. "I'm sorry," he said. "That was very
clumsy of me."

When Hannah felt the strong bands relax around her, she
let her own arms drop to her sides. As the man stepped
back, she looked up to stare at his half-frown. A slight
shiver slid along her arms in response to the sudden chill
as the mist seeped into the space between their bodies, and
she had to force her lips into a smile. "Don't apologize. I
was the one who moved without warning." She glanced
down at the water and sighed. "Well, I guess we don't
have to worry about arranging my hair."

"Why not?"

Hannah looked back up to him. "I heard my comb fall
into the pond."

Quint shook his head as he lifted his right hand. "I probably pushed a small pebble into the water as I grabbed this."

"Oh, thank you." Hannah stared at the silver comb lying
in his palm. "I would hate to lose that."

Quint glanced at the item resting in his palm, then looked
closer at the design that time had tarnished on the otherwise
gleaming spine. Billowing clouds were etched in the silver,
along with two birds in flight, one on either side of a soaring
balloon attached to a square basket.

"How unusual," Quint remarked softly.

Hannah watched him staring at the slice of silver and
answered just as quietly, "It was my mother's." When
Quint glanced at her, she looked away, feeling suddenly
shy. She had to force herself to smile up at him and speak

lightly. "Well, I suppose we should see about getting my hair under control."

Quint replied with a nod; then without a word, Hannah bent her head to let her hair fall forward. She stared at the ground as she captured her hair and twisted her tresses into a long rope. She took a deep breath and set her teeth with determination as she once more wound it into a knot at the top of her head. Then, without looking up, she spoke to the man standing at her side. "I'm going to turn around so that you can hold my hair in place for me. Then I'll take the comb from you and try to bury it deep enough to keep this silly mess in place."

Hannah turned as she finished speaking. She removed one hand from her tightly coiled hair and held it out, palm up. Quinton dropped the comb into it, then took the slender hand still anchoring the coil of hair and covered it with both of his. He felt the coolness of her long fingers beneath his for but a second before Hannah slid her hand away, leaving Quint's fingers pressed against the silken crown of hair.

The smooth knot began to loosen, so Quint cupped his hands gently around it, then stood guarding the gossamer threads with his outstretched fingers while Hannah worked the silver comb into the golden strands. Her hair felt like satin beneath his palms, and the soft scent of lilac rose to assail his senses. His breathing slowed, and for a moment he was only aware of the feather-light texture of her hair and the smell of early summer.

When Hannah touched his hand softly with one slender finger and said "Thank you. I think we have it this time," he jumped slightly, then slowly lifted his hands from her hair.

Hannah turned to look up at him. She felt the twisted cluster atop her head shift slightly, but the solid bite of the comb's teeth against her scalp told her that it was secure. She smiled.

"Thank you, sir. You did a fine job. I believe you could hire out as a lady's maid, if you so chose."

Quint's lips quirked into a smile, but no response came to his mind.

"So," Hannah went on, "if you need a reference, you can certainly come to me. I'm currently residing with Squire Summerfield at the manor house. My name is Hannah Bradley." She hesitated. "And you are . . . ?"

Quint frowned. He had heard every word she said, but with only the barest comprehension. His normally well-ordered mind seemed to have been rendered numb by the warmth still prickling the palms of his hands and flowing through his body. He tried to concentrate on the young woman's words, but he could only stare and wonder why he'd never seen her before. As he continued to gaze into Hannah's violet-blue eyes, he saw them widen questioningly. Forcing his mind to work, he answered her question.

"I'm . . . Quinton."

He smiled as he replied, a full, wide smile like the one he'd given her when she first looked across the pond and into his eyes. Hannah felt her knees weaken. Quinton, her mind echoed. Mr. Quinton, most likely, if he was indeed a servant. She'd had very little exposure to the serving class, but somehow this man, with his proud bearing and aristocratic features, differed sharply from the few servants she'd met at her uncle's.

Yet he didn't seem at all like the smattering of upper-class gentlemen she'd met since arriving in England. Mr. Quinton, especially when he smiled, was completely without the air of arrogance and disdain she'd noticed in her uncle's acquaintances. She liked the way the corners of his eyes crinkled and the way his dark curls tumbled onto his forehead with a boyish charm that belied his obvious maturity.

Quint was aware of Hannah's assessing gaze and was

pleased to see her small smile. He found himself staring at her full, curving lips, thinking how soft and warm they looked, how very inviting. For a moment he found himself imagining how her mouth would feel beneath his, and his lips parted in anticipation.

A slight breeze brushed Quint's cheeks. He blinked and straightened, aware that he had actually begun to bend toward Hannah, and let the rational part of his mind scold him.

Hannah blinked as well. She felt as if she could stare into this man's green eyes for the rest of the morning, but she knew that this would only result in calling her uncle's anger down on her. Then even more restrictions would be heaped upon her. Unless she hurried now, she wouldn't have time to make herself presentable for breakfast. She released a regretful sigh as she spoke.

"I'm very happy to have made your acquaintance, Mr. Quinton. However, since I no longer need a lady's maid, perhaps you might lend your hand to the job of guide."

Quint raised his eyebrows slightly. "You're lost?"

"Yes. And if I don't return to the manor house soon, I will be in quite a bit of trouble."

Quint's eyes narrowed. She had mentioned that she resided at Summerfield Manor. "Is the squire a demanding employer, then?" Quint frowned as he asked the question. He was aware that Squire Summerfield enjoyed exercising his authority, but had never heard that the man was particularly hard on his servants.

The question made Hannah blink in surprise, then smile widely as she shook her head. "Oh, I don't work for the squire. I'm his niece—from America."

She saw Mr. Quinton begin to color. Her tinkling laughter filled the air as she glanced down at the lavender cotton dress she had thrown on before donning her warm gray cape. "I don't blame you for your assumption," she said as she grinned up at him. "I'm hardly dressed as befits my uncle's standards. I doubt even his servants would be caught wearing something this old."

Hannah twisted her lips into an embarrassed grimace. "I'm not even supposed to be here. I was hoping to dash out and find the cottage where my mother once lived and get back before anyone knew I'd gone out, so I wore one of my old gowns." She sighed. "Now I must hurry back to the house and change into something more appropriate for breakfast."

The slight flush disappeared from Quint's face as he stared down at Hannah. His mind began working on a rational level, associating this mention of a cottage with the other bits of information he'd gleaned about this young lady.

"Did you say that you're an American?" he asked suddenly. His voice was sharp with anticipation, and before Hannah could do anything more than nod briefly, Quint spoke again, his voice vibrating with the excitement of discovery. "Then you must be Regina Higdon's daughter."

Hannah's lips widened into an immediate smile. "Yes! Did you know my mother?"

Quint's laugh was a short bark as he shook his head. "Not exactly. I was but a lad of five when she left St. Albanswood. But I knew *of* her. Your mother and father have been the talk of the village for years." He shook his head and grinned. "To this very day, down at the Beak and Bill, the story of how quiet, reserved Regina Higdon ran off with the crazy American balloonist, Matthew Bradley, is recounted over and over to the younger lads."

"My parents have become a legend, then?" Hannah's lips quivered into a soft smile as she gazed up at Quint.

"Absolutely." Quint nodded. "Of course, the sport of ballooning is a fairly common pastime in this part of the country. Still, your father has a special place when the subject turns to tales of glory in the air. None of the men who knew Matthew Bradley have forgotten his skill and sense of adventure, and they've continued to enjoy speculating on his exploits, especially his work as a spy for the United States government.''

Hannah's smile faded slightly at the mention of the War between the States. Her father had never really liked to speak of the days he spent in a balloon, spying out Confederate troop movements, so she knew the stories Mr. Quinton spoke of were mostly conjecture, as similar tales had been in Boston. The most her father would ever say of that struggle was that far too many men had paid an unbearable price.

''And if their gossip wasn't enough to keep the memory of your parents alive''—Quint's voice pulled Hannah out of her dark thoughts—''the squire's wife made a point of sharing her sister's letters with her friends, passing on your mother's descriptions of her travels with your father.'' Quint shook his head with a wry grin. ''The tales of their adventures with Buffalo Bill's Wild West Show still provide fodder for exaggeration and speculation at the tavern.''

A small smile lit Hannah's features as she recalled her own adventures with her parents, the circuses and the fairs. Then the smile disappeared. All of that had happened before her mother's illness forced Hannah and her mother to seek shelter with Aunt Amelia in Boston, where they were often separated from the man who gave joy and light to their existence.

Now both her parents were gone, the stuff of legends indeed. Hannah had learned to live without her mother slowly over the past eight years. She wasn't certain she would ever come to terms with the loss of her father.

Quint saw Hannah's lips stiffen, then watched them tremble. The last of the smile faded from her lips with a sigh as she spoke. ''I'm afraid the adventures of Regina and Matthew Bradley ended some time ago.''

"Of course." Quint's mouth fell into a straight line. "Your father's letter announcing your mother's passing arrived shortly after Betsy Summerfield's funeral."

Hannah nodded. "Yes. My father always drew comfort from the thought that Mama and Aunt Betsy were reunited at last after being separated when Mama left with Papa."

Hannah tried to smile as she looked back up to Quinton. When he saw the pain and longing in those violet-blue eyes, he searched for words of sympathy, but could find none. His own mother's death, in a carriage accident with her lover in Paris, coming so shortly after she deserted her husband and two young sons for a "gayer, happier life," had left Quint without any sense of loss, only a bitterness that twisted any happy memory he had of the woman.

Silence stretched between Hannah and Quint. The mist continued to drip softly onto the forest floor as Hannah stared at her feet. Quinton scowled as he tried to think of something to say that might pull the sadness from the girl's heart.

"I owe you an apology," he said at last.

Hannah glanced up quickly, a small frown lowering her light brown eyebrows. "For what?"

"For assuming you were a servant." His mouth twisted into that lopsided grin that Hannah had noted earlier as he went on. "Of course, that wasn't my first impression."

"Oh?" Hannah lifted her brows and her lips began to twitch at the teasing glint in his eyes. "I almost hesitate to ask you what that might have been."

Quinton shifted his gaze and stared at the mists swirling over the surface of the pond. This wasn't the sort of conversation he was accustomed to carrying on with young ladies. He wasn't sure it was a good idea to reveal his folly, his fantasies, but when he looked back at Hannah and saw her eyes shining with anticipation, he shrugged and spoke. "Well, for one second I mistook you for a wood nymph."

Hannah blinked. Noting his sheepish smile, she laughed

warmly. "What a lovely mistake to make. I think the mists must have been playing tricks on both of us today. When I first saw you, I couldn't decide if you were an enchanted prince or a poacher."

"A poacher?" It was Quinton's turn to lift his eyebrows.

Hannah nodded. "I think it was the rifle. Then I realized you must be my uncle's gamekeeper."

Quinton stared down at Hannah. The rational part of his mind told him that he should clear up the matter of his identity at this point, but he rejected the idea almost the moment it came into his head. He'd spent most of his life doing exactly what was expected of him. He had no desire to try living up to whatever expectations this enchanting young woman might hold of someone who possessed the title of earl. For once he simply wanted to enjoy the magic of the moment.

For as long as possible Quint wanted to keep the world outside the forest at bay, even if it meant pretending to be something he wasn't. Here, within the gray fog, he felt like a different person, one who had no past and no future to concern him, only the present. It was as if the surrounding mist encased every moment, allowing him to extract each separate element from it. And for as long as this condition lasted, he wanted to savor these moments as they came.

"Oh, dear."

Hannah's words made Quint glance at her quickly. He reached out to take her hand protectively as he asked, "Is something wrong?"

"Yes. Here we stand talking"—Hannah smiled up at Quint—"which I am enjoying immensely. But time is slipping away. If I don't hurry, I shall be late for breakfast and in for a scolding. Can you point the way back to the manor for me?"

"I can do better than that." Quinton tugged on her h
"Come, I'll lead you out."

Hannah let her hand nestle in his large, warm one as he turned to lead her off the bridge and onto a narrow path that ran beneath some tall elms. The wispy fog parted before them to swirl around the tree trunks lining the path, and their footsteps were muffled within the gray that surrounded them.

Quint tightened his fingers around Hannah's as he led her through the gauzy haze. For one moment he had an almost irresistible desire to pivot and lead her the other way, back toward Blackthorne Hall, where he could lock her up in the tower room like Rapunzel and keep her all to himself.

He smiled at that whimsical thought. Immediately the logical side of his mind spoke up, telling him that the abduction of Hannah would serve no practical purpose at all. Her presence in his life wouldn't help him restore his home, and it certainly wouldn't save him from the marriage he'd agreed to. Locking her away would most likely only make Hannah angry, for she struck him as the sort of person who jealously guarded her freedom.

Quint glanced over at the young woman walking next to him, thinking of the stories he'd heard of Matthew Bradley. Hannah seemed to be very much his daughter, straightforward and unconventional in thought and behavior. Yet he had seen real concern in her eyes as she contemplated the idea of being late to breakfast and improperly attired.

"Miss Bradley, do you mind if I ask you a question?"

Hannah looked up at him with a smile. "Not at all. But please call me Hannah."

Quint's brow quirked up at this confirmation that this was not a young woman who stood on ceremony. "Would you explain to me how it is that someone who is so unorthodox as to make a living flying balloons would be so strict about ⸺ daughter's appearance at breakfast?"

⸺nnah stopped walking so suddenly that Quint almost ⸺ grasp on her hand. She stared up at him for a moment, then shook her head slowly. "It isn't my father who will scold me, Mr. Quinton, it's my Uncle Charles." Hannah paused and swallowed, then allowed her lips to curve softly as she glanced past Quint's shoulder and spoke again.

"My father never cared a fig about mealtimes, of course. He ate whenever he was hungry, wearing whatever he happened to have on at the time. He was just as likely to sit down to a formal meal attired in dusty traveling clothes as he was to munch on a boiled egg wearing a top hat and tails." Hannah paused again, then forced her eyes back to Quint's and carefully controlled her voice as she continued. "But my father isn't here to argue with Uncle Charles on my behalf. Papa died three months ago."

Quint stared at Hannah. The gray mist surrounding them gave the silence between them texture, making the air almost more real than the tree limbs blurred by the fog. Quinton swallowed as he stared into Hannah's wide violet-blue eyes, then spoke quietly. "I'm sorry. I didn't know."

Hannah attempted to curve her tight lips into a small smile. When that effort failed, she shrugged.

Quint took her hand. "I should have paid more attention." He glanced at her dress as he spoke. "Lavender and gray are mourning colors, and—"

"No, they aren't." Hannah's sharp words cut into Quint's as she lifted her blunt chin. Her eyes shone, and she blinked rapidly. "That is, they *are* considered colors for mourning, but that's not why I'm wearing them. My father stipulated in his will that neither my great-aunt Amelia nor I should wear mourning or retreat from life in any way. My father felt that death was a natural occurrence, just another part of life's journey."

Hannah paused to take a deep breath, then went on more slowly. "My father believed in living each day as fully as possible, you see. He missed my mother terribly when she died, of course, but he impressed upon me that for us to go into a year of mourning would not bring her back.''

As Hannah finished speaking, it occurred to her how relatively easy this had been for her father. He wasn't the one who had to walk day after day through an empty house that held only sad reminders of her mother's presence. He could escape to the air, above his fairs and circuses.

A sharp pain knifed through Hannah's chest as she blinked away the traitorous thought and forced herself to shrug as she glanced at the man next to her. ''So I am to go on now, just as we did then.''

Hannah braced herself, waiting for the inevitable arguments about behaving as society expected, the words she'd heard repeatedly from her uncle and her cousin Carolyn since her arrival in England.

Quint looked into Hannah's defiant eyes and experienced a moment of sharp regret, knowing that he would never meet the man who had raised this combination wood sprite and realist.

''Your father must have been a very wise man,'' he said quietly.

''I doubt that my uncle would agree with you.'' Hannah's lips tightened. ''My father never managed to accumulate much money, you see. His was the wealth of new and wonderful experiences, something no one can take from you.''

In the second it took Quint to blink, he contrasted his life of routine and responsibility with that of a man who flew above the clouds without worrying what anyone said about him. This was a dangerous thought, one that challenged everything Quint believed about prospering and looking toward the future. He shoved it to the back of his mind and concentrated on Hannah's features as he spoke. ''The cronies in the tavern will be sad to hear of your father's death.''

Hannah's eyes widened. "You mustn't tell them. At least not until Monday."

"Why not?"

"My uncle would prefer that no one know until Cicely's betrothal celebration is over." Hannah's lips tightened as she shrugged. "And in this I agree with the man. My father's passing should not be allowed to cast a pall over my cousin's life."

Hannah was Cicely's cousin. The realization slipped into Quint's mind, accompanied by a sickening twist in his stomach and a feeling of dull-wittedness that this hadn't occurred to him earlier. He should have made the connection as soon as Hannah gave her name, would have if he hadn't put so much energy into systematically shaking off any thought of the world that existed outside the strange mist that seemed to bind him to Hannah.

Quint still didn't want to think of anything beyond the edge of the forest. He ignored the mention of his intended and asked, "Was your father's passing sudden?"

Hannah's eyes glistened with unshed tears as she shook her head, then glanced at the ground. "No. He was sick for about eight months. The doctors never could agree what was wrong with him. He just grew weaker and weaker until he faded away."

Quinton frowned. That was hardly a fitting ending for the saga of Matthew and Regina Bradley. His hand tightened around Hannah's as he spoke softly. "The lads at the Beak and Bill will never believe that, you know."

Hannah looked up sharply to find Quint gazing at her intently. He smiled gently as he spoke again. "And neither do I. In fact, just last week I believe I heard a story about an American balloonist who was blown off course and into the side of a mountain. They say the crash was a spectacular sight. That *was* your father, was it not?"

Hannah blinked and stared at Quint a moment. When her

lips began to tremble he started to fear that he'd said the
wrong thing. Then the corners of her lips lifted and parted
in a trembling smile as she nodded emphatically. "Of course
it was. And I know my father would like for the lads at the
Beak and Bill to hear every detail."

"I'll be glad to oblige. Every legend should have a proper
ending." Quint felt his throat tighten over his words. He
quit speaking, surprised at his emotions. He hadn't had time
for sentimentality when his own father died, not after learning how the man had lost or entailed most of the Blackthorne
estate. The strongest feeling he'd been able to manage was
pity, knowing that his father had allowed his wife's treachery to destroy him.

Quint had long ago vowed to allow no woman to cloud
his mind so. Yet as he stared down at Hannah's brave smile,
he found himself struggling to keep his mind working on a
rational level in order to battle his growing desire to lower
his lips to hers, to kiss away the slight tremble he could
still see, to help ease the pain in those wide violet-blue eyes.

"Mr. Quinton, thank you."

Hannah's words were soft, yet they jolted Quint far
enough out of his bemused condition to allow him to nod
and clear his throat. "You're welcome. Now, I believe you
are in a hurry. We'd best step lively if we're to have you
home and attired properly for your kippers and toast."

Hannah smiled again, wishing she could better express
her gratitude for the solace his words had offered her. For
one second she considered rising on her toes to kiss him
lightly. Her heart pulsed wildly as she imagined his firm
lips on hers. Her body still held the memory of the feel of
his lean form, making a hot blush rise to her cheeks that
robbed her of her moment of daring. She was forced to
lower her head to hide the flame coloring her cheeks when
Quint's hand tightened over hers and she accompanied him
down the path.

As Quint held a low-hanging branch up so that Hannah could pass beneath, it occurred to him again that he should correct her misconception about his station in life. Once more he rejected the idea.

Quint had never found it easy to speak at any length with many people. In order to compensate for not having had the time or money to attend Oxford, he'd spent a great deal of time in his grandfather's library educating himself, only to find that his contemporaries had used their time at the university to engage in racing horses and courting ladies. Thus, beyond the subject of horses, he had little common ground for easy conversation with men belonging to the same station in life as he.

He normally had even less to say to women. His mother's treachery had left him with a deep distrust of the fairer sex, an impression that had deepened when he attended his first Season and learned that no matter how taken with his looks the young ladies were, they had little interest in marriage to a man with a title but no money.

Except for Felicia. Lovely Felicia, who joyfully agreed to be his bride, only to come to view her marriage to Quint as an inescapable prison.

Of all the women he knew, only his grandmother held his respect and admiration. And now she had coerced him into a marriage he didn't want.

Quinton frowned at this last thought. His grandmother had undoubtedly chosen his second wife with more intelligence than he had used with his first. The squire wanted to marry Cicely to a titled gentleman, and the Blackthornes needed her dowry. Besides, Cicely was young, tractable. Marriage to her would not upset the well-ordered life Quint's situation demanded.

Quint glanced at Hannah. Even watching the path to elude the rocks and roots beneath her feet, she displayed a liveliness and naturalness that other women lacked. It was hard to imagine that Hannah and Cicely were related at all, so very different was this vital young woman from her shy cousin. Quint had the distinct feeling that the man Hannah married would find his entire life turned upside down.

A strange sense of sorrow and loss twisted within Quint as he reflected on this, which made his scowl deepen. This was hardly a characteristic response for him. Suddenly wary of searching his heart for the source of his discontentment, he cleared his throat and said the first thing that came to his mind.

"Watch your step. The path falls away to your right here."

Hannah stepped carefully over a large root, then glanced to her right to see that the path had risen above a shallow dale filled with gray mist, like a witch's caldron. When she looked up she noticed that the haze seemed a mere film on the path and that the trees now grew farther apart.

"Are we nearing the end of the forest?"

Quint nodded in reply.

Hannah shook her head. "I was beginning to think these woods had no ending. I guess it was very foolish to come in here by myself. I should have waited for Cicely."

Quint glanced at her sharply and Hannah smiled. "Ever since Cicely and I started corresponding, when we were very little, we have been planning for the day we could visit our mothers' childhood home together. Cicely has been too busy to do much of anything with me, because of all the plans for the betrothal party, so I decided to strike out on my own this morning. I had somehow gotten the impression that the forest was not very large."

"It isn't very wide," Quint replied. "But it's quite long. As for the Higdon cottage, it's hard to find even on a sunny day. The last time I saw the building, it was covered in leafy vines."

Hannah shivered as she walked along next to him; then

she shrugged. "Well, I certainly would never have found it in this fog." She paused and shook her head. "I've never been in mist this thick. It's quite strange, don't you think? I've had the strangest feeling all morning that I've somehow stumbled into an enchanted wood." She paused again as she looked up at Quint with a rueful smile. "I keep thinking that once I step out into the light, I'll turn to see that you've completely disappeared."

Hannah stopped walking and looked up at Quint with a mischievous grin as she continued to speak. "Or perhaps I'll find that you've turned into some mythical beast, a guardian of the forest of some sort. Which shall it be?"

Quint had to force a smile to his lips as he turned to gaze into Hannah's wide dark eyes. Part of him had felt the mystery also, but the most recent mention of Cicely had finally brought the sensible portion of his mind into command, the part that recognized duty all too well and had no use for fantasy.

"I firmly doubt that either one will happen," he replied. He heard a strange note of sadness echo in his voice and forced a cheeriness into his next words. "I shall just stay myself"—he paused, and the next words came directly from his heart—"someone who hopes you will consider having as a friend."

Quint's words and the warm look in his eyes pleased Hannah inordinately. She nodded, then felt her cheeks grow warm as she began to walk forward again, still smiling at Quint. She could hardly feel the ground beneath her soft shoes. A strange warmth and lightness seemed to take possession of her body, and she felt suddenly as if she were floating upon the mists surrounding her as she replied, "That's perfectly accept—"

Hannah's last syllable ended in a cry of dismay as her foot hooked under a root protruding into the path. Quint reacted quickly, tightening his right hand on hers and reaching for her with his left. The momentum of her fall was too strong for his effort, though, and he barely had time to wrap his arms about her protectively before they fell to the ground and began rolling down the hill together like a bundle of twigs.

Hannah lay in the circle of Quint's arms as they tumbled. She held her breath as she spun around and around until they reached the bottom of the knoll and the alternating twirling and pounding ended.

She lay atop Quint, his arms still around her, her cheek pressed to his chest. She forced herself to breathe slowly as she listened to his heart pound, noting that her own pulse throbbed with the same rapid cadence. After a few moments Hannah placed her hands on Quint's chest and pushed herself up to gaze into his face. Her eyes locked with his.

"Are you hurt?" she breathed.

Chapter 3

Quint's head throbbed, and pain arced across his back from the force of the fall, but he was only half aware of these sensations. He was far more conscious of the feel of Hannah's shapely form atop his, where the tips of her breasts teased his chest and the gentle pressure of her legs upon his sent hot blood pounding through his veins.

He opened his eyes and saw that Hannah's hair had escaped its comb again. Above him floated the ethereal face of a wood nymph. Her features appeared blurred, and all he could see was undulating waves of golden hair framing violet-blue eyes and dusty pink lips.

Quint closed his eyes to clear his vision. When he felt Hannah's cool hand against his cheek, he opened his eyes again to gaze into hers.

"Mr. Quinton, are you hurt?" she repeated.

Quint shook his head slowly as a smile twisted his lips. No, he wasn't in pain, unless one counted the burning ache of desire. Though his head was still spinning from the dizzy tumble, he could now see Hannah with complete clarity. Her parted lips seemed to call to his as his body throbbed beneath the slight weight of her slender form, clouding his mind to everything but his physical needs.

Never taking his eyes off Hannah's, Quint placed his right arm about her waist, then rose onto his left elbow to a half-sitting position. When Hannah moved as if to pull away from him, he tightened his arm about her waist and held her close, savoring her warmth and the feel of her soft curves against him. He stared into eyes the color of the sky at dusk, eyes that spoke of the magical time before the setting of the sun, eyes that were filled with wonder. His lips softened into a wistful smile as he lowered his head to hers.

Hannah found her gaze trapped by the deep green of Quint's eyes. Her hands, splayed out over the hard curve of his chest, could feel an intense heat, a warmth that seemed to hold her as securely as did the arm that encircled her waist. His soft smile drew her eyes to his mouth, and suddenly her lips tingled strangely. She felt no fear, only an odd expectancy when he began to lower his head. His warm lips touched hers with a gentle force that made her own lips soften and part as she slid her hand up from his chest to curve around the back of his neck.

Quint's mouth closed more firmly over Hannah's. Her eyes fell shut in response to the thrilling warmth spiraling down the center of her body, and her head lolled to one side as Quinton's lips moved slowly over hers with ever deepening pressure. Her head began to spin. She felt as if she were twirling around and around in the mist, being pulled into some magical world where new, unexpected sensations and emotions awaited her.

Quint's pulse pounded with growing desire as he tested the softness of Hannah's lips and explored the supple warmth of her mouth. When his arm tightened around her waist, drawing her closer, a flash of pleasure heated his blood. As he intensified his kiss, his hand slid up her back to the base of her skull to tangle in the silk of her hair.

Hannah foundered in a world of newfound sensation and enchantment. The fingers of her right hand sifted through Quint's hair, while her left hand traced the hard muscles of his back. Her breasts swelled against the solid curve of his chest as her legs, bared in the fall, pressed against the velvet strength of Quint's buckskin-clad thighs.

A river of fire surged through her veins as Quint slid his hand down her back, then gently caressed her bottom. A strange heat swirled through her belly, and her head began to spin again, as if she were once more rolling down the hill. His tongue teased her lips farther apart and slid in to fill her mouth with a sensual pleasure that rendered her weak and hot and elicited a soft, low moan from her throat.

It was this sound, small and muffled, that drew Quint from the swirling world of passion and brought him to his senses. He blinked and lifted his head to stare down at Hannah's closed eyelids. She lay in his arms, absolutely still for a moment until a frown formed over her eyes and she opened them.

"I'm sorry." Quint's voice was deep with a rough edge. "That was very wrong of me."

Hannah didn't say a word. She knew very well how improper their behavior had been, but was too honest to pretend that she hadn't thoroughly enjoyed what had passed between them. She let him help her to her feet, then looked up to him with lips that trembled into a smile of resignation.

"You mustn't apologize, Mr. Quinton. What just happened has convinced me that this must indeed be an enchanted forest."

Quint could think of no reply. His body still throbbed with desire, though he strove to ignore the clamor of his senses and attempted to regain control over his reactions to the young woman who smiled so suddenly as she spoke again.

"Neither one of us is behaving normally. How else could one explain the fact that you mistook me for a wood nymph and I thought you were a prince?"

Quint lifted his eyebrows and his lips curved of their own accord. "Or a poacher."

Hannah glanced down to smooth her wrinkled skirt, then sighed as she looked up again. "I think, considering the circumstances, that I'd best get my hair atop my head again and hurry back to the manor before the magic becomes more capricious and we find ourselves turned into a couple of frogs, forced to live in the pond."

Quinton nodded wordlessly. He held Hannah's hair for her again, breathing deeply of its lilac scent and savoring the silken feel of it as she worked the comb into the golden coil once more. His body ached to inch closer, to experience the satin of her curves once more, but he held himself conscientiously at attention. When her hair was finally secure, he gently took her arm to help her up the slope, then guided her down the path and through some bushes.

Hannah blinked as they came out onto an open field, then stared across the green grass at her uncle's immense brick and timber house. Sunlight breaking through gaps in the gray haze glinted on the slate roof, telling her that she was going to be very late to breakfast.

But this no longer bothered her. No matter how severe her uncle's scolding turned out to be, she would bear it easily. She would have the memory of a special morning to keep her spirits high, and the hope that she might see this man again soon.

Hannah turned to Quint and said simply, "Thank you."

He smiled down at her. "It was my pleasure." Then he lifted his eyes to stare at the house. A frown formed above suddenly solemn eyes as he glanced once again at Hannah. "You'd best be going now."

* * *

The gas lamp on the wall threw a yellow glow onto the dressing table in Hannah's blue and gold room. Hannah sat before an oval mirror, staring at her own reflection within the gilt frame while Letitia, the plump, dark-haired chambermaid whom Uncle Charles had promoted to lady's maid for Hannah's convenience, put the finishing touches on Hannah's upswept hair.

Staring back at her was a very different person from the young woman who had run out of the house that morning dressed in a simple lavender frock and gray cape.

A mauve silk dress molded itself to Hannah's slender curves. A web of ecru lace edged the low, wide neckline and skimmed her shoulders to form small cap sleeves above her long ivory gloves. Her mother's single strand of pearls encircled her neck, and two teardrop-shaped pearls dangled from her earlobes. Her hair was swept up into a soft bun atop her head, with a few loose tendrils of honey-colored hair wisping around her squarish face.

Hannah sighed and as she stared at herself, hoping that Letitia's handiwork would please her uncle, perhaps make him forget his ire at her late arrival at breakfast that morning. Fortunately the squire had been too preoccupied to give Hannah more than a brief, harsh lecture on his house rules before turning to his oldest daughter, Carolyn, to discuss the plans for the weekend-long celebration of Cicely's engagement.

Hannah frowned at her reflection, remembering how very quiet and pale Cicely had been, taking only nibbles of toast between tiny sips of tea. Hannah had wanted to speak to her cousin, to offer the reassurances she knew the timid girl would need, but directly after breakfast Carolyn had whisked her younger sister off, leaving Hannah to her own devices.

Hannah's lips curved into a small smile. She'd spent much of the day wandering in her uncle's garden, while her mind

meandered down misty paths till it encountered the image
of one particular dark-haired man. Even now the vision of
Mr. Quinton's lopsided smile made her grow warm. The
memory of his lips upon hers made them tingle and part
with sudden longing and her body glow with remembered
pleasure.

Hannah wasn't disturbed by these feelings. She had been
waiting all her life for this moment, certain that she, like
her mother, would find love in an instant of magic. She
gave no thought to the fact that Mr. Quinton was still barely
more than a stranger to her. The fact that she had met him
in the same forest that had seen her parents' first charmed
encounter strengthened her conviction that the passion
which had flared between them had been fated, inescapable,
and beyond reproach.

"Will that be satisfactory, miss?"

Letitia's high-pitched voice broke in on Hannah's
thoughts like a slash of cold water on her face, forcing her
to look at herself in the mirror once more. Slowly she
nodded, then turned to the plump form dressed in black and
white. "You've done wonders, Letitia. I almost don't recognize myself done up so elegantly. Thank you."

The maid smiled shyly and opened her mouth to reply,
but it was Great-Aunt Amelia's voice that echoed through
the chamber. "My goodness! Do I have the correct room?
I was looking for my niece, Hannah Bradley."

Hannah grinned and turned to the woman standing in the
doorway, then blinked at the change in her tiny white-haired
aunt. Normally Great-Aunt Amelia dressed simply, prefer-
ring shirtwaists and skirts to lace and satin. Tonight Amelia
looked every inch the Boston society lady she'd once been.
Her dress was of dark burgundy satin. The neckline dipped
in a wide V from her shoulders and was inset with matching
burgundy lace, which also formed the sleeves that puffed
up and out before ending in a tight band just above her long

black gloves. The woman's snowy hair was piled up on her head in a style that gave the illusion of height to her five-foot frame.

Hannah walked over to her aunt. Small herself at only five feet three, she still had to bend down to give the old woman a hug. "Aunt Amelia," Hannah breathed, "you look wonderful tonight."

The white head dipped forward slightly, and the tiny face broke into a web of wrinkles. "Thank you, my dear, and so do you. I'm glad we took the time to shop in London when we first arrived. Now, are you finished dressing?"

At Hannah's answering nod, her aunt spoke briskly. "Wonderful. I just stopped in to see Cicely, and she asked to speak to you as soon as possible."

The note of concern in Aunt Amelia's voice made Hannah rise quickly. She started forward, then paused just long enough to nod and smile at Letitia before following Aunt Amelia out the door and down the wide hallway to her cousin's room.

Hannah's knock was answered by a blond maid. The young girl held the door open as Hannah stepped into a light room where rows of yellow fleurs-de-lis marched up and down white walls. A yellow silk coverlet graced the large postered bed, while matching fabric fell from a cornice high on the wall behind it and draped both sides of the tall windows.

The sound of rustling silk drew Hannah's attention to her left, where a young woman with hair the color of sun-bleached flax sat perched on a stool in front of a dressing table and mirror. Cicely Summerfield had turned her back to the rectangular mirror. Her sky-blue eyes gazed across the room at Hannah out of a porcelain-pale face as she pressed her full lips into a thin line.

Hannah moved forward, immediately recognizing the fear

behind her cousin's tense air, but before she could reach Cicely, a harsh voice made her stop.

"What are you doing in here?"

Hannah lifted her gaze from her cousin's eyes to the dark-haired woman who stood behind Cicely. Lady Carolyn Emmerly, wearing a bright yellow dress with a revealing décolletage, glared back at her. Before Hannah could reply, Cicely spoke in a low, shaky voice. "I sent for her, Carolyn. I wish to speak to her before I go downstairs."

As Lady Carolyn looked down at her younger sister, the jewels scattered in the woman's medium brown tresses sparkled in the light of the small chandelier. Cicely glanced up and spoke even more softly. "Please, Caro. I promise to be down soon. Take Belinda with you so that I can talk with Hannah a few moments. She knows how to help me."

Carolyn tightened her lips, but nodded. Hannah remained in the center of the room trying to ignore the narrowed look that Cicely's sister shot her as she walked toward the door. Hannah turned toward the door just in time to see Aunt Amelia smile and wink as she followed Carolyn and the maid into the hall.

Hannah swiveled back to her cousin as the door clicked shut. Cicely hadn't moved. Her light blue eyes gazed straight ahead in an unfocused stare. Hannah took a deep breath. She'd seen this many times during the year she and Cicely had spent together at a French finishing school. It had happened each time they were preparing for a ball or a formal tea. Hannah forced a curve to her lips and warmth to her voice as she moved forward.

"Cis, that's a beautiful dress. I don't remember when I've seen anything so lovely. Did you help design it?"

Cicely blinked and lowered her pale eyebrows in a puzzled frown. Then she turned on her stool to face the mirror and stare at the blue watered silk dress as if seeing it for the first time. Slowly she nodded.

Hannah wasn't surprised. Her cousin had an exquisite sense of style. This dress, with its low rounded neckline trimmed in white rosettes that skimmed across Cicely's white shoulders, was the perfect complement for her delicate looks. Elbow-length gloves ended just below the soft fall of her sleeves, and a five-strand collar of iridescent pearls encased her slim neck.

"And that necklace finishes off your look perfectly." Hannah spoke softly as she came to stand next to her cousin.

Cicely nodded slowly and lifted her gloved fingers to caress the smooth choker. "Thank you. The pearls arrived today." She paused, and her whisper of a voice seemed to catch in her throat as she went on. "They are a gift from the earl."

Hannah placed her right hand on Cicely's shoulder, feeling the coolness of her cousin's skin even through her kidskin gloves. Hannah spoke softly. "Your love has wonderful taste."

Cicely blinked and jerked around to stare up at Hannah. "What did you say?"

Hannah's brows moved together at the startled look she saw in her cousin's eyes. "I said, your intended has wonderful taste." She paused, then smiled. "Of course, when you wrote to me last fall that you'd met the man you wanted to marry, you slyly failed to mention his name and the fact that he was an earl."

Cicely took a deep breath and stared past Hannah as she spoke. "That's right. I . . . I was being very superstitious, I suppose. I was afraid to say much until he made his intentions clear." Her voice trailed off as she released a sigh, then continued softly. "I'd almost forgotten that letter. Fall seems so long ago."

A haunting sadness echoed in Cicely's words, a sadness that struck a chord in Hannah's heart. The image of a man lying beneath a plain brown blanket flashed into Hannah's

44 *Elane Osborn*

mind, a man fighting for his every breath while the leaves on the trees outside blazed with color. Slowly Hannah nodded. "Yes, it does seem as if an eternity has passed since then."

Hannah felt something cover her hand and looked down to see Cicely's gloved fingers holding hers.

"Oh, Hannah"—Cicely's voice quivered as she spoke—"I'm so sorry about your father. I'd always hoped to meet him one day."

Hannah glanced into Cicely's eyes and saw a film of tears threatening to flow over the girl's lower lids. She bent to hug her cousin and whisper, "And Papa wanted to meet you, too. I know he'd have loved you as much as I do." Hannah straightened and grinned down at her cousin. "But he would have insisted that you smile more often and learn not to be so frightened of everything."

Cicely straightened her shoulders. "I'm not afraid of everything." Her voice was much stronger. "Not after spending a year with you. How can you suggest that after I helped you set those pigeons loose from the roof of the school?"

Hannah smiled as she watched some color blossom in her cousin's cheeks. Her own mood lifted and she laughed as she shook her head. "Oh, that *was* an adventure, wasn't it? Especially as no one could prove we were the culprits. You're right, you *did* become more courageous by the end of the year, or you never would have braved Madame Lavoisier's wrath." She paused and lifted her brows. "So why are you quaking in your room at the thought of a mere ball in your honor?"

Hannah watched with dismay as Cicely's smile faded. The young woman pressed her lips together and lifted her shoulders in a helpless shrug. "You know I've never liked large groups of people. And I detest being the center of attention. I just wish I could simply get married and have it done with.''

Cicely stopped speaking abruptly. Her features tightened as she stood and stepped across the mustard-colored carpet to her open window, where she stared out into the evening as she spoke. ''But of course, Father must have his way. No matter what I might prefer, we must have a house full of nobility for him to impress with his wealth and possessions.''

Hannah was puzzled at this sudden outburst from her normally placid cousin. She bit back a sarcastic comment on the squire's lack of sensitivity as she walked over and took her cousin's hand in hers. Hannah smiled as she was forced to look up at the taller girl.

''I know you dislike crushes, Cis. However, since this ball is being held for you, I'm afraid there's no avoiding it.'' She squeezed her cousin's hand. ''Try to remember how it used to be at Madame Lavoisier's. You were always very tense and frightened before a grand occasion then, too, but once you got caught up in the glitter and excitement, you forgot your worries and had a wonderful time.'' Hannah paused and gave her cousin an encouraging smile. ''Let's go down now, and before you know it you'll be on the arm of your earl, relaxed and happy.''

Once more Cicely stiffened. Her eyes widened and she opened her mouth, but before she could speak the door opened. Both girls turned to Cicely's maid standing on the threshold, her hands clasped in front of her ruffled apron.

''The master says you are to come down directly, miss. I'm sorry.''

The maid curtsied briefly and left. Hannah looked at Cicely and saw the young woman take a deep breath, then smile weakly. ''I suppose we'd better do as he says.''

Cicely's voice was soft, the words spoken in a dull monotone that made Hannah frown as she followed her cousin toward the open door and the stairs beyond.

At the bottom of the stairs, in a foyer lit by a huge crystal chandelier, Quinton Blackthorne and his family stood behind the Summerfields as the guests awaited Cicely's entrance. Quint frowned at the tightness in his chest as he clasped his hands behind his back.

To get his mind off the feeling that a trap was slowly closing around him, he glanced behind him to where his younger brother stood at the edge of the crowd. Noting that Parker's normally ruddy features were pale beneath his auburn hair, Quint stared at the young man for a moment, wondering if his brother was ill. He couldn't remember a time in all of Parker's twenty-six years that he'd seen the young man look so very serious.

A low cough from the woman next to him made Quint shift his gaze to his right. His grandmother looked every bit as sober as his brother. A high collar of black lace encircled her neck above a low scoop neckline inset with the same black lace. Her iron-gray hair was dressed simply but regally atop her head. Each earlobe sparkled with a large solitaire diamond, and smaller gems winked in the silver broach pinned in the center of her collar.

As the shimmer of the stones caught Quint's eye, he reflected on the talents of the artisans at Petrie and Yarrick. No one who saw the pin or the earrings would suspect the gems were paste, especially when his grandmother wore them with such pride.

The source of Lady Evelyn's pride was the knowledge that she had sacrificed the genuine stones for much needed improvements on Blackthorne Hall. Quint's jaw tightened as he turned once again to look at the stairway. His grandmother's pride was his shame. He knew that the diamonds had been his grandfather's wedding gift to her, and he was determined to replace the paste with real stones as soon as he received Cicely's dowry money.

"Cicely would be down by now if it weren't for Hannah."

The harshly whispered words caught Quint's attention. He glanced at Lady Carolyn, who stood directly in front of him next to her father, Squire Summerfield. Her yellow satin dress rustled as she leaned closer to her father and went on, "I can't imagine why Cicely insisted on having that girl come to her room. As far as I'm concerned, my little sister is far too impressionable, but she absolutely refuses to listen to me when I tell her that Hannah is nothing but trouble."

Squire Summerfield stood tall and straight, still lean and fit at fifty-nine. His long face was only slightly lined, and just a few strands of silver glinted in his light brown hair as he turned to listen to his daughter continue her tirade.

"*You* saw today how it is with that girl," Carolyn went on. "Up at dawn and into the forest without your permission. I just hope she obeys your orders tonight and doesn't disgrace us in front of our guests."

Quint glanced at the squire as he spoke to his daughter. "Don't concern yourself, my dear. Hannah has been warned. If I see any sign that she's forgotten my orders, I'll simply lock her in her room until our guests have left."

Quint frowned at these cold words, then fought a shiver as he imagined the carefree wood nymph he'd held in his arms that morning shut away like a caged bird. Without closing his eyes Quint was able to conjure up an image of Hannah's laughing lavender-blue eyes, wide with the promise of open skies and gaiety.

The crowd seemed suddenly to melt away from Quint. The red-carpeted stairway dissolved from sight, to be replaced by a gnarled tree twisting up through gray mist. In less than a moment his mind had taken him to an altogether different world, where he gazed at delicate features framed by soft waves of long golden hair. Quint's heart began to race, and warm blood flowed through his veins. The burdens of his everyday life were lifted from his shoulders and he began to smile.

This sort of thing had happened to him repeatedly during the day. Once he left the woods and returned to his duties at Blackthorne Hall, Quint had assumed that he'd escaped whatever spell the misty forest had cast upon him. But as he went about his daily routine, more than once he'd found his thoughts wandering through the gray woods, searching for that elusive nymph. Only by sheer strength of will had he been able to force his normally disciplined mind back to the matter at hand.

"She's coming now."

Carolyn's sharp words shattered the hazy world Quint had slipped into. As he blinked away the misty woods and focused on the stairs, his shoulders instantly tensed. He reminded himself once again that the events of that morning had been an aberration, something best forgotten. He was announcing his betrothal to Cicely Summerfield tonight, an act that would bind the two families together and at last restore the land and wealth that his father's gambling had lost.

Quint's jaw tightened with determination as he watched Cicely move stiffly down the stairs toward him. He tried to concentrate on the way her light blue dress enhanced her arctic beauty, but he couldn't help thinking that the pale face beneath the flaxen hair held all the animation of a porcelain doll as Cicely gazed at some spot at the rear of the crowd.

Quint tried to force some warmth into his heart by reminding himself what a sweet, unspoiled young woman Cicely was. She was quiet and sensible, the voice of logic whispered in his ear, the perfect choice for a man who didn't trust the idea of marriage, who feared the power a woman could wield over a man's heart. Cicely was not that sort of woman. She was the kind who would easily slip into the ordered routine of the Hall without making excessive demands on his time or attention.

But even as Quint attempted to concentrate on the woman he was bound to marry, he caught sight of a slender figure in pale mauve descending the stairs behind Cicely. He raised his eyes, and his stiffened jaw went suddenly slack as he met her violet-blue gaze.

Quint drew in a soft involuntary gasp as he recognized Hannah. There was no mistaking her, though she no longer resembled a lost waif or a wayward wood nymph. The simple lines of her silk dress accented Hannah's slender curves, and Quint's body grew warm with the recollection of holding her soft form to his. Her upswept honey-gold hair shimmered in the light of the large chandelier, making his fingers tingle as if they were once more caressing those silken strands.

Again he looked up into her wide eyes, and in that moment all the other people in the room once more seemed to fade into the oak paneling as he watched her float down toward him.

Hannah saw Quint the moment she came around the last curve of the stairs. She spied his dark head in the crowd behind her uncle and saw that his deep green eyes were staring at Cicely, like all the others eyes in the room below. Hannah stopped and gazed at him in wonder. What was he doing here? Surely her snobbish uncle would never include a gamekeeper among his guests.

As soon as that thought flashed through Hannah's mind, she was forced to bite her lower lip to keep from laughing at herself. "Mr. Quinton" obviously wasn't a servant at all. No servant would possess a well-tailored cutaway jacket like the black one that stretched across his broad shoulders, nor would a gamekeeper look so at home in the starched white collar that rose above his black bow tie.

Hannah smiled and began to descend again, trying not to hurry as she anticipated letting him tease her for having made the same wrong assumption about his station in life as he'd made about hers. She longed to skip down the stairs and into the circle of the man's arms, but she forced herself to move sedately, reminding herself that they were no longer within the protective shelter of the forest.

Her steps slowed as for one heart-stopping moment it occurred to her that Mr. Quinton might have been released from the spell of the early morning mist, leaving him indifferent to her or, worse, embarrassed by those magical moments they had shared. Hannah's fears were eased the second Quint's eyes met hers. He blinked in surprise, then stared at her in open wonder and admiration as she followed Cicely into the room.

As the two young women reached the bottom of the stairs, Hannah became vaguely aware of the low murmur of voices and the fact that several figures had crowded forward. But her attention was totally focused on the dark-haired man who walked slowly toward her. Standing on the step behind her cousin, Hannah eased her lips into a welcoming smile. She watched Mr. Quinton's lips begin to curve, then stiffen suddenly when someone said, "Good evening, Your Lordship."

Hannah recognized her cousin's soft voice. Cicely's words had barely reached Hannah's ears when she saw Mr. Quinton blink, then shift his gaze to her cousin. Hannah watched in numb confusion as he took Cicely's hand.

Wide but empty blue eyes met Hannah's as Cicely turned and spoke quietly: "Hannah, I would like to present the Earl of Chadwick, my future husband."

Cicely gave her head a half-turn so that she was not quite

facing Quinton as she finished the introduction: "Your Lordship, this is my cousin Hannah Bradley."

Hannah's eyes darted from her cousin's pale profile to the green eyes beneath darkly frowning brows. Quint's gaze held hers for a long moment before the man spoke in calm, even tones. "It's a pleasure to meet you, Miss Bradley."

On the periphery of her vision Hannah saw Quint's gloved hand move toward her. She glanced down as she lifted her own hand and let his long, lean fingers close over hers. His grasp was firm and warm. Hannah felt a burning sensation pass through her gloves, a heat that seemed odd when the rest of her body was so very cold.

She raised her gaze to Quint's once more and saw him lift his brows, as if trying to prompt a response from her. Sudden anger flashed through her at his cool reaction to the situation. Hannah straightened her shoulders and, with proper slowness, dipped her head and spoke in frigid, even tones. "Thank you, Your Lordship. I'm pleased to make your acquaintance as well."

Chapter 4

Beneath the crystal chandelier glimmering above the ballroom, Hannah danced across the smooth parquet floor in the arms of Cicely's older brother, Hartley Summerfield. As she attempted to follow his demanding lead, she concentrated on the music while watching the other dancers swirl around them. The sight of black coattails that floated behind the men twirling around the room in the arms of women in long dresses of every hue did little, however, to keep Hannah's mind off her cousin's torturous dancing or the disappointment and anger that filled her. Even with all the distractions available, she wasn't able to forget how "Mr. Quinton" had made such a complete and utter fool of her.

"You dance quite well, Cousin Hannah."

Hartley's voice pulled Hannah's mind from her angry thoughts, and she glanced up into her cousin's narrow face, noting again how much he resembled his father. Like the squire, he was tall and lean and possessed the same pale gray eyes, light brown hair, and long face.

Hannah wasn't sure how to reply to Hartley's compliment on her dancing ability. He hadn't added "for a Colonial," but his voice held a mocking tone that had said just that. Hartley's wry, pointed humor had grated on Hannah ever since she first met him, but Cicely had written glowing letters describing how kind her older brother was to her, and so Hannah was determined to ignore the quirks that irritated her.

"Thank you for the compliment, Cousin Hartley." Hannah kept her voice soft, her tone light. "I'm trying very hard not to disgrace your family."

Hartley's pale eyebrows dropped into a slight frown and he glanced away. Hannah was just congratulating herself on treating him to some of his own medicine when he looked back into her eyes. His lips twisted into an impudent smile as he spoke. "No, we wouldn't want you to disgrace us in the presence of our new relations." He paused and lifted his pale eyebrows. "So tell me, cousin, what do you think of the Countess of Chadwick?"

Hannah blinked, trying to conjure up a memory of the woman. She had been introduced to her shortly after being formally presented to Quinton, but she retained only a vague image of a tall woman with a regal bearing, iron-gray hair, and silver-framed glasses.

"Impressive," Hannah replied at last. "Most impressive."

Hartley's head fell back as he laughed silently. When he looked down at Hannah again, his eyes glimmered with merry tears. "That, dear cousin, is an understatement. Our countess is stronger of will than most men I know. Look, there she is now, interrogating poor old Feniwick."

Hannah glanced over Hartley's shoulder as they danced past the woman in question. One gnarled hand rested on the head of a silver-tipped, black cane as the countess looked down through her lenses at a portly gentleman with a shiny pate.

"One must admire her spirit, I suppose," Hartley went

on. "Somehow she manages to keep everyone in awe of her in spite of her imitation gems and a wardrobe that is ten years out of fashion."

Hannah frowned as the movement of the dance took the woman out of her line of sight. "Why would a countess choose to wear such things?"

Hartley's laugh was a sharp bark. "Because despite their impressive titles, the Blackthornes have no money. I suppose I should say they *had* none. Tonight all that will change with the announcement of Quinton's betrothal to my little sister. The next time I see Lady Evelyn, I've no doubt the twinkle in her earlobes will be genuine."

Hannah glanced quickly at her dance partner. Hartley's lips were twisted into a disagreeable smile that made her frown as she asked, "What do you mean? You can't be suggesting that the earl is marrying Cicely for her money."

"I'm suggesting just that." Hartley raised his brows. "It's done all the time, you know, even among the best of families. *Especially* among the best of families. Of course I've never really counted the Blackthornes among the best. Other than my friend Parker, they're all too stiff-necked to be any fun, always going on about duty and such. Except Parker, of course." Hartley shrugged. "Perhaps that's because the Blackthornes haven't been very lucky in recent years. My sister's intended has already been married once, you know."

Hartley twirled Hannah in a tight circle, then continued speaking without missing a step. "Poor Felicia. She died before she and Quint had been married a year. She did bring some money into the Blackthorne coffers, but apparently not enough, so Quint must marry again."

With those words Hartley swung Hannah in another violent circle that made her lose her step and left her breathless. Her mind was whirling; she felt dizzy from the sudden motion and the shocking information Hartley had imparted.

Did Cicely suspect that her earl was marrying her only for her dowry? Was this even true? She'd heard Hartley exaggerate more than once in the short time she'd known him.

"What do you think of him?"

Hartley's question made Hannah lower her brows in a puzzled frown. "What do I think of whom?"

"Of Parker. Quint's brother. You met him in the foyer—the tall, thin chap with the brownish-reddish hair."

Hannah recalled being introduced to a young man with auburn hair, but was still so stunned at learning Quinton's identity that she only had the most indistinct picture of Parker in her mind. "Yes, I remember. I only spoke with him for a moment, but he seemed nice enough."

"He is," Hartley replied crisply. "I always thought it was a shame he wasn't the eldest. Not that his being three years my junior has affected our friendship. I'm not known for my maturity, you see. But Father would much prefer that I consort with fellows who have titles."

Hannah cocked her head to one side as she stared into her cousin's gray eyes. "I'm beginning to think your father is something of a snob."

"Oh?" Hartley raised his eyebrows, and his voice lost all amusement. "Well, you shouldn't judge us until you know our circumstances, young cousin. This isn't America where everyone spouts lies about equality. Here we admit that titles and money mean everything, to squire and earl alike."

The music stopped. Hartley smiled insolently as he bowed. Hannah curtsied in return, then turned to walk off the dance floor in the direction of the curtained French doors that ran along one side of the room. The vigorous dance had left her breathless and her cousin's words had raised serious questions in her mind, but before Hannah was halfway across the ballroom, the violins struck the first chords of the next dance.

When she spotted a tall gentleman with streaks of white in his jet-black hair making his way toward her, Hannah recognized the Duke of Ludmore immediately. Her uncle Charles had introduced her to the older man just before the first dance of the evening. The duke had been a far better dance partner than Hartley, and he was not unattractive for a man nearing his fifties. But his almost black eyes had stared into hers with a piercing intensity that had kept her fighting off shivers.

Hannah had been trying to avoid the man ever since. Now she studiously ignored his gaze as she slipped between the couples beginning to cluster on the dance floor, then made her way to the windows and stepped out into the cool night air.

The heels of Hannah's shoes clicked softly as she crossed the flagstone terrace to the stone wall bordering the garden. She looked up at the sapphire sky, focusing on the round silver ball of a moon and took a deep breath as she mulled over her conversation with Hartley.

It was impossible for her to believe everything he'd said, and yet she knew some of it must be true. She turned Hartley's words over and over in her mind, concentrating on his insistence that Quinton's betrothal to her cousin had come about out of economic considerations rather than love.

Hannah's fingers tightened on the edge of the rock parapet. Cicely deserved better than that; she deserved a man who would love and cherish her. The man Hannah had met in the woods earlier today would be capable of the sort of gentle love Cicely needed, unlike the cold, grasping man Hartley had described. Which man had Cicely fallen in love with? Certainly not the stiff, formal earl that Quinton Blackthorne appeared to be when he escorted Cicely onto the dance floor.

The soothing strains of a waltz floated onto the terrace from the house behind her, but this had no effect on Hannah's emotions, which continued to twist and churn within her. All day long she had cherished the memory of each moment she'd spent with "Mr. Quinton." The enchantment of the forest encounter had lingered long after the sun had dispersed the last of the morning mist.

Hannah's lips twitched into a bitter smile, and her stomach tightened into a knot as she wished she could wipe all recollection of the morning's meeting from her mind. The man's betrothal to her cousin meant she had no right to think of him at all.

But her attempts to forget those moments were futile. Little remembrances were everywhere. Even now, a small breeze caressed Hannah's arms, instantly evoking the memory of Quinton's fingers on her flesh. She glanced down at the ivy trailing along the stone fence and recalled the deep green of his eyes. Some unseen force tightened its hold on her heart, and Hannah closed her eyes and told herself she was very foolish to have allowed herself to become so enamored of a complete stranger.

"Hannah."

Her name, spoken hesitantly in a deep voice, made her swivel around. Quinton stood two feet away, his face pale in the moonlight, his eyes dark and shining.

"I need to speak with you," he said. "I need to explain about this morning."

Hannah shivered as his voice seemed to reach out and caress her. She felt an insidious warmth rush through her, a warmth she knew she had no right to feel. She straightened and shook her head. "That will not be necessary, Your Lordship. I'm only happy that I could provide you with a little entertainment on such an important day in your life."

Hannah stepped forward, planning to stalk past him, but Quinton took her arm and turned her to face him. Only inches away from him now, she looked defiantly up. The expression she saw there made her eyes widen and some of the ice around her heart melt. She saw no sign of the haughty earl she'd noticed earlier, only a man with dark eyes full of concern and sorrow.

Quint gazed into Hannah's wide dark eyes. There were so many things he wanted to say, and even more things he wanted to do. He stared at her angry, compressed lips and longed to kiss them to softness, but he knew he wouldn't. His fate was sealed, and he wouldn't allow himself to repeat the morning's transgressions. Still, he felt a strange need to explain his actions somehow, an urgent desire to keep her from hating him.

"Hannah." Quint forced himself to speak. "I wasn't looking for amusement this morning, nor am I in the habit of assaulting innocent young women lost in the woods."

He paused, opened his mouth as if to say something further, only to shut it again. Hannah watched him lift his head and stare past her to where the forest lay in the blackness of night. A moment later he looked down at her again.

"You mentioned a sense of enchantment about the forest this morning, remember?" he asked.

Hannah nodded slowly.

Quint tightened his jaw, then took a deep breath. "Well, I felt it, too. You see, my mother used to tell me stories about those woods, about wood nymphs and elves." He stopped and glanced to one side, as if embarrassed to mention this, then looked back into Hannah's eyes as he went on. "I don't think about those fanciful tales often, but for some reason they were on my mind this morning. And somehow, between half believing you might be a fairy queen and the haunting atmosphere of the mist, I apparently forgot how to behave properly."

Hannah stared up at him silently as Quint's lips twisted into a self-deprecating smile. "You may think me a fool if you like," he said. "I know this is a ridiculous explanation for what passed between us there, but I have no other to offer." He leaned closer to look intently into Hannah's eyes, and his voice deepened. "Please believe me when I say that I meant no disrespect, to you or to Cicely. I look upon what happened as completely inexplicable, not to mention inexcusable. But I do hope you can forgive me." He paused. "You did say you wanted to be friends."

Hannah's blood pounded in her ears as she stared up into Quint's moonlit face. Her flesh tingled where his fingers encircled her arm, her body was flushed with sudden warmth, and she felt her lips part with the memory of his mouth on hers.

Hannah felt her chest rise and fall more quickly, then blinked in sudden anger, this time at herself. The man had offered her an apology, and it was obvious that he was sincere in this. She could hardly refuse to forgive him, especially when she remembered how she had shamelessly returned his kisses.

Hannah glanced away into the blue of the night, recalling the gray morning fog and the feeling that she had been lost somewhere out of time. Perhaps his explanation for the force that had brought them together wasn't so absurd after all. A feeling of immeasurable sadness welled up in her chest. Regardless of the explanation, the morning's events would have to remain both out of time and out of mind.

Hannah looked into Quint's eyes and nodded solemnly. "I'll put this morning completely out of my mind." She paused, and her lips curved suddenly. "I suppose worse could have happened to us, especially when you consider what the Bard did to Oberon in *A Midsummer Night's Dream*."

Quinton's lips twisted into the half-grin that had become so achingly familiar to her in such a short time. "You're right," he said. "I have no desire to share my bed with a donkey, though I probably deserve to be turned into one."

"No." Hannah's voice rang with conviction. "It was all

a mistake. And we *should* be friends. I know Cicely wouldn't take it at all well if I were to be ungracious to her fiancé.''

Quint was still frowning into Hannah's eyes. Thinking that he needed to be further assured of her forgiveness, she gave him as wide a smile as she could manage and said lightly, ''Let's just forget anything happened at all.''

Quint nodded slowly, but in his mind all he could think of was the exhilaration he'd experienced in Hannah's presence that morning. He felt it even now, and beneath that emotion he felt something deeper, the growing need to pull her to him again and once more taste her sweet lips, and knew that he wasn't likely to forget anything at all.

Quint forced himself to loosen his grasp on Hannah's arm and took a step back. He gave her a small bow, then turned and crossed the flagstones to the French doors and slipped into the lighted room beyond, leaving Hannah to shiver as she remembered the look of resignation that had crossed his features, and to ponder the coldness that had gripped her heart.

Inside the ballroom, light cascaded onto the dancers. Charles Summerfield stood at the far end of the room, his thin lips curving as he watched his guests swirl beneath the glittering prisms of the huge chandelier. His eyes followed his daughter's pale blond head as Cicely moved gracefully around the room in the arms of the very wealthy duke of Ludmore. Then his gaze narrowed as he caught sight of Hannah stepping into the room by way of the French doors.

Only moments before, he'd seen Quinton enter through that very same doorway. The squire scowled as he watched Hannah gaze around the room, catch sight of Quinton not three feet from her, then turn with a quick jerk and walk toward the refreshment table, where her aunt Amelia stood.

''You can't tell me you're not enjoying yourself, Father.''

Hartley's jovial words made the squire turn quickly. His son's thin lips curved in a satisfied smile, and his pale gray eyes glinted with pleasure as he surveyed the titled throng that filled his father's "humble" manor house.

"You've truly outdone yourself this time." Hartley met his father's gaze as he spoke again. "Lady Anne is most impressed, as is her dear father. Lord Kendrick just spent a good time chatting horses with me, in fact. He's most impressed with our stable and seemed extraordinarily pleased when I led Lady Anne out onto the floor for a second dance."

At these words the squire's frown eased somewhat. He nodded as he replied, "That's most gratifying news my boy. But don't let this go to your head. Although Lady Anne seems quite taken with you and her father appears pleased by your attention to her, you're not without competition."

The squire stared at his son a moment longer, then brushed at a nonexistent piece of lint on his immaculate black jacket before turning to gaze at the colorful blur of dancers as he went on. "Lady Anne might be as plain as a mud fence and just as interesting, and her father might owe his very soul to creditors, but he's still the Earl of Kendrick and very aware of the value of that name. Since the man had the misfortune never to sire a son, and his only male relative died last year, you can be certain he's going to choose Anne's husband very warily. We must tread carefully if we are to assure him that *you* are the right man to inherit his title."

Hartley lifted his thin eyebrows slightly. "You hold the notes on many of his debts, Father. I assumed that this fact would tip the scales in my favor."

"No!" The squire twisted around to glare at his son. "We can't count on that. The man has a great deal of pride, if nothing else, and if this matter isn't handled properly he might marry his daughter off to someone else just to tweak our noses.'' He lowered his slender brows in a scowl. "This isn't another of your larks, Hartley. This is your future and the future of the Summerfield name. Don't act the fool.''

Hartley's hands tightened into fists at his side, but he simply smiled at his father. "Sir, I give you my word, all will go as planned. I will marry Lady Anne, and one day a grandson who bears your name will be born to the peerage.''

The squire nodded, and a small smile lifted the corners of his mouth as he turned to watch the dancers come to a stop at the end of the number. The smile widened as he noticed the Duke of Ludmore escort Cicely from the dance floor and lead her toward her fiancé. But as the couple approached Quinton, Squire Summerfield saw that the young earl's attention was not on his betrothed; it was directed somewhere across the room.

Once again the squire's gray eyes traced the direction of Quint's gaze, narrowing immediately when he caught sight of Hannah Bradley deep in conversation with her white-haired aunt.

"Father, you're frowning again.'' Hartley spoke in a low voice. "Is one of the servants behaving incorrectly? I'll see to it if you wish.''

The squire shook his head. "No. It's your silly little cousin again. It seems Hannah has attracted Quinton's eye.''

"Oh, really? How utterly diverting.''

The mocking amusement in his son's voice made the squire twist around and glare at Hartley once more. "There's nothing at all entertaining about it.'' His words came out in a low growl. "Just moments ago I saw them reenter the room separately from the terrace. Quinton was frowning deeply, and Hannah looked distinctly distracted. As Carolyn reminded me, Hannah is very like her father, totally lacking in regard for social conventions. I refuse to have the girl destroy my plans for Cicely.''

"Father, don't let yourself get so upset." Hartley fought to keep a straight face at his father's ire. Seeing a chance to prove his intelligence and maturity to the man, he spoke in a smooth, even voice. "Hannah can't cause any trouble. Cicely and Quinton officially announce their betrothal tonight, and the wedding is planned for next month. Nothing is going to stop that.''

The squire shot his son a doubtful look, and Hartley pressed his point. "Have you forgotten how desperately Quinton needs money? The meager amount Hannah's father left her for a dowry is nowhere near enough to tempt Quint to throw away his last chance to restore his beloved Blackthorne Hall.''

Hartley glanced across the room at his small cousin, and a sly smile twisted his lips. "But after the marriage takes place, this attraction might be something we want to encourage.''

His father grabbed Hartley by the lapels and pulled him into the foyer. "What godforsaken reason do you have for saying something like that?''

Hartley lifted his shoulders in an elaborate shrug. "I know it's no secret to you that your daughter's affections lie with someone other than her betrothed.''

"Parker." The squire spat out the name.

"I have reason to believe so . But don't get into a lather. Parker might resent the fact that he's only the second son, but he's full of noble ideas. That's probably what attracted our little Cicely to him in the first place. Anyway, Parker is resigned to the fact that Cicely and Quinton are going to be married. I just thought it might cheer my old friend if Quinton were to develop an outside interest. Parker would be more than happy to offer his comfort to Cicely, if she somehow learned of this from a concerned friend—or relative, perhaps."

The squire clenched his teeth more tightly with each word his son spoke. He longed to slap the silly smirk off Hartley's face, but forced himself to control his rising anger and speak with utter coldness.

"You really *are* a fool."

Hartley jumped slightly at his father's vehemence, then blinked as his father went on. "You know my plans, my desires. My grandchildren are going to be aristocrats. The brilliant match I made between Carolyn and Viscount Emmerly has already netted us a little lord and lady. You have agreed to do the same, and so has Cicely. There will be no talk of affairs, especially in her case."

The squire released his hold on the front of Hartley's jacket. "I refuse to allow your silly little sister to jeopardize all my work and plans by creating any question about the paternity of her children. Not that I think Cicely would have the courage to do such a thing even if she had the desire. But just in case, I believe I shall offer to purchase a commission in the navy for Parker."

Hartley frowned for a moment, then shrugged. "I suppose that's the best idea. I'm not absolutely positive about Cicely's feelings for him, but I know Parker's besotted with her." He stared ahead blankly for a moment, then spoke softly. "It's a pity. I shall miss having Parker to bounce about with. He's quite an amusing friend."

"That's only because he has no idea what a totally disloyal soul you are, my son." The squire chuckled dryly as the two men turned to reenter the ballroom. "Parker's friendship has served you well, of course. Because of your connection to the brother of an earl you've received a far better entrée to society than most sons of country squires. But as soon as you settle with Lady Anne, you'll be so far above Parker that to continue the friendship would be an embarrassment. It's best he be gone.''

A look of pain crossed Hartley's features, an expression his father didn't see as he gazed around at his ball. The squire smiled with satisfaction as he noticed that Cicely was once again dancing with Quinton, and that Hannah now moved around the room in the arms of Parker Blackthorne.

Totally unaware that her uncle was watching her, Hannah laughed as Parker finished recounting yet another scrape he had shared with Hartley.

"And the farmer never learned who the culprits were?" she asked.

Parker lifted reddish brows. "Of course not. That would have spoiled things entirely. Did you ever let Madame Lavoisier know that you and Cicely released all her pigeons?"

Hannah's eyes flew open as she looked into Parker's hazel eyes. "Did Cicely tell you about that?"

"Who else?" Parker nodded, then spoke slowly. "Cis and I are old friends. She's told me so much about you that I feel I've known you all my life."

Hannah glanced down to hide her puzzled frown as Parker twirled her around. It was strange that this man should have heard so much about her from Cicely when she couldn't for the life of her remember her cousin giving Parker more than a passing mention in any of her letters.

"But don't worry." Parker spoke in a conspiratorial whisper that made Hannah glance back up. "Your secrets are safe with me. No one here will force from my lips the stories of your escapades."

Hannah gave him a saucy grin. "What escapades?"

"Oh, I don't know. How about the time you parachuted out of your father's balloon into the middle of a lake?" Hannah's mouth fell open, and Parker shook his head in mock seriousness. "No, no one would believe that without proof. Perhaps you could show us how to juggle, or demonstrate your talents with the cards. You are quite adept at the shell-and-pea game as well, I understand.''

Once more Parker spun Hannah around as she stared into his laughing eyes. When they stopped, she was breathless and giddy, and a little worried. ''No one is to learn of these things.'' She looked up at him earnestly. ''My uncle will be furious if he finds out you know all this.''

Parker shook his head and smiled down at her. ''Don't worry. I won't say anything. Cicely told me not to.''

His last words were almost a whisper. Hannah saw Parker gaze off for a moment before giving her a little smile as he spoke in his normal tone of voice once more.

''You'll be down to see the race tomorrow, won't you?''

''Race?''

''Well, two races actually. We've arranged for several balloonists to assemble in the morning for a hound and hare race. Perhaps you'd care to participate.''

Parker's eyes twinkled, and Hannah reluctantly shook her head. ''Not unless you can spirit me into one of the baskets without my uncle learning of it.'' Hannah sighed. ''Never mind. It would never work.''

''I don't suppose the squire wants you racing horses, either. That's what we're doing in the afternoon. Would you care to watch?''

Hannah's lips curved slightly. ''I suppose that would be permitted. Where will it take place?''

''Well, it will start at the end of the drive. It's to be a steeplechase of sorts, but just into the village, around the church, and back, so we'll have but one steeple to chase. Most of the mounts will be from the squire's stable, of course, and Hartley's horse, Midnight, is the best of the lot. I don't imagine the purse will be too interesting, unless I can get Quint to race Hippocrates.''

Hannah felt her face grow warm at the mention of Quint's

name, but forced herself to ask calmly, "Your brother keeps a stable?"

"A stable?" Parker gave a quick laugh. "Just barely. We have a couple of carriage hacks, and I have a fair mount, but Hip is the only horse we have that is truly worth his oats and hay." He paused, frowning, then went on in a quiet voice. "The Blackthornes did keep a good stable once, though. I was very small when the horses had to be sold off, but I remember the filled stalls, the smell of horse and hay, the excitement of standing next to Quint and watching a blooded stallion send clods of dirt flying as he raced around the track."

Over the sound of the slowing music, Hannah could hear Parker's sigh. His eyes met hers, with a sad expression that didn't match his jaunty smile at all. "But the horses are all gone now. The squire bought most of them, I understand. I think Quint would like to start up again, but Grandmother is against it. I guess you can't blame her, after Father lost everything gaming. Raising horses is every bit as much a gamble as wagering, I suppose, but I've seen the pleasure Quint has gotten out of raising and training Hippocrates, and I think he'd be good at it."

Hannah felt a deep ache in her throat as she asked, "What does Quint say about this?"

Parker shook his head and gave her a wide smile. "He always tells me to go about my business and leave the worrying and planning to him and to Grandmother. It would be fine advice if I had any business to be about."

Hannah could find no reply to that, but fortunately at that moment the music stopped and so did the dancers. Parker bowed, and Hannah curtsied, then turned to walk over to where her aunt sat against the wall.

"Nice young man?" Aunt Amelia lifted her white eyebrows.

Hannah's lips curved as she smiled down at her aunt. "Very."

Amelia narrowed her eyes slightly. "Well, I must say I was glad to see you dancing with someone closer to your age. Most of the men who have partnered you are near your father's age and far from fit-looking. Your uncle Charles has apparently gone to work sooner than I expected."

Hannah glanced down at her aunt, then lowered herself into the chair next to the older woman before asking sharply, "What do you mean?"

Amelia cocked her head to one side and slanted her eyes at her niece. "Oh, come now, my girl. You don't really think your uncle wants to be saddled with the two of us for long, do you? It's my suspicion he's using this ball to pick out a prospective husband for you."

Chapter 5

Hannah's hand stopped suddenly in the process of smoothing the skirt of her mauve dress. She turned to her aunt, stared into the tiny wrinkled face for a moment, then blinked once.

"Oh, blast. You're right, of course. Can he do that? Make me marry someone I don't care for?" She shuddered as she thought of the piercing look in the eyes of the Duke of Ludmore. "After all, I'm not his daughter."

Amelia put her small hand over her niece's. "Don't look so frightened. I'm here to see you don't suffer a fate like that."

"I'm not frightened, I'm angry. You have no idea the strange questions I've been asked as I danced with some of these men. Now I understand. They were trying to see if I would be acceptable in their proper British world. Who knows what Uncle Charles has told them about me?"

Hannah paused as she glanced around the room. When she caught sight of the squire standing near the doorway, her eyes narrowed and her voice grew hard. "My father never did like the man. He said Uncle Charles was the kind who would take full charge of controlling the moon and the

stars if he could. I thought Father was exaggerating, until
we arrived and the squire began ordering you and me about.
Even then I told myself this was only because he had so
much planning to do for this celebration. Well, Uncle
Charles might run this house like some high and mighty
lord, but he's not going to run me. If he thinks—''

''Oh, my girl,'' Aunt Amelia broke in, her voice soothing
and commanding at the same time, ''rein in those horses.
Fighting the man will get you nowhere. And you must
admit, finding a husband to care and provide for you
wouldn't be such a bad thing at this point. Your father hardly
left you a wealthy woman.''

Hannah swiveled around to face her aunt. ''No, he didn't
leave me much money, but Skylark is mine. If I had my
way I'd be traveling the fair circuit right now, earning my
living as he did. Madame Blancharde did quite well, you
know. I feel another female aerostat, especially one with
my competence, could make good money.''

When Hannah saw her aunt's face harden, she went on
quickly, ''Besides, my father left me a much more treasured
legacy, the memory of the love he shared with my mother.
I will not settle for less than that kind of love. And I assure
you that I could never come to have any such feelings for
a man like the Duke of Ludmore, no matter how much
money he might have.''

Amelia squeezed her niece's hand again and shook her
head. ''I'm not suggesting you even try, my darling. But
there are a few younger men here. Parker Blackthorne seems
to be quite nice. He's not as handsome as his brother the
earl, but he has a shy humor I find quite attractive. What
do you think?''

Hannah followed the direction of her aunt's gaze and
easily spied Parker's auburn hair across the room, where he
stood next to Hartley.

She sighed. Her aunt was right. Parker wasn't as handsome as Quinton Blackthorne, but the young man did have the ability to laugh. Dancing with him and listening to his amusing stories, she'd forgotten the disappointment and heartache that had plagued her ever since she'd learned that Quinton was not free to be hers.

Hannah continued to look at Parker, considering his good points. He had very nice hazel eyes, she remembered, large and attentive and never cynical like Hartley's. Parker was obviously athletic as well. He was tall and leanly muscled like his brother.

That thought was all it took to make her remember Quinton's hard form pressing along the length of hers. This memory brought those sensations immediately to life, igniting Hannah's senses. Without conscious volition, her gaze moved to the right and unerringly found the tall, black-haired man. All evening, ever since their talk on the terrace, she'd been careful to avoid looking at him. But somehow, no matter where she was or whom she danced with, she seemed to sense exactly where Quint was.

Hannah stared at Quint a moment and saw him flash his rare boyish smile at Cicely as they spoke with another couple. The dart of pain that pierced her chest was so sharp and sudden that she almost gasped. Instead she frowned, both at Quint and at her reaction to him. This strange response was completely unwanted. He belonged to her cousin. But Hannah knew it would be a long time before the magic of her moments with Quint faded from her memory.

Hannah glanced back at Parker. He was nice, but there was no magic in his touch, and his smile didn't twist her heart around as Quinton's did. Hannah shook her head and turned to her aunt.

"As I said, I will not marry unless I can be certain of having the kind of marriage my parents had. And no one, neither Uncle Charles nor you, can force me to."

With those words Hannah stood and stalked across the

room with every intention of mounting the stairs to her bedroom and thwarting her uncle's plans. She was barely conscious of the crowd surrounding her until she felt someone grasp her hand and heard Cicely's soft voice call her name.

Hannah turned slowly. Cicely gave her a tight smile, then glanced at the man by her side.

"You haven't danced with the earl yet, Hannah. There's to be one more number before supper, and I would like for you to dance it together so you can come to know each other."

Cicely turned to Quint. "That is all right with you, isn't it, Your Lordship?"

Hannah's heart skipped a beat, then began racing erratically. The last thing she wanted was to move around the room in this man's arms. She held her breath, hoping Quint would deny his fiancée's request, but he simply nodded and reached out to take her gloved hands as he replied to Cicely, "Of course it's all right."

Before Hannah could think of a reasonable excuse to escape this torture, the orchestra started playing, Quint took her right hand in his left, placed his other hand lightly on her back, and they were dancing.

Dancing with Quint was nothing like any of her earlier experiences on the ballroom floor. Unlike Hartley, Quint moved smoothly around the room. Hannah fell into step with him immediately, and soon they were gliding across the floor with effortless grace. Hannah was intensely aware of the strength of Quint's arm around her and the feel of his fingers holding hers. Despite her attempts to regard this as just another dance, she felt her heart pounding wildly and tightened her lips in vexation at her inability to control her reaction to his nearness.

"You know," Quint said, "if you wish Cicely to think

that we are becoming friends, you really should smile a little.''

Hannah looked up to his solemn green gaze, then lifted her shoulders in a slight shrug. ''I don't feel much like smiling.''

''I'm sorry.''

Quint's left eyebrow dropped into a half-frown of concern, and Hannah shook her head.

''Don't look so worried,'' she said. ''It's not you I'm angry with; it's my uncle Charles.''

''Oh? What's he done?''

''It's not something he's done, but something he is planning.'' Hannah's eyes narrowed as she looked up to Quint. ''According to my aunt Amelia the man is trying to arrange a marriage for me.''

A dark frown shadowed Quint's green eyes as he nodded very slowly. ''Well, the squire is very good at that sort of thing. He'll most likely arrange a very advantageous match for you.''

Hannah stared at Quint, barely breathing as she moved with him across the floor. His words had lacked all feeling, and his face was void of expression. Here was the stiff formal man she had seen with her cousin earlier, a man who was more of a stranger to her now than he had been when first she saw him in the woods.

''I don't want to make an advantageous match.'' Though Hannah spoke softly, her voice trembled with defiance. ''I will only marry someone I truly love.''

One black eyebrow quirked up. ''That's a very nice sentiment, but hardly very practical.''

Hannah shook her head slightly. ''I've never heard it said that there was anything practical or logical about love.''

Hannah felt her throat close over this last word, remembering in an instant how her own irrational emotions regarding this man had turned her life upside down. Despite her anger at Quint's cool assessment of her situation, her body registered only the pleasure of being held in his arms, the warmth of his hand around hers, and the sensual ease with which he moved.

"We were discussing marriage, not love." Quint's words broke into Hannah's thoughts. She frowned up at him as he went on, "They are usually two very different things, no matter how we may wish otherwise."

Quint's reasonable tone made Hannah want to scream. Instead she replied in a level voice, "Not always. My parents were very much in love and very happy in their marriage."

"So were my grandparents," Quint replied. "And after seeing their happiness together, I tried for that the first time I married. It didn't work. Perhaps I should apologize for my cynicism, but I've seen love matches cause more pain than joy, and I've come to believe that practicality is a much more reliable criterion in choosing a mate."

A cold hand closed over Hannah's heart as she gazed at Quint's implacable sculpted features. Again she shook her head.

"Hartley told me you were marrying Cicely only for her dowry. I didn't believe him."

Quint raised his brows slightly, then lowered them to a frown as he gazed into Hannah's eyes. "And did he also mention that Cicely is marrying me only for my title?"

He paused a moment, then smiled tightly. "I thought not. Well, she is. Cicely is no more in love with me than I am with her. In fact, I have every reason to believe that she is very much enamored of my brother."

Hannah's eyes widened as Quint gently twirled her around in the middle of the floor. She shook her head, then missed the next step. Quint smoothly guided her back on track, never taking his eyes off hers.

"You don't believe me, I can tell." His lips twisted into

a wry smile. "I'm sorry to disillusion you so. But if you are going to survive here, you should know how things are. Otherwise you'll make very dangerous blunders."

"I've already done that." Hannah's voice was low and hard as she stared up into Quint's eyes. "And you're right . . . I don't believe what you said about my cousin. Cicely isn't the kind of woman who could blithely marry someone for a title, then live under the same roof as the man she truly loves."

"Parker lives in town, at his club. And Cicely has been trained by a master, her father. She is doing exactly what is expected of her." Quint paused and looked deep into Hannah's eyes. "I may sound heartless, but I do plan on doing my best to make your cousin happy. I would never have agreed to marry her if I thought that she and Parker had made any plans. But given their situation—Parker's position as a near penniless younger son and Cicely's loyalty to her father—there was never any hope of their marrying each other."

"So they just forget about their feelings?" Hannah shivered as she glared up at Quint.

"Most likely they will, in time. The heart can ache for only so long. Then it scars over and becomes numb."

Hannah stared up in mute disbelief at his callous attitude as the music slowed to an end. She followed him numbly across the room to where Cicely waited for them. At her cousin's insistence, Quint escorted both women into a huge hall filled with linen-draped tables, where he seated Hannah and Cicely at the far corner of a long table, then took his place between them.

Hannah's hands tightened in her lap. She wanted to excuse herself, but after one look at Cicely's wide, unfocused eyes, she knew she had to stay. Still, she felt as if she had been placed in a glass cage, forced into a situation where she could do nothing more than observe.

A few moments later Parker escorted his grandmother and Aunt Amelia to the table, followed by Lady Anne Kendrick, a tall, thin woman in a peach-colored gown, with medium brown hair framing plain, pleasant features. She was in the company of her father, the Earl of Kendrick, and Hartley.

Hannah watched as Hartley sat next to Lady Anne, and immediately began speaking.

"I hope you and your father will be comfortable at the family table tonight," he said to Lady Anne. "I know you are acquainted with my sister and her fiancé. Most likely with the countess as well."

Lady Anne's thin lips parted in a wide smile as she nodded at Lady Evelyn. "Of course. The countess and my father are old friends. Papa and Lady Evelyn's son often used to bid against each other for the same horses, when we could still afford to keep a stable."

Lady Evelyn nodded in acknowledgment, but her lips pursed as they tightened. Hartley spoke again, his words somewhat rushed. "Well, allow me to introduce you to my cousin from America, Hannah Bradley, and her aunt Amelia."

Hannah nodded and managed a smile to acknowledge the introduction. A moment later her smile disappeared as her uncle Charles and the Duke of Ludmore approached the table and took the last remaining seats.

Hannah couldn't remember when she had enjoyed a meal less. The other diners murmured often over the excellent fare as course followed course, but to Hannah everything tasted like paste as she became aware of strange undercurrents flowing between the people surrounding her.

Hartley kept the conversation lively during the meal, with Parker chiming in occasionally. Hannah noticed that the auburn-haired young man seemed to become more loquacious with each glass of wine, and more than once she caught

Cicely glancing at Parker with an expression that held concern and some other emotion Hannah couldn't identify.

Hannah refused to believe Quint's claim that her cousin was in love with Parker. Regardless of Cicely's timidity, Hannah was certain the girl had more backbone than to allow her father to force her to marry someone she didn't care for, especially if Cicely cared deeply for someone else.

A light dessert of iced raspberries in chocolate sauce had been placed before Hannah, when Lady Anne's voice echoed across the table and drew her from her thoughts.

"I can't tell you how much I'm looking forward to tomorrow's races." Her enthusiasm rang down the table. "I've never seen a balloon ascent before, but I understand they are beautiful to watch. Of course, Father is no doubt more interested in the horse race in the afternoon."

Lord Kendrick nodded and glanced at Hartley. "I'm looking forward to seeing that magnificent black beast of yours in action."

"I'm sure that Midnight will be happy to oblige." Hartley smiled. "He loves nothing more than a good hard race." He paused and looked down the table at Quint. "You are going to give my horse a run for his money by racing Hippocrates tomorrow, aren't you? Your mount is likely to be the only real competition my horse faces."

Quint lifted his slender brows slightly. "Yes, we'll be there. And thank you for the compliment."

"Well, I believe in giving the devil his due, old man. I still can't believe you found such a prize. Tell me, Quint, how did you come to own that magnificent beast? I attend all the sales. I can't believe I'd overlook a horse like Hippocrates."

"Oh, it was just Quint's blasted luck again."

Hannah, along with everyone else, looked at Parker, who wore a nonsensical smile as he leaned forward to look at Quint.

"Tell them the story, old boy, about the deal you came upon at the fair while selling the oats." Parker straightened as he finished speaking and looked down the table. Without giving his brother a chance to speak, he went on. "Hip was the sorriest excuse for a colt I ever saw. Quint not only bought him but paid far more than I would have paid for that spindly collection of bones."

Quint shrugged. "Hippocrates *was* thin as a colt. And to be honest, I can't really say why I bought him."

"I'll tell you why," Lord Kendrick spoke up. "Because you are your father's son. Old Blackthorne made many a mistake in his life, but never when it came to choosing horses."

Quint frowned slightly as he took a sip of wine, then shrugged. "You might be right about that. Father used to take me along when he purchased horses. I suppose I learned something from him. Either that"—he paused with a smile—"or I just had enormous luck, as my brother suggested."

"Ah, yes, luck." Parker took a long drink from his glass, then smiled down the table. "Are you willing to try that luck of yours out tomorrow on the balloon race? I'm piloting one, as is Hartley."

Quinton shook his head. "Never having been up in a balloon, I shall have to decline."

"That's true. You are always involved in far too serious matters to accompany us into the skies. What a shame." Parker frowned into his glass, then lifted his brows and stared down the table at Hannah. "I know. You can go up with Hannah. She even has her own balloon, don't you, Hannah?"

Hannah was aware that everyone else at the table had turned to stare at her as she gazed back at Parker. Her mind whirled as she felt her uncle's gray eyes on her. How had

Parker come to know about the balloon that the squire had
reluctantly agreed to store for her?

Hannah glanced at Cicely and saw the girl look away
quickly. Hannah frowned again. Parker certainly seemed to
be the repository of all her cousin's secrets. Were secrets
the only thing they shared?

Hannah blinked away her suspicions as Parker spoke
again, "Well, what do you say, girl?"

Hannah shifted her eyes to Quint. He lifted one black
eyebrow but said nothing.

"Certainly she'll do it." Cicely's voice rang out loud
and strong, drawing the attention of everyone at the table.
Hannah stared at the suddenly smiling young woman as she
spoke again. "I'm sure few of you are aware of this, but
my cousin is an excellent balloonist. My father was saving
that fact to surprise you with tomorrow. However, since the
subject came up tonight I want to add that I shall be honored
if Hannah agrees to help the earl meet his brother's challenge."

Cicely lifted her wine goblet. "A toast! To all those who
fly tomorrow. Good wind and sunshine."

"You fool."

Hartley pulled Parker into the hallway, away from the
crowd moving back to the ballroom. Parker glanced down
at the fist that clutched the front of his black waistcoat, then
back into Hartley's scowling face.

"Fool? Why? I know I'm a bit foxed, old man, but so
what? I've seen you drink a little too deeply from the goblet,
and I've said nothing of it to you."

"Yes, but my drinking hasn't caused you to lose the
prospect of a titled bride."

Parker shrugged and his lips parted into a silly smile.
"Probably not. But then, most women, titled or no, aren't
interested in second sons, are they?" He paused, and before

Hartley could reply he went on in a sober, bitter tone. "At least not to the point they consider marriage."

Hartley stared at his friend a moment, his features softening a little. "How many times do I have to tell you that if it were left up to my sister, I'm certain she *would* marry you, even without a title or money. It's my father who has forced her into marriage with Quint. And it's my father who will be most displeased if I fail to impress Lady Anne with my abilities in the air tomorrow."

Parker's brow wrinkled into a puzzled frown. "So? Impress the lady. You're a capable aerostat. What have I to do with that?"

"You've lessened my chances of winning that balloon race, that's what. First by goading Quinton into going up with Hannah, then by suggesting that Hannah pilot her balloon."

"It wasn't all my doing, you know. Cicely's the one who made the girl agree." Parker lifted his head to gaze into his friend's eyes. "Why did Cicely do that, I wonder? She wasn't herself tonight. I do believe she even frowned at me as she raised her glass in that toast."

"And with good reason, fool." Hartley tightened his fingers around Parker's vest and pulled the loose-jointed man toward him again. "Cicely warned you that no one was to bring up Hannah's ability to pilot a balloon. Besides, not only are you drunk, but you've spent most of the evening sniping at your brother, when you should just stand up to Quint and tell him that Cicely should be marrying you instead of him."

"I can't do that." Parker jerked away from Hartley and took two long steps before pivoting back. His ginger-colored eyebrows met in a deep scowl. "Grandmother thinks I am worse than useless as it is." His hard-edged voice sounded completely sober. "If I botch up her one chance at restoring the family honor and position, she will never forgive me."

He shook his head as he stepped up to Hartley. "And speaking of botching things up, just what do you think would happen if I should succeed in such an unlikely move? I believe your father has threatened to disown those of you who marry against his wishes. Despite whatever feelings Cicely holds for me, I doubt she cares enough to spend her life in genteel poverty. As if I'd ask it of her."

Hartley sighed and shook his head. "I don't know. *I* certainly wouldn't want that, but Cis has strange ideas."

Hartley stared off to one side for a moment, then frowned as he blinked and turned back to Parker. "All of this is beside the point. We were talking about *my* marriage prospects. They will be greatly reduced if your idiocy and your juvenile jealousy cause me to lose that race. As my father has reminded me, the Earl of Kendrick doesn't care for losers. Do you remember what he used to do to his horses if they lost too many races? Yes, he shot them. I have to win that race tomorrow or he will scratch me as a possible husband for his daughter."

Parker took a deep breath and released it in a forceful sigh. "You'll win. We have our plan, remember? I'll run interference with my balloon and make it look like I'm a bumbling idiot up there, getting in the way of everyone else while you get to the target first."

Hartley shook his head. "That was a fine plan before. But I doubt that you could even keep up with Hannah, let alone get in her way, if Cicely's stories about the girl's expertise have any truth to them."

Parker stared at his friend a moment, then shrugged. "Then bind and gag your cousin till the race is over. Quint can't pilot the balloon himself."

"You *are* foxed, aren't you?" Hartley shook his head, then turned to pace back and forth for a few moments. He stopped suddenly and looked up with the beginnings of a smile. "No, binding and gagging certainly wouldn't work.

For one thing, the plan lacks subtlety. But you're on the right track.''

"You have a plan? Tell me."

"Not now, not in your condition. Just stay close to me tomorrow as race time approaches. I may need your help."

Chapter 6

"Ludmore is unhappy." Squire Summerfield spoke in a low, even tone.

Hartley clasped his hands behind his back as he crossed the dew-dampened lawn toward the field where the balloons were being readied for flight.

"I take it the duke's horse lost again."

"You know it did." The squire turned to glare at his son. "I warned you about getting greedy. He's suffered too many losses too close together now."

Hartley lifted his pale brows as he met his father's gaze. "I didn't realize the man's pockets were so shallow or that the contents of the late duchess's jewelry box were so meager."

"The duke still has many choice pieces at his disposal, young man, of that I'm certain. That's not the point. He has become suspicious, and we can't afford that."

Hartley drew in a deep breath of cool morning air, then sighed. "Well, then, I suppose his luck will have to change for a while."

The two men stopped about ten feet away from a long bag of silk hanging empty from a tall gibbetlike pole as a man dressed in brown attached a hose to the mouth of the uninflated balloon.

"Yes, and not just at the track." The squire lowered his voice. "He's interested in Hannah."

Hartley turned in surprise. "That little sparrow? Why, in God's name? Doesn't he know she has no money?"

"Of course he knows. I'm wiser than to try to fool a man on that account." The squire's lips twisted into a small smile. "Actually, my honesty about Hannah's lack of wealth might possibly have eased the duke's suspicions somewhat. And as to his attraction to your cousin, the man is known for his weakness for young blondes."

The squire turned to his son suddenly. His smile had faded and his eyebrows lowered into a scowl. "I don't want you to involve yourself in this matter. I hardly trust you to handle a young woman as skittish as Hannah. I shall deal with her. I just wanted you to be aware of the situation."

Hartley tightened his jaw and nodded stiffly. "Of course. Well, I have the Lady Anne to impress with my abilities in the air. I'd best join the others. Are you going to watch?"

"Of course." His father turned and looked across the field until he spotted a young woman dressed in blue, with all but the back of her golden hair covered by a matching hat. "If for no other reason than to keep an eye on your cousin."

"Not so close, now, little lady. This isn't a plaything, you understand."

Hannah gazed up at the half-filled silver balloon towering above her like a bloated mushroom cap. She lifted her skirt and took a step back to accommodate the short man dressed in tan knickers, jacket, and cap who was working the machinery that pumped helium into the oversized silk bags. Hannah grimaced as her skirt rustled.

The high-necked dress of sky-blue satin was not going

to be the most comfortable outfit for this excursion, and the broad-brimmed blue hat trimmed with pink flowers was far less practical than the simple straw hat she usually tied on when she took to the air. If she'd had her choice of clothing she would have worn a simple skirt and shirtwaist, but her uncle insisted she dress formally. At least she'd had the good sense to leave off her corset so she could move more easily.

Figuring she had moved away far enough, Hannah stared at the silver fabric straining against the hemp netting as it bobbed slightly in the breeze. The supporting pole had been removed, and as the balloon swelled, so did her heart. *Skylark* was going to fly again.

Several yards away, silk stripes of blue and gold began to take on a more rounded form, indicating that another balloon was almost full. Just beyond that, a fully inflated globe of bright orange, trimmed with gold festoons, swayed within the grasp of the ropes that were staked to the ground, still unattached to the round wicker basket sitting nearby.

Three other balloons, each in a different stage of readiness, towered behind her. Hannah turned around, surveying the sight, and tears filled her eyes as memories of her father flashed through her mind. The whisper of the rubberized silk against the netting, the hiss of the gas entering the envelopes, the brilliant colors of the silk and the blue of the beckoning sky above brought vividly to mind the many times she had accompanied her father into the ether.

"Is this the famous *Skylark* that Cicely told me about?"

Hannah turned to see Parker standing behind her. His face was very pale beneath his dark red hair as he stared at the inflating bag.

"Yes." Hannah felt her throat close over that single word. She coughed slightly. "This was my father's most prized possession. I thought it would be at least a year before

I could fly in it again. I want to thank you for suggesting this last night.''

Parker coughed lightly, too, then gave her a lopsided smile that reminded her very much of Quint's. "I have a feeling that you and I are the only ones pleased with this. I noticed the squire scowling at you a few moments ago, and I have a fuzzy recollection of Hartley scolding me for bringing up the subject last night.''

"Well, I hope he wasn't too hard on you. I suppose I can understand their concern.''

"Yes, it can be dangerous up there.''

Hannah gave Parker a sharp look. "Oh, I don't think for one moment that either my uncle or Hartley is worried about my safety. Uncle Charles is only anxious about what his guests might think of me. It's certainly not uncommon for a woman to ride in a balloon, but I think he feels that no true lady should know how to pilot one. I imagine Hartley feels the same way.''

Parker shrugged and grinned weakly as he rubbed his forehead. "I wouldn't know about that; I don't recall much of what Hartley said.'' He paused and looked back up to the billowing ball of silver. "Is this the same balloon that swept your father and mother away after their marriage?''

"No, but it's identical to that one. Father had several balloons, all the same color and all named *Skylark*. That way, when he returned to a city he'd visited before, people would recognize him and clamor for rides. The balloons need to be replaced when they become torn or worn out, so I expect that this is the last *Skylark*. They are very expensive.''

Hannah's voice trembled as she spoke these last words, and her eyes stung with sudden tears that could not be blinked away. She gazed at the blurred silver orb, dreading the day when this last reminder of her father would exist no more.

A warm hand closed over hers, and Hannah glanced up into Parker's hazel eyes, seeing concern and care. "Don't cry," he said. "It never brings them back. I cried for weeks after my father died, and that's what everyone told me."

Hannah lifted her free hand to wipe the moisture from her cheeks. "I know that, and I imagine you did, too. Papa told me not to weep for him, but sometimes it just happens."

Parker gave her a quick smile as he released her hand. "Well, if truth be told, I imagine your father would probably be disappointed if you didn't grieve a little. But you are all right now, aren't you?"

Hannah nodded.

"Good. I seem to remember Hartley saying he needed to see me before the race, so I'd best find him. But I did want to wish you luck."

"Thank you." Hannah smiled back. "I need to be off, too. I should find your brother and give him some quick instructions. May the winds be kind to you."

Hannah gave him a wide smile, then watched him walk away. She started to move in the opposite direction, but stopped and turned to see that *Skylark* was almost completely inflated. She gazed at it for several moments, committing the sight to memory.

At the edge of the field, Quint leaned against a rock wall, gazing at the breathtaking sight of the huge colored balls bobbing and swaying beneath the pale morning sky. But even his appreciation of this magnificent sight didn't ease the twisted knot in his stomach, couldn't make him forget watching Parker stand so close to Hannah and take her hand in his.

The rational, reasonable portion of Quint's mind strove for control over his inappropriate anger and jealousy. As he had numerous times in the last two days, he told himself it was insane to feel this way about a woman he had just met, a nymph he'd held in his arms for one brief moment.

Yet that one moment haunted him so. That short time in the gray mist rose to mock him with a vision of a life and a love that would never be his. It was impossible for him to see Hannah without longing to pull her into his arms.

He had felt some measure of control returning last night, when he danced with Hannah and explained his views on love and marriage, and when he woke this morning, he felt as if he had his emotions in check. He'd risen before the sun, seen to his morning duties with all the single-minded attention he'd devoted to those mundane concerns before his meeting with Hannah.

Then he had come down to the field. The multicolored balloons rising above him like a garden of giant flowers budding forth had touched that portion of his mind that responded to beauty and fantasy. He watched one balloon after another fill to graceful glory beneath a pink and yellow sunrise, and he suddenly felt bereft. His heart and soul hungered for the freedom these monsters of the air promised, but he knew his life was inexorably bound to earth, and to Blackthorne Hall.

It was then that he'd spied Hannah and Parker in intimate conversation beneath the billowing silver balloon, and his hands had tightened into fists as his stomach twisted into a clump of futile anger.

Quint watched Hannah turn away from the balloon at that moment and cross the field toward him, her attention on the uneven ground beneath her feet until she reached him. When she looked up, her blue eyes widened in surprise and for one moment a joyful expression brightened her features. Quint's heart lifted, then dropped when she blinked and her lips tightened into a polite smile.

"Good morning, Your Lordship."

Hannah's voice was soft and held no sarcasm, but the earl frowned as he replied, "Quint will do just fine." He paused, then forced himself to smile and speak more lightly.

"After all, you are to be my captain today, aren't you? I've been standing here awaiting my orders."

The teasing lilt to Quint's voice made Hannah take a deep breath. She allowed her lips to curve into a smile as she told herself that her sudden anger at the man had been childish, and reminded herself of what her father had taught her: that a balloon pilot must learn to deal with the caprices of the wind. Now she must learn to accept the whims of fate that had brought the same man into her life and Cicely's.

"There isn't much I can tell you at this point," she replied. "It's all quite simple and very complicated at the same time. If you're willing to follow my orders without question, we'll do fine. I am aware, however, that some men have trouble with that idea."

Quint's lips twisted in a wry smile. "It shouldn't be a problem for me. I've been doing my grandmother's bidding for years. Where's Cicely?"

"I don't know." Hannah looked up at Quint's question. "She told me she would be down to see us off."

They stood in the midst of a fair-sized crowd consisting of balloonists and men and women who were there to observe the ascent and await the results of the race.

Several servants circulated through the crowd carrying silver trays holding glasses of sparkling champagne. Both Hannah and Quint had just refused to take a glass when Parker and Hartley stepped up to them. Hartley held a silver goblet in his hand.

"You don't mean to refuse to join our toast, do you? We must celebrate Quint's maiden flight and initiate him into the fellowship of aerostats." Hartley looked from Hannah to Quint with a smile. "Come, now. I have a special toast prepared." He handed the silver goblet to Hannah, then took two glasses from the servant's tray and handed one to Quint as he took the other.

"Parker!"

Hartley spoke sharply. Hannah glanced to one side to find Parker staring at the goblet she held. His reddish brows remained in a frown for a moment as he continued to gaze at the silver vessel in Hannah's hand. Then he blinked and looked up.

"What?"

"It's time for the toast." Hartley lifted his glass and soon a sea of goblets rose above Hannah, sparkling in the sunlight.

"To a successful first flight for my future brother-in-law and the brave young woman of the skies, my cousin Hannah Bradley."

Hannah blinked in surprise at Hartley's words, then watched as all around her people started to drink. Hannah stared at the pale amber liquid in the silver goblet she held. She didn't care at all for the taste of champagne, but knew it would be rude not to drink it after that special toast. Slowly she lifted the rim to her lips, then tipped her head back to down the bitter fluid as quickly as possible.

Moments later Hannah stood with the others and watched the weighing-off procedure of a balloon formed of alternating vertical strips of red, yellow, and blue silk. The middle was banded in bright red, where the balloon's name, *Intrepid,* was emblazoned in brilliant gold letters. Eight men surrounded the wicker basket attached to the multihued monster above, swaying in the slight breeze. When the men in the car tossed two heavy canvas bags to the ground, Quint leaned toward Hannah.

"Shouldn't the rest of us be in our balloons as well?" he asked.

Hannah shook her head. "The *Intrepid* is the hare balloon. It rises first, and the pilot maneuvers it off some distance and then drops a sandbag, like the ones used for ballast. That marks the target. Once the hare has moved out

of the ascension area, the rest of us—the hounds—will take
off and do our best to follow. The winner of the race is the
balloon that drops its sandbag nearest to the target.''

A loud voice emanated from the *Intrepid*. ''Hands off.''
Hannah turned her attention from Quint to that balloon. The
men surrounding the basket released their hold on the rim,
and the basket rose, though only a scant six inches. ''Hands
on!'' rang across the field and the men once more grabbed
the basket and pulled it to earth.

''What are they doing?''

The soft feminine tones made Hannah turn to her right
to find Cicely standing at her elbow. ''There you are. We'd
been wondering if you were coming down.''

Cicely gave her cousin a little smile. ''I'm sorry. I felt
too tired to rise very early this morning. But I'm glad I
wasn't too late to see you two off. Will the race begin
soon?''

''Yes. They'll be sending the hare balloon up any moment, as soon as they finish testing the basket for proper
balance. The pilot is trying to throw out enough ballast to
allow the balloon to rise, but not so much that he goes up
too high or too fast.''

Hannah looked back to watch the pilot jettison a single
sandbag along with several handfuls of sand from another.
Hannah smiled. ''This is definitely an experienced pilot who
seems to know his business. I think the next attempt to rise
will be successful.''

A moment later the hands-off order was given again, and
this time when the men released their hold the basket quickly
rose beyond recall. Hannah held her breath, watching the
huge balloon rise majestically, rotating slowly as it ascended
like a giant's toy top into the blue heavens. She leaned over
to speak quietly to Quint.

''Now watch the top of the balloon. If the pilot indeed

knows what he's about, he'll release some of his gas before he rises too high.''

Hannah lifted her face to watch the ever rising balloon, then spoke quickly. ''There it is. A thin bluish vapor rising above the balloon. Do you see it?''

''Yes.''

Quint and Cicely answered in unison. Hannah turned to find them staring at each other above her head. She spoke quietly to Quint. ''I'm going over to *Skylark* now and see if everything is ready. There's no reason for you to hurry yet. The *Intrepid* is still moving straight up. We can't ascend until it's completely out of our way.''

Hannah took a step away, then turned to her cousin and smiled. ''I want to thank you, Cicely, for helping to bring this about. I forgot how much I missed it all. I hope your father didn't give you too much of a scolding for chiming in with Parker.''

Cicely gave her cousin a tight smile that spoke volumes about the talking-to she'd received from the squire, but she simply shrugged as she replied, ''It wasn't too bad. He's only worried for your safety, you know.''

Hannah fought to keep from grimacing at the polite lie. ''Tell him he has nothing to worry about. I'll return to ground, with the balloon and your future husband intact.''

Hannah managed a smile as she finished speaking. Then she turned on her heel and walked away to give Cicely a chance to be with Quint for a few moments. Frowning angrily at the envy twisting in her heart, Hannah hurried across the grass to the silver balloon. At the basket she was greeted by the same small man who had filled her balloon earlier.

A concerned expression narrowed Albert Dunstan's features as he realized that this young woman was planning to fly the balloon. The moment she reached for the rim of *Skylark*'s basket he began to scold her for her foolishness in trying to pilot a craft that only men were meant to handle. But after five minutes of conversation, Mr. Dunstan was smiling, impressed by Hannah's expertise and caught up in her infectious excitement.

"I can't believe you are the daughter of Matthew Bradley," he said. "He was a one, wasn't he? Oh, the stories we've heard about his adventures. Is it true that at one point he held the record for the greatest number of solo flights across the United States?"

Hannah turned her attention from inspecting the wooden block and tackle used to secure the netting rope to the wicker basket and simply nodded in reply. Once again memories of her father had formed an aching knot in her throat that trapped her voice.

"Oh, yes, the stories that have been told about him are numerous." Dunstan paused, and his wide smile faded. "I was sorry to learn he had passed on. Just this morning we learned of it. It's a real shame. But in this business, we are aware of the risks. I'm sure he didn't suffer, miss. I'm told when you fall from such a height, you're gone before you hit the ground."

Hannah blinked and stared into the man's yellow-green eyes. Fall from what height? Then a deep voice echoed in her memory: Quint saying, "It would be far better if someone hinted that your father went down in a balloon somewhere." Hannah blinked again and managed a trembling smile.

"Yes, I was told he died instantly," Hannah replied softly. "It was painful to lose Papa, but I know that is how he would have chosen to go."

Dunstan nodded. "And in such splendor. I understand that this Grand Canyon is a marvel of natural beauty."

The Grand Canyon? The grief throbbing in Hannah's chest dissolved in a flash, replaced by the desire to laugh out loud. When Quint decided to embellish a legend, he certainly did it with style.

"Is it time to get in?"

Quint spoke from behind Hannah. She turned to him and nodded, then introduced him to Mr. Dunstan and watched as Quint climbed gracefully into the wicker car. Hannah stood looking at the rim of the basket, which was even with her chest, and wondered how she would manage to follow him without making a spectacle of herself.

Apparently Dunstan could read her mind, for he spoke quickly. "Just a moment, miss. Let me fetch you something to step on."

A few moments later he returned with one large wooden box and a smaller one. He set them on the ground, and Hannah gracefully ascended the makeshift steps. As she leaned forward to rest her hands on the basket edge, planning to jump lightly into the car, Quint's hands closed around her waist. Before she could protest, he easily lifted her up and in, setting her down lightly in front of him.

"Thank you." Her voice sounded small and breathless as she looked up into his dark green eyes. Quint stared down at her, his warm fingers still lightly touching her hips.

"You're welcome."

His voice was low. His eyes continued to hold Hannah's, and for one long moment it was as if they were back in the forest, shielded from the rest of the world by a gray mist of their own making.

"They've given the order to weigh off, miss."

Dunstan's gravelly voice broke the spell. Quint removed his hands, and Hannah stepped quickly away. Several men from the village surrounded the basket, and Cicely stood behind them, watching. Hannah smiled at her cousin, then turned to Quint.

"I want you to throw out the ballast. This is your race. I'm here only to advise you."

It took only two tries for them to reach the proper balance for flight. While they waited for the other pilots to get ready, Hannah explained the basics of ballooning. She pointed to the four-foot ring of iron above them, where the ropes from the net covering the balloon converged before being fastened to the wicker car. Two lighter ropes hung from the mouth of the balloon and were looped loosely around the ring.

"This one is the valve rope," she said. "We pull it to release a small amount of gas from the top of the balloon to control our rise when necessary. The gas expands as we go higher, you see, which is why the mouth of the balloon is open. If it weren't, the balloon might burst from the force of the expanding gas. We'll also release some vapor if we overshoot the air current we want, but I'll watch for that and tell you when it's necessary."

Quint gazed up through the opening to stare at the gaping interior of the balloon, then frowned. "But what if we release too much? How do we rise again?"

"That's what the sandbags are for." Hannah tipped her head to indicate the large pile of sandbags in each corner of the five-foot-square car. "If we need to rise, we toss out a bag, sometimes more than one, sometimes just a handful of sand. Now look at this other rope, the one painted red."

Quint looked up from his inspection of the bags on the wicker floor as Hannah continued. "This rope is attached to the rip panel. We don't want to pull it except in a dire emergency. It releases the gas in one big rush, allowing the silk to rise to the top of the netting and form a parachute to slow our descent."

Again Quint nodded. "And what's all this?" He pointed to several dials on one edge of the basket, then at several items on the floor.

"A barometer, a thermometer, and a compass. We shouldn't need them today; we will be navigating by line of sight." She pointed upward. "Those small flags will

catch the breeze and tell us which direction the air is blowing. And here''.—she directed his attention to several items
attached to the rim of the basket—''we have a grappling
hook, which we'll use when we land, and blankets to keep
us warm if we hit a very cold current. But I don't know
what's in that hamper on the floor. Dunstan?''

Hannah looked over the rim of the basket into the man's
upturned face. ''What's this hamper for?''

Dunstan grinned. ''Miss Cicely had me put it in. She
seemed concerned lest you miss a meal.''

Hannah turned to thank her cousin, but Cicely was no
longer standing near *Skylark*. Hannah glanced around, then
spied Cicely standing about fifty feet away beneath a pure
white balloon. The sun glinted on Parker's reddish hair as
he sat on the edge of the car and reached down to take
Cicely's gloved hand.

With the strange blend of clarity and distance found in
dreams Hannah watched her cousin laugh as Parker pre-
tended to be in danger of falling out of the basket. Cicely's
feelings for the man were clearly etched on her pale features.
Hannah frowned as she glanced down at her gloved fingers,
clutching the edge of the basket. Her head began to spin as
she remembered all the little clues she'd overlooked, Cicely's nervousness in Quint's presence, the way she always
referred to him as ''the earl,'' and her total lack of joy at
the prospect of marriage.

Hannah looked up at Quint, and met dark green eyes
looking closely at her. ''Well,'' she said, forcing herself to
speak, ''I would say we are all ready to go as soon as we
hear the word.''

Word came moments later with the cry of ''Hands off!''
Eight pairs of hands released their hold on the edge of
Skylark's wicker car and stepped back. Hannah watched as
the men seemed to fall away from her, growing smaller and
more distant by the moment.

There was no sense of lift as they rose. The only motion she could feel was the slow turning of the basket as it moved away from the ground. Hannah's mind was instantly freed of all worry as she was filled with expanding elation, the feeling of complete freedom that she experienced each time she took to the sky. Her lips curved into a wide smile of their own volition. Then suddenly she found her vision blurring and she frowned.

Her head began to spin far faster than the turning of the basket, and she reached out to grab the edge of the wicker car. She heard a loud roaring in her ears, like a thunderous wind. Then the sound eased to a mild hum, and Quint's voice seemed to come from much farther away than the tiny basket should allow.

"Hannah, is something wrong?"

Chapter 7

Quint stared at Hannah. Beneath the brim of her sky-blue hat, her face was as pale as a blank sheet of paper as she gripped the edge of the basket. "Hannah, is something wrong?" he asked again.

Hannah responded to his question this time, first blinking then turning slowly meet his gaze. Her eyes seemed too large, until she blinked again and shook her head.

"How very strange. I've never become dizzy on ascension before." She paused, then smiled. "But I'm fine now."

Quint continued to frown as he looked at her. "You're sure you aren't ill? You looked as if you might faint. If you don't feel well, I suggest we forget the race and land this thing."

Hannah shook her head again. "No, I just felt giddy for a moment. I really shouldn't have drunk that champagne so quickly, when I hardly ever drink anything stronger than tea." Her eyes crinkled up as she gave him another smile. "Don't look so worried. I promised Cicely I would return you to her in one piece, and I shall do so. Now forget about me and enjoy your ride."

Hannah stretched her arm out and down to indicate the

view. Quint searched her features a moment longer, noting that a little color had crept back into her cheeks, then took her suggestion and turned to look over the edge of the basket.

The world beneath him bore no resemblance to the world he knew so well. A broad green patch of land opened up beneath them, dotted with small clusters of figures he knew to be people, figures the size of small insects. When he lifted his head, he could see square fields of varying shades of green, bisected by the tan line of the road. He looked to his left, where the village lay, and he could just barely make out the cluster of roofs that made up St. Albanswood.

As the balloon rotated slowly, Quint found himself staring at a miniature of the squire's manor house, looking like some little girl's dollhouse rather than the impressive Elizabethan structure of brick and timber that the squire was so proud of.

"Quint, I think we're high enough now."

Hannah's voice sounded strangely subdued. Quint turned to find her eyes fixed on the ground below. Before he could ask if she was all right, she turned to him with a bemused expression and spoke again. "Reach up and pull on the valve rope. It takes a hard tug because the valve is held shut by a stiff spring. You need to hold it open to the count of five, then release it." Her lips eased into a small smile. "And remember, don't touch the red rope."

Quint grinned as he reached up to disengage the proper rope from the ring above, then followed Hannah's directions to the letter. After refastening the bit of hemp, he turned to gaze below again.

The basket had rotated some more, and he could see that the balloon was now gliding eastward over the forest that separated his land from the squire's. He gazed at the darker green patch below. The woods he knew so well looked like a flat, irregularly shaped head of broccoli gleaming in the sun.

Quint glanced over at Hannah. She stood a foot and a half away, holding tightly to the edge of the basket. Her knuckles were white, and her face held a strange faraway expression.

Quint felt a deep yearning to be near her. He raised his arm, intending to reach out and draw Hannah to his side so that they could gaze down at the forest together, but a voice at the back of his mind warned him this wouldn't be wise. He forced his arm back to his side. It was dangerous enough, he told himself, just knowing that Hannah was also haunted by memories of their time in that forest, a time so magical and yet so real that it intruded upon his thoughts at every turn.

"Is that Blackthorne Hall?"

Hannah's voice was soft, but her question made Quint start and blink away his thoughts of the forest below and the wild desires those memories stirred in him. He looked in the direction Hannah indicated and gazed at the tall gray tower rising from the green lawn at the edge of the woods.

"Yes," he said. "That is my home."

Quint stared at the square Norman tower that rose above the west side of the house. It looked no taller than his little finger, yet he could remember climbing the circular stairs to the tower room as a child, staring out at the world below, and thinking how far above everything he was.

The balloon floated closer. His home, the house he'd worked so hard to restore to the grandeur of his grandfather's days, looked insignificant from this height, like a pasteboard replica sitting alongside some little boy's train track. Viewed from this perspective, all the sacrifices he'd made for that stone toy seemed suddenly very foolish.

Quint took a deep breath, filling his lungs with cool, sweet air. Once again he found himself in a magical world, a realm of silence and light, where all the cares he'd carried on his shoulders were lifted away from him as he was borne aloft.

All at once Quint felt that none of the things he'd been so concerned about mattered, not family name or honor, not money or social position. He had everything he would ever need in life right here in this basket: sunshine on his face, fresh cool air ruffling his hair, and Hannah Bradley standing next to him. Quint's lips parted in a wide, exuberant smile, as he turned and spoke her name softly.

"Hannah."

The word sounded like a caress even to his ears. Hannah turned to him, her eyes wide. He opened his mouth to tell her how he felt, to share the joy in his soul. Instead he looked into pupils that had dilated so completely that her irises appeared completely black. His heart contracted at the sight of her unfocused gaze.

"Hannah. What's wrong?"

The young woman before him opened her mouth. Her lips moved, but no sound passed them. Quint's body stiffened as she shook her head slowly and her eyelids began to droop. He ordered his arms to reach for her, but before he could do more than touch her, Hannah swayed, then slipped slowly to the floor of the basket. Just before the brim of her hat fell forward to cover her face, he saw her eyelids close completely.

Quint knelt on the floor, scooped her up in his arms, and pushed the hat to one side. As it slid onto the wicker floor, he stared at her expressionless face and called her name. He watched her eyelids, but they didn't so much as flicker. Fearing the worst, he put his ear to her chest and listened. For several long seconds he heard nothing. He pressed his ear closer, then released a relieved breath when he heard the soft, dull thud . . . thud . . . thud.

Quint straightened, looked around, then reached up and jerked on the netting that held a blanket. After resting it behind Hannah's head, he laid her down again, then stared at her inert form.

She'd said she rarely imbibed strong spirits, but he couldn't remember seeing one glass of wine cause anyone to collapse so completely. The wicker floor bit into Quint's knees as he leaned forward to listen to Hannah's shallow, uneven breathing. He shook his head, then stood. Somehow he would have to get back to the ground and find a doctor.

Quint stepped to the edge of the wicker car. When he looked past the basket's rim he could clearly see the other six balloons below him and to his right, converging on a spot near an empty field, with the rainbow-hued hare balloon hovering just beyond them. The tension in his muscles eased slightly as he told himself he only had to wait for the wind to blow him that way; then he could call to one of the other pilots and get instructions for landing.

As he stared at the other balloons, a feeling of utter helplessness swept over him. He was completely at the mercy of the wind. An angry frustration filled him, tightening his hold on the ropes holding the basket to the balloon, as he chafed at being forced to wait when he was accustomed to controlling his destiny. Then, as he gazed in powerless fury at the other balloons, he noticed that they appeared to be moving away from him.

Quint glanced up to see that a little flag attached to the rope above him was flapping in a breeze that ran counter to the direction he wanted to go. He clenched his jaw as he remembered Hannah explaining how air currents switched at different heights, then looked back down to the cluster of balloons to see that they appeared to be growing smaller and more distant by the moment.

For what seemed like a long time Hannah had been vaguely aware of floating in a dark, warm place where nothing could touch her. Occasionally she thought she heard someone call her name, but when she tried to open her eyes, her lids felt far too heavy to budge. Each time the voice came closer. It held an urgent note that intruded on her comfortable world. She felt powerless to obey the call, but a strange chill had entered that world, and the voice seemed to boom from right above her head.

"Hannah! Hannah, you must wake up. The balloon is going down!"

Hannah's heart began to pound at these words. Her father, it was her father calling to her. Something had happened. Was he the one who grasped her arms, who shook her so violently? She summoned all her will and concentrated on her heavy eyelids, forcing them open.

"Good girl, Hannah. You have to help me."

Hannah stared at the face that seemed to sway above hers. The features blurred, but she was certain they didn't belong to her father.

"Hannah, can you hear me?"

The deep voice made her frown and squint. Her vision cleared, and she recognized the man whose fingers bit so painfully into her upper arms.

"Quint, you're hurting me."

Hannah's words sounded strange and far away to her ears and felt odd on her thick tongue. She felt Quint relax his hold on her as he bent forward so that his dark eyes bored into hers as he spoke again. "Hannah, you have to get up. I need your help."

Hannah shifted her gaze beyond Quint's tousled dark curls to the mouth of the balloon above. Suddenly she knew where she was, and the urgency in his voice made sense. She drew in a startled breath and sat up in one quick motion. Getting to her feet was more difficult, but Quint put his arms around her and all but lifted her into a standing position at the corner of the basket. Hannah closed her fingers tightly over the wicker rim, then leaned forward, only to gasp and pull back when a spray of water hit her face.

Hannah wiped the stinging salt water from her eyes and stared out at a gray-green sea of surging waves beneath darkly lowering clouds. She glanced down and saw that the waves were licking the bottom of the basket as they rose and fell. She swiveled to face Quint.

"Release some ballast!"

"I've done that. Repeatedly." Quint shouted the words as he frowned out at the water. He looked into her eyes and said, "The sandbags are all gone, Hannah."

Hannah wanted to ask a thousand questions. She wanted to know what had happened to make her lose consciousness, why all the ballast was gone, and how they had come to be over water. But she knew there wasn't time for questions.

She looked around the basket, spied two blankets on the floor, and bent to lift them. When she struggled to raise the heavy tangle of wool, Quint's arms were suddenly there to assist her, and in moments the blankets went over the side and were floating upon the waves below.

Hannah drew her lower lip between her teeth, waiting to see if the balloon would lift a little. Slowly the sinking blankets and the waves seemed to move away, first a foot, then two. Finally, at four feet above the water, the balloon stopped rising.

"Should we throw out anything else?" Quint's voice came over her right shoulder. Hannah turned to him. "What else do we have?"

He shrugged. "Not much. There are the instruments attached to the rail and the rope and anchor hanging outside the basket. Oh, and the food Cicely sent."

Hannah stared down at the waves below. They were no farther away than when she had looked a moment before, but no closer either. "Let's wait a bit." She turned to him. "What happened?"

Quint raked his long fingers through his tousled black hair and shrugged. "I hardly know where to start. Nothing has gone right since you fainted."

Hannah shook her head. "I didn't faint. I never faint."

Quint's lips twisted into a wry half-smile. "Perhaps 'passed out' would be a better term. Let this be a lesson to you: Never again down your champagne so quickly."

Hannah's lips twitched at the teasing note in Quint's voice; then she shook her head and frowned. "It couldn't have been the champagne alone. It tends to make me light-headed, but I hardly drank enough, regardless of how fast, to make me lose consciousness—certainly not for any length of time, and not so completely." She shuddered. "What an awful feeling. It was as if I'd been shut up somewhere inside myself. I was able to think but not speak. Then complete darkness washed over me. I really don't think mere champagne could do that."

Quint had prepared another chiding remark about her ability to hold her liquor when the memory of a silver goblet being lifted to Hannah's lips made him stop. His green eyes darkened beneath his intense frown.

"Hartley." Quint paused. "That idiot must have put something in your champagne."

At Hannah's startled look, Quint went on, "God, I knew he wanted to impress the Kendricks, but I never thought he'd be so desperate as to endanger someone's life to further one of his schemes."

Hannah's brow wrinkled. "Quint, we can't be sure of this."

"You don't know your cousin very well, do you?" Quint stared into her eyes as his hand closed tightly over hers. "Hartley's determination to come out first in every endeavor is matched only by that of his father. Look, you said yourself that mere liquor couldn't affect you so strongly."

Hannah nodded slowly, trying to think rationally as

warmth from Quint's fingers flowed into hers. "Well, I don't think my cousin meant any evil," she said at last. "Whatever he gave me, it's apparently not permanently harmful."

"What are you saying, not permanently harmful?" Quint released a short, harsh laugh. "Because of whatever he put in your champagne, we're stuck in a sinking balloon in the middle of the English Channel with no way to get help."

Hannah glanced around. "So that's where we are. And how . . ." She broke off as she caught sight of something off to her right. "Look. Over there. We're not in the middle; we're nearing land."

Quint turned and narrowed his eyes at the darker gray line between the sea and the sky, then nodded. "You're right." He swiveled back to look down at Hannah. "But what country is that? I've become completely turned around."

Hannah fought the smile that tugged at her lips. He sounded so very forlorn, much like a lost little boy. "Tell me what happened, Quint. What went on after I passed out?"

"I hardly know where to begin." He paused, glanced out over the water, then returned his eyes to Hannah's. "It all started when I realized we were in a different air current from the other balloonists. I could see that they were lower than we were, and I remembered what you'd said about letting out some gas to descend. I guess I pulled too hard on the valve rope, because *Skylark* dropped very quickly. I was afraid it was going to crash into the ground, so I threw out two bags of sand."

Hannah's heart sank. She tried to keep her face motionless, but her features must have revealed her thoughts.

"Too much, right?" Quint asked. When Hannah nodded, so did he. "I've since figured that out. Anyway, after that, the balloon rose again and ended up in the same current. I tried letting out just a little gas this time, but apparently I was too gentle, because we just kept moving toward the Channel.''

"That's not your fault, Quint." Hannah spoke as soon as he paused. "I hardly gave you any instructions, and even if I'd explained air currents more thoroughly, the only way to learn how to utilize them is through lots of experience. And by the time you reached the shore, chances are that even the lower air currents were pushing you over the water.''

Hannah stopped speaking as a puzzled frown formed over her eyes. "That explains two of the sandbags. What happened to the others?''

Quint sighed and shook his head. "I kept throwing them over. At first I was trying to get up to a landward air current. I stopped that when I realized my efforts were futile, although a few times I did think the balloon was moving back toward shore." His features twisted into an expression of disgust. "But when the clouds moved in, I lost all sense of direction. Soon after that, I noticed that the balloon was gradually dropping toward the water.''

"That's to be expected.''

Quint glared at her casual response. "And why is that?''

"The gas cools when you get over a large body of water. Then it contracts, making the helium heavier, and the balloon sinks. So I suppose that explains what happened to the rest of the sandbags.''

"I'm afraid I made a mess of this.''

Quint stared out at the rolling sea, and Hannah reached out to take his hand in both of hers. "Not at all. We're both alive, so you've done better than most first-time pilots might have, given the same situation. Now, did I hear you mention that hamper of food Cicely sent with us?''

Quint looked down at Hannah as if she had just asked

him if he'd ever seen a horse sprout wings and fly. "What do you want with that?"

"I want to eat, that's what. I become weak when I get hungry, and I'm still a little dizzy from whatever it was I drank. Since we'll need all our wits and strength when we get closer to the shore, I want to eat while I have the chance."

Quint had enjoyed many picnics in his thirty years, but never one in such an odd situation. However, with Hannah's encouragement he gamely joined her on the wicker floor, sitting cross-legged as he munched on cold chicken and sampled an assortment of cakes to the accompaniment of the basket's rhythmic creaking and the occasional sound of a wave breaking on the water below.

"You don't want any of this, do you?" Hannah pulled a bottle of champagne from the hamper, and Quint shook his head. "Good, it will serve as ballast then, should we need it. Do you want to eat anything else?"

Again he shook his head. Hannah packed everything back in the hamper except a napkin full of naked chicken bones and two unopened tins, which she lifted for his inspection. "Caviar and pâté," she said. "I hate them both, but if you want to keep either, tell me now or they go over the side and into the deep."

Quint shrugged. "I can't abide either of them myself, so over they shall go. But why keep any of the food?"

"We'll soon reach land, I hope, and we might set down some distance from a town. It's coming on evening, and I'd like to keep the food, if we can, so that we can pass the night in some comfort."

Quint looked deep into Hannah's violet-blue eyes. "You really think we will reach land and escape from this thing in one piece?"

Hannah shook her head. "Two pieces." She grinned. "I'm one, you're the other." With these words she got to her feet, then asked, "Oh, and by the way, how's your French? The prevailing winds flow in a southeasterly direction from England. There's a chance we could be swept to Belgium, but a landing in France is more likely."

Quint stood as she finished speaking. "My French is fine, thank you, though I haven't used it in some time."

Hannah nodded absently as she went to the edge of the basket and stared intently forward. Quint turned in the direction of her gaze and saw that what had once been a thin gray line on the horizon was now a thick band of white.

"France, definitely," he said.

"Oh?"

"Yes. Those cliffs are made of chalk, like the ones near Dover on the English coast. If we land there, we should be somewhere near Calais."

"Well, then, my French lessons at Madame Lavoisier's will be of some use, after all."

Quint's lips curved into a smile as he glanced down at the water beneath them. His smile faded immediately. "Well, Miss Bradley," he said, "if we keep sinking, we will get no chance to test our skills in that language."

Hannah looked over the edge of the basket. Once more it had dropped to barely a foot above the rising and falling waves.

"Nonsense." Hannah spoke with grim determination as she tossed the caviar and pâté over the side. Faced with her bravery, Quint felt his own will harden, and he bent to retrieve the bottle of champagne.

"Do I send this over now as well or wait until later?"

The jaunty smile curving Hannah's lips eased the heaviness in Quint's chest. "Send it over now," she said. "We need all the lift we can get. And see if you can't get that rope and hook off the side, too. They're useful when landing, but they'll do us no good at all if they keep us from getting over those cliffs. Oh, and tear those instruments off the basket too, and get rid of them.''

"Yes, sir, Captain.''

Hannah grinned up at him. "You're following orders wonderfully. I'll be sure to see to it you receive a commendation from the queen.''

When all was tossed out, Hannah was relieved to see that the basket had again lifted away from the sea, this time to an altitude of almost twenty feet. She turned her back on Quint as she gazed at the approaching cliffs, trying to assess their height, but though she could now clearly see the spray leap up toward the white surface, she couldn't tell if *Skylark* was high enough to clear the rocky summit.

Hannah glanced up at the angry dark clouds above and saw the navy blue flags on the balloon's ropes flapping wildly in the wind. She then looked down at the turbulent surface of the sea and realized they must be caught in a storm rushing toward shore.

"We're not high enough.'' Quint spoke so calmly that Hannah lifted her head to look forward quite slowly. When she saw the cliffs this time, she gasped. He was right. If they kept going as they were they would be dashed into that solid white face with the same deadly force as the breakers crashing against the cliffs.

"Throw out the food.''

Hannah bent over the hamper and handed Quint several items, but he brushed her hands aside. Before she could get out her words of protest, he grasped the handles on the sides of the hamper, stood, and threw it out of the car in one swift motion.

Hannah and Quint turned at the same moment and stood side by side watching the cliffs come closer, staring at the forbidding surface, hoping to see the upper edge sink below their line of sight. They held their breath as the waves below began dropping away. When the balloon's rise stopped, they both whispered, "Blast!" From what Hannah could guess, they would reach the cliff in fifteen minutes or less, and they needed a lift of at least another three feet to clear the summit.

"Hannah." Quint's voice was still calm. "We don't have anything else to send over."

Hannah narrowed her eyes at the approaching wall. This was no way to die, no way for an adventure like this to end.

"We have our clothes," she said.

Chapter 8

Hannah turned to find Quint staring at her as if she had suggested they might try flying without aid of the balloon. He narrowed his eyes at her. "You aren't serious."

"I certainly am. The first men to cross the Channel, in 1785, had to throw their clothes overboard for exactly the same reason. They were about to plunge into the water and drown."

Quint shook his head. "Hannah, have you considered how difficult it will be to get anyone's help in returning to England if we appear in total dishabille?"

Hannah looked into Quint's darkly frowning eyes and began to laugh. "Quint, before we worry about anyone's sensibilities, we must first manage to *survive*! If we arrange that miracle, I'm sure we can handle whatever follows. Besides, I wasn't going to suggest we remove everything we're wearing, just the heaviest items to start with, like your boots and jacket, and my shoes and this ridiculous dress."

Hannah bent to unlace her ankle-high boots. By the time she stood with them in one hand and her blue hat in the other, Quint had stripped off his jacket. He threw it over the side of the basket, then asked, "Is it necessary to remove your dress?"

Hannah tossed her shoes to the wind, then watched her hat spin as it sailed through the air before she answered. "Most definitely. All these yards of satin are very heavy. I have several extra underskirts that can go as well, and I'll still have enough underclothing on for decency's sake. My costume won't pass muster in London or Paris, but I doubt the French peasants will give it a second thought." She paused and glanced at Quint's gray waistcoat. "That can go as well."

As Quint began to work on the buttons of his vest, Hannah found herself staring at his lean fingers. After a moment she turned, lifted her blue skirt, and reached up to the waistband of the ivory-colored underskirt just beneath it. Trembling fingers pulled at the strings there, then searched for the tie to the second underskirt. When she felt the material gape from her waist, she gathered the fabric in her hands, pulled it down, and with a few quick wiggles slid the underskirts past her hips and let them drop to the wicker floor.

A moment later she had the bundle of ivory muslin in her arms. She lifted it to the rim of the basket and tossed it to the wind. She turned to find Quint watching the underskirts billow and flutter away and saw that he no longer wore his waistcoat.

His tie was missing as well, and the top two buttons of his shirt were undone. The dark, curling hair on his chest contrasted sharply with the white shirt stretched across the muscles there. Hannah stared at Quint in quiet fascination, her eyes moving slowly from his chest up to his neck. She hadn't seen him like this before. His bared throat made him look younger, vulnerable, while the hard muscles hinted at beneath his shirt gave him the appearance of strength, of power.

Heat coiled in Hannah's stomach, then spread to her lower limbs, rendering them suddenly weak. She reached out to grab the side of the basket, then lowered her eyes as a warm blush heated her cheeks. As she stared at the floor, she noticed that Quint's feet were bare, and something about his white toes wiggling on the wicker floor made Hannah forget her earlier reaction and smile. She looked back up to meet his eyes and said, "You could have kept your socks."

Quint grinned as he turned to her. "They stayed in my boots when I pulled them off. I don't seem quite as adept at removing them as my valet."

"Well, would you mind acting as lady's maid again and undoing all these buttons?"

Hannah turned away from him as she spoke, presenting a long row of tiny pearl buttons running down the length of her spine. Quint reached for the top one and unfastened it. The cold, damp air had made his fingers stiff, but as he moved from one button to the next, slowly revealing more white, satiny skin, his hands and his entire body grew warm. As the dress opened farther, the ivory fabric of her camisole formed a barrier between the tips of his fingers and the flesh they had brushed, but didn't prevent him from fantasizing about the warm, supple flesh it covered.

"Is that the last?" Hannah's voice held a quiet urgency as she glanced back over her shoulder.

"Just one more." Quint's voice was low and harsh-sounding.

"Leave it, and help me out of this any way you can."

Hannah's tone of voice left no room for questions. Quint didn't need to glance toward the shore to know that they must be rapidly approaching the cliffs. He bent and stretched his arms out to grab the hem of her dress in his hands, then stood, pulling the material up with him, lifting it high above Hannah's head and raised arms. Before the hem of the skirt cleared the top of her head, Hannah's muffled voice commanded, ''Throw it over the side, quickly.''

Quint did as he was ordered, and the blue satin floated up and away on a gust of wind, then dropped quickly toward the green sea below. Quint didn't watch its fall to the ocean. He turned instead, to stare forward at the waves dashing on the craggy bluffs.

The cliffs weren't as near as he'd feared they might be. They were still several hundred yards away, and it appeared that the basket might just have sufficient height to clear the rocky crest.

''We're going to make it,'' Hannah breathed.

''I think we just might.'' Quint's heart pounded wildly against the wall of his chest. He turned to Hannah just as she removed the heavy silver comb from her hair and saw her wildly waving tresses fall about her shoulders to curve over the sleeveless muslin bodice like spilled honey. The memory of the silken feel of her hair called out to him and he lifted his hand to seize one long spiraling curl, but when he saw her raise the comb and realized her intent, he changed the direction of his reach to close his fingers over hers.

When Hannah looked up to him, her violet-blue eyes were wide with surprise. Quint shook his head. ''That was your mother's. It can't weigh enough to make any difference to us now. Give it to me; let me keep it safe in my pocket. You'll want it later.''

Hannah's eyes seemed to shimmer for a moment as she handed him the comb. Then she laughed, the tinkling sound floating in the wind as she spoke. ''You're right, of course. And after all, it would hardly do for me to appear before the peasants we're likely to encounter with my hair down around my shoulders.''

Quint stared at her as he dropped the comb into his pocket. Her eyes were still gleaming, no longer with unshed tears but with wry merriment. "You really aren't afraid of what's to come, are you?"

Hannah tilted her head to one side, considering his question. "No, I suppose I'm not, though by all that's logical I should be."

Quint stared at Hannah, seeing a small sprite with dark gold curls flying in the wind. Her eyes held his with a look of total trust and a hint of suppressed excitement; her lips curved in a defiant smile. Quint gazed at those lips, remembering the kiss that had so shattered him three mornings before. Recalling those moments made joy surge through his veins along with a deeper physical pulsing.

"Hannah Bradley, you are unlike any other woman I know."

His soft, husky voice sent warm shivers coursing through Hannah's body. Suddenly the looming cliffs were only incidental to her. All that was important in life was the man whose hands now rested at her waist, whose dark eyes held hers with such easy power, and whose lips were close to hers.

Quint's mouth closed over Hannah's with a mingling of tender care and desperate urgency. Her lips parted eagerly beneath his kiss. She moved closer to him as his arms encircled her slight frame. Her breasts tingled as they pressed against his chest, and her body became flushed with the heat radiating from his powerful form. She suddenly felt as light as a feather, as if she were being lifted up to the heavens on some warm, powerful breeze. A moment later, when his lips parted from hers, she gasped at the shattering sensations coursing through her.

Quint forced his eyes open and stared down at Hannah's upturned face. Her long lashes lay dark and curling against her cheeks; her lips were a dark pink, soft and still slightly parted. His body throbbed with a wild surging, pounded like the wild surf crashing against the cliff, and he lowered his lips to hers once more.

This second kiss was deeper than the first. When Quint slipped his tongue into Hannah's mouth, her body was jolted with wave after wave of pleasure that made her cling to him with frenzied strength, as if he were the only thing anchoring her to life. Quint tightened his arms around her, urging her supple form closer to his body, as if this would somehow bind them and keep the wildly blowing wind from tearing them apart.

A loud crash below them made them both break off the embrace. For one brief moment they stared at each other; then at the same time they turned and looked forward.

Hannah gasped and Quint pulled her close to him as they stared at the fast approaching cliff. Quint could see over the top of the jagged rocks, but he wasn't sure the basket would clear them. His lips widened in a taut smile when Hannah's arms tightened around his waist, but he didn't take his eyes off the approaching wall. He took a deep breath and held it as a gust of wind caught them, pushing them forward. The rocks drew closer and closer.

Death was right in front of his eyes one moment. Then, a second later, Quint felt the basket lift and watched in silent amazement as the edge of the cliff passed beneath the basket.

"We did it!" Hannah turned to Quint, her face full of excitement, flushed with the glow of victory.

"Yes, we did." Quint gave her a warm, slow smile that added an extra dimension to the joy she felt. Then he lifted his brows. "Now how do we get this thing to stop?"

Hannah sighed. Her smile faded, leaving a worried expression on her face. "I suppose you mean safely," she said. "Well, that depends on what we find below."

She turned and gazed forward in the dimming light, squinting at the dark mass several hundred feet in front of them, then shook her head.

"Blast! Trees. I was hoping for a nice soft field. Even a vineyard would have been preferable to a forest."

Quint looked in the same direction. The forest seemed to be rushing toward them. "Can we land before we reach the trees?"

Hannah hesitated a moment, then shrugged and turned to him. "We'll have to try. Quick, climb up into the ring and untie the red rope."

Quint raised his arms, grasped the iron circle and pulled himself up to roost among the encircling ropes. "The red one?" he shouted down. "Are you sure?"

Still peering through the half-light, Hannah nodded vigorously. Without taking her eyes from the green sea of treetops quickly approaching, she turned her head slightly and called back, "Yes. Unhook it and when I give you the word, pull on it with all your might. Do you understand?"

"Yes!" Quint shouted back. He reached up to unloop the red rope. He didn't understand what he was doing or why, but he trusted Hannah's knowledge of this strange craft. He tightened his fingers around the rope, every muscle in his body tensing as he waited for her command.

It wasn't long in coming. Hannah squinted at the rocky ground below, then spotted a wide, tan strip running along the edge of the trees. A road. With luck she could get the balloon to drop there, where she and Quint were less likely to find themselves thrown head first onto a large boulder. Crossing her fingers and sending a quick request for assistance to her father's spirit, she counted to three, then turned to Quint and shouted, "Now! Pull it now!"

Quint jerked on the rope with all his strength. The force of his downward thrust sent him toppling from his perch, but he held on to the end of the red rope as he dropped through the center of the ring. He landed on his feet on the wicker floor and began to sway, but Hannah's slender arms encircled his waist to steady him.

When he looked down into her upturned face, he saw that she was staring upward. He looked up also and saw the silver material float to the top of the netting above, then spread out and catch the wind. He felt the basket slow somewhat, and lowered his gaze to see that they were no longer approaching the trees but were dropping out of the sky like a spent shot of lead.

"Hold on to the side of the basket, Quint," Hannah shouted from behind him. He turned to see her clinging to the wicker and moved back to stand beside her. He hooked one hand over the rim of the car behind Hannah's back and crossed the other in front of her, then closed his fingers over the sharp edge of the basket as she looked up and spoke again. "Bend your knees slightly, brace yourself, and hold on tightly."

Seconds later the basket crashed into the ground with a force that buckled Quint's knees and almost knocked him to the wicker floor. He tightened his grip on the edge of the car as he felt the balloon rise again, only to bounce back to earth a moment later with a teeth-rattling jolt.

The car rose yet again. Quint braced himself, expecting it to smash back into the earth. Instead, it tipped forward, turning both Hannah and him nearly upside down as it scraped along the earth. Quint's arms ached with his attempt to maintain his grip on the jolting basket as he supported Hannah as well as himself. His cramping fingers began to slip, and he clenched his jaw, but the next sharp bounce ripped his hands from the wicker.

This last jolt made Hannah bite her lip as her hands were also torn from the side of the basket. She gasped as she felt herself falling, and cried out in pain as her shoulder struck the other side of the basket and her weight, combined with Quint's, drove the wicker car into the ground.

Hannah closed her eyes for a second, lying in the suddenly motionless basket, wishing she could simply stay there.

Every muscle in her body ached with tension and cried out for rest, but she knew that rest would have to wait. If the wind caught the fabric of the balloon again, they would once more be pulled forward helplessly and possibly dashed against a boulder or a tree trunk.

She lifted herself up on one elbow, only to find herself facing Quint as he did the same thing. "We have to get out immediately," she said.

Quint responded by sitting up quickly, then rising to a crouch as he took Hannah's arm in one hand and held her waist with the other. Then, half carrying and half dragging her, he climbed out of the basket onto the dirt road.

He and Hannah stood together and silently surveyed their surroundings. The battered brown basket lay before them, the near corner crumpled and broken. Hannah's gaze followed the taut ropes to her left where they were stretched out between two tree trunks. She could just catch a glimmer of silver fabric twisted within the netting on the floor of the forest beneath the branches of the towering trees.

Hannah suddenly felt as deflated as *Skylark*. Her legs began to tremble, slightly at first, then with more force. To keep from falling, she slowly lowered herself to the hard dirt of the road, then stared at Quint as he sat down next to her.

"Now what?" he asked.

Hannah shrugged as she stared into his green eyes. Her arms hung limp at her sides, and her hands rested on the gritty earth.

"I don't know," she replied. She frowned at the weak sound of her own voice, and as she saw Quint's half-scowl deepen she could almost hear her father chide her: *You're alive, Hannah girl. Smile. You did well.*

Hannah's lips curved. "I don't know," she repeated with more force. "I only promised to get us safely to the ground. You can figure out how to get us back to England."

Quint's lips eased into a grin as he looked into her crinkling eyes, amazed anew at Hannah's resilience. He couldn't think of any other woman or man who would have come through such an experience with such good humor. He lifted his hand to her cheek and shook his head.

"Well, Miss Bradley, I'll do my best."

Hannah's smile trembled as she gazed up at Quint. With his black hair curling wildly onto his forehead and the jaunty smile gleaming down at her, he looked every bit the hero of her childhood dreams. She longed to lean toward him, to touch her lips to his, to feel their tender strength once again, to experience the exhilaration that had lifted her soul when he kissed her.

But they had been facing death then. The ground was solid beneath her now. That kiss belonged with the ones they had shared in the misty forest—shining memories to store away to keep her warm when she was alone and Quint was married to her cousin.

Hannah swallowed, then spoke softly. "Well, have you a plan, Lord Blackthorne?"

Quint frowned at the slight edge in her voice when she spoke his name. He *had* formed a plan, a nebulous one that involved lowering his lips to Hannah's as he pulled her close to him to caress away her aches, then holding her body to his to assuage the growing need in his loins. But looking into her suddenly sad eyes, he knew he'd need to come up with a different scheme.

Quint let his hand drop from her face. The magic was gone once again. Reality stared him in the face, and duty and responsibility again became his masters. He turned to look up the road to his right, then down at Hannah again.

"I suppose we'd best start by walking along the road and hope we find a village, or at least a farmhouse."

Hannah nodded. Quint got to his feet and helped her to rise, then took her hand to start down the road.

"Wait!" Hannah spoke as she tugged on Quint's hand, making him turn and look at her sharply. "Please," she went on, "we can't leave my balloon like this."

Quint shook his head. "We can't take it with us, Hannah."

"I know that. But let's at least place the silk in the basket and put it somewhere out of sight. Maybe I can get someone to keep it for me until I can send for it."

Quint hesitated for a moment as he saw her turn and look at the overturned basket with an expression of anguished loss on her face. Then he spoke softly. "Of course. But let's hurry. Dusk will fall soon, and I don't like the look of those clouds."

It took almost half an hour to gather the netting and fabric and pack it into the basket, then drag the heavy wicker car a safe distance into the forest. Quint's muscles ached from the exertion, and his spirits drooped. One look at Hannah told him she felt exactly the same way. Once more he took her hand, and when she looked up at him he gave her an encouraging smile. "We'll walk until it gets dark. If we don't come across a village or farmhouse, we'll search for shelter in the forest."

Hannah nodded wearily and gave him a weak smile, then turned to walk barefoot alongside him, trying not to cry out each time she trod on a rough clod of dirt or sharp rock.

Her feet felt as if they were on fire by the time dusk started to ease into night. She was ready to ask Quint to stop and look for a place to sleep before it became too dark to see, when she caught a glimmer of light in the distance. Before she could speak, Quint's hand tightened on hers.

"Hannah, look. I think there's a farmhouse ahead."

Hannah, too tired to speak, merely nodded in reply. She did manage to walk a little faster when he tugged on her hand to urge her forward, however, and several minutes later was rewarded with the sight of the dark silhouette of a building rising near the side of the road.

The single light she'd seen became two, shining out of square windows. As she and Quint moved closer, she could see that they were situated on either side of a narrow door above three stone steps. Hannah and Quint mounted the steps wordlessly, both silently aware that they had little choice in accommodations, and both too tired to discuss the matter.

They stood patiently after Quint knocked on the door. From within the house they heard the scrape of a chair against the floor, followed by low-toned murmurs, then one higher-pitched word. Hannah felt a drop of moisture strike her shoulder, then another as they waited for the door to open. When that didn't happen after several more moments, Quint knocked again as a light drizzle began to fall.

Once again deep voices echoed through the planks of wood. Hannah glanced at Quint, then back at the door when she heard the sharp click of a latch opening. Light poured out onto her face as the door swung inward, making her blink as a small female form filled the half-open door. Hannah squinted against the brightness at dark hair topped with a white cap as a high-pitched voice called out, "*Qui est là-bas?*"

"We are two weary travelers in need of shelter," Quint answered in English. When Hannah turned to him with a questioning look, he gave her a quick warning glance that made her bite back the French translation that had sprung to her lips.

"*Je ne comprends pas.*" The woman shook her head and started to shut the door.

Quint's hand shot out to hold it open. "No, please. We need a place to stay," he said.

The woman shook her head, but a deep voice echoed from behind her, "*Madeleine, ouvre la porte.*"

Hannah felt her tense muscles relax when the woman followed orders and pulled the door open. With Quint's hand resting on the small of her back she mounted the stairs and stepped into the room.

Hannah got a brief impression of white walls and blue-checked gingham at the windows before her attention was drawn to a large man with graying brown hair and square, plain features standing in the middle of the room. "Good evening. Please feel welcome." He spoke slowly in heavily accented English. "I wish to apologize for my wife. She is normally most gracious."

Hannah smiled at the small woman who had come to stand next to the man. The woman nodded in return, making the white lace cap atop her head bounce.

"Please don't apologize." Hannah spoke in English, since the man was obviously comfortable in that language. Although she didn't understand Quint's glance or his failure to use French, she had seen a definite warning in his glance. "I fear we must have startled her, knocking after dark. And finding two such bedraggled creatures would make anyone nervous."

The woman looked up to her husband, who translated quickly, glancing at a narrow stairwell to his right occasionally before turning back to Hannah and Quint.

"You have met with some misfortune. Please, take a seat by the fire."

Hannah crossed the shining wooden floor to a braided rug that lay in a large oval before the wide hearth. She lowered herself to one of two benches, then looked up to see that Quint remained standing by her side.

Hannah frowned up at him. He glanced at her quickly before turning to the man and woman who stood side by side on the other side of the hearth. "Thank you both for letting us in. I think perhaps introductions are in order. I am Quinton Blackthorne, and this . . . is my wife, Hannah."

Hannah immediately turned her attention from the couple across from her to Quint. He didn't return her look at all, just stood tall and rumpled-looking in his dirty shirt and stained black pants as the other man spoke again.

"We are pleased to meet you, Monsieur Blackthorne. I am Émile DuBois, and this is my wife Madeleine." The man's dark eyes narrowed as he studied first Hannah, then Quint, before speaking again. "Please forgive my curiosity, *monsieur*, but it is obvious that you are no less than a gentleman and your wife a most proper lady, despite the state of your dress. Are there thieves on the road, perhaps, who set upon you?"

"Yes, let us hear this story."

The voice that echoed across the room was sharp-sounding, with only a hint of accent to identify the speaker as French. Hannah turned toward the narrow stairwell. A slender male stepped into the room and continued to speak. "Was it indeed thieves, Monsieur Blackthorne, or are the woods full of gendarmes awaiting your signal before they burst into my sister's house?"

Hannah stared at the speaker a moment, a short, wiry man with golden hair and a mustache. Behind him she caught a glimpse of another man. She had the impression of a wide face and straight coal-black hair, but her attention slipped quickly from him as the first man stepped forward into the room, lifted a pistol, and aimed it carefully at Quint's head.

Chapter 9

Hannah stared at the cocked hammer of the small pistol, then let her eyes follow the barrel to the black hole trained on Quint.

"Pierre, *non!*" the small woman cried out as she moved over to the slender young man. His blond head turned toward her as she approached. He spoke rapidly in oddly accented French, the words tumbling forth faster than Hannah's mind could translate them.

Émile followed his wife and began speaking as well. Soon a three-way jumble of French filled the room, and Hannah managed to comprehend only a few disjointed words and phrases. They all used the word "fool" at least once. She also caught "gendarmes," "suspicious," and finally a phrase she thought sounded like "listen to what they have to say."

This last came forcefully from Émile's lips and echoed in the suddenly silent room. Pierre stared at the taller man a moment, then turned his narrow gaze to Hannah and Quint. Hannah stifled a gasp as the man placed his thumb on the pistol's hammer, then released it slowly and lowered his arm to his side, holding the weapon loosely.

"My sister's husband suggests I listen to your story of woe," he said. The thin lips beneath his blond mustache twitched into a tight smile. "Let me warn you. Émile tends to be very trusting, but I am not and neither is my brother, Antoine. We want to hear the truth."

"You shall do so." The amusement lacing Quint's voice made Hannah glance up in surprise and watch his eyebrows lift slightly as he went on. "But I have a warning for you as well. Our story is most outlandish."

Pierre cocked his head to one side, and his smile widened slightly. "Ah, well. This is good to know. Please proceed."

Hannah listened as Quint recounted their adventures and watched the faces of the three people standing in front of her. It was obvious that Émile hung on each word. He kept his eyes on Quint at all times, even when he bent to give a quick, whispered translation to his wife from time to time.

Pierre was also obviously interested. His dark brown eyes narrowed and widened as Quint spoke, but he maintained a wary stance while a cynical smile continued to twist his lips.

Hannah shifted her gaze to the dark-haired man who stood almost behind Pierre. His round head topped Pierre's by just enough to allow Hannah to make out dark brown eyes set in heavy features beneath black hair that hung in a straight fringe to his eyebrows. Shifting her gaze slightly, she saw that he had a much broader build than the man in front of him, with thick legs and heavy forearms.

As Hannah stared at the man, she suddenly remembered a picture she had seen once of a hooded man wielding an ax over a kneeling figure. The sudden, ghoulish image made her shiver. She pulled her gaze from his stocky figure back to Pierre just in time to see the blond man's thin lips twist as Quint explained how they had hidden the balloon in the forest before starting down the road to look for shelter.

"You are right," Pierre said quietly when Quint finished.

"That story *is* outlandish. I do not believe a word of it."

"But it's true." Hannah leapt to her feet. "I assure you. We will show you the balloon, if you like. It can't be much more than two miles down the road."

Pierre shrugged. "Perhaps it is. Perhaps it isn't."

"Don't be ridiculous, Pierre. Look at them." Émile gestured toward Hannah and Quint. "Why would anyone make up a story like that?"

"Why does anyone do anything?" Pierre turned to his brother-in-law. "They could be thieves who have worked up this ruse to get into your house and rob you. Antoine and I have seen such things happen in Paris. I would hate to see you suffer such a fate."

Émile shook his head and began speaking again in rapid French. Pierre shook his head as well, and Émile spoke louder. This same pantomime was acted out twice more. Hannah managed to understand that Émile was insisting that Quint and Hannah be allowed to stay in the house and Pierre was refusing. At last Pierre shrugged, turned to the dark-haired man behind him, and spoke softly as he gestured toward a spot on the floor near the rear wall.

Hannah saw Antoine step behind Émile and Madeleine to bend and remove a small rug, then returned her attention to Pierre as the man spoke again.

"My sister and her husband insist on extending you their hospitality. However, my friends, I cannot allow myself to trust you so completely. I apologize for my lack of manners, but I do not trust easily. So, we have reached a compromise Émile and I. You may stay, but you will spend the night locked in the cellar."

Hannah's heart skipped a beat as she looked at dark-haired Antoine. Then her blood began to pound in her ears as she lowered her gaze to the black hole beneath the trapdoor he held open.

"I'm sure that will be satisfactory."

Quint's words were all but drowned out by the sound of rushing blood in her ears as Hannah continued to gaze at the gaping black hole. Slowly she shook her head and lifted her eyes to Pierre. "We are telling the truth." She paused to swallow and ease the dryness of her throat. "Please, if you wish, I will take you to the balloon and prove it to you."

Pierre's dark brown eyes narrowed as he looked into hers. "I am sorry." He spoke softly. "I pride myself on being a gentleman, *madame,* but I must refuse. It is too dark and wet to search now, and I see that you are weary. The cellar is clean, and we will see to it that you are not uncomfortable."

Quint had taken Hannah's hand while Pierre was speaking. She looked up to find Quint's green eyes gazing down at her and his lips curving in an encouraging smile. "We'll be fine, Hannah. After what we've experienced today, a night in a cellar will be nothing."

Hannah nodded numbly and let Quint draw her to the opening in the floor. As he released her hand and began to descend a crude staircase made of planks, she glanced around at the others, seeing apology on the faces of Émile and his wife and a triumphant smile on Pierre's narrow features. The completely blank look in Antoine's black eyes made her shiver and look down as she stepped gingerly onto the first of the wide wooden steps leading into the dark hole.

Hannah was still three steps from the bottom when the cellar door slammed shut with a crash that left her in total darkness. She jumped and gasped, then stood teetering on the edge of the step. Her arms swung in wide circles as she fought to keep from falling, and a small cry escaped her throat.

"Hannah?" Quint's deep voice echoed softly in the dark. "Are you all right?"

The moment he called her name, giving her floundering

senses some point of reference, Hannah regained her balance. However, the fear of darkness that had plagued her all her life tightened her throat and held her motionless.

"Hannah!" Quint spoke louder this time. She jumped slightly again and forced herself to answer. "Yes . . . I suppose I'm fine. I almost fell, though, and I'm afraid if I try to step down I'll lose my balance again."

"Don't move, then." Quint's voice was soothing, and Hannah felt herself relax slightly. "Just put your arms out in front of you and stand still. I'll find you."

Hannah was only too happy to follow his orders. She stood with her arms stretched forward, toes curled tightly over the edge of the rough step, until she felt Quint's touch. His long, warm fingers closed over hers, and she released the breath she'd been holding.

"It's all right now." Quint's deep voice caressed her nerves. "I have your hand. Just step down slowly."

Hannah did as he said, moving gingerly down the next two steps. When she placed her bare feet on the cold, rough floor, she shivered and stepped closer to Quint.

Quint still held Hannah's hand tightly. When he felt the shiver tremble through her, he drew her to his chest and placed his arms loosely around her slender form, then said, "Yes, it *is* cold in here."

Hannah let her cheek rest for a moment on the solid warmth of Quint's chest. He was an island of reality in the total blackness that surrounded her. She felt her fear of the darkness retreat somewhat as his warmth engulfed her, allowing her to speak past the fear that had constricted her throat. "It's not just the cold that made me shiver; it's being shut up here, where I can't see what's around me. I'm afraid to move from this spot."

Quint's right hand moved up and down Hannah's arm in a warming, reassuring motion as he chuckled and said, "Don't tell me you are afraid of mice and bugs."

The inky blackness surrounding them made Hannah's throat tighten again. She tried to answer, but all she could do was shiver again, violently. Quint laughed softly. "And here I was thinking you were the bravest person I'd ever met."

The sting Hannah felt at Quint's teasing words drew indignant words from her lips as she pulled back from his surrounding arms and spoke up to where she figured his face was. "I *am* brave, when I can see what I'm up against. I am perfectly capable of dispatching all sorts of bugs and even rodents all by myself, thank you. But I have to be able to see them first."

"Hannah." Quint's voice still echoed with amusement. "I doubt that you have anything to worry about. From what I observed of the room upstairs and that woman in her starched apron, I would be willing to wager that any vermin in the area learned long ago to stay away from her house." He paused a moment, then went on. "Now, we can't just stand here in the middle of the room. I suggest we find a place to sit down."

Hannah shook her head adamantly. "You can sit down if you wish. I am perfectly capable of standing all night, thank you. And if I do need to sit down, I'll do so on the stairs."

At least then she'd have some idea where she was, she thought, something concrete to hold on to in the total darkness. She pulled away from Quint's light grasp and turned in the direction she thought the steps were as she continued speaking, "In fact, I think I shall—"

"Shhh." Quint's hand tightened on her arm. "Listen."

Hannah frowned, but obeyed his order. From above her, where she imagined the cellar door to be, she could hear a low, angry murmur, followed by a short, deep reply. A moment later a higher-pitched voice joined in. This went on for several moments; then all was silent again.

"Could you understand what they said?"

Quint spoke quietly and Hannah replied just as softly, "No. The words were too muffled, and they speak too fast. I think they are using a dialect as well. Breton, most likely. I tried to understand their arguments earlier, but very little made sense—especially when Pierre suspected us of having gendarmes posted in the bushes one moment and then accused us of being thieves the next."

"I wondered about that myself." Quiet speculation echoed in Quint's voice. "He's certainly a suspicious fellow. Of course, so am I. I didn't want to let on that we spoke French after all the whispering that went on before someone came to the door, just in case something strange was in the air. Actually, I wouldn't be surprised to learn that Pierre and Antoine are indeed up to something larcenous. Smuggling, perhaps."

"What would they be smuggling?"

"Who knows? It's become an old and honored profession in some areas, espe—"

A soft creaking sound coming from the door in the ceiling made Quint stop speaking. He reached out to pull Hannah to him and took a step back as the door opened. A soft light trickled down the stairway; then a narrow face appeared in the opening.

"Good evening again." The light caught the gold of Pierre's mustache as he stared down to them. "I told you we would make you comfortable. Here is your bedding."

Hannah watched him toss a bulky bundle on the stairs and followed its bouncing trail to the floor, where it bumped softly into her shins.

"My sister has provided food and drink as well, so that you do not doubt her worth as a hostess."

Hannah glanced up to see him holding a large oval basket covered with blue and white checked fabric, which he set on the second step from the top. She eyed the basket hungrily until she saw him move away from the opening and heard the creak of the hinges as he began to shut the door.

"Wait!"

Hannah's voice rose in a squeak.

Pierre's narrow face popped into the opening again. "*Oui?* What is it, *madame*?"

Hannah's brows lowered into a puzzled frown at the title. Then, remembering Quint's lie that they were man and wife, she went on to ask the question uppermost in her mind. "Could we have a light of some sort? A lantern perhaps, or at least a candle? To eat by, you understand."

Pierre turned and Hannah listened closely to the quick murmured conversation between the man and his sister, but again could not hear the words distinctly. When she saw him move away again, her heart froze in her chest as she awaited the dread darkness.

"Here." Hannah blinked at the small flickering object Pierre placed next to the blanket. "You can eat by the light of this candle. After that you should sleep. It is late, and by all accounts you and your husband have had a most trying day, *n'est-ce pas?*"

With his mocking laughter ringing down the stairs, Pierre moved out of the frame of light. The hinges groaned again, and the door slammed shut. Hannah held her breath, her eye on the candle stub in its pewter holder as she watched the flame dance wildly from side to side. At one point it flickered down to almost nothing, and its slight glow became only the dimmest of light. Hannah gasped as she placed her foot on the bottom step, then sighed with relief when the little flame reappeared, to point upward like a yellow finger at the closed door.

Hannah stepped forward, preparing to mount the stairs, but Quint's hand closed around her wrist and held her still. "I'll get the basket and the candle," he said. "You spread something on the floor for us to sit on."

Hannah nodded, then with one last worried glance at the swaying flame, turned to do as Quint asked. Moments later they sat on a thick coverlet fashioned of brightly covered swatches of material sewn in a pinwheel design to a thick woolen blanket. Hannah curled her feet under her, glancing around the circle of light as Quint opened the basket and produced thick slices of cheese and bread.

Quint placed a slice of cheese between two pieces of bread and handed the sandwich to Hannah. When she made no move to take it from him, he looked more closely at her, to find her staring off into the dark.

"Hannah?" His voice was soft, but she jumped as if he'd shouted and turned to him as he continued. "I'm sure there's nothing there except the normal boxes and barrels found in cellars. If it will make you feel better, I'll take the candle around and light everything up for you. But not until after I've eaten. Now, are you hungry or not?"

Hannah nodded as she reached out to take the sandwich. It galled her to let Quint continue to think she was frightened by bugs and mice. Vermin were a simple fact of life to one who had spent as much time traveling with fairs and circuses as she had. But she would rather he think that was what was bothering her than reveal her childish fear of the dark.

Madeleine DuBois had nestled a bottle of wine and a pitcher of water in the center of the basket along with two earthenware mugs. Hannah refused the wine and washed her sandwich down with the fresh cool water. Neither she nor Quint spoke during their little meal. Hannah kept glancing around the dark room, though as her stomach filled she found her irrational fear receding somewhat.

As Hannah took her last bite of cheese, she gazed across at Quint, sitting cross-legged and looking perfectly at ease with his bare feet tucked beneath his legs. The open neck of his rumpled, dusty shirt revealed the thick, dark hair on his chest that had so fascinated her earlier.

Hannah watched him raise his mug to his lips slowly. He was looking directly at her, but his gaze was unfocused, as if he were seeing right through her. Hannah glanced down at her torn and stained garments. The low-cut neckline of her corset cover skimmed the upper curves of her breasts, and the garment nipped in tightly at her waist, while the thin fabric of her underskirt clung tightly to her hips and the curve of her outstretched leg.

Warm heat rose quickly to Hannah's cheeks. Hoping Quint's distraction would last a moment longer, she turned and grabbed the closer of the two remaining blankets, threw it around her shoulders like a shawl, and held it together in front of her.

"Getting cold again?"

Hannah lifted her head at Quint's question and nodded quickly, taking refuge in another lie as she felt the blush lighting her cheeks spread down her body until even her bare toes began to feel hot.

"Well," he said, "do you want to check around the room while our light still lasts?"

Hannah glanced at the candle and saw that little more than an inch of wax remained beneath the dancing flame. She nodded, then rose as Quint picked up the holder and stood. With the blanket still tightly held to her, she followed him around the room as he lifted the candle to reveal one harmless shadowy corner after another.

Just as Quint had said, the cellar was full of barrels and boxes here, lumpy gunny sacks and more boxes there, and wooden bins filled with carrots and turnips under the stairway. The dirt floor was dry and free of debris, and not once did the moving light send anything scurrying from one shadow to another.

"All right now?"

Quint turned to Hannah as they stepped back onto the coverlet. She looked up at his smiling face and gave him a sheepish grin. He answered her by smiling wider before he spoke. "Now, don't be embarrassed. After the way you so coolly controlled the situation in the air today, I was beginning to think you were invincible. I was also beginning to feel decidedly inferior."

His light tone and words made Hannah frown. "And now that you know I'm afraid of bugs and rats you feel superior?"

Quint shook his head. "Hardly. Just a little less outmatched."

"Why should you feel outmatched because I know how to pilot a balloon and you don't? Few people do, you know." Hannah's eyes narrowed and her voice hardened. "Is it because I'm a woman?"

Quint looked into her angry eyes and lifted his brows in surprise. "Yes, I suppose it is." He paused a moment, then went on before she could voice her indignation at his attitude. "And that really surprises me. Considering my relationship with my grandmother, one would think I would be quite accustomed to the idea that either gender can be equally capable in all areas. I apologize."

Hannah felt as if the bubble of righteous anger in her chest had suddenly burst. "Well,"—she blinked and shook her head as she sat down—"that's amazing. If you truly mean what you say, you are just about the only man I've met, aside from my father, who isn't frightened by a woman who knows something he doesn't."

Quint sat on the other side of the candle. As he spoke, his lips curved into that twisted smile that always made Hannah's heart turn over in her chest. "Well, that's because few men have been raised by the likes of Evelyn Blackthorne."

Hannah hesitated, uncertain how to approach the subject of the countess. "Your grandmother is a very impressive woman," she began. "She seems very self-possessed."

"I believe the word is 'iron-willed.' " Quint's lips curved wryly. "And I would venture to guess that one could say the same about your Aunt Amelia. Small and tiny she might be; however, I've a feeling she isn't one to cross when she's angry."

Hannah shook her head with a wry grin. "Definitely not. When Aunt Amelia's mind is set on something it's best to go along with her." She hesitated. "I can smile about that now, but when my mother and I first moved in with her, I found this trait infuriating. Then, after my mother died and I realized this woman had full charge over me, I became very rebellious."

"You two seem to have worked things out."

Hannah smiled and nodded. "Yes, but I'm afraid that Aunt Amelia and I had a difficult year right after my mother died. Looking back I can see that I was hurt and angry and that she was the only one for me to take it out on."

Quint frowned as an old wound throbbed in an almost forgotten part of his heart. He knew the kind of anger she spoke of, the need to strike out at someone, the longing to return a blow, only to find nothing but a blackness that mocked the futility of his fury.

"It's amazing what pain does to the human mind." Quint stared at the unwavering yellow flame between them. "We consider ourselves so very civilized, so far above our animal brothers, yet when something hurts us deeply we growl and slash out, figuratively speaking, of course."

He paused, then went on quietly. "I was quite terrible to my father after my mother's death, even though the man's anguish was very apparent to me. I suppose somehow in my seven-year-old mind I thought there must have been something he could have done to keep my mother with us. I loved her so much that I couldn't bear to place the blame where it really belonged, which was with her, first for abandoning us, then for loving someone more than she loved us, and finally for dying.''

Hannah watched him speak. A miniature flame was reflected in his eyes. His voice was low, with a curious quality to it, as if he was examining these feelings for the first time. His frown pulled his eyebrows closer together, and his lips tightened and twisted as he mentioned his mother's death.

Hannah felt her own lips draw into a tight line as his words entered a dark corner of her soul, shining a light on a bit of truth she had buried away there. She blinked in surprise and her thoughts sprang to her lips.

"I used to get angry at my father, too, whenever he left for another circuit. I knew he had to leave, understood that ballooning was how he supported us, but when I watched him sitting in the wagon that held *Skylark,* folded in its basket, I became furious.'' She lifted her eyes to find Quint looking at her. "But it hurt too much to be angry at him, so I took it out on Aunt Amelia. Amazing.'' She shook her head. "I treated her awfully, fighting her at every turn for six months, and she simply smiled. Then, one day I discovered that I had no fight left in me.''

Quint felt a small smile on his lips and lifted his brows. "Oh?''

The doubt echoing in that one word made Hannah shrug. "Well, not against Aunt Amelia. I finally realized she wasn't trying to make me into one of those simpering Boston society women, that she just wanted me to know how to move through their world with ease as I found my own way. After that, we became the best of friends.''

Quint's lips quirked up slightly. "Interesting. That's exactly how I view my grandmother—as my best friend. I guess that does make me a rather strange fellow.''

Hannah tilted her head to one side, stared at him a moment, then shook her head. "Well, it must have limited your nights of gaming and drinking, but I wouldn't say it makes you strange.''

"It does, you know." Quint narrowed his eyes. "I was never at any one school long enough to make friends, and then I inherited Blackthorne Hall and the exalted title of earl, along with my father's pile of debts. That ruined any chance of attending a university. As a result, I'm afraid I deserve my reputation as a recluse and as something of an eccentric. Felicia certainly thought so, at least after we'd been married awhile.''

Hannah glanced at him sharply, then gave a short nod. "That's right. Hartley mentioned you had been married before." She hesitated as she glanced down at her interlaced fingers, then back up to Quint's dark eyes. "He told me she died very young. Was she ill long?''

A hard look narrowed Quint's eyes as he shook his head. "She was never ill.''

Hannah bit her lower lip. This was none of her business, but after Hartley's dark hints she couldn't keep from asking, "What did she die of?''

Quint's lips took a bitter twist. "It depends on whom you talk to. Some would tell you she died of neglect. Others would say I frightened her to death.'' Quint paused as he looked long and hard into Hannah's eyes. Then he shrugged. "There's a bit of truth in both stories.''

Chapter 10

A chill rushed through Hannah as she gazed into Quint's dark green eyes. She pulled her blanket more tightly around her and asked softly, "What is the *real* truth?"

Quint lifted his brow. "Does anyone ever know the real truth about anything?" His voice echoed bitterly in the small room. Beneath the caustic tone Hannah discerned a note of pain as he shrugged and went on more quietly. "I was very busy when we were first married, overseeing every part of my estate, accounting for every farthing I spent. Grandmother had always helped me with the books, but she had suffered a stroke shortly after Felicia and I married."

Quint sighed. "Poor Felicia must have been very confused. I spent hardly any time with her after our wedding, after a courtship in which I couldn't bear to be away from her side." Quint's lips twisted wryly as he glanced at Hannah. "Most people who know me find this hard to believe, but I fell madly in love with Felicia the moment I saw her. Just meeting her had the most extraordinary effect on me." Quint stopped speaking to gaze into Hannah's wide eyes.

Just like the effect you have had on me, Hannah Bradley. The thought reverberated through his mind as he stared at her rapt features framed by wisps of golden hair, feeling the magic pull that had first captured his heart when he saw Hannah struggling with that curtain of gold in the silver mist.

But was it the same? After nine years he could barely remember Felicia, could only vaguely recall a round face and quiet brown eyes. But he knew he would always carry a picture in his mind of every detail of Hannah's face, from her wide dusky eyes and short nose to the way her pointed chin tipped up whenever she grew thoughtful.

"And Felicia loved you back?"

Hannah's breathless question made Quint blink. His lips twisted wryly as he answered. "I don't think I gave her a chance to think about it. We met in May and were married in July. She was the fourth daughter of Baron Woolrich, who had very little money left for a dowry. My grandmother had hoped I'd find someone who would bring in a little more silver, but this was one decision she had promised to leave completely to me."

He sighed as he shook his head. "And for the first two months I was the most considerate and attentive of husbands. Then the harvest came in and required all my attention. Once I received the profits, I had to make arrangements for new equipment and see to some of the householders' repairs before the winter. By the time the snows came to keep me inside, my bride was most perturbed with me. She missed her busy life in London and her important friends."

Quint's eyes didn't waver as he stared at the candle silently for a moment before he continued in a subdued tone. "Felicia urged me to move to the town house, but I couldn't afford to give up the rent it was bringing in. I assured her that once spring came there would be plenty of things to keep her busy in the village. I said she would make new friends to keep her occupied. Unfortunately, I was right."

Something about the deepening of his voice and the harsh

edge to his words told Hannah what had happened. "She found a lover?"

He nodded, staring at the candle with empty eyes. "When I first heard the rumors, I was incredulous. Then I saw her sneak off one night. I followed her, heard her talking to a man in the garden, but the moment I stepped in, he disappeared. I was so furious I couldn't speak. I just grabbed her arm, pulled her up the stairs to her room, and slammed the door. She was gone the next morning. We found her in a ditch, her neck broken, her horse grazing nearby. Apparently she'd been unable to tighten the cinch, for the saddle was dangling to one side."

His voice trailed off, leaving Hannah searching her mind for the proper words of consolation. He saved her from having to make any comment when he lifted his head and looked into her eyes. "So you see"—he smiled wanly—"both opinions are true. I did neglect her, and I suppose it could be fairly said that her fear of my anger killed her."

Hannah gazed into Quint's eyes, seeing pain and self-recrimination. She shook her head. "What a silly girl she must have been."

"What do you mean, silly?" Quint frowned.

Hannah shrugged. "She must have been an empty-headed fool to be unable to find something to occupy her time. She sounds to me like some of the spoiled misses I met at finishing school, with their heads full of nothing but new dresses and balls and the latest gossip." She stopped and looked at him sharply. "Cicely isn't like that, you know. She's very sensible, though a bit shy. But that will work well for you. I'm sure she'll do wonderfully in the country, especially after you have children."

Quint gazed at Hannah. Once more he'd completely forgotten about Cicely. It was as if the only reality was what he could see within this quickly fading circle of light where Hannah's quick understanding offered warmth. But now that

Cicely's name had come up, it was as if she were sitting between him and Hannah, a reminder of duty and convention.

"I hope so," he said finally. "I want her to be happy."

Quint spoke with quiet force. Hannah gazed at him, remembering how matter-of-factly he'd spoken about marrying Cicely for her dowry. This still sounded coldhearted to her, but after seeing her cousin with Parker, it had become obvious that Cicely had agreed to this arrangement with complete knowledge that Quint was no more in love with her than she was with him. All she could do was hope that somehow they would find happiness together.

Hannah lowered her gaze as she shivered once more, then blinked as a flicker of light caught her eye. She looked at the candle, and her eyes widened as she saw the flame start to sputter. Before she could say anything, the little yellow tongue stretched upward one last time, as if reaching for freedom, then disappeared completely.

Her hands tightened around the blanket she held around her, and she bit her lip as complete blackness engulfed her. Quint's voice floated in the darkness, light and amused.

"I guess that means it's time to lie down. Let me just get this candle holder out of the way." He stopped speaking, and Hannah could hear something sliding over the surface of the quilt. "Ah, got it." Again there was silence, broken only by the shuffling sound of Quint stretching his long form out on his side of the coverlet. "Well," he said, "I've certainly slept on softer surfaces, but I think I shall be asleep in no time. It's been a most unusual day, wouldn't you say?"

Hannah nodded slowly, then realized he couldn't see her and forced herself to speak. "Yes, most unusual."

Still she didn't move.

"Hannah, aren't you going to lie down?"

Hannah heard his words, but she couldn't answer. The

darkness had moved closer; she could feel it like a solid wall around her, holding her in, suffocating her. Soon she knew she would not be able to hear or feel anything.

"Hannah!"

Quint's voice was sharp and closer to her. Hannah jumped when his hand closed around her wrist. When she felt him next to her, the wall moved away somewhat, and she took a deep, shaky breath.

"What's wrong, Hannah? It's not the rats and bugs again, is it?"

Hannah's lips tightened as she shook her head. "No." Her voice was small, choked by embarrassment.

"It's the dark, isn't it?"

Hannah nodded, and her cheeks flamed as feminine laughter echoed out of the past.

"Hannah, am I right?"

She forced herself to answer. "Yes." She paused, then forced herself to go on. "I know it's silly. They tried to cure me time and time again, but nothing worked."

"Who tried? Your parents? Your aunt?"

"No. The teachers at school. They said it was ridiculous for a great big girl like me to be afraid of the dark. They tried to force me to sleep without a light, but I couldn't do it. I would stay awake night after night, and when I finally did doze off, I would start screaming when I woke up in the dark. Finally they had to relent and let me have a candle by my bed."

"Do you know what caused this fear?"

"Yes. When I was very little, about three, I was playing with some older children. I hid inside an old trunk in a circus wagon. I let the lid fall down, and somehow one of the latches caught. When no one found me I tried to get out, but I couldn't. I screamed and screamed, but no one came. I finally screamed myself hoarse. There was no air. I couldn't see or hear a thing, and soon I could hardly breathe. Mama said they found me just in time to keep me from suffocating.''

"Did you tell your teachers this?"

"Of course, and many were very sympathetic. They just thought I should have outgrown my fears."

A long pause followed Hannah's last words. Then Quint spoke again. "Do you think you could relax if I held you? You wouldn't feel alone then."

Hannah bit her lip as she considered his offer. She remembered far too well how his arms felt around her, the pleasure, the comfort she'd found in them. The thought was tempting, but she felt that to accept would be wrong. Even if Cicely truly didn't love Quint, there was a legal and moral bond between them that forced Hannah to shake her head as she spoke. "No, that won't be necessary. I'll be fine as long as I sit up. It's only when I lie down that the fear gets too bad."

"Hannah." Quint's hand touched her shoulder, then slid up her neck to rest warmly on her cheek. "You have to sleep. I need you to be alert in the morning to help me persuade our hosts to let us go." He paused, then spoke again. "How about if you curl up on the coverlet and just let me hold your hand?"

Hannah took a shaky breath. "All right." Slowly she lay down a foot away from Quint with her right hand resting in his and her left clutching the blanket. The soft sound of his breathing soothed her taut muscles as she waited for the familiar heaviness of fear to clutch her chest and rob her of her breath as it always did.

Her heart pounded so loudly she was sure Quint could hear it. It continued to race, but her chest rose and fell in a rhythmic fashion with complete ease and she continued to be aware of the heat of his strong fingers.

"How are you, Hannah?"

"I'm fine."

Quint chuckled and she almost smiled herself at the surprise in her voice.

"Well, sleep then. And remember, if you should awaken, that I'm right here."

"Thank you, Quint."

Hannah felt warmth from his hand move up her arm and wash over her form. Her heartbeat slowed, though it still pounded with a strange intensity. The heat rinsed the tension from her muscles, and she let her eyelids drop over her eyes. On her lids she saw a misty picture of Quint standing in the fog, helping her through to a dawn that blossomed on the edge of her mind, and she drifted into heavy sleep.

Quint lay next to her, listening to her even breathing, intensely aware of the slender form next to him. He closed his eyes, willing himself to sleep, but the day's happenings fluttered across his eyelids in vivid color. Strange feelings flowed through him as he reexperienced the vibrant sights and emotions, the exuberant sense of freedom he'd known in the air, the strange detachment he'd felt when death seemed to approach, and the deep connection he'd felt to the woman next to him.

Quint frowned into the darkness. This sort of experience had no place in his life. It might be all well and good for others to look for adventure, others who had only their own lives to consider. But he had too many people depending on him. He had made promises long ago that remained unfulfilled. Promises that a part of him forgot each time he was close to Hannah Bradley.

Hannah never knew how long she'd been asleep or what woke her. She had a vague memory of falling from a great height and of her body suddenly jerking with a sudden force that made her gasp and open her eyes wide.

The total blackness engulfed her immediately. She gasped again, but could hear no sound. She was once more in a world without sensation, unable to see, to hear, to feel. Terror gripped her and her breath came in short, quick spurts as her hands groped for something to hold on to, any object that would give her some sense of place so she could pull herself out of the dreaded emptiness.

When Hannah's fingers closed over Quint's arm he woke with a start. For two beats of his heart he struggled to remember where he was. The answer came in a flash, and when he heard the ragged breathing echoing in the dark, he knew what must have happened.

"Hannah."

He turned toward her, covering the hand grasping his arm with his free hand, but she made no reply.

"Hannah, I'm here with you. Do you hear me?"

Again there was no response. Quint reached over and curled his free arm around Hannah's waist and pulled her closer to him. Her lithe form was rigid and shaking, and yet he could feel a warm heat radiating from her as he drew her closer to his body.

"Hannah, can you hear me?"

Hannah shivered, only half feeling Quint's arms around her, but his firm, soothing words seeped through the barrier of her fear. She nodded with a jerky movement as she closed her fingers over the material of his shirt, hungry for any sensation.

Quint bent his head till his mouth was near Hannah's ear. "Take a deep breath."

Hannah obeyed the silky whisper, drew cool air into her lungs, held it, and when Quint ordered her to release it, she did so quickly. Her knotted muscles eased a little, and her body woke to the feel of the solid form pressed close to hers.

She opened her eyes, but the darkness was still there, threatening to swallow her into that bottomless void that haunted her nights. She arched forward, hungry for the reassurance of closer contact.

The unconsciously seductive movement set Quint's body on fire. He tightened his arms around Hannah's quivering form, trying to control his lust even as he offered reassurance. "You're safe, Hannah."

His voice was a husky whisper in Hannah's ear. She shivered with the sudden mixture of cold and heat that shimmered through her.

"Can you hear me?" Quint asked, and Hannah nodded.

"Are you all right now? Talk to me."

Was she all right? Hannah bit down on her lower lip, but could feel only the slightest pressure. She was doing better than when she first awoke, but she knew if Quint let go of her for even a second, she would once more be swallowed up by the numbing blackness.

Hannah turned her head and opened her mouth to answer his question at the same time Quint bent his head to repeat it. His lips brushed hers, sending a shock of desire trembling through him, and without thinking he lowered his mouth to capture hers and move over the supple velvet of her lips.

Hannah reacted to the feel of his kiss with a hunger born of her desperation to fight off the nothingness that threatened her. She parted her lips and pressed them to his, responding mindlessly to her urgent need for his touch. She shut her eyes to the darkness around her and concentrated on the sensation of his moist lips caressing hers and his arms drawing her against the hard contours of his body.

She released her hold on Quint's shirtfront and placed her open hand on his chest, gasping against his mouth as her palm registered the heat of hair-roughened skin. She slid her hand up, exploring the hard planes of his chest, then curved her fingers over the rigid strength of his shoulder.

The rational portion of Quint's mind never got a chance

to be heard. He was only aware of holding Hannah, of the warmth beneath the thin fabric covering her. He caressed her back, his long fingers spread out wide to touch as much of her as he could until they slipped past the top of her camisole and encountered naked flesh.

The warm satin feel of her skin made his heart race, sending heated blood surging through his veins. He began to move his hand upward again, angling around to brush up over the soft flesh covering her ribs until the tips of his fingers touched the lower curves of her breast.

Hannah was lost in a world of sensation. Quint's strong hands caressing her bare skin awoke a coiling heat in her stomach and a strange pulsing in the area between her legs. As his hand closed over her aching breast she moaned against his lips. When his tongue slid into her mouth, her tongue met it, delighting in its velvet moistness.

Her body pulsed with fevered warmth that seemed to crave the heat of Quint's body, and rejoiced when he unbuttoned her camisole, then slipped it from her shoulders. He slid his lips from her mouth, and she sighed with pleasure when they closed over the sensitive skin on the side of her neck, as his fingers circled first one bare breast, then the other, making them tingle with need.

Quint touched his tongue to Hannah's neck, tasting a hint of salt, then trailed the tip of his tongue slowly down the slender column of her throat and across her upper chest to tease the hardened tips of her breasts. He heard Hannah gasp with pleasure as he closed his mouth over one pliant nipple, then ran his fingers down the center of her abdomen until they encountered the string holding her underskirt closed. He released its bowknot and eased it over her slender hips and down her legs.

Hannah gasped again as Quint brought his hand up to spread his fingers out over her belly. The heat churning beneath his hand coiled tighter. She wrapped her arms around his shoulders, holding tightly to him as the floor seemed to rotate beneath her. When Quint's fingers moved down to brush the curling triangle between her legs, she gasped, and when he touched the pulsing warmth there, she moaned his name.

Quint lifted himself up on one elbow and bent forward to capture Hannah's mouth in a hard kiss. She writhed beneath him, clinging to him tightly, making his desire for her an urgent need. Abruptly he sat up and forced his anxious fingers to undo the buttons on his shirt and pants.

Once Quint had removed his clothes, cold air touched his naked skin, jolting his passion-drugged mind. For one second the voice of reason made itself heard, whispering that he was taking advantage of Hannah's fears. But Hannah's voice was louder.

"Quint, where are you?" Her words were uttered in a husky whisper. "Please . . . come back."

Without the sensations provided by Quint's body and hands, Hannah found the darkness closing around her again, found herself slipping into a world without feeling. When Quint's hard form stretched out against hers again, she turned in his arms eagerly, hungry for his warmth, longing for his touch, craving fulfillment for the need pulsing through her.

Their lips touched again as Quint pulled her close. She softened against his firm, muscular form, enjoying the feel of his sculpted thighs caressing hers, the hair-roughened curves of his chest pressing against her naked breasts, and the solid plane of his abdomen resting on hers. She became aware of the hard ridge of his manhood pressing into her lower stomach, and the pulsing sensation between her legs increased.

She arched forward as Quint gently rolled her over on her back, raised himself up to slip his hand down the front of her body, then gently brush his fingers over the triangle of curls once more. With each pass of his hand Hannah felt the combination of pleasure and pressure grow there. When he finally touched her, sliding his finger over the soft moisture, she moaned at the sudden pleasure his caress elicited.

Hannah frowned when Quint removed his hand, then moaned softly against his mouth when she felt his manhood against her, moving slowly. She lifted her hips, hungry for further contact, heard Quint's deep moan answer hers as she felt something hard and warm pressing into her, gently but firmly.

She gasped as he entered her. A spasm of pain mingled with her growing pleasure, becoming one as Quint held himself still within her. He kissed her deeply, the thrusting action of his tongue filling her with renewed need, then began moving his hips once more. Hannah clung to him as she arched her lower body toward him, no longer even slightly aware of the darkness surrounding her as she concentrated on the growing sensual ache.

The feeling of pleasure grew with each contact till it took Hannah to a dizzying height and held her there a moment before bursting into a thousand fragments of pulsing delight. As spasms of pleasure rippled through her, she felt Quint jerk hard against her and heard a deep growl rumble in his chest as he tightened his arms around her body.

Hannah's breath came in ragged, uneven gasps as she buried her face in the hard curve between Quint's neck and shoulder. Her entire body felt flushed, her muscles relaxed to the point of feebleness. She held her eyes tightly closed, unwilling to lose sight of the bright lights dancing on her eyelids, and let her mind float down and wander into a moonlit dream in which warm lips caressed her neck and a deep voice whispered her name in a tone that mingled joy and anguish.

* * *

"Hannah, wake up."

The voice seemed to be part of Hannah's dream. She smiled and curled tighter into the warmth that surrounded her.

"Hannah. You must wake up."

This time the words were spoken sharply. Hannah opened her eyes and stared up through the gray light seeping in the tiny window set high on the wall behind her. Quint sat in front of her, fully dressed, a dark frown over his eyes.

"Hannah, you must get dressed, before the men come to get us."

Hannah blinked, becoming aware that beneath the blankets she was completely naked. She opened her eyes and stared ahead, not seeing Quint, but remembering what had happened during the night. Her recollections had the misty feel of a dream, but she was aware that it had all been very real.

"Hannah. Are you . . . in pain?"

Again Hannah blinked, bringing Quint's concerned face into focus. She shook her head. "No, I'm not in pain."

"I understand." Quint stood. "I'll turn around while you dress."

Hannah stared up at his back, feeling heat rise to her cheeks. It hadn't occurred to her to be embarrassed until he made this assumption. She hadn't had time to think about how she did feel, but she knew that shame hadn't occurred to her.

Spying her clothes arranged neatly in front of her, Hannah sat up and slipped her camisole on. As she placed the tiny buttons in the holes, she recalled the feel of Quint's fingers pulling each one open, remembered how desperately she had needed his touch.

She drew her lower lip between her teeth as she stood and stepped into her underskirt. What had passed between her and Quint should never have happened. He was betrothed to her cousin. In the cold light of dawn it was clear to her how wrong she had been to let Quint comfort her, to let . . . no, to ask him for more. But this had all come about in the dark, when she was vulnerable, barely capable of thought.

Hannah slowly tied the string at the waist of her underskirt into a bow. There was nothing she could do to right this particular wrong; neither could she blame Quint. She clearly remembered how she had clung to him, returned his every kiss and caress, welcomed each new sensation. How could she fault him for taking what she had so eagerly offered?

Of course it must not happen again, ever. Hannah straightened her shoulders and raised her eyes to the back of Quint's dark head and spoke quietly.

"I'm dressed now."

Quint turned slowly. Beneath his frowning brows his green eyes met and held hers. "Hannah, we must talk about last night. We—"

Quint's words were cut off when the sound of hinges creaking echoed through the room. He and Hannah turned to see the trapdoor open slowly.

Chapter 11

Hannah and Quint stared at the ceiling as the rectangle opened up completely. A second later Émile DuBois looked down at them. *"Bonjour,"* he said. "I hope you have rested well and that you can forgive us for our poor show of hospitality. Please come up and join us. Madeleine has prepared breakfast."

Quint spoke quietly. "Thank you very much. Hannah?"

He turned to her, looking into her eyes as he offered her his hand. Hannah, recalling Pierre and his gun, closed her teeth over the inside of her lower lip, but lifted her hand toward Quint's to let his fingers close around hers. She and Quint had a role to play, that of man and wife. Any suspicious actions on her part could reveal that lie and perhaps cost them their lives.

Hannah glanced at Quint's broad back as he led her up toward the tantalizing scent of bacon and coffee. She blinked as she stepped into the room above, where the whitewashed walls reflected the early morning sun. Two streams of light slanted onto the pine table that stood in front of two windows curtained in blue and white gingham. Several baskets of bread and fruit sat in the center of the table, surrounded by six place settings.

Pierre and Antoine were sitting at two of these places. Antoine barely lifted his dark head when Hannah and Quint entered. His small dark eyes darted over to Hannah a moment, then back down to the food on his plate as he lifted a loaded fork to his wide mouth. Pierre looked up from his food as well and gave Hannah a jaunty smile.

"*Bonjour, madame.* I trust you slept well. I did, until Émile dragged me out of bed before first light to go on a little hunting trip. We found your balloon and have it in Émile's wagon, and I owe you and your husband a thousand apologies for not believing your story. Please sit down and let my sister's wonderful cooking begin to make amends."

Hannah glanced at Pierre as she lowered herself onto the woven seat of the chair Émile pulled out for her. The slender young man seemed sincere in his regret. "We must apologize as well, I'm afraid," she said with a smile, "for appearing in such a strange fashion so late at night. You were right to be cautious. Our story is even difficult for me to believe."

"No." Émile spoke as he took his seat at the head of the table. "Pierre is right to be embarrassed. But now we will make reparations. First you shall enjoy this meal my wife has prepared for you, and then you can tell us how we can help you."

Hannah cast a relieved look at Quint, who dipped his head in an answering nod as he stirred milk into his bowl of porridge. Noticing that the others were already eating, Hannah turned her attention to her meal. Her stomach was so tightly knotted that she thought at first she would not be able to eat, but she found the cereal soothing, and her appetite increased.

She gladly accepted a plate of fried eggs and two thick slices of bacon that Madeleine silently served, then smiled at the woman as she took her place at the end of the table opposite her husband. *"Merci, madame."* She limited her thanks to these simple words, reluctant to reveal that she knew any more French for fear Émile and Madeleine would think she had been eavesdropping on them as they conversed in their own language.

Émile answered for his wife. "You are most welcome. Believe me when I tell you that Madeleine is most pleased to be able to offer you such a meal. She is distressed that her brothers have disgraced the family in such a way."

Hannah watched Émile and Pierre exchange angry glances before Pierre turned his attention to Hannah and Quint. "I have already told these people I am sorry. I, too, wish to offer my services to make restitution for my error in judgment."

"Thank you," Quint replied. "Our needs are very simple, actually. We must get back to England as soon as possible."

Émile glanced at Pierre once more before turning to Quint. "We are to go to Calais today. I have things to sell at the market there. I would be honored to give you a ride in my wagon if that would help you."

"That would be perfect." Quint turned to Hannah. "Several boats leave from there, bound for Dover, each day. From Dover we can take a train to Hastings, which is only about fifteen miles from St. Albanswood."

Hannah looked up from the last of her breakfast, prepared to agree to the plan. When she looked at Quint, she hesitated. His shirt was gray and rumpled, and with the dark stubble shadowing the lower half of his face, he looked less like an earl and more like the poacher she had once feared he might be.

Hannah knew she couldn't look any better. Her hair fell in tangled waves as she glanced down at her wrinkled undergarments. A blush rushed to her face as she looked back up to Quint. "We have no money for passage," she said. "And look at us. Do you think anyone would let us on a boat dressed as we are?"

Quint stared at Hannah. Her hair hung to her waist, twisting and curling about her face in a tousled manner that reminded him sharply of the pleasures they'd shared in the night. Just recalling their lovemaking made Quint's body respond, and as he felt his manhood rise, he frowned. Ever since waking this morning the voice of reason had berated him for what had happened, even as his body glowed with sated pleasure.

With a blink, Quint forced his thoughts back to the present. He rubbed his hand over the rough, suddenly warm skin on his face, then raked his fingers through his black curls to clear his thoughts. "You're right," he told Hannah. "We *are* a sorry-looking pair."

"That can be repaired." Émile spoke up. "My wife and I will provide you with clothes, as well as money for the boat."

Quint turned to the man. "We will take the money as a loan only. I can send someone to return the sum to you tomorrow."

"No." Émile shook his head. "We should have believed you. We pride ourselves on helping those who stop on our road. It will be our gift, in return for the poor night's lodging we gave you."

Quint continued to frown, but nodded slowly. "We shall accept, then. However, I would ask that you please keep Hannah's balloon safe here until I can send someone for it. I will insist you take payment for retrieving and storing it for us."

The man seemed to hesitate a moment before he nodded. Then Quint turned to Hannah, lifting his brow as if to ask for her agreement to this plan. Hannah could only give him a tremulous smile. Her heart was too full of gratitude for

his thoughtful gesture, and her throat too tight to allow her
to speak.

An hour later Hannah and Quint stood on the stone steps
in front of the house, giving their thanks to Madeleine
DuBois for the food that filled them and for the clothes the
woman had found for them.

Hannah felt cool and comfortable in the long-sleeved
peasant dress of pale blue. Its more than ample girth was
tucked into a dark blue skirt and covered by a long white
apron. The woman had brushed Hannah's hair and helped
her twist it up and anchor it at the nape of her neck with
the silver comb Quint had returned to her.

Sturdy clogs encased Hannah's feet, making her step
carefully as she followed Émile to the wagon where Quint
waited. As he took her hand, Hannah glanced up at his
clean-shaven face, then lowered her gaze to inspect the blue
blouse he wore over tight trousers of rough brown material
tucked into scuffed boots.

Hannah, frustrated by the tension between them, felt her
hands tighten into fists at her sides. She longed for the
easygoing banter she'd shared with Quint in the woods and
again in the balloon, the feeling of mystical oneness she'd
sensed before the coupling of their bodies came between
them.

In an attempt to lighten the atmosphere, she forced a
smile to her lips, then looked at Quint and spoke as brightly
as she could. "Well, Lord Blackthorne, don't we look like
a couple of proper beggars?"

Quint's lips twitched into a half-smile as he helped Hannah up into the back of the wagon. "Yes," he replied, "but
at least, dressed like this, we'll be allowed on one of the
ships." He paused as he swung himself up next to her, then
shrugged. "I suppose we'll have to answer all sorts of
questions before they believe we truly are British subjects,
but Émile has been more than generous with the money he

gave us, so I suppose that will help things along.''

As Émile took his place on the seat of the wagon, Hannah and Quint settled themselves behind him facing the rear of the wagon in comfortable niches between the boxes and barrels arranged in the center.

Hannah was just leaning back against the forward wall of the wagon when she glanced over to see Pierre and Antoine stop at the door where Madeleine stood. Pierre, wearing a slouching cap made of mustard-colored fabric, smiled at his sister. Madeleine shook her head twice before bestowing a quick, reluctant kiss on his cheek, then turned to Antoine's dark, silent figure to do the same.

Both men were dressed in the local peasant garb of loose blue shirts over darker-hued pants. Antoine's black hair and most of his face were covered by a dirty white canvas hat with a broad, drooping brim. He placed his large hands on the edge of the wagon and in one smooth motion pushed himself up and around to sit facing backward with his legs dangling off the back of the conveyance.

As Hannah watched him, Antoine drew a knife from the leather scabbard at his side. Her eyes widened at the sight of the wide shiny blade that narrowed into a deadly point. Her heart nearly stopped pumping, until she saw him bring forth a short stick with the other hand, and begin to angle the knife along the piece of wood in a smooth, controlled stroke that sent a long, pale tendril curling to the ground.

Hannah heard a dry chuckle and looked over to find that Pierre had made a place for himself in a spot about three feet in front of her. He sat facing her from his cross-legged position and grinned. "He can do that all day, my brother. He never makes anything, just whittles quietly, leaving piles of shavings wherever he's been."

"That's far superior to leaving people totally exhausted from listening to your never-ending chatter."

Antoine's deep voice startled Hannah. She had begun to

wonder if he was a mute. The fact that he spoke perfect English, with even less of an accent than Pierre, made Hannah glance at Antoine in surprise. His small dark eyes glittered and his full lips twitched into a ghost of a smile before he turned away to watch the progress of his knife as it slipped along the edge of the wood.

"Is everyone settled?" Émile called back over his shoulder. After receiving three affirmative answers he clucked to the horses, and they rattled forward, pulling the swaying wagon behind them.

At first trees lined both sides of the road. Then the foliage on Hannah's right thinned and disappeared as the path moved closer to the edge of the cliff. The road dropped gradually until they were even with the surging sea. Hannah glanced at Quint, who met her gaze, lifted his expressive brows, and gave her a small smile. "If the wind had blown a little harder to the east," he said, "our landing wouldn't have been near as exciting. You wouldn't have been forced to discard that lovely dress."

Hannah shrugged and smiled widely. "The memories I have will last far longer than the gown would have. It turned out well, as adventures go, wouldn't you say?"

Quint gazed into her eyes for a long moment. There was so much he wanted to say to her. But with Émile and Madeleine's brothers well within earshot, all he could do was smile tightly. "Well, since I can't remember taking part in anything remotely adventurous before, I really have nothing to compare this with. All I can say is that my life has not quite been the same since I met you, Hannah Brad-ley."

A quick blush heated Hannah's face in response to the warm look in Quint's eyes. Somehow she knew he wasn't just referring to what had passed between them the previous night. She wanted to reply that meeting him had changed her life also, by adding a richness of emotion she'd never known before, but she could not say the words.

Hannah stared at Quint as her mind opened to the truth of her feelings for him. She was hopelessly in love with him, and had been almost from the moment they met. She had no control over this emotion. It had sprung from the very depths of her soul, without regard for logic and reason.

A bittersweet ache twisted in the center of her chest. It was all so ironic, meeting him in the same wood where her father had first come upon her mother. Where their love had bloomed into a flower, hers was doomed to die on the vine.

Hannah turned away from the warmth shimmering in Quint's green eyes to gaze thoughtfully at the ocean rising in blue green waves to crash into foamy white spray on the rocks lining the shore. She might not be able to stop loving this man, but she had to begin to school her features. He belonged to someone else, to Cicely, and her cousin must never learn how he and Hannah had betrayed the girl's trust.

Beneath the sound of the crashing waves, a soft rattling sound drew her attention to Pierre. She watched him shuffling a deck of cards, handling them with a quick deftness that spoke of hours of experience.

Pierre fanned the cards, face down, in his hand then extended them toward Quint as he spoke. "*Monsieur*, would you take a card out of this deck, *s'il vous plaît?*"

For the first time that day the corners of Hannah's lips twitched into a smile of honest amusement as she watched Quint draw a single card out and look at it. Pierre spoke quickly again. "Do not show me the card. Memorize it and place it on top of the deck."

When the cards were once more in a compact rectangle, Pierre held the edges between his thumb and forefinger and held the deck out to Quint, who slid his card on top. Pierre cut the deck and placed the bottom half on top of Quint's card, then began flipping the cards over and tossing them onto the wagon bed one by one, revealing their faces. Approximately halfway through the deck, he laid down the five of diamonds, then stopped and lifted his eyes to Quint. "That was the card you picked."

Hannah could hardly control her urge to laugh at the expression of amazement on Quint's face as he nodded. Pierre's answering smile was so full of arrogance that Hannah gave in to temptation.

"Oh, I don't believe that," she said. "That isn't possible. Are you sure it was the five of diamonds?"

"Of course I'm sure," Quint replied.

"Well, it was just luck, then. Either that or Pierre has some way of marking the cards so he knows which one you are looking at."

"*Madame*, I assure you that is not the case." Pierre turned to her with a wounded look in his dark eyes. "You are welcome to try it yourself. Hold the card so that I cannot see even the back if you doubt me."

Pierre fanned out the cards and extended them to Hannah. She looked down at the blue and red design on the cards, then reached out to take the corner of a card just to the right of center. She drew it to her, cupping the card in her hand protectively and stared at the sober king of spades for a moment. She turned the card slightly so that Quint could see it. Then, still holding it in her palm, she turned her hand over, slid it between Pierre's thumb and finger, and placed the card on top of the deck.

Pierre cut the cards again, his nearly black eyes on Hannah's the entire time. Once he'd placed the bottom half on top he dropped his gaze and began to turn the cards over one by one. He flipped them slowly at first, then after he had gone through over half the pack he tossed them down as quickly as he could turn them over. When the entire deck lay on the bed of the wagon, he lifted narrowed eyes to

Hannah. His mouth tightened beneath his narrow mustache. "Where is it?" he demanded.

Hannah considered teasing him a few moments longer, but there was no amusement in his hard dark eyes. "This?" she asked as the two of diamonds suddenly appeared in her fingers.

Pierre stared at the card as Quint reached for Hannah's wrist. "Hannah, that isn't the card you showed me. Yours was the king of spades."

Hannah smiled, her eyes still on Pierre's. "I know, but *this* card was on the bottom of the deck, and Pierre knew it." She turned to Quint. "We both placed our cards on top of the deck, remember? When he cut the cards, in my case, it would have placed the bottom card right behind the king of spades. When Pierre turned the cards over, he would know that the card after the two of diamonds was the one I had looked at."

Quint stared at her. "I have two questions. How in the world did you know that? And how did you take the bottom card."

"I have the identical questions, *madame*."

Hannah smiled at Quint, then turned to Pierre with an apologetic look. "I learned several card tricks from a magician who was traveling the same fair circuit as my parents and I one year. Professor Stonegate also showed me how to palm a card. That's when you hold something in such a way that no one can see it."

"I am aware of that." Pierre spoke in an aggrieved tone, and Hannah widened her smile. "I know. I watched you shuffle. You are very skilled with your hands, and you control the deck well."

Pierre's lips curved into a reluctant smile at her praise. "It takes much practice to do what you have done."

Hannah sighed. "One has much time to practice when traveling from town to town in a wagon. I probably wouldn't have remembered how to do this if I hadn't worked on my skills during the voyage from Boston to London, just to pass the time.''

''You say you know other versions of this trick. Would you show me?''

Hannah cocked her head to one side. ''I did promise Professor Stonegate I'd keep them a secret, but since he doesn't travel in Europe, I suppose showing you one or two would not hurt.''

Quint leaned back and watched as Hannah's slender fingers manipulated the cards—until he started to imagine her hands moving erotically over his skin with similar skill. With an angry frown at his wayward thoughts he swiveled forward to stare beyond the head of the horse drawing the wagon.

They were obviously nearing the outskirts of a town. As they approached the collection of buildings, the road they had been following joined with a wider one, and they took their place in a long, uneven line of wagons and carts headed for the busy port.

About a quarter-mile later, Émile pulled to one side of the road and turned to speak over his shoulder. ''Pierre, *nous sommes voici. Faites vite.*''

Hannah glanced up, startled. ''Here we are,'' Émile had said, but she could see no sign of the dock he had mentioned. However, he had also exhorted Pierre to hurry up. Assuming she and Quint were to get out there also, she started to stand.

''No, *madame*.'' Émile shook his head. ''Only my wife's brothers are to disembark here. You and your husband are to stay with me. I will take you to where the boats for England leave.''

Hannah turned around to bid farewell to Pierre and the enigmatic Antoine, only to find that they were both gone. She lowered herself to the bed of the wagon just as Émile clucked again to the horses and the conveyance jerked forward. Hannah glanced over at Quint to find him staring at the back of the wagon with a curious frown; then she turned to watch the tall brick and plaster buildings slide slowly by.

Several moments later a masculine voice rose above the clopping of the horses' hooves, and the wagon clattered to a stop once again. Hannah turned to see two men in blue uniforms approaching Émile, one on either side of the wagon. They stared at him closely. Then the one on Hannah's side of the vehicle stepped up to look at her face for a moment before standing on tiptoe to examine the inside of the wagon.

"Can I help you?"

Hannah understood Émile's question perfectly although he spoke in rapid French. The uniformed man turned to look up from beneath his black-billed cap, and his thick brown mustache rose and fell as he asked Émile what road he had just traveled. Hannah understood each word, and Émile's response was just as clear in her mind, confirming her suspicion that the others had used a local dialect when speaking around her and Quint.

The official drew two folded pieces of paper from his pocket, handed them to Émile, and asked if he had seen anyone who resembled these men. A few moments later she saw Émile shake his head and return the papers to the officer.

Light blue eyes shifted beneath the billed cap to trap Hannah's gaze. "*Madame et monsieur,* would you look at these drawings and tell me if you recognize these men? They are known as the Bertrand brothers and were last seen leaving a home just outside Paris yesterday morning. We have reason to believe they robbed the owner of all her jewels, and we suspect they will attempt to take them out of the country."

Hannah took the papers and held them so that both she and Quint could examine them. The uppermost drawing revealed a thin face that could have belonged to any of a hundred men, since the features were so nondescript. Hannah shook her head, then stared in mute horror at the other picture.

There was no mistaking the heavy features, the black hair, the wide brow, and the small eyes above the wide mouth. This was unquestionably a picture of Antoine. Hannah looked up at Quint. His eyes met hers and held her gaze for a long moment before he took the pictures and handed them to the police officer. "No," he said. "We have not seen them."

The man looked closely at Quint, then glanced at Hannah before waving Émile on. Once more the horses started down the road. The hollow echo of hooves striking the cobblestone street filled the air as Hannah and Quint gazed silently at each other.

An hour later they stood on the dock watching a ferryboat that had just arrived from Dover. Émile had left them a half-hour earlier, apologizing again for his inhospitality the night before, and not once mentioning Pierre and Antoine or remarking on Hannah and Quint's ability to understand the police officer's French.

Hannah glanced from the brick wall of the ticket office behind them to the crowds streaming off the ferry that had just crossed the Channel. Her shoulders drooped, and she could see that Quint's frown had deepened even further.

"Well, we knew it might be difficult to secure passage," she said with a sigh. "We have no papers to prove our identities, and as the ticket seller says, he cannot let us go without some proof that we aren't fugitives trying to escape French justice. I suppose we are fortunate he hasn't had us taken off to jail."

"I suppose." Quint shook his head. "Well, I guess we shall have to send a wire to Hastings and have a message relayed to your uncle, then wait until someone comes over for us.''

Hannah glanced down the street where Émile had disappeared. "If we have to stay in France, we should see if—"

"My God, Blackthorne, it *is* you." A loud, deep voice broke into Hannah's words. She twisted around to find a portly man in a top hat shaking his head at Quint as he went on. "What *are* you doing here, old boy? And dressed like . . . what? A local peasant? I'd not have recognized you at all if I hadn't heard your voice. Be a good boy and satisfy my curiosity."

Quint grinned, his teeth gleaming as he shook the man's large hand. "Ralston, I warn you, you won't believe me. First, allow me to introduce Hannah Bradley. She's the daughter of the famous American balloonist, Matthew Bradley. Hannah this is Lord Ralston, the Duke of Rawley."

Hannah acknowledged the introduction with a smile, then watched the man's broad face as he listened to Quint recount their adventure. His full lips, wreathed in a dark beard and mustache, widened into a smile of delight at the tale, and the yellow and black checked waistcoat that showed between the lapels of his black coat shook as he laughed.

"That's an unbelievable tale, my boy. And all the more so because you are the one telling it."

He turned to grin down at Hannah. "Good for you, Miss Bradley. For years now I've been telling this lad that there's more to life than work and duty, urging him to get out in the world and have some fun. Now he's done it with a vengeance. What a wonderful story!" He shook his head and glanced back at Quint. "Only wish I were going to be in London to tell this tale. Had to escape early this year. This Season has been one of the fiercest in memory."

Quint lifted a brow. "But you haven't been caught yet."

"No." Ralston gave a short, hearty laugh. "No, but I

suppose sooner or later I shall be forced to find a wife. Got to get an heir eventually, and all that. But for now, it's off to the cool air and warm folks of Lucerne. Now wait . . .'' He paused. ''Say, didn't I hear that you had gotten yourself engaged?''

Hannah felt a warm blush start on her cheeks and saw Quint frown. She spoke quickly. ''Yes, he just became betrothed to my cousin, Cicely Summerfield, who is most likely wondering if we are still alive. We were hoping to cross to Dover, then hurry down to St. Albanswood by train, but the officials won't let us board without identification.''

''Well, that's preposterous.'' Ralston glanced from Hannah to Quint for a moment, then nodded decisively. ''I've some time before I have to catch my train for Switzerland. Let me talk to the fellow for you.''

Hannah leaned against the warm brick wall of the ticket office while Quint and Ralston spoke with an official. She glanced at the high, wispy clouds, then looked around, idly watching a fishing boat tie up not far from the ferry.

A spot of mustard yellow caught her eye. Hannah glanced to her right, to see two familiar figures standing near the stern of the white ship. Pierre and Antoine were talking to a third man, who was tall and slender with a long, sharp-featured face. As she stared she saw Pierre and this man exchange small leather pouches.

Hannah blinked in surprise, then realized that if she had done that a second earlier she would have missed seeing the exchange. As she continued to look at them, the tall man looked around, and before Hannah could avert her gaze, his eyes met hers. She found herself staring into the most unusual eyes she had ever seen, such a pale shade of blue that they appeared almost white.

She blinked again, forced herself to look down at her feet, then frowned. Pierre and Antoine were suspected of being jewel thieves. Shouldn't she tell someone what she'd seen? After Émile left them, she and Quint had discussed the drawings they had seen. They agreed it was probably best that they had lied to the officials about recognizing the men in the drawings. Émile and Madeleine were obviously not involved in whatever Pierre and Antoine were doing, but the fact that the brothers had stayed at their house would cast suspicion on those two nice people.

But Émile was gone now, and what Hannah had just seen seemed to bear witness to Pierre's guilt. Perhaps someone should be notified. Hannah looked up again, then stared at an empty space where the three men had been. A moment later Quint waved two tickets beneath her nose, and before she could do anything but glance up at him, he linked his arm with hers to usher her onto the ferry that was preparing for its return trip to Dover.

Hannah turned at the top of the boarding ramp to wave good-bye to Lord Ralston, then turned to Quint to see him staring at the broad figure in the black suit and top hat through narrowed eyes.

"That was a wonderful piece of luck," she said. "If we hadn't met him, we might have been stuck here for days."

Quint nodded absently, then frowned as he turned to look down at her.

Hannah gazed at his solemn features and asked, "Is something wrong?"

He gazed down at her a moment longer. Of course something was wrong. The special sense of joy he felt in Hannah's presence existed no more, and though he realized he was to blame for letting the passion between them flare in the night, he feared she might be blaming herself.

He longed to talk with her, but it was hardly a subject one could discuss in public. That conversation would have to wait for a private moment, after he'd had time to consider the possible ramifications of their passion.

"No." Quint shook his head. "Nothing is wrong. I was

just thinking that it looks as if the crossing might be rather rough, with the clouds moving in. Do you want to find a place inside or brave the chance of rain and sit out here?''

Hannah glanced up at the tattered bank of white clouds and shrugged. ''Let's sit on deck. If it gets too cool, we can always move to cover.''

Quint nodded, and Hannah followed him along the crowded deck, all too aware of the strange stares they received from the well-dressed men in their dark suits and top hats escorting women whose pastel frocks swayed gently as they walked. Quint strode purposely forward as he made for two seats beneath a wide awning.

Hannah lowered herself onto one of the wooden chairs. She glanced over to see Quint settle into his, then stare toward the railing in front of them. A whistle blew overhead. Hannah turned to look past the railing and watch the dock begin to move slowly past, then turned back to Quint and spoke softly.

''Something *is* wrong. What is it?''

Quint turned to her slowly, opened his mouth to speak, then shook his head before letting his lips curve slightly. ''It's nothing, really. I've just been thinking I probably should have sent a wire to let our families know we are alive and well. It's too late now. We'll send one from Dover. Depending on what time the next train for Hastings leaves, we might be home in time for dinner.''

He stopped talking abruptly and gave Hannah a tight smile. ''These seats recline, if I remember rightly. I think I shall see if I can sleep some. Makes the time go quicker.''

Hannah watched him adjust his chair, then lean back and close his eyes. She gazed at the harsh lines of his face for a moment, wondering about the sudden change in his demeanor.

She closed her eyes as a shard of pain pierced her heart. It was foolish to grieve over someone who was meant for another, she told herself. And a waste of emotion, when she should be bracing herself for the scolding she would receive from her uncle when she arrived back on his doorstep. She was certain he wouldn't take kindly to her having had an adventure, no matter how unwilling, with his daughter's betrothed.

Quint's thoughts were running along the very same lines, but his worries involved graver matters than the squire's anger. Something in Lord Ralston's amused smile, his sly wink, had made Quint realize just how serious his situation was. He wanted to look at Hannah, to see how she was doing, but he didn't want her to see his concern until he had a chance to think through all the options.

Chapter 12

Quint stood next to Hannah on the platform as the westbound train for Hastings pulled into the Dover station. He glanced up at the gray sky, assessing the threat of rain, then looked down at the woman next to him.

Hannah gazed around the platform in open interest, greeting, with a smile and a lift of her nose, the curious stares produced by the strange clothing she and Quint wore. Quint felt a smile tug at his own lips as a strange joy filled his chest that ran counter to all logic.

A few moments later he lowered himself into one of the brown leather seats in the private coach he'd secured for them. As he glanced at Hannah, gazing raptly out the window, his frown began to return. Was it some Blackthorne curse that attracted the men of the family to unsuitable women? What was it about Hannah that made him want to pull her into his arms against all reason?

Quint stared at the knot of silken hair atop Hannah's head. He shook his head as he thought back over the surprises this young woman had provided him with. His lips curved into an involuntary smile as he recalled Pierre Bertrand's stunned expression when Hannah tricked him at his own card game.

Hannah glanced at Quint at that moment. "You're smiling," she commented. "You must be pleased to be on English soil again."

Quint glanced down at her and nodded. "Yes, especially when that eventuality was in doubt for a while. But that's not what made me smile. I was thinking about how you fooled Pierre at his own trick. You took us both by surprise."

Hannah studied Quint's features, wondering which man she was talking to, the carefree adventurer or the formal Earl of Chadwick. Was he genuinely amused, or did his smile only mask his disapproval of her unusual talent? Hannah's fingers closed into nervous fists in her lap. She glanced down at them as she spoke. "Well, that really wasn't kind of me." She paused, then glanced up with a worried look. "You won't mention this to anyone else, will you? My uncle believes people will think less of me if they learn about all the odd accomplishments I picked up on my travels with Papa. He's sworn both Cicely and me to secrecy."

"Cicely knows about your card tricks?"

Hannah cocked her head to one side. "Yes, as well as the juggling and the puppets and . . ." Her voice trailed off as she saw Quint's eyes slowly widen with each "and." "Didn't she tell you? Parker seems to know all about it."

"Parker has been Cicely's confidant for years." Quint's smile disappeared as he continued in a dry tone. "Cicely doesn't tell me about such matters. I think she regards me as far too advanced in age to be interested in card tricks."

Hannah gazed up at his suddenly sober features. At that moment his ten-year advantage on her showed in the serious set of his lean features. Deep lines bracketed his mouth as his smile faded. Speaking of Cicely must have reminded him of his obligation to his betrothed, Hannah decided, an

obligation that could not be laid aside even in the face of
Cicely's feelings for Parker, or Quint's for Hannah.

Hannah felt certain that Quint's attraction to her went
deeper than a sensual response, no matter how sane and
sensible he liked to consider himself. But she also knew
how important Blackthorne Hall was to him, and if Hartley's
hints were true, and Quint was at risk of losing his home,
she was certain the voice of reason would prove stronger
than the lure of desire. His next words seemed to affirm
that thought.

"You were right to think I was glad to be back in
England," he said. "I travel very little, but when I do, I
always seem to enjoy the return trip the most. I like coming
home."

Hannah shrugged as she struggled to fight off a sudden
sadness. "I like leaving best myself. It's a time full of
excitement and promise." Her lips twisted into a wry smile.
"But then, for most of my life home was a place I was
forced to stay while my father did the leaving. I've never
had a home that I cared for the way you love Blackthorne
Hall."

"That's a very English trait, I think, love of home."
Quint crossed one lean leg over the other and laced his
hands over his knee. "We British seem to have this very
strong attachment to home and hearth, while you restless
Americans appear to thrive on travel. Perhaps it's because
that land of yours is so very large, with such wide horizons,
while we're bound to this little island, mired in history and
tradition that tie us to our homes whether we live in a grand
mansion, a crumbling old castle, or a vine-covered cottage."

Quint turned to gaze out the window again as he finished
speaking, thinking of all the differences between the two
of them. Hannah loved excitement, while he longed for a
quiet place by the fire after a day's work. He cherished

tradition while she loved the promise of new beginnings.

He suppressed a sigh as he watched the landscape move by, knowing that each mile they traveled brought them closer to a fate that might make them both miserable. He began to hope fervently that his assessment of the situation was wrong, and he prayed that everyone would be so happy to see him and Hannah alive that no one would question the impropriety of the night they'd spent alone together.

Hannah stared at the light rain that had just begun to fall outside the partly open window as the train approached Hastings. She took a deep breath, drawing in the fresh scent of moisture on the green surroundings that passed in an ever slowing blur as they pulled into the tiny station. She felt a hand on her shoulder and turned to find Quint standing in the aisle, frowning down at her.

"Let's get ready to leave the train. If no one has come to meet us, we'll need to hire a carriage to take us to your uncle's."

Hannah nodded and stood silently. Quint's tone had been curt, impatient, as if he was now weary of their adventure and wanted to get the last of it over quickly.

Looking for a carriage for hire proved to be unnecessary, for just moments after Quint had handed Hannah out of the passenger car, they heard a voice shout down the platform. "There they are!"

Hannah looked up to see a crowd of people, many wearing coats to protect their finery from the elements, all marching down the platform beneath a canopy of open umbrellas. She blinked against the rain as she searched their faces, seeing emotions that ranged from excitement to curiosity to unabashed anger.

That last sentiment was etched deeply in her uncle Charles's sharp features. His footsteps seemed to echo louder than the others and his top hat bounced slightly atop his head as he strode in front of everyone else. Hannah took a deep breath and braced herself for the coming storm.

"Well, miss, pray tell us, just where have you been?"

Hannah took a deep breath, forced a smile to her lips, and shrugged. "We've been to France!"

"France?" at least seven other voices echoed. She nodded, but before she could speak, Quint broke in.

"Yes, to France. But this is not the place for explanations. It's a very long story, and I would prefer to tell it somewhere dry and warm."

Several cries of protest greeted his words. Hannah heard someone mutter, "Well, if you didn't plan on explaining things here, why did you send the telegram?" This question was greeted by nods and angry murmurs. Hannah braced herself to get a thorough drenching while she and Quint recounted their tale.

She was saved when a loud clap of thunder ripped across the sky overhead, followed by a torrent of wind-driven rain that had all of them scurrying for the protection of their carriages.

Quint grabbed Hannah's hand as they ran with the pack of people. As they approached the carriages, Hannah spied her aunt's white head leaning out of one of them waving a sodden handkerchief. Hannah made for that carriage, and Quint followed her in, pulling the door shut behind him.

"Tell the driver to pull out."

At Amelia's commanding tone Quint shouted out the window to the driver. Immediately the carriage jolted forward, and as the clop of the horses' hooves rose to drown out the sound of the pounding rain, Hannah began to shiver.

"Here, dear girl, put this around you."

Hannah gratefully shrugged into the shawl her aunt placed around her shoulders, then glanced at Quint as her aunt spoke again. "And here's a carriage blanket for you, young man. My, you look as bedraggled as a couple of drenched kittens. Whatever were you all doing standing around in the rain?''

"We were being ordered to tell our story." Hannah smiled at her aunt, then sighed. "I suppose they can't be blamed for wanting to find out where we've been."

Amelia's snowy brows lifted. "Well, yes. We've all been in an uproar since you two failed to return yesterday afternoon."

"Were you worried?" Hannah placed a wet hand over her aunt's small wrinkled one.

Amelia shrugged as she looked up at her niece. "Of course, a little." Hannah smiled at the shimmer of moisture in her aunt's blue eyes that belied her nonchalant tone. "I'm aware that even the best pilots have been known to have accidents," Amelia continued, "but I've always had complete faith in your abilities, so I just sat and waited to hear from you."

She paused and patted Hannah's hand. "Now, I won't plague you for details. You look tired, and you're going to be questioned at great length as soon as everyone is settled in your uncle's place. Both of you just rest till we get there."

Hannah took a deep breath and smiled, and Amelia shifted her attention to Quint. Hannah saw her aunt lift her eyebrows, as if asking him a silent question. Quint frowned and shook his head before he turned to stare out the window.

Hannah frowned, puzzled by the silent exchange, then suddenly found that she was too weary to think. She leaned back against the leather seat and tried to gather her strength for the questioning they were about to face.

Their carriage pulled up before the manor house, and Hannah and Quint were quickly ushered into the parlor. It was occupied by several people who rushed forward and began a babble of questions as the two of them entered the room.

"Hush, now!"

Parker's voice rose above the clamor. Hannah looked behind her and saw him standing at the door to the room with Cicely on his arm. He gave Hannah a quick smile, then spoke again. "The rain at the station prevented any of us from hearing their story, so please keep your curiosity in control until everyone else arrives."

As soon as he finished speaking, Cicely crossed the blue and red carpet to take Hannah in her arms and whisper quietly, "Oh, Hannah, I was so frightened for you. Are you truly all right?"

Hannah nodded and forced a smile to her suddenly tight lips. "I'm fine. And look, I kept my promise."

Cicely's puzzled frown told Hannah that her cousin had no clue as to what she meant. Hannah nodded toward Quint and grinned. "I told you I'd bring him back in one piece, and I did."

Cicely nodded, then turned slowly to Quint. Her lips seemed to quiver slightly as she slipped her hands from Hannah's and dropped them to her sides as she approached her fiancé. "Quinton, I'm glad to see that your adventure has left you looking well. And I want to thank you for seeing to it that my cousin returned safely."

Quint looked into Cicely's pale blue eyes for a long moment, searching for a hint of warmth, any suggestion that she might have been truly concerned about his welfare. He saw nothing but polite gratitude, and he had a sudden desire to laugh out loud. Fortunately at that moment Squire Summerfield stepped into the room and spoke firmly.

"Everyone, please find someplace comfortable to sit. The servants are bringing in extra chairs, and as soon as you are seated, the earl will begin his tale. We have been held in suspense for far too long."

Hannah watched well-coiffed heads nod and heard murmurs of agreement above the rustling of silks and satins. Amazingly, the room was silent in a matter of moments.

When her uncle turned expectantly to Quint, Hannah decided there was no reason the burden of explanation should rest solely on his shoulders.

"Our story is a very simple one." Hannah managed a small smile as she stepped forward. All eyes turned to her as she went on, "I became giddy shortly after the balloon rose into the air, and I fainted, leaving Lord Blackthorne to pilot the balloon alone."

This announcement brought about a wave of whispered comments that made Hannah stop speaking. She glanced at Quint. His dark brows were lowered in a frown as he stared at the crowd, but he shifted his gaze to Hannah a moment, and she thought she saw him twitch his lips in a tight smile before he began speaking.

"Unfortunately," his booming voice crushed the hubbub immediately, and he went on, "I have no skill in that area. The balloon drifted into a southeasterly current, and by the time Miss Bradley regained consciousness we were well over the Channel, on our way to France."

Hannah stood stiffly at Quint's side while he continued to hold the crowd in silent thrall with the rest of the story, altering the truth in a few key places. When he stopped speaking, the silence lasted for a scant minute. Then the questions began tumbling forth one after another.

"My God, weren't you frightened?"

"How far did you have to drop once you pulled the rip line?"

"You mean to say you were absolutely at the mercy of the wind? You couldn't have found another current to take you back?"

This last question was asked in a sharp, doubting tone that made Hannah glance quickly at the older woman in peach who had asked it. "No, we couldn't," she answered firmly. "Over the Channel there is a strong prevailing wind that runs in a southeasterly direction. For this reason there have been many successful balloon crossings from England to France but very few going the other way.'' The woman shrugged and lifted her brows as Hannah finished.

Then a deep voice echoed across the room. ''You haven't explained why you are dressed like peasants. What became of your clothes?''

Hannah met the Duke of Ludmore's dark scowl as he waited for an answer. She had almost been disappointed when Quint failed to describe how they jettisoned their clothing, for that would have made the story all the more suspenseful. Now, as she stared at the suspicion narrowing the duke's eyes, she realized why Quint had left that part out. As a hot blush began to rise from the base of her neck, she searched her mind for a plausible explanation that would allow her and Quint to avoid a scandal.

''We tossed our footwear out to lighten the basket while we were over the water.'' Quint spoke before Hannah could think of anything. ''Because our clothes were in tatters after we were tossed about in the wicker basket during our rather rough landing, Émile and Madeleine DuBois were kind enough to lend us something more presentable to wear home.''

''These DuBois people took you into their home and made you feel welcome despite your ragtag appearance?'' Another masculine voice rose sharply at the end of this question and, before Quint could answer, continued in a chiding manner, ''I hope the accommodations were to your liking.''

Hannah froze at the sly suggestion beneath the innocent-sounding remark. A smirk twisted the lips of the young man who had spoken. Her uncle stood directly behind the man, and Hannah could see the squire scowling deeply as Quint answered.

''The lodgings weren't what I normally request when I travel, of course.'' His easy smile echoed in his tone of voice. ''I was offered a pile of hay in the barn, and Hannah was given the honor of sharing a bed with the daughter of the house.'' Hannah managed to keep herself from blinking at the blatant lie, and continued to gaze at the people in front of her as Quint continued. ''Mademoiselle Antoinette is far from slim, and I am told that the bed was rather narrow. I think I received the best of the deal.''

Hannah forced herself to smile as laughter filtered through the room. She saw that her uncle's frown had lessened considerably as he stepped forward. The squire looked at her sharply for a moment before turning around to speak to the crowd.

''Dinner will be served within the hour. I'm sure our travelers wish to freshen up before that time, as will many of you.''

The squire turned then, as if dismissing his guests, and approached Hannah and Quint. He spoke in a low tone, his voice barely audible beneath the rustling and whispering of the departing crowd, but his anger was unmistakable.

''Quinton, I sent a servant to Blackthorne Hall to fetch a change of clothing for you, and I've been informed he's just returned. I want both you and Hannah to change and meet with me in my study in half an hour. We have much to speak of before dinner.''

The squire turned on his heel and strode toward the door where Hartley and the Duke of Ludmore waited. Hartley's narrowed eyes caught Hannah's attention, and a cold chill touched her flesh as she watched all three men disappear down the hall.

''Hartley's been very worried about both of you.''

Cicely's soft comment made Hannah turn to the young woman who stood between Aunt Amelia and Parker, but before Hannah could remark on that, another voice reverberated through the room.

''As have I.''

Lady Evelyn Blackthorne's sharp voice drew Hannah's glance back to the doorway. Looking very regal in her high-necked black silk gown, the gray-haired woman leaned on her cane as she stepped forward, her eyes fixed on her older grandson.

Quint left Hannah's side, crossed the carpet, and took the old woman in his arms. Hannah watched Lady Evelyn's sharp features twist with emotion as her arms went around Quint's back. Hannah blinked back sudden tears. Even the warm greetings she'd received from Cicely and her aunt hadn't displayed that much tenderness.

Hannah felt someone take her hand. She looked down to see Aunt Amelia's fingers tightening around hers, and when Hannah lifted her eyes, her aunt spoke softly. "Let's do as your uncle asked and get you dressed. I want you to lie down for a few moments, if you can. I have a feeling our little chat with the squire won't be a pleasant one."

Up in her room Hannah and her aunt scarcely spoke as Hannah changed her clothes. What few words did pass between them consisted of questions regarding which gown she ought to wear and how she should dress her hair. They decided on a pale pink silk with a simple off-the-shoulder neckline, short sleeves, and a skirt that draped gracefully from Hannah's slender hips to the wide ruffle at the hem.

Hannah sat at the dressing table, staring at her pale reflection as Letitia swept her hair into a simple figure eight, which she anchored at the back of her head with the silver comb. Hannah nodded absently when her aunt commented on how flattering the style was. Her thoughts were down in her uncle's study. A frown wrinkled her brow as she wondered why her uncle had insisted that Quint be present when the squire's anger would most assuredly be directed at her alone.

* * *

As Squire Summerfield crossed the Aubusson carpet in front of his white marble fireplace one more time, he took out his pocket watch and glared at it.

"Are they late?" Hartley looked up from the pipe in his hand, and rested his other arm across the back of the dark blue Louis XIV couch on which he sat.

"No." The word snapped out as the squire swung around, frowning. "But I'm impatient. This is not something I can take lightly. Ludmore is very angry at the turn of events."

The squire's narrowed eyes warned Hartley not to comment on anything beyond the duke's interest in Hannah as Carolyn turned from the window next to the hearth. "I warned you," she said as she released the dark blue velvet fabric, letting the heavy draperies fall back into place. "I told you Hannah would be a problem. But you didn't believe me. Fainted, indeed. Very clever, my little cousin."

A muscle twitched in Hartley's jaw as he stared at the smoke ring he had just released, and he blinked as his father replied, "Yes, I mean to learn more about this fainting business. If I can prove that Hannah engineered this fiasco, perhaps the situation can be salvaged."

Hartley sent a questioning glance to his father, but before he could speak, the double doors opened and a servant ushered in Hannah and her aunt Amelia. Cicely, in a dress of pale plum, entered the room behind them and turned to her father.

"Would you like me to mingle with our guests while you speak to Hannah, Father?" she asked.

"No." The squire looked at Hannah as he answered his daughter. "I'm afraid your presence will be required here as well."

Hannah tried to keep from shivering as she gazed into her uncle's cold gray eyes and wondered why her cousin would have to stay. Before she could ask him, a rustling sound behind her made her turn to watch as the Countess of Chadwick was escorted through the door by both of her grandsons.

Quint once more looked every bit the earl. His black cutaway coat fit his broad shoulders to perfection, and the stark white of his shirt accentuated the blue-black of his hair, which had been carefully combed free of the unruly waves she'd become so accustomed to in the last day and a half. Quint's green eyes met Hannah's and held them for a long moment. Then his chest rose in a sigh as he gave her a brief nod before turning to Squire Summerfield.

Parker was dressed formally as well. Hannah saw him send a quick glance to Hartley, hesitate as if considering joining his friend on the couch, then step to one side and stand next to Cicely.

No one spoke. The only sound in the room was the soft swish of the door as the servant pulled it shut. Hannah watched it slowly close, feeling her chest tighten by the second, waiting for the click that would set in motion whatever fate had in store for her.

"Squire Summerfield." Quint's voice drowned out the final sound of the closing door. "I believe I know what it is that you wish to speak about, and I think it unnecessary that this conversation be prolonged or any more unpleasant than necessary. Cicely?"

Hannah watched from beneath a puzzled frown as Quint turned to her cousin. As he stepped over to Cicely, he moved away from his grandmother, and Hannah found the old woman's gray-green eyes staring at her from behind the silver frames of her spectacles. Lady Evelyn held Hannah's gaze for several seconds before turning disappointed eyes to her grandson.

Quint stood in front of Cicely, looking down into her pale blue eyes. He gazed for a moment at her porcelain features and saw an expression of fear cross them. He forced a smile to his lips as he took her hand, feeling it tighten within his grasp.

"Do you have any idea why your father called us all in here?" he asked.

Cicely started to shake her head, then stopped as she glanced at Hannah. "I know it has something to do with *Skylark* running away with the two of you. I expect that my father wishes to express his displeasure."

Quint cast a quick glance at the squire, then looked back to Cicely. "I'm sure you are correct. And he is well within his rights to be angry. You see, because of that balloon flight, I am no longer free to marry you."

Hannah gasped at the same time Cicely did, then stood holding her breath, watching her cousin blink in confusion. "We are not going to be married?" Cicely asked softly.

"No."

Cicely blinked again, and for one second her lips twitched into a smile. The smile vanished as she took a deep breath and turned to her father. "Is this true?"

The squire straightened as his eyes glinted at Quint. "It is a distinct possibility," he replied. "The matter deserves more discussion, I think, before a definite decision is reached."

Quint stepped forward. "I don't see any reason for discussion. Hannah and I were gone for over twenty-four hours without benefit of a chaperon, in a situation that would cause a scandal under any circumstance. Due to the number of people who are aware of this, I'm sure Hannah's reputation has been compromised beyond repair. Since this happened when she was trying to help me meet a challenge, I feel it is my duty to do the only thing possible: marry her."

Chapter 13

Hannah's pulse slowed as Quint's words echoed in her mind. She stared at him a moment, certain she must have misunderstood him. Her gaze shifted to the old woman standing behind Quint. The Countess of Chadwick met Hannah's eyes with a level stare that told her nothing. Slowly Hannah turned to her right, to find her aunt Amelia looking up at her with deep concern in her dark blue eyes, and suddenly Hannah knew she hadn't imagined Quint's words.

Her heart began to pound wildly as she looked from one person to the next. Cicely's eyes were wide blue pools that looked as disbelieving as Hannah felt, while Parker's hazel eyes appeared darker than usual beneath his frowning ginger eyebrows.

It wasn't until she looked at her other two cousins that Hannah became certain this was not some elaborate hoax. Carolyn's and Hartley's pale gray eyes met hers with an icy cold glare that made her shiver. But their angry expressions weren't responsible for the deeper chill that took hold of her. It was a word that Quint had used when he announced his intention to marry her. That one word had caused icy fingers to clutch Hannah's heart and hold her frozen where she stood.

Just one chilling word: *duty*.

Only her intellect was not numbed. A flame of resentment started a jumble of thoughts racing through her mind as her cheeks burned. This could not happen. Hannah was completely aware of the truth behind these people's suspicions, but no one could have any way of knowing what had transpired in that cellar in France. Cicely shouldn't have to suffer a broken heart, nor should Quint be forced to forfeit his chance to restore his home simply because of gossip.

On top of that, Hannah absolutely refused to be regarded as an obligation by any man. "Uncle Charles." Hannah turned to the tall, stiff figure. "This is ridiculous. Lord Blackthorne was a perfect gentleman during the last day and a half. He should not be burdened with me, especially when he is already spoken for. Tell him his kind gesture is not necessary."

When Hannah began talking, the squire lowered a furious frown at her, but by the end of her speech his brows had lifted and his eyes narrowed speculatively. "That is an interesting statement, Hannah," he said. "I believe you, of course, but as the earl hinted, society is not so kind in these cases. If you don't marry Quinton, I fear there will be little chance of finding a husband for you."

"Uncle Charles." Hannah spoke very slowly, as if to a small child. "I never expected to find a husband here in England. I came only because my father's will stipulated that I do so. I will be happy to take my inheritance, return to America, and make my way there."

"That is out of the question, my dear."

Aunt Amelia's curt words made Hannah swivel around. The woman's dark blue eyes glinted up at her niece as she spoke again. "Your father's will was very specific about the amount of time you are to remain here. There will be no returning to America for at least a year, and that is a very long time to force your uncle to shelter someone who has created a scandal.''

Hannah's eyes opened wide in disbelief. "Perhaps so, but a marriage lasts a lifetime. That is assuredly too long to force someone to keep me.''

Amelia's brows drew tightly together as she pulled herself up to her full height, making Hannah draw back slightly. She knew that stance all too well, recognized a mind made up and a will that would see her orders obeyed. Hannah braced herself for the flurry of words she knew would come, but before Amelia could speak, Parker stepped forward.

"Hannah, they're right.'' She turned to find him looking into her eyes with no hint of his usual mirth. "You must marry. But I agree that there is no reason to destroy the arrangement my brother has made with Cicely. I am unattached, and although I have nothing to offer you but an honest name, it is yours for the asking.''

As Hannah stared up at Parker's very serious face, she blinked back the tears pricking her eyes. She was deeply touched by his offer, but she didn't want to be a burden to any man.

Before she could formulate a reply, strong fingers closed over her wrist. She looked up to find Quint frowning down at her as he spoke. "There's no need for any further discussion on this matter. I was the one you were with; therefore I will see this through. You and I will be married at the earliest possible date.''

Hannah stared into Quint's eyes. If she hadn't known they were green, she would have sworn they were solid black. They glittered with a strange light that made her shiver and want to pull away, but his hand gripped her wrist tightly, trapping her at his side.

Another shiver danced down her spine, but in its chill wake an ember of anger burst into flame. Hannah swung around and glared at the squire. "You are my guardian. Tell the earl I refuse to marry him just to conform to the conventions of a society of which I'm not even a part."

Her uncle stared quietly at her for a moment. He glanced up at Quint, then back at Hannah, scowling once more. Before he could speak, the sharp, commanding tones of Lady Evelyn made everyone turn to her.

"Miss Bradley, you have no say in the matter at this point."

The old woman shifted her gaze to Parker as she went on. "My younger grandson's suggestion simply will not do. Too many people are aware of the circumstances surrounding your disgrace, and I will not have it said that the Earl of Chadwick has allowed another man to do the honorable thing in his place."

Lady Evelyn turned back to Hannah. "It would have been better if you'd thought of all this before you pulled such a silly prank as feigning an attack of the vapors. You may not care what British society thinks of you, but my family and that of your uncle must deal with these people on a daily basis. This situation will cause enough gossip as it is. You will do as you are told, and with as much grace as you can muster, so as not to cause further talk."

Hannah stared at the woman. She wanted to protest, to explain that she had not done anything to bring this farce about, but the situation had become so overwhelming that she could only shake her head weakly.

"Grandmother." Quint's voice was sharp. "Hannah did not play any prank. I'm convinced that someone placed something in her champagne that morning. She was most definitely drugged."

"Drugged?" Parker stepped forward. "Are you sure of this?"

Quint glanced at his brother. "I've yet to see a fainting fit that caused the victim's eyes to dilate so far, or that lasted so long. I suspect the champagne Hannah drank contained laudanum. At one point her pulse and breathing were so faint that I thought she had died.''

"That's nonsense." Hartley's lazy voice rose from the sofa. "Who would do such a thing?"

As Parker pivoted slowly to stare down at his friend, Quint replied evenly, "I have no idea. It's not important at this time. As my grandmother pointed out, the die is cast." He turned to the squire. "I would appreciate it if we could carry out this wedding with as much speed and decorum as possible."

"Of course." Squire Summerfield had been gazing thoughtfully at his son as he nodded. Now he lifted his eyes to Quint's. "I will announce the plans at the end of dinner. And speaking of that, I believe we will be just in time to sit down with the rest of the guests if we leave now."

Hannah blinked at the finality in his tone. When Lady Evelyn voiced her agreement, Hannah felt a chilling numbness take possession of her limbs. She stared in blank disbelief as everyone turned to walk toward the door, Parker offering an arm to both his grandmother and Aunt Amelia, while the squire escorted Cicely. As Carolyn and Hartley exited together, Hannah told herself she should follow, but her legs wouldn't cooperate. She felt herself begin to sway, but before she could fall, Quint's fingers tightened again around her wrist and his other hand slid to her waist.

"Hannah, take a deep breath and look at me."

She did as he asked, drawing air slowly into her lungs and lifting her eyes to his. Quint's were once more the deep green she remembered, and his frown was obviously one of concern, for that emotion colored his voice also as he spoke in a soft undertone. "You will have to come to dinner with us, laugh, and seem unconcerned by the turn of events. You can argue with me all you want afterward. Do you understand?"

Hannah stared at him for a long moment. She still felt a strong urge to protest this arrangement, for she had no desire to wed a man who viewed marriage to her as a burdensome necessity. But a deep weariness pulled her spirit down. She was outnumbered.

Slowly she nodded. Quint bent his head toward hers, still holding her gaze with his, and Hannah felt her heart leap with sudden joy when she saw a look of anticipation enter his eyes. Sudden heat weakened her limbs further, and her lips parted as his mouth drew closer to hers.

"Quinton? Hannah!"

They both jumped and turned to find Lady Evelyn standing in the doorway, glaring at them impatiently. "We are waiting for you to enter the dining room with the rest of us."

A moment later Hannah felt rather than saw dozens of pairs of eyes follow her as she walked next to Quinton and took her place next to him, near her uncle's seat at the head of the table. She sat quietly, forcing herself to smile at the people around her as the serving girls placed bowls of soup on the plates in front of them. When she lifted her spoon to her mouth, she was vaguely aware of the warmth of the liquid on her tongue, but she could not taste the soup, or any of the courses that followed.

During the meal Hannah briefly answered whatever questions were put to her, only half conscious of her replies. She was only truly aware of the man sitting next to her, the man who had held her in his arms the night before, whose very glance could set her pulse racing.

Her emotions shifted constantly. One moment she was remembering the feel of his lips on hers, certain that Quint felt as drawn to her as she did to him, and the next minute her mind reverberated with his cold reference to *duty*, dashing all joy from her soul.

About halfway through the meal it occurred to Hannah

to wonder how Cicely was faring in all this. She turned her attention from the poached sturgeon on her plate and glanced down the table at her cousin. Cicely was sitting between Aunt Amelia and Parker, talking in an animated fashion that made Hannah's heart lift some.

No matter how the instructresses at finishing school had tried, they had never succeeded in teaching Cicely the art of hiding her emotions. It was blatantly apparent that her cousin was not unhappy in the least with the turn of events. Yet even this knowledge eased the heavy sense of dread in Hannah's chest only slightly. Quint would lose so much because of this change of plans that he was bound to resent her.

As the last course was being cleared away, Lady Evelyn rose, signaling that the women were to withdraw so the men could enjoy their cigars and brandy. Hannah stood with the other ladies, but just as she began to turn from the table, her uncle got to his feet also and cleared his throat.

"While we are all here together," he said, "I would like to make an announcement. My daughter Cicely has called off her engagement to the Earl of Chadwick."

A wave of murmurs caused the squire to pause, but after a second he raised his voice and went on. "My niece, Hannah Bradley, will be married to the earl in our local church within the week. I invite all of you to stay and celebrate this union with us."

No one moved for several moments. Then once more Lady Evelyn took charge and started for the door. Hannah fell in step behind her, followed by the other women. As Hannah mounted the stairs to the second-floor drawing room, she could feel the quick glances of the women behind her as sharply as if they were darts.

Once they reached the green and gold drawing room, Amelia came to stand on Hannah's left side while Cicely moved to her right. Hannah watched in surprise as Lady

Evelyn positioned herself next to Aunt Amelia to parry some of the delicate but potentially deadly thrusts of the women who approached.

Hannah breathed a sigh of relief when the men joined them. Someone asked for music, and Cicely obliged by sitting at the piano in front of the gold damask draperies to play and sing pleasantly, giving Hannah a chance to sit quietly and think.

Immediately she wondered about Quint's reaction to all this, and she glanced across the room to see him standing next to the squire. The ploy was obvious to her. Both men were doing their best to dilute the scandal that hung in the air. Hannah decided they made a very unlikely pair of conspirators, and the thought almost made her smile.

Almost, but not quite. She fought the sudden weariness that crept over her as two more young ladies followed Cicely to the piano to display their musical talent. In order to keep from falling asleep in her chair, Hannah glanced idly around the room, studying the mixture of expressions ranging from rapt attention to complete boredom.

Her wandering gaze stopped when it chanced upon the Duke of Ludmore, trapped by the cold, dark look in the man's eyes as he stared back at her. A cold chill prickled along her arms. Hannah hadn't seen the man since before dinner, when he had fixed a similar angry glare upon her while Quint told their tale in the parlor. She didn't understand the fury in his gaze, and as he continued to stare at her, anger of her own began to thaw some of her fear. She had just decided to cross the room to question his rudeness, when the piano fell silent.

Ludmore was lost to her view as several people stood and excused themselves for the night. Lady Anne Kendrick and her father were among them. The tall young woman stopped her father at the door, then crossed the room to give Hannah a hug.

''What a lark your adventure must have been,'' she whispered in Hannah's ear. ''Please let's get together tomorrow so you can tell me the details.''

Hannah smiled up into Lady Anne's brown eyes. Then, as the woman rejoined her father, a strange tingling sensation crept down Hannah's spine. She turned slowly to her left. Hartley and his father stood with the Duke of Ludmore in a corner; all three of them were regarding her with the same intense stare. When they noticed her looking at them, they all turned away from her to confer quietly together.

Hannah shook away another shiver, then glanced around the nearly empty room. Directly in front of her one of the French doors had been left partly open. Almost without thinking, she stood and crossed the soft green carpet. As she stepped out onto the balcony, she pulled the door shut behind her, then gazed up at the black sky and watched a cloud float away to reveal a moon almost as full as it was the night of her cousin's ball.

Hannah released a sigh. Had that truly been only three nights ago? So very much had happened in the last few days that it was no wonder her head was spinning. Hannah stepped forward to the wooden balustrade. Her eyelids fell shut as she closed her fingers over the cool railing, fighting a dizzy sensation.

They snapped open again when she heard a soft click behind her, and her fingers tightened on the smooth wood as she clenched her teeth. She was weary of the company of people who wanted to poke and prod her with questions. She yearned to turn and lash out at whoever had come to disturb her one moment of solitude. But she knew she had to control her anger. Silently, stiffly, she waited for the questions to start.

''Hannah.'' Quint's deep voice echoed softly through the night.

Hannah drew in a sharp breath, then stood staring at the

moon, torn between the desire to greet him with a smile and the urge to run away. She heard the hollow echo of his boots on the wooden balcony too late to do any more than pivot toward him as he reached her side.

Moonlight slanted across one side of his face, and she could see that he was once more frowning slightly. His hands closed over her upper arms gently, and the warmth of his fingers seeping through the thin silk of her sleeves made the muscles in her legs grow weak until she swayed slightly as she continued to gaze up at his shadowed face.

"We have to talk, Hannah."

Quint's voice was low, his tone firm. These things should not have made Hannah angry, but they did. In the second it took her to blink, a frantic resentment built up in her chest and strength flowed back into her limbs. She pulled quickly back from his hands as she replied with controlled fury.

"Yes, Your Lordship, I would say we need to talk." All the pain and fear that had been layered one upon the other since Quint announced he would take responsibility for her ruined reputation echoed in her chilly tone. The muscles in her jaw grew so tight that her words came out with difficulty. "Unfortunately it seems that anything I might have to say regarding the rest of my life has been rendered null and void by a decision in which I had no say. Just what is it you wish to discuss? Marriage plans, perhaps? Why? My uncle will take charge of the wedding just as he does everything else."

Quint started to reach for her again, but dropped his hands to his sides as he shook his head. "Hannah, I don't blame you for being angry. I want to apologize for the manner in which all this has been handled." He paused a moment, then went on slowly. "These are not the best circumstances in which to embark on something as solemn as a marriage. I realize that most women expect to be wooed, that they expect a certain amount of romance before the ceremony.

I'm sorry I can't offer you that luxury. My position—in fact, whatever chance I have at all of improving my fortune—demands that we move swiftly and put this scandal behind us. I hope you understand.''

Even before he finished speaking, Hannah felt the anger drain away from her. "I do and I don't,'' she replied, then lifted her head. She could just see his dark eyes in the dim light. "Quint, there has to be some way around this. None of this was your fault, and yet you are the one who will suffer. I may be losing my independence, but you stand to lose a small fortune.'' She paused and glanced to one side as her chest tightened. "You can't be happy about that. Besides, the last few days have shown that you and I are very different people, with next to nothing in common.''

Hannah stood stiffly as Quint closed his hand over her right shoulder, then lifted one long finger to touch her left cheek and gently coax her to look up at him. He gazed into her eyes, and his mouth curved into a gentle smile. The ache in Hannah's breast deepened, then shattered when he lowered his head.

Quint's lips brushed across hers tenderly at first, a feather-light contact, like the first tentative kiss they had shared on the forest floor. Then his mouth closed warmly over hers, moving slowly, provocatively. Hannah responded immediately, parting her lips beneath his, melting against him as his kiss deepened and he thrust his tongue between her teeth, sending delightful sensations spiraling through her.

Quint slid his hand down her arm in a warm caress, then pulled her into a tight embrace as Hannah lifted her hands to his shoulders. His lips continued to move over hers, expressing a deep hunger that found an answering need in Hannah. She tightened her arms around his neck and moved closer to him as he drew her even closer.

When Quint finally lifted his mouth from hers, Hannah's eyes remained closed as she waited for him to kiss her again.

When the kiss didn't come, she opened her eyes to stare into his amused green ones.

"Hannah." Her name was a husky whisper on his lips. "Hannah, I think we have more in common than either of us has been willing to admit."

An embarrassed heat engulfed Hannah's body. Quint's words were clear. They shared a physical bond, lust, and he found this diverting. She tried to pull away from him, but he held her close.

"You may laugh, but this isn't amusing to me." Hannah's voice trembled with emotion as she tried unsuccessfully to escape his hold again. She swallowed, then went on in a tight voice. "But I suppose I should be relieved to learn that you take your *duties* in such a light-hearted manner."

Quint's smile disappeared and he lifted a gentle hand to her cheek, but Hannah took the opportunity to pull away from his grasp and hurry toward the French doors. Quint grabbed her arm one more time to pull her back, but a loud click made them both look up as a tall lean form stepped onto the moonlit terrace.

Squire Summerfield turned toward them immediately, as if he knew precisely where he would find them. "Quinton, please excuse me. You and I have some papers that need signing immediately, if you would be so kind as to come to my study. And I'm sure my niece needs to get some rest. Don't you, Hannah?"

Hannah nodded and took one step toward the door her uncle held open for her. She was prevented from going farther by the strong hand that captured and held hers as Quint came around to look down into her eyes.

"Your uncle is right." He spoke softly. "Get some sleep, Hannah. My grandmother always says things look better in the morning. We'll talk again before the wedding.''

He released her fingers then, but not before lowering his lips to brush the back of her hand, leaving her flesh warm and tingling long after she had gone to her room.

Chapter 14

Chapter 14

The tinkling of china woke Hannah the next morning. Hannah frowned as she opened her eyes to see a small woman standing next to her bed, breakfast tray in hand.

"Hannah."

It was her aunt Amelia who spoke so softly. Hannah sat up quickly, brushing a shock of hair from her face, and reached out to take the tray from her aunt.

"Are you playing at lady's maid today, Aunt?" she asked as she placed the tray, holding a teapot, cup and saucer, and silver-domed dish, on the table beside her bed.

Amelia gave Hannah a grin and a shrug. "Out of necessity, yes. All the servants are quite busy, you see. Your uncle sent for the Reverend Mr. Smythe very early this morning, and the good man has informed the squire that he will be able to celebrate your wedding tomorrow."

Hannah had just swung her legs over the edge of the bed and reached for the silver cover. At her aunt's last words, her hand stopped, suspended over the ornate silver knob as she stared at the woman. There wasn't a trace of amusement in the dark blue eyes that gazed back at her. Hannah swallowed, and slowly pulled her hand back as she shook her head.

"Why so soon?"

"It seems that the squire's guests are anxious to return to the London scene. And of course, dear Charles wants one last chance to impress these people with his wealth and his gracious style of entertaining. He has coerced them to stay by promising that the event will take place at the earliest possible moment. I'm sure he would have married you off today, but Mr. Smythe insists that he needs to secure the proper papers."

Hannah stared at her tightly clasped hands and shook her head. "This is like some horrible nightmare." She looked back at her aunt. "Do you realize that five days ago I didn't even know the man I'm about to marry?"

Amelia narrowed her eyes and smiled slightly. "Yes. And that is a very short acquaintance on which to base a marriage. But it wasn't so very long ago that it was perfectly normal to meet one's husband for the very first time at the altar itself."

Hannah shuddered and her aunt's hand closed over hers. "My dear, I'm sure many a medieval lady would have given her best tapestry to have spent a fraction of the time with her intended that you have spent with Quinton. At least you've been with him enough to learn that he is not abhorrent to you—that is, if my observations are correct."

At the wry amusement in Amelia's last words Hannah's face grew warm. No, Quinton Blackthorne was not abhorrent to her. She had been attracted to him from the moment they met. But they had hardly met under normal circumstances.

Hannah stared at the teapot. She had almost come to believe their shared jest that the forest had indeed exerted some kind of enchantment that day, some spell that had made them both act far differently than they usually did.

How else could one explain such easy laughter from a man who made a habit of immersing himself in his work to the point of deadly seriousness? How else could she explain her ease in his presence, her lack of restraint when she lay in his arms and allowed his lips to capture hers?

Without warning, the memory of the passion that had engulfed her in the dark lit a flame of desire in Hannah's stomach, giving rise to a quick blush that seemed to sweep over her entire body. She was well aware of her aunt's sharp gaze, and found it impossible to raise her eyes to meet Amelia's knowing look. Slowly she lifted the domed cover from her breakfast.

"That's a good girl. You'll need some nourishment today." The wry amusement in Amelia's voice made Hannah glance up to the older woman's encouraging smile. "The squire wants to see us in his office in an hour," Amelia announced with an arch of her white eyebrows. "He says he has business to discuss with us. I'll come back in about twenty minutes and help you dress."

She turned as she reached the door. "Oh. I thought you might like to know that you have Hartley to thank for your 'fainting' spell."

Hannah looked up quickly, and Aunt Amelia smiled. "As I was passing by your uncle's study I overheard the two of them discussing the matter in rather loud voices. It seems your cousin—"

"Didn't want to lose the balloon race," Hannah finished. At her aunt's look of surprise, Hannah went on, "Quint guessed as much. Apparently Hartley is trying to woo Lady Anne."

"Poor girl." Aunt Amelia winked at Hannah as she opened the door. "Fortunately Lady Anne is as sensible as she is poor. I seriously doubt that Hartley has a chance with her."

When the door closed behind her aunt, Hannah took a

bite of scrambled egg and chewed slowly. She wasn't hungry, but she didn't want to meet with her uncle on an empty stomach. Now the scolding she'd been dreading would come. There had been no mistaking the anger in her uncle's eyes ever since her return, and she was certain that only the presence of his guests had kept him from lashing out at her for destroying Cicely's betrothal.

Hannah frowned as a sip of tea with sugar and cream, warm and soothing, slid down her throat. She needed to speak to Cicely, to tell her cousin how sorry she was for all of this.

But was she sorry? Hannah took a small bite of buttered toast. Certainly she regretted having caused Cicely so much embarrassment. She wished she knew her cousin's true feelings in this matter, for she hated to think of anything hurting her, especially something her own actions had brought about. But could she truly say she was unhappy that she instead of Cicely would walk down the aisle to marry Quinton Blackthorne?

No, she thought. She wasn't sorry at all. Oh, she was nervous, at the very least, and unsure of what this marriage would be like, and she regretted it would mean Quint would have to go without Cicely's dowry money—money that the Blackthornes needed and that Hannah could not provide.

But, Hannah told herself, there was so much more to life than money. What about the joy, the excitement, and the laughter she and Quint had shared? What about the feeling she couldn't shake that she had somehow found the one man who could complete her, and whom she could in turn complete?

As Hannah ate another bite of egg her smile took a wry twist. This was her father's legacy to her, a capacity for joy, and this was what she would offer her husband. True, Quint had been all business with his talk of duty last night, but after they were married, she would see to it he learned to relax a little. She could ride with him, perhaps, as he inspected his property. They could have picnics in the forest and, within its misty grasp, find once again the magic that brought them together in the first place.

Hannah took one more bite of toast, then rose and slipped into her periwinkle dressing gown. Teacup in hand, she walked to the window. Taking a sip of the warm liquid she lowered herself to the seat to stare out into the woods where she and Quint had met such a short time ago.

There was no fog lying over the ground today. The sun shone brightly on the treetops. Three birds darted up to the sky, then wheeled around and dove back into the green depths. Hannah lifted her eyes and noticed what she had failed to see in the mist that day, the square stone battlements rising like gaping teeth atop the tower of Blackthorne Hall.

Closing her eyes, Hannah remembered how the Hall had looked from the air, like a miniature castle set on an island of green lawn surrounded by a sea of trees. After tomorrow it would be her home.

Home. Hannah shivered. Home had never had a warm, cozy meaning to her. For much of her life home had been a prison, a place to wait until her father returned from his most recent travels. What would it be like to have something as solid and permanent as Blackthorne Hall to call home? And to belong to that house and to a man like Quint, who was inexorably tied to that house, who would not always be leaving?

Hannah bit her lip at that disloyal thought and placed her cup and saucer on the window seat as she pulled her knees up to her chest. It wasn't as if her father had wanted to leave her and her mother so often. He'd had to earn a living. If he had been a shoemaker instead of a balloonist, he would have been with them all the time.

"Hannah?"

Cicely's soft voice invaded Hannah's thoughts. She

turned at the query in her cousin's voice and blankly stared
at the blond girl a moment. Cicely stood in the half-open
doorway, wearing a white shirtwaist and a brown skirt. With
her wide blue eyes expressing uncertainty, she looked just
like the lost schoolgirl who had once won Hannah's heart.

"Come in. Please." Hannah smiled and rose from the
window seat as Cicely stepped into the room and shut the
door behind her. "I'm glad you came, Cis, I've been wanting to talk to you."

Cicely crossed the floor and took Hannah's hand in hers.
"And I've wanted to talk to you, too. Oh, Hannah, I'm so
sorry."

Hannah blinked up at her cousin and shook her head.
"*You* are sorry? Whatever for?"

"Why, for suggesting you take Quinton up in your balloon. Now you are going to be forced to marry him."

Hannah's frown deepened as her cousin shook her head
sorrowfully. "Cicely . . ." Hannah paused, hesitating over
what she was about to say. "You make it sound as if you
think marrying Quint will be something horrible."

Cicely glanced away, then met Hannah's eyes once more
as she shivered and shook her head. "Not horrible, not for
you, I hope. But I don't love him, Hannah. I never did."

Hannah opened her mouth to speak, but Cicely hurried
on. "I know you and I always shared secrets, but this was
different. I didn't want you to know how miserable I was.
There was absolutely nothing you could have done to stop
my father's plans." She paused, then shrugged. "At least,
I didn't think there was."

Hannah looked up at her cousin, saw Cicely's lips begin
to twitch at the corners. Hannah felt her own lips curve as
she shook her head. "Well, leave it to me to perform the
impossible." They looked at each other for a long moment,
then collapsed into laughter, holding on to each other as if
they were back in finishing school, rejoicing over another

sneak attack on their art instructor, Mademoiselle La Rouge.

A few moments later they both recovered, blinking and taking big breaths as they straightened away from each other. Then Hannah frowned and glanced up sharply.

"But, Cis, you did write and say you were in love." Hannah paused, then asked quietly. "It's Parker, isn't it?"

The smile faded from Cicely's lips, and an incredible look of sadness shaded her eyes. But when she opened her mouth to speak, it was Aunt Amelia's voice that answered: "Of course she's in love with Parker."

Both Hannah and Cicely turned to see Amelia step into the room and shut the door behind her, smiling her elfin smile.

"How did you know?" Cicely spoke in a breathless, stunned voice, and Amelia's smile widened as she stepped forward.

"I pride myself on being a great observer of the human condition. Of course, with you and Parker I hardly needed to strain. One would have to be blind to miss how you feel about each other."

Hannah took her cousin's hand. "Well, now that this is out, I want to hear all about the two of you."

Cicely's smile disappeared. "There isn't anything to tell."

"What do you mean? You admit you're in love with him, and Aunt Amelia seems to believe he feels the same for you." Hannah's eyes narrowed. "You don't mean to tell me your father refuses to allow you to marry him just because he's a second son?"

Cicely shook her head. "Parker has never asked me to marry him." She paused and sighed. "You see, he and I have never discussed our feelings for each other. We've been friends all our lives, you know. We grew up together, confiding in each other. Then last fall I began to feel something deeper for him. I thought he felt it, too, but before things could go any further, my father informed me that he'd arranged for me to marry Quinton."

"Couldn't you have refused?"

Cicely shrugged. "I suppose so, but it wouldn't have done any good. Father always gets his way."

"Not always." Aunt Amelia placed a hand on Cicely's arm. "Quint may be getting married, but Hannah is going to be the bride. And speaking of that"—she stepped toward the mahogany wardrobe as she looked at Hannah—"you need to decide what dress you are to be married in. What do you think of that pale lavender satin we purchased on Regent Street right after we arrived in England?"

In response to Hannah's numb nod, her aunt pulled the large wooden door open and reached into the wardrobe. "I'm sure we can locate a length of netting for a veil, and you have silver slippers that will go nicely. I'd like you to try the dress on now. If it looks right, we'll send it down to be pressed."

Hannah stared at the shimmering satin in her aunt's arms as the woman crossed the room. She started to remove her dressing gown, then shot a startled look at her aunt. "I don't have time for that right now. Have you forgotten our meeting with Uncle Charles?"

"No. But I did forget to mention that we have been given a reprieve. The earl sent word that he has important business to tend to today. Quinton apparently insists on being present when the squire speaks with us, so our meeting with Charles will be postponed until after dinner tonight."

"Important business?" Hannah breathed.

Amelia shrugged. "Yes. His note didn't say what the nature of that business might be, but he did request that you and I pack up everything except the items we shall need for the next two days. You are going to be moving to Blackthorne Hall, my dear, and apparently so am I. I've ordered our trunks to be sent up so we can begin to pack."

"Oh, Miss Amelia, that won't be necessary." Cicely stepped forward. "You don't have to go to all that trouble for such a short distance. We can have the servants lay your things in the carriage and transport them over to your new rooms."

Amelia laid the satin dress on the bed and shook her head. "No, that won't do. According to the earl's note, the countess and I as well as you and Quinton will depart for London the day after the wedding. Again, he didn't explain."

"Well," Hannah's tone was dry. "Apparently the earl is very long on orders and deplorably short on explanations."

Cicely caught her lower lip between her teeth, then released it as she spoke. "I think I should go check on those trunks for you. The servants are quite distracted, with all they have to do."

Hannah watched her cousin leave, then turned to her aunt with a smile. "And to think I wanted to apologize to Cicely for taking her betrothed from her. My cousin owes me her life."

Hannah felt none of the morning's elation that evening at dinner. Quint had arrived just before the meal was to be served, and they had been able to exchange only the simplest and most formal of greetings before being ushered to their seats.

Hannah sat at the far end of the table, smoothing imaginary wrinkles out of the skirt of her blue-green gown. She had been placed at her uncle's elbow and was extremely conscious of his stony anger. She took some comfort in knowing that his fury was directed at Quint as well as at her, a notion she'd received when her uncle had inquired stiffly as to the success of Quint's venture that day, only to receive an enigmatic smile and a nod for an answer.

The number of guests had dwindled noticeably from the

night before, a fact that probably had added to the squire's anger, for the meal was a masterpiece of beautifully prepared dishes. Hannah was relieved to see that the Duke of Ludmore was not seated at the table, but still she had absolutely no appetite. She spent the entire meal pushing food around her plate with her silver fork, trying to keep her eyes from straying to where Quint sat about three places away from her on the opposite side of the table.

Hannah lost her battle to control her gaze more than once, for Quint looked even more handsome than usual this evening. The twinkling lights of the crystal chandelier painted dark blue streaks through his neatly combed black hair. Again he wore the formal black cutaway coat that suited him so well.

The light from above accentuated the aristocratic lines of his face. Hannah watched him smile politely at a woman in a low-cut pink gown, and felt something sharp twist in her breast. When she realized that something was jealousy, she blinked and forced herself to stare down at her plate again.

Dinner seemed as if it would never end. Course after course was placed in front of her. After the soup came baked haddock. A clear consommé led into brandied pheasant, which was followed by carrot soufflé and asparagus in wine sauce, and finally a dessert consisting of a light cake covered in chocolate syrup.

When Lady Evelyn stood at the end of the meal, Hannah rose along with the other women, wishing she could avoid facing their curiosity in the drawing room. Her prayer was answered when her uncle stood and asked the men to excuse him and the earl, as they had several matters to discuss.

When the squire glared at Hannah, she knew that she was one of those matters. For a moment she almost wished she could follow the women, then decided that whatever her uncle had to say to her would be easier to face than the snide smiles she'd seen directed her way during dinner.

Once more Hannah found herself in her uncle's blue and white study, where four ornate chairs were arranged in front of the squire's desk. Hannah fought a shiver as she sat in the brocade chair nearest the marble fireplace. Aunt Amelia seated herself next to Hannah as Lady Evelyn gathered her skirt into her hand in preparation to take the chair Quint held for her.

Having seen to his grandmother's comfort, Quint went to the last chair and brushed the tails of his coat to one side as he sat, then glanced up to study the young woman across the narrow semicircle who would soon be his wife. Seeing the trepidation in her wide lavender-blue eyes made his lips stiffen. He placed his hands on the smooth wooden armrests and tightened his long fingers around the curved edges as if to keep himself anchored there.

All evening he'd been fighting an insane desire to sweep Hannah into his arms and carry her out the door and away from all the prying eyes and sly, knowing smiles. Then, in the dark safety of the woods, he would be free to hold her, to experience again the joy and freedom and pure physical pleasure that was Hannah Bradley.

The squire gave a low cough, and Quint blinked away this picture as he watched the man approach his desk. The expression of superiority and disdain twisting Summerfield's lean features made Quint's scowl return as he gripped the arms of the chair with even more force.

Hannah shivered again as her uncle passed behind her chair. She shot a glance at Quint, and when she saw his knitted brow, she grew even colder. A tense silence filled the room as the squire stepped behind his large, ornate mahogany desk to place his hands on the green blotter and stare over the collection of pens in their holders.

"Well, Hannah." His cold eyes rested on her face. "In case you have been wondering, this meeting is being held to discuss the dowry that you will bring to the earl. I expect the meeting to be quite brief.''

He paused to give more weight to his words, his pale eyes narrowing and his lips curving unpleasantly. Hannah caught the inside of her lip between her teeth and gazed back at him. After a moment he glanced down as he lifted a sheet of paper from the desk.

''According to the papers drawn up by your father's Boston solicitor, Matthew Bradley left you exactly two thousand pounds. Some of that you have spent already, I assume, in paying for your transportation here. I also believe you purchased several dresses in London before you arrived on my doorstep.''

He paused lifting one eyebrow as he glanced at Hannah. ''I take this to indicate that you inherited your father's attitudes toward spending as well. As I remember, he put little stock in savings.''

Hannah's fingers curled into a tight ball within the folds of her skirt. There was nothing she could say in her defense. Her face began to blaze as she realized how damning this must look to Quint. Two days ago he had expected to marry a woman who would provide all he needed to fulfill his dreams. Now he was saddled with one who spent money without any consideration for what the future might bring.

Aunt Amelia, however, did have something to say. ''I'm afraid I have to correct you on that point, Charles.'' Hannah glanced over as her aunt pulled herself up taller in her seat. ''None of that money came from Hannah's dowry. What was spent came from my purse.''

The squire lifted his brows and nodded. ''Fine. Then Hannah brings to the Blackthornes the full sum of two thousand pounds.'' He glanced back at the paper in front of them. ''To that we can add Matthew's half-interest in a flying machine, stock in a silver mine in a place called

Virginia City, and part ownership of the Bramble Brothers
Traveling Circus.''

He looked up with a smile. ''According to the solicitor,
the flying machine has crashed, the silver mine has yielded
nothing in the last five years, and the Bramble Brothers
were forced to disband their circus in some place called
Omaha. Quite a wizard at investing, our Matthew.''

Hannah's embarrassed glance strayed to her left, where
both Quint and his grandmother sat tall and stiff in their
chairs. Quint's scowl was deeper than before, and the countess's mouth was held in a hard, pinched line.

Hannah's jaw tightened and she lowered her eyes. Her
face felt as if someone had dashed hot liquid over it. The
only sound in the room for several moments was the crack-
ling of the fire behind her. Then the rustle of skirts caught
Hannah's attention, and again her aunt's strong voice echoed
with suppressed anger.

''Charles, if you are finished with what you have to say,
it is my turn to speak.''

Hannah watched her aunt rise, then turn to Quint and his
grandmother.

''I am well aware that this dowry is not anywhere near
the amount you were promised in return for marrying
Cicely.'' Aunt Amelia spoke in a quiet, even tone. ''Per-
sonally, I find it absurd in this day and age to continue this
medieval practice, but I hope, young man, that you know
better than to measure the worth of the woman you are
marrying by the wealth she does or does not bring with
her.''

As Aunt Amelia paused, Hannah glanced at Quint. She
thought she saw his lips twitch before her aunt went on.
''However, I will not have my niece feel that she is a total
burden upon you. I have funds at my disposal that I wish
to add to my niece's dowry. Ten thousand dollars, to be
exact.''

Hannah gasped softly and looked up at her aunt, who was still staring at Quint. Hannah glanced at him once more. All traces of amusement had disappeared from his features.

"That is very generous of you, Miss Bradley." He dipped his head in a brief nod. "I'm sure you know you are under no such obligation to make this offer, and do so only because you care so much for your niece. I know I speak for my grandmother as well as myself when I tell you we are honored to have you become part of our family."

Quint rose and offered his hand to Lady Evelyn as she got to her feet. Hannah stood at the same time, and when the countess turned toward the door, Hannah prepared to follow.

"Hannah."

Her uncle's sharp voice made her stop and turn to face him. His thin lips curled unpleasantly: "I would like to have a few words with you, alone."

"I don't think so." The earl's voice cut off Hannah's reply. She swiveled. Quint wore a smile every bit as unpleasant as the squire's. "There are several matters I wish to discuss with Hannah before tomorrow," he said.

Hannah stood, tense and watching, as the two men glared at each other. Then her aunt's hand closed about her wrist.

Amelia spoke in a calm, dry voice. "My niece is quite tired, Lord Blackthorne. I would like her to get a good night's sleep. Do you think whatever needs discussing can wait until tomorrow, perhaps after the wedding?"

Quint turned to Amelia, his full lips easing into a smile. "Certainly."

He shifted his gaze to Hannah then, and his face once again became sober. He seemed to hesitate a moment, then walked forward and took her hand.

"Sleep well, Hannah."

She could only nod. Her hand throbbed with a strange heat, and she was mesmerized by the strange, dark look in his eyes. When he lifted her hand and bent forward over it, her breath caught in her throat.

Quint's lips just barely brushed the back of her hand, as they had the night before, but the soft contact sent strange shivers racing up Hannah's arm. She watched as he seemed to hesitate, his mouth but a hairbreadth from her hand. She braced herself for another scintillating shock, but instead Quint straightened and lowered her hand till her fingers slid away from his.

He turned to take his grandmother's arm and usher the countess out of the study. A second later, Aunt Amelia led Hannah through the doors and up to her room. Hannah walked as if in a dream. Each step felt slow and laborious. She couldn't remember ever feeling so suddenly weary, and when she commented on this upon entering her room, Aunt Amelia smiled.

"My girl," she said, "a scene like that would tire anyone. I'm exhausted myself. The only thing that kept me on my weary old feet was my joy at seeing your uncle bested on all sides."

Hannah smiled weakly at that comment. But as she prepared for bed, she couldn't help feeling that scene had marked the end of only the first act in this drama. Her blue-green dress swished to her feet, and her skin puckered with a sudden chill as the memory of her uncle's cold gaze rose ghostlike before her tired eyes.

Chapter 15

Quint stood near the altar. His gaze skimmed the colorful wide-brimmed hats of the women sitting in the first three rows, then focused on the rear of the stone church. His heart pounded with a deep thud-thud while in his mind a small voice whispered, *This is daft.*

The voice was right, Quint decided. There wasn't one whit of logic to what had happened to him in the last six days, and even less sense in the fact that a part of him was irrationally pleased with the turn of events.

Quint's breathing slowed as he thought of that part of him, the secret man who had taken over his body and mind, off and on, since that fateful meeting in the woods. He knew where this part of him came from. It was an inheritance from his parents, latent until now and related to his mother's stories of elves and fairies and his father's penchant for games of chance.

A quick glance at his grandmother, sitting in the front row in her customary black, revealed a worried frown behind her silver glasses. Quint's own brows lowered to match that expression. The irrepressible lunacy that Hannah incited in him had to be controlled. None of his responsibilities had

219

disappeared because of that meeting, none of his promises could be forgotten simply because a wood nymph had cast a spell on him.

Quint saw his grandmother look up at him, and smiled to reassure her, as well as his more reasonable side, that the spell was only temporary. Restoring the house, the lands, and the reputation of the house of Blackthorne would remain his first priority. Lady Evelyn nodded at him, a gesture he was about to return when a flash of dark and light at the back of the church caught his eye.

Hannah stood at the head of the aisle, on the arm of her uncle Charles. Her dress, made of a material that seemed to be a blend of lavender and silver, was cut in a simple style. A high collar of satin encircled her slender neck above a sheer yoke that dipped in the center like the upper half of a heart. The rest of the close-fitting bodice was satin, as were the wide sleeves that narrowed at the elbow and ended in a point over the back of each hand. Her long full skirt fell in a graceful, shimmering sweep from her narrow waist.

Hannah's hair cascaded over her shoulders and down her back in long honey-gold waves beneath her misty veil. A garland of yellow rosebuds, so pale they were almost white, sat atop her head, and long ribbons the color of her dress twisted among her golden tresses like slender ropes of silver.

No music accompanied Hannah and her uncle as they started down the aisle, only the low whispers of the guests. Quint ignored the murmurs and kept his eyes on Hannah's, his heart pounding in time to her slow steps, until she came close enough for him to see the uncertainty in their violet-blue depths.

Hannah forced her wobbly legs to support her. She refused to lean on her uncle's arm. He was a cold, ruthless man, and she wouldn't give him the satisfaction of knowing that the harsh words he'd poured into her ears as they waited in the vestibule had had any effect on her.

But they had. Even as she approached Quint and met the solemn expression in his eyes, she could hear her uncle's words echo in her mind: ''Enjoy today, my little lady. As amazing as it is to me, Quinton seems quite taken with you. Of course that won't last long. Before a month is out he'll tire of you and see you for the liability you are.''

Hannah kept her lower lip trapped between her teeth as she walked the last few steps. Her gaze was still held by Quint's, but she couldn't fathom the emotions that lay within their dark green depths. She saw him offer his hand, and gratefully she removed her arm from her uncle's and stretched her hand out to Quint's.

His fingers were warm and dry as they captured hers; then he tucked her hand within the crook of his elbow as they arranged themselves self-consciously in front of the tall, gray-haired minister.

The Reverend Mr. Smythe began speaking, but his voice was a dull droning in Hannah's ears. Her mind refused to focus on the words, but their meaning was far too clear. Hannah was being joined to the man standing next to her, a man who was handsome and intelligent, a man who looked upon marrying her as a duty to be performed.

The vicar's words echoed loudly in Quint's mind. They were words that vibrated with his every fiber, words concerning duty and responsibility. He would protect this woman, would honor her, would . . .

Quint glanced at Hannah as he repeated his vows. Love. What did he know of that? In his life it had meant only pain and desertion. Would he *love* Hannah? He cared for her, certainly. He wanted her, absolutely. Standing next to her, breathing the perfume rising from her flowers, he couldn't deny the need that ate at him, and had from almost the first moment they met.

But love? Love meant trust; it meant opening his heart in a way he never wanted to open it again. Mentally Quint removed that word from the vows he agreed to as he slipped the delicately carved gold band on Hannah's finger. Yet when the final words were spoken and he turned to meet Hannah's gaze, his heart pounded wildly. The rational part of his mind warned him to move slowly, even as he lowered his lips to hers, touched them lightly, then lifted his head to look into her eyes once again.

The uncertainty was there still, but he saw something else, a widening of her eyes, a parting of her softened lips that invited further contact. Quint began to bend his head once more, but a soft, only half-heard snicker from the front pew made him frown and straighten.

Hannah watched Quint move away from her. Her lips were still warm from the soft caress of his mouth, and for the first time that day the rest of her felt warm as well. Her lips tingled and longed for further and deeper contact. She stared into his eyes, only to see them grow darker as he moved farther away from her. When he took her hand to walk her down the aisle, his fingers were once more cold, and so was she.

"That was a very nice ceremony."

Parker smiled down at Hannah as they danced across her uncle's ballroom. Hannah glanced away from where Quint stood talking to two older gentlemen, looked up at Parker, and said, "Was it really? I'm afraid I wasn't paying attention."

Parker stared at Hannah a moment, then tossed his auburn head back and laughed. "Oh, dear. Grandmother is going to be most distressed."

"Oh?"

"Yes. Don't you know that the Blackthornes are supposed to take all this pomp with the utmost seriousness?"

Hannah lifted her eyebrows. "Well, I would say that she

and Quint are more than capable of carrying that banner all by themselves.''

Parker glanced at his grandmother, who sat watching, somber-faced, as the dancers moved by. Then he shifted his gaze to Quint, who was deep in conversation with a tall, portly man with silver hair and long, wide whiskers.

''Ah, yes, I see what you mean. Well, you have to understand Quint. He's not a bad sort, just unlucky enough to be the elder son.''

''Does that mean he cannot dance with his bride at his own wedding?'' Hannah heard the sharpness in her tone, and the pain beneath the anger. When Parker looked into her eyes, she stared past him.

''Oh, well,'' he said. ''Again, you have to understand Quint. Until this season, with all the talk of him marrying Cicely and being forced to attend balls and such, Quint was never one for dancing and getting out. And Lord Ellesly over there is a specialist on horse breeding, you know. I fear my brother is so thrilled at a chance to speak to the man privately that he's completely forgotten his husbandly duties. He'll come around soon, I'm sure.''

At the mention of husbandly duties Hannah felt herself blush. She glanced away and spied Cicely speaking to Aunt Amelia, then looked back at Parker.

''Well, if talking about horses is Quint's excuse, what is yours?''

''Mine? Madam, I *am* dancing.''

Hannah cocked an eyebrow. ''With your new sister-in-law. What about the woman you love?''

When Parker's face fell into a dismayed expression and his step faltered slightly, Hannah smiled up at him and went on, ''Cicely is no longer betrothed. Why haven't you asked her to dance? Why haven't you tried to console her on her loss?''

Parker blinked. ''Console her? What for? I've never seen

her so happy. She's free now. She no longer has to—'' He broke off suddenly and turned a deep shade of red as Hannah smiled.

"She no longer has to what? Dread being married to Quint? Well, that's true. So she's free to marry you."

Parker glanced at Cicely, and for one moment an expression of hope lit his face. Then he shook his head and looked back at Hannah. "She may be free of Quint, but there's still her father. Look. Just now he's dragging some old coot over to her. Another titled fellow, I'm sure. No, Cicely doesn't have time for the likes of me, not for dancing and certainly not for anything else."

The music began to slow as Hannah lifted her brows and smiled at her new brother-in-law. "Parker, have you ever thought of simply asking her? Believe it or not, we women much prefer to have some choice in these matters."

With that the dance ended. Hannah grinned up into Parker's startled face, then turned and walked toward her aunt.

Quint looked up from his conversation with Lord Ellesly and watched Hannah walk away, noticing how the sway of her slim hips made her lavender-gray gown sweep back and forth over the smooth floor. The old man next to him continued speaking about horses, but Quint hadn't heard a word since he noticed Hannah laughing up at his brother.

Quint had no trouble recognizing the sharp sensation twisting in his stomach and chest as jealousy. He'd felt it before, when he learned that his first wife had taken a lover. Quint turned away from Hannah, tried to focus on the bewhiskered jowls of the man speaking to him. Jealousy was most uncomfortable and, he told himself, highly irrational.

He had always been aware that women felt more comfortable with Parker. The boy had an engaging sense of the absurd and seemed to feel completely at ease in the presence of women. It was only natural that someone as lighthearted as Hannah should enjoy Parker's company. There was no reason at all to feel jealous.

There was also no reason that this interminable evening couldn't be put to an end at this point. Everyone had raised a glass to his health and Hannah's. All had partaken of the excellent food and imbibed enough liquor to ensure the success of the evening. It was definitely time to go home.

Quint stared across the empty dance floor again, to where Hannah stood talking to Cicely. He glanced briefly at the taller girl. Cicely was indeed a beautiful young woman. In her pale green dress, with her silver-blond hair artfully drawn up on the top of her head, she looked almost regal. All the clothes her father had bought for her and the schools he had sent her to had borne fruit. Cicely would have brought an air of reserve and propriety to the title of Lady Chadwick had their marriage come to pass.

Quint shifted his gaze to Hannah. In her flowing, mist-colored gown, her dark golden hair flowing about her, she looked regal as well, every bit the fairy queen of his mother's tales, a wood nymph who didn't belong in a ballroom. Hannah should be waltzing in some moonlit forest glade. And if not that, she should be in his arms, in his bed.

That thought brought a fierce tightening to Quint's loins. He knew he couldn't stand there one moment longer, wasting precious time. Hannah was his now. There was no longer any reason not to savor the taste of her lips, explore the softness of her flesh.

Quint interrupted whatever it was Lord Ellesly was saying. "Your Lordship, please excuse me. I fear I cannot continue this conversation at this time. Perhaps on Friday, at the Duke of Uxley's soiree?"

Quint bowed and walked toward Hannah, only vaguely aware of the bemused expression on the older man's face. All his attention was on the slender form in lavender-gray.

Hannah fought sudden weariness as she listened to Cicely

describe the strange conversation she'd just had with her
sister Carolyn. She started to smile at her cousin's tale,
when suddenly she stiffened. Her body grew suddenly
warm, and slowly, without consciously willing it, she turned
to see Quint striding purposefully across the dance floor.
Cicely must have seen him, too, because the young woman's
words trailed off into silence.

Hannah's heart began to race as Quint grew nearer. His
eyes held hers intently, and as he reached her, she had to
tilt her head back to look up at him. "Hannah." His voice
was deep, his eyes dark beneath that habitual scowl of his.
"It is time we left for Blackthorne Hall. I shall order our
wraps and the carriage. Would you be so kind as to inform
your aunt that my grandmother and I will be in the entry
hall in five minutes?"

Hannah blinked at the abruptness of his orders, but her
suddenly warm, weak muscles refused to tighten in response
to the anger his attitude provoked. She managed only to
nod wordlessly, then watched him blankly for a moment as
he strode away.

"Oh, Hannah." Cicely spoke in a soft undertone. "I am
so sorry." She smiled apologetically. "But I must admit to
being relieved. You will handle the earl far better than I."

Hannah smiled wanly. This Quint, the public person, was
nothing like the man who had acted lady's maid for her in
the forest and soared with her in the clouds. Would that
man ever reemerge, or was he trapped forever behind a
facade of social convention?

"Hannah?" Cicely's voice was slightly louder. "I think
we'd best get Aunt Amelia and make our way to the entry
hall."

When Hannah arrived in the vestibule with her aunt and
cousin, Quint was standing by the door, his dark coat but-
toned and his top hat in hand. Next to him stood the countess
in a coat of purple silk with a gray fox collar.

Uncle Charles was there as well, standing stiffly as the servants helped Hannah and her aunt into their wraps. Hannah could feel the man's cold gaze upon her. She sensed his anger and disapproval and remembered his words from earlier in the day.

Hannah felt a chilling cold pull her into its grasp, a cold that neither her heavy gray cape nor Cicely's warm parting embrace could dispel. She felt Aunt Amelia's dry hand close over hers as they followed Quint and his grandmother to the waiting carriage, but even her aunt's unspoken support couldn't melt her frigid heart. Quint handed the two older women in. When his icy fingers closed over Hannah's, she looked up suddenly.

The moon lit his features from above. She couldn't see the expression in his eyes, but as she stood there a moment, her hand in his, she saw his lips curve slightly as he spoke in a low undertone. "We'll be home soon. Try to relax."

Hannah attempted to do as he asked. At first, sitting next to Quint as the carriage began to rock behind the trotting horses, Hannah found she could take a deep breath and order her tight muscles to relax, and each time the swaying conveyance made Quint's arm brush against hers, she felt some heat return to her limbs.

The ride was short. No one spoke until they drew up to Blackthorne Hall, where Quint got out and handed down the three women.

Hannah emerged from the carriage first and gazed up at the tall stone structure that Quint called home. The square tower rose to her left, and in front of her the stone entranceway curved upward into a pointed Gothic arch. Five wide stone steps led up to a dark carved oak door that echoed the shape of the entry.

Hannah mounted the steps as the door opened inward. Quint ushered the three ladies into the entry hall where a white-haired butler took their wraps, draped them over his arm, then stood to await further instructions.

"Barrows, we are all quite fatigued. Please have someone show Miss Bradley and"—he paused and looked at Hannah—"Lady Blackthorne to their rooms."

Hannah stared up at Quint, fighting the sudden urge to laugh as she realized that *she* was now Lady Blackthorne. It sounded wonderfully impressive, terribly proper. And impossible to live up to.

The urge to laugh went as quickly as it had come, and with it the small smile that had begun to curve Hannah's lips. Quint apparently saw this, for he lifted her suddenly drooping chin so that she was forced to look into his eyes as he leaned forward and spoke softly.

"I shall be up soon, Hannah."

He gave her a small smile that could have meant a thousand things, then turned and started to mount the stairs behind his grandmother. A small, perky woman with a white cap on her dark head and a wide smile on her lips stepped up to Hannah and her aunt.

"I'm Sarah, Your Ladyship." She dropped into a quick curtsy, just long enough for Hannah to realize that the woman was addressing her, then spoke again. "I would like to show you to your rooms."

Several moments later Hannah entered a large room with a mahogany ceiling embossed with ornate circular medallions. A large wardrobe stood to her left, a wide hearth blazing with an inviting fire lay in front of her, and next to that sat an overstuffed chair covered in plum-colored velvet.

Hannah's gaze was drawn to the enormous curtained bed on her left. The coverlet and heavy draperies tied to the tall posts with silver cords were of wine red. Large pillows of matching fabric lay at the head of the bed, and over the footboard were draped two garments of silver-gray.

"They're a wedding present from Cicely." Aunt Amelia

spoke from behind her. "She wanted to give you something very special."

Hannah turned to her aunt, who smiled from the doorway as she waved. "Good night, my girl."

Sarah turned to show Amelia to her room, but before she stepped out the door, she gestured toward the ivory screen in the corner and advised Hannah that a hot bath awaited Her Ladyship's pleasure and mentioned that her maid would be along in a moment to help her prepare for her bath.

Hannah glanced around the room again as the door shut behind her. Two gas lamps with large round globes hung on either side of the bed, casting a soft light over the room. As Hannah stared at the rose-patterned rug, she noticed worn spots between the flowers and the green leaves. As she crossed to the screen, she passed in front of the overstuffed chair and noted spots where the velvet was wearing away on the wide arms.

Hannah peeked around the screen, formed of ivory lace gathered onto a mahogany frame, and stared at the ornate gold and cream footed tub. Although the rest of the furnishings in the room showed the wear of time, the tub gleamed in the light of the dancing fire. Soft swirls of steam rose from the clear water, and suddenly Hannah knew she wanted nothing more than to submerge her tense body in the warm water.

She sat down on the chair to remove her shoes and stockings, then stood and lifted her heavy satin skirt to loosen the strings on her muslin underskirt and let it fall to her feet. She had begun to unfasten the satin-covered buttons running down the back of her gown when a soft knock sounded on her door. Her "Come in" produced a tiny uniformed woman, who closed the door behind her softly, then stood regarding Hannah with worried blue eyes.

"Oh, Your Ladyship, I'm sorry to be late." A white cap bobbed atop ginger-colored hair as the girl dropped a quick curtsy. "I was only just informed you were here. My name is Liza. Please let me help you."

Hannah smiled, then turned to present her back. As the girl finished unbuttoning her, Hannah spoke over her shoulder. "Don't worry. You aren't late. I was in a hurry to get into that bath while the water is still hot."

Moments later Hannah was lowering herself slowly into the tub, savoring the warmth as it captured each part of her in its liquid embrace. When most of her body was submerged, she let herself sink back until her neck was resting on the rounded edge of the tub. The heavy knot of hair, which Liza had arranged atop her head, shifted slightly. As it tugged on the front of her hairline, it eased away the last of the tension that had lodged there.

Hannah lay still for several moments, her eyes closed, her mind focused on nothing but the warmth and security that swirled around her. She heard the door open softly, and a few moments later Liza's voice echoed softly. "Lady Evelyn ordered some hot cocoa for you, my lady. I'll fetch it and come right back to finish getting you ready."

The door clicked shut and Hannah's eyes opened quickly. My lady? No one was going to let her forget her new status for very long.

Hannah's heart began to thud slowly as she thought of the maid's other words. She was going to return to "finish getting her ready." Hannah's thoughts flew to the gossamer gray nightgown and matching silk robe she'd seen on the bed, and her face grew even warmer. What was it Quint had said? That he'd be up soon?

Hannah gazed into the fire. She knew what to expect when they were at last alone. The memory of the passion she'd shared with Quint in France rose to haunt her constantly. Still, her lips trembled as she recalled the concern in her aunt's tiny face yesterday afternoon as the woman had offered her words of encouragement. "Hannah, my girl, as I mentioned earlier, this is not the first marriage that has begun on such short acquaintance, my dear.'' Her aunt's words echoed in her mind. ''Since you have an idea of what to expect, I won't need to discuss your wedding night, beyond suggesting that you do your best to let yourself enjoy your husband's attentions.''

Hannah remembered the surprise she'd felt at these words. It must have shown on her features, for her aunt had blushed, then smiled as she shrugged. ''Yes, I know of such things. It's true that I have never had a husband, but I did love a man once, very much. He was killed before we could be married, but not before we knew the full measure of each other's love. You may be shocked if you wish, but that experience taught me that to deny pleasure is to deny life. And who knows? What starts as only physical desire may grow into the kind of love I know you want, given time and patience.''

Time and patience. The words echoed in Hannah's mind as she sat up and began to slide the smooth, softly scented soap over her skin. Patience was a virtue she had come into the world totally lacking. But she certainly had plenty of time at her disposal—a lifetime in which to coax the Quint who had captured her heart away from the serious position to which he had retreated.

Hannah rinsed the soap from her arms and back, then glanced around with restless impatience. She hadn't heard the door open again, but she no longer felt like sitting in the tub. A thick towel hung over a tarnished brass towel rack nearby. Hannah reached for it as she stood, then wrapped it around herself as she stepped out of the tub. She gazed into the fire for a long moment as she ran the rough material over her body, then slowly let the towel drop to her feet as she stepped toward the edge of the screen.

Hannah bent forward as she tucked a loose, damp tendril of hair into the thick coil atop her head. As she rounded the thin barrier, she looked up, then stopped and stared, unable to believe for a moment what she was seeing.

Across the room, leaning against one of the tall bedposts, stood Quint. His arms were crossed over an emerald-green brocade dressing gown that ended just above black velvet slippers. Hannah's eyes flew to his, dark beneath his half-scowl; then she noticed the small lines fanning out from their corners. Her gaze moved down to his mouth, which twisted into a small smile as he stared openly at her.

Hannah was acutely aware of her nakedness, but could think of nothing to do but stand there, wondering what Quint was doing there now, before she'd had a chance to dress. As she stared at his mouth, his smile grew wider and he spoke, answering her unspoken question.

"I've come to see if the position of lady's maid is still open."

Chapter 16

Quint tightened his crossed arms as he gazed at Hannah. It took all his control not to stride across the room, sweep her up into his arms, and slide his hands over her pale, silken skin.

After intercepting the maid outside the door and telling her that her services would not be needed again that evening, he'd silently entered the room. The sound of splashing water had drawn his eyes to where Hannah was silhouetted on the screen, slim and shapely as she rose from the water. His breath had caught in his throat and his body had begun to throb as her towel hid her curves, then dropped to reveal the grace of her slim thighs as she stepped to the edge of the screen.

Now, raw desire tightened his loins, but the look of surprise and fear on Hannah's face warned him to move slowly. She reminded him of a young filly, long-legged with large eyes filled with doubt. He forced himself to keep his eyes on hers and to display a self-possession he was far from feeling.

Hannah stared back at Quint. The black velvet lapels of his dressing gown crossed over his chest in a deep V that revealed a wide expanse of muscle covered with dark curling hair.

A hot blush rose to Hannah's cheeks as she realized there was nothing beneath that dressing gown but warm flesh and lean muscle. For a moment she couldn't think clearly, so stunned was she by the unexpected sight of him standing in front of her and her own strong reaction to the message in his eyes. She gazed at him a moment longer, then forced herself to speak.

"It seems that I am very much in need of some sort of assistance. If you would bring my dressing gown to me, I would be most grateful."

Quint turned to lift the silken garment from the foot of the bed. His eyes held Hannah's as he approached her, holding the robe open for her. He stood behind her while she slipped her arms into the sleeves, then let the thin material slip from his fingers as she pulled it close around her and knotted the thin belt around her waist.

Hannah turned slowly to Quint. She lifted her head to stare once more into his eyes. They were dark, so dark she could see no traces of green. As she gazed up at him wordlessly he placed his hands on her shoulders, then slowly moved his fingers in a circular caress that started her heart racing once more.

"You made a most beautiful bride, Hannah."

Again Quint spoke in a deep, strained voice that sent Hannah's senses skittering with a strange thrill. She saw his lips twitch in a half-smile as he reached up to remove the hairpin holding her loose topknot. His smile grew wider as her hair tumbled down around her shoulders in a mass of honey-gold. She tried to smile back, but her lips would not respond. They felt numb and warm at the same time, and she could barely speak.

"Thank you Quint. It was a nice wedding." She hesitated. "The ring is beautiful."

Quint lifted her left hand to examine the wide openwork band. It shone like gold lace, catching the light as he touched it.

"I saw it in a shop when I was in London yesterday. It looked like you, delicate but strong, like something the queen of the wood fairies would wear." The ring slid easily up Hannah's finger as he spoke, making Quint frown. "It's too large," he said. "I'm sorry."

Hannah looked up into his dark eyes. "Don't be. I didn't expect a ring at all."

"No ring?" One black eyebrow quirked up. "How would anyone know you'd been captured forever?"

His eyes stared into Hannah's with ever growing intensity, and her skin beneath his hands grew warmer. She didn't even try to speak this time; she simply shrugged, then held her breath as she saw his head begin to bend toward hers.

The first contact of his lips was incredibly soft, almost a phantom kiss. Hannah closed her eyes as his mouth brushed hers. She felt a slow fire slide through her at that ever so slight contact and parted her lips invitingly.

A second later Quint's lips touched hers again, a soft caress that slanted over hers first one way, then the other. His hands slid down her arms. Hannah lifted her hands to his shoulders as his eased from the curve of her hips to the small of her back, where his long fingers spread out as he drew her closer to him.

Hannah gasped softly; then Quint's mouth closed over hers possessively. He kissed her deeply for a long moment, the moist softness of his tongue teasing her slightly parted lips. She opened her mouth beneath his, sliding her hands up along the muscles of his shoulders to draw her body closer as his tongue slipped between her teeth and lit a fire deep within her.

Quint tightened his arms about Hannah, let his hands caress the tempting curve of her buttocks. His fingers easily spanned the firm, rounded muscles, then tightened to mold themselves to her curves as he drew her closer to him, groaning as the contact between them increased and his hardness pressed into the softness of her stomach.

Hannah gasped as she felt the rigid length against her. The warmth and fire in her stomach spiraled lower, and her knees threatened to buckle with sudden weakness. As she sagged against Quint, his mouth released hers. He drew a ragged breath, then touched his lips gently to her cheek and trailed a long kiss across to her jaw. He tightened his hold on her again, his breath warm against her neck.

''Hannah.''

He uttered her name on a whisper, a whisper breathed into her ear that spoke of desire and need. An answering need welled up within Hannah, and she breathed his name softly.

Slowly Quint lifted his head to look once more into her face. Her eyes were wide, her cheeks flushed a soft pink, and her parted lips a deeper rosy color. Quint drew on every ounce of restraint he possessed to control the urge to drag her to the floor and complete their lovemaking right there in the center of the room. His entire being throbbed with a yearning he'd never before experienced.

Earlier in the evening, when he could still think clearly, he had given a great deal of thought to this moment. He didn't want to repeat that desperate coupling in the basement. There had been no time to woo Hannah in the manner she deserved. He couldn't offer her his heart fully and freely, but at least he could see to it that her wedding night was one of slow, sensual pleasure.

He longed to capture her mouth once more, but he forced himself to smile, and he coerced words from his clouded mind. ''This isn't the proper place for this, you know.''

At the surprised lift of Hannah's eyebrows he smiled again and tilted his head to indicate the bed behind them. Hannah peered around his shoulder at the impressive piece of furniture, bathed in bright light, then looked back up at Quint.

Hannah hesitated. She knew what was to come; her body was already pulsing with longing. But she found herself longing for the very darkness that had once frightened her so. Without the cloak of night to hide her responses, she felt as frightened and vulnerable as if she were truly a virgin.

He saw the hint of fright enter her eyes, the same look he'd seen in those of an unbroken colt being introduced to the bridle for the first time. Once more he smiled. Then, without saying a word, he released his hold on Hannah, sliding his left hand down her arm to capture hers. Still looking at her, he drew her toward the far side of the bed.

The bedcovers had been turned back. The white sheets glowed a pale yellow in the light from the overhead lamps, but as Hannah stared at the expanse of pristine fabric that light dulled slightly. She looked up to see that Quint had turned off the gas lamp on the wall and released sheer gray curtains from behind the heavier burgundy ones to hang like a wave of mist around the bed. Before she could question Quint, he was tugging on her hand, pulling her around the foot of the bed, releasing the other ties encircling the posts as he went, until they stood beneath the lamp on the opposite side.

Hannah watched as Quint turned that light out as well, then glanced at her with one dark eyebrow raised. She looked back at the bed. The area within the confines of the curtains was wrapped in a soft mist of sheer fabric, lit softly by a small lamp on the bedside table.

Her lips curved slightly. All the enclosure lacked was the soft smell of damp earth and a bower of leafy trees to reconstruct the ambience of their first meeting. Sudden tears stung her eyes at Quint's thoughtfulness as her throat tightened around a slight knot.

The tears shimmered in the pale light as she looked back

up at the man who was her husband. Her smile widened as she told herself that at last she was in the presence of that elusive part of him that had so captured her imagination and her heart. Without thinking, she rose on tiptoe to press her lips warmly to his.

As her mouth touched his, Quint dropped her hand and placed both hands on her waist to hold her up to him. When her lips parted invitingly, he thrust his tongue in to gently explore the warmth and moisture. He felt her sway toward him, but his hands held her back for a moment as his fingers curved beneath the slender belt at her waist, then tugged. Her gown parted as the belt came untied, and seconds later he had released the knot on his own belt.

He pulled her to him then, gasping against her mouth at the feel of her skin against his, as the soft curve of her stomach yielded to the shaft that throbbed in response to the sweet contact.

Hannah's legs brushed against Quint's. The lean, hard muscles roughened with hair that touched her thighs contrasted sharply with the smooth ridge of muscle pulsing against her abdomen. A strange fire flared within her, spreading along her skin. She turned her head to one side, pulling her lips from beneath Quint's to gasp for air.

Quint made no attempt to recapture Hannah's lips just yet. He, too, found it necessary to draw in deep drafts of air as he held her tightly to him. His hands glided over the silk of her dressing gown, sliding over her skin until, craving the feel of his hands on her flesh, he tugged on the material as he stepped away from her slightly and watched as the gray cloud drifted down to settle at her feet.

In one swift motion he shrugged out of his dressing gown and parted the curtain with his right hand as his left one closed over Hannah's to urge her onto the bed. She glanced up at him only briefly before climbing onto the soft mattress, moving to the center of the bed, then turning to face him, curling her legs beneath her as she sat up.

Quint let his gaze caress her naked form. Her skin gleamed with the iridescence of pearls, and her golden hair fell like a sheer curtain over her full breasts. Every curve and valley cried out to be explored.

Hannah kept her eyes on Quint as he knelt on the bed, then moved forward to join her in the center, where he sat down beside her and took her face in his hand, his fingers lying along one side of her jaw, his thumb on the other. With exquisite slowness he lowered his lips to hers. He kissed her deeply while taking her in his arms and laying her back against the coolness of the sheets.

They stretched out facing each other on their sides. Quint pulled Hannah to him with one arm, while the other hand slid up her hip and over her rib cage to close over the fullness of her breast.

Hannah felt her breast swell beneath his gentle fingers. A sharp shaft of pleasure spiraled downward to add to the pressure that had begun to build between her thighs. The muscles in her buttocks tightened, as if that might ease the pressure somewhat. Instead, she brushed against Quint's arousal.

The contact made both of them gasp. Their lips parted for just a second, long enough for Hannah to look into his eyes and see his frown of concentration, long enough for her to feel a quick, irrational stab of fear.

Quint saw the widening of her eyes. Swiftly he lowered his head to cover her mouth with his, to kiss her deeply, to feel her muscles once more relax.

Gently he rolled her onto her back. The palm of his hand brushed over the hardened tip of her nipple as he continued to kiss her. Slowly he slid one leg over hers, dipped his knee between hers, then shifted his weight, holding himself suspended over her.

Hannah felt her legs part. Her mind was clouded with the sensations coiling through her, her will wrapped in a mist of pleasure as she felt Quint, smooth and hard, begin to slide slowly over the curls at the joining of her thighs. The contact was light at first. Then he urged her legs to part more and lowered himself farther, sliding down to caress the moist tender flesh beneath the curls.

Hannah's neck arched back, and her hips lifted to invite further contact. Quint couldn't control the groan that rasped in his throat as the tip of his manhood slid over her, then moved down to nestle a moment in the warm opening below. He heard her answering moan and repeated the motion again, then yet again as she began to move in rhythm with him. Each time he pressed a little deeper within her, and each time it became more difficult to force himself to withdraw.

Hannah's eyes were closed, and her mind was a blank. She was aware only of the feel of Quint's hand caressing her flesh, of the thrusting of his tongue in her mouth in rhythm to the motion of his hips, of the sweet tension between her legs, the warm, demanding urgency that kept building each time Quint pressed himself to her. Her hips moved of their own volition, lifting when he thrust down, descending as he raised himself.

Quint groaned again as his need burgeoned. He raised his lips from Hannah's, then lowered them to her ear and whispered, "I need you Hannah. I need you now."

Hannah's body cried out for release from the spiraling, growing pressure. Aware that Quint's need held the answer to hers, she nodded.

Quint tightened his arm around Hannah and lowered himself slowly into her, then held still a moment as he lifted his head to look into her eyes.

Hannah gazed up at his tense features, into his almost black eyes. Neither spoke. Hannah felt a soft throbbing

SKYLARK 241

within her, and as Quint lowered his mouth to take hers with deep tenderness, she felt that lethargic warmth flood her again, relaxing her muscles and reawakening the aching need.

Quint began to move within her again. Hannah rocked beneath him, their bodies working in unison, rising and falling more and more quickly. Hannah felt the strange sensation intensify, build with more promise until it reached a moment of wonder and bliss, then shattered into a throbbing pleasure that had her holding on to Quint with a strength she didn't know she possessed.

Quint's arms tightened around Hannah as well, as with one deep thrust his pleasure joined with hers. They lay pressed together, throbbing ever more slowly, until they felt their bodies drain of all tension and only a soft memory of pleasure warmed their loins.

Hannah didn't remember falling asleep, but hours later she woke to a dim light, feeling Quint's arms around her, his long powerful body lying behind her, cupping her to him. The soft glow from the lantern still lit the curtains and a small smile curved Hannah's lips as she wondered if he had remembered her fear of the dark, or if like her, he had simply fallen asleep where he lay.

Hannah sighed softly and snuggled closer to his warmth. It seemed her fears that he might treat their marriage as only one more duty had been groundless. She could see now that Quint's reserve had been for the benefit of her uncle and his guests only. The remembered look of sated pleasure and joy on his softly smiling face as he pulled her to him and closed his lids over the sleepy satisfaction in his eyes left her feeling that perhaps her aunt was right, that even forced marriages could result in the deep love she'd always longed for.

Hannah smiled and let her eyelids droop closed. She

longed to wake Quint up, to tell him her feelings. But she was too warm and relaxed to move. The morning would be time enough.

Morning was barely a flicker of light on the horizon when Quint woke to the soft glow of the lantern. He lay still a few moments, savoring the soft body cradled to his, then slowly opened his eyes and stared at the streams of golden hair falling over his wife's shoulder.

His wife. Quint's eyes flew open. Slowly, carefully he eased his arm from beneath Hannah, then slid out of bed, watching for any sign that he'd disturbed her rest.

He found his dressing gown where he had let it fall to the floor on the other side of the bed. After he shrugged into it, he turned again to gaze at the sleeping woman lying in the gray mist created by the filmy curtains.

She seemed no less magical to him now than before he had explored her body's secrets and made them his, for he knew he'd only touched the surface. He knew so little of her thoughts and her needs. He only knew he couldn't bear it if she slipped out of his life. He had to find a way to hold her, to bind her to his world.

He could hold her, he told himself. If he could gentle a freedom-loving horse, accustom it to bridle and saddle, then he could tame Hannah's need for excitement, curb her longing for freedom, and keep her by his side.

Quint drew the covers up over Hannah's arm, then turned and crossed to the door to start his morning.

Chapter 17

When Hannah woke the second time, it was to pale sunlight slipping past the edges of the heavy draperies at her window to create a soft gray mist within her curtained bed. A slow smile curved her lips as she rolled over to greet her husband.

The place where Quint had lain the night before was empty; only a deep indentation in the pillow remained as evidence of his presence. Beyond the sheer curtain, the small flame in the lantern flickered a mocking greeting.

Liza came in a moment later, and once the maid had lit the fire, Hannah expressed a desire to dress. A half-hour later, wearing a high-necked white shirtwaist and a dark blue skirt, she followed Liza to the dining room.

"Quinton? Oh, he's an early riser." Lady Evelyn looked up from her plate and gazed across the table to Hannah. "He ate an hour ago. I imagine he's off on that horse of his checking on everything before we leave for London. Please, come sit with us." She indicated the spot next to her, across from Aunt Amelia. "There's plenty of food on the sideboard. Just help yourself."

After glancing at her aunt, who greeted her with a warm smile and a nod of encouragement, Hannah stepped over to

243

the mahogany sideboard and placed a few spoonfuls of potato and a serving of kidneys on her plate, then slid into the chair next to the dowager countess. A servant poured her some tea, and she ate in silence for several moments.

"Almost all of the trunks the squire sent over have been packed off to London, along with most of the servants. Normally the town house is rented out for the season. Quint only agreed to keep it for our use this year and participate in the rituals of society because of his engagement to Cicely." Hannah looked up sharply at these words but Lady Evelyn spoke again, in a calm, imperious tone.

"I would appreciate it if you ladies would see to it that your personal items are packed quickly and your portmanteaux brought down to the entry hall after breakfast so Barrows can finish loading the carriage."

Hannah nodded wordlessly. She could think of no appropriate reply, so she took another bite of boiled potatoes in white sauce and a sip of tea. A few moments later she found that the knot in her stomach had robbed her of her appetite. She lifted her napkin to the corner of her mouth and looked across to see that her aunt had put her fork down and was staring out the window behind Lady Evelyn.

"Aunt Amelia?" Her aunt turned, and Hannah went on, "I'm finished eating. If you are also, we should probably go up and complete our packing."

Her aunt nodded and smiled a small, secret smile that made Hannah blush. She glanced down as she placed her napkin beside her plate and began to rise. Lady Evelyn's sharp voice stopped her. "Before you go, I think we should have a little talk."

Hannah glanced over and lowered herself back into her seat as the countess turned to Aunt Amelia. "Miss Bradley, I would appreciate it if you would stay as well."

Lady Evelyn then turned to Hannah and said, "Lady Blackthorne." Hannah blinked at this reminder of her new title, then lifted her eyes to meet the spectacled ones set within Lady Evelyn's stern features as the woman continued, "Our acquaintance has been brief, and the circumstances under which we have become part of the same family are rather strange."

Hannah heard her aunt's blue silk rustle and glanced over to see Amelia's features harden. Hannah felt herself stiffen defensively, but forced herself to nod and reply, "Yes, I suppose the events of the last several days do seem rather odd."

Lady Evelyn lifted her brows a moment, then nodded in return. "Well, I want you to know, that although I am less than happy with the outcome, I do not hold you to blame. Quinton has explained the circumstances to me in detail, and it does appear as if fate has decided to send an unexpected twist into his life."

She paused and coughed delicately into her hand as a serving girl removed her plate, then looked at Hannah once more. "However, what has transpired can have a definitely unwholesome effect on my family's fortunes. From what was mentioned in your uncle's study the other night, I know you are aware that the Blackthorne's are . . . shall we say, somewhat financially embarrassed."

She stared at Hannah, who nodded as the knot in her stomach coiled tighter. Lady Evelyn folded her hands together on the table in front of her, and went on. "This affects you in several ways, my dear. First of all, you must understand that Quinton's time is very valuable. He's started several ventures, based on the money he expected to receive upon his betrothal to Cicely Summerfield. He will be quite busy dealing with these while we are in London and will have very little time available for social functions, except in the evenings.

"Second"—the woman lifted her chin slightly—"I want you to deport yourself with the utmost decorum while in

London. There is bound to be gossip floating around about you and Quinton. This unpleasantness can be overcome only if your behavior is most circumspect.''

Hannah lifted her chin as well, and her hands tightened into fists in her lap. However, before she could reply, her aunt's voice rang out sharply.

''My niece is no schoolgirl in need of a lecture, Your Ladyship. She's attended some of the best finishing schools, where she mastered all the social arts. I'm sure you will find her behavior above reproach.''

Lady Evelyn listened to Amelia without blinking. When the woman stopped speaking, the dowager countess turned to Hannah with a curt nod. ''I'm sure your aunt is correct. However, in the next week or so, when your every move will be scrutinized closely, you will have to watch everything you do and each syllable you utter, until society is sufficiently certain of your acceptability. Frankly''—Lady Evelyn raised one brow—''I find many of these people boring and silly. Normally I wouldn't care a fig for what they thought.''

She paused and Hannah looked at her sharply to find the woman smiling tightly. ''However,'' she continued, ''we Blackthornes have little left to us but our good name. It is that name, literally, that my grandson banks upon. The way we handle this notoriety will have a great effect upon any success Quinton and I are to have in reaching our goals.''

Hannah stared at the woman a moment longer. She wanted to be angry, to be filled with resentment over the woman's words, but she wasn't. Everything Lady Evelyn had said was true. The threadbare rugs and worn furniture bore mute testimony to how far the family's fortunes had fallen. Hannah, remembering the echo of pride in Quint's voice when he spoke of his home, began to understand for the first time the sense of ancestry and history the British invested in their houses.

"Lady Evelyn," Hannah said evenly, "I give you my word that I will do my best to behave in a way that will reflect favorably upon you and your grandson. As my aunt mentioned, I'm not unschooled in manners and comportment. However, if there is any area in which you feel I need instructions, I shall be most willing to receive them."

Her grandmother-in-law looked into Hannah's eyes for a long moment before nodding. "Thank you. We will talk more on the carriage ride to London."

Hannah glanced out the window at the scenery that moved by to the clopping rhythm of the two bay mares pulling the carriage. She fervently hoped Lady Evelyn's assurances that they were fast approaching London were correct. The rocking, jolting ride, along with the forced inactivity, had made her sore, stiff, and anxious to stretch her legs.

She had seen Quint only twice all day, and for just a few moments each time. He'd arrived back at Blackthorne Hall in time to oversee the final loading of the carriage. Then he had handed his grandmother and Aunt Amelia into the black conveyance. When Hannah stepped up to his side, he took her hand as well, then looked down into her eyes and gave her a brief smile before asking, "How are you this morning?"

Quint's words had sounded formal and stiff. The wide smile of greeting curving Hannah's lips faded as she blinked up at him, seeing once again a man in whose mind duty and family name were uppermost.

"Fine, thank you," she had answered in a small voice before stepping into the carriage and leaving him to mount Hippocrates and ride ahead.

She didn't see him again until noon. They stopped at a white half-timbered inn, nestled in the small village of Chillwickel, and Quint joined the three ladies for a lunch of shepherd's pie and ale. He was silent during most of the meal, with a decidedly distracted air about him. Once or twice he pulled a small notebook and pen from his breast pocket and jotted something in it before returning to his food.

Shortly after the third such occurrence, Hannah excused herself to walk out in the woods behind the tavern. Forcing her anger and disappointment down, she breathed deeply of the fresh moist air as she walked along a little path that led to a small stream.

The water ran clear, dashing over and around stones, the soft rushing sounds soothing Hannah's taut nerves. She sat on a large rock to watch the stream leap and swirl at her feet.

It was here that Quint found her. She didn't hear his footsteps, and when he placed a hand on her shoulder she gasped and jumped up in fright. Quint smiled down at her and spoke in a warm voice. "I'm sorry. I didn't mean to startle you."

Hannah straightened her shoulders. "That's all right. I probably shouldn't be tarrying here. It must be time to get back in the carriage."

Quint shook his head. "Not yet. Grandmother is still eating." He paused and his eyebrows slid into a slight scowl. "I want to apologize for my behavior at lunch. I should have been more sociable."

Hannah looked into his face and saw the tight vertical lines between eyes that looked tired and drawn. Remembering the late hour at which they'd fallen asleep the night before, and his grandmother's words regarding his business concerns, she felt a stab of guilt over her petty feelings of neglect.

"No. Don't apologize." She took his hand as she spoke. "Your grandmother explained you have much to do while we're in London."

"Yes." His frown deepened. "Since most of the men I

need to speak with will soon be returning to their country homes for the rest of the summer, I'll be quite busy. Hannah''—his fingers tightened around hers—''I have several meetings this afternoon and evening. I may be out very late, so I will understand if you cannot wait up for me.''

Hannah gazed up at him, then turned to stare into the stream. What did he mean? Was he saying he would prefer not to be expected to come to her bed at such a late hour? With so much to do, perhaps he felt he needed a good night's rest.

A deep ache filled her breast, but she forced herself to smile and looked back up at him. ''Let us see what the night brings.''

Quint looked into her eyes and smiled suddenly. Just as suddenly he lowered his lips to hers, took her into his arms, and drew her close as his mouth moved slowly over hers. When he released her, Hannah held on to his upper arms to keep from swaying and stared up at his grinning face. A smile of her own curved her lips, a smile that grew wider with anticipation as he bent toward her once more. However, before their lips could meet, the driver's voice calling for Lord and Lady Blackthorne echoed down the path, drawing them back to their journey.

Now, as the carriage rocked over the road, Hannah glanced out the window again, craning her neck to catch a glimpse of Quint riding ahead on his steel gray horse, but she could see nothing.

An hour later, when the carriage clattered to a stop in front of the Blackthorne's town house in Mayfair, she learned that Quint had arrived earlier, changed his clothes, and taken a hansom cab to his first appointment.

Hannah stood next to Lady Evelyn and gazed around the high-ceilinged vestibule, noting the richly carved moldings and the impressive sweep of stairs that curved gently upward. The stairway was of rich, warm oak, the banister smoothed and polished, the balusters carved and turned with superb craftsmanship.

Sensing someone behind her, she turned to smile at Barrows and allowed him to remove her cape as she studied the deep red pattern of the Aubusson carpet. When she looked up, she found Quint's grandmother smiling slightly.

"It's beautiful, isn't it? Would you like to see the rest of the house?"

Hannah nodded and turned a questioning eye to her aunt Amelia who also indicated she wanted to inspect her new surroundings.

The tapping of Lady Evelyn's cane was muffled by the thick carpets as she led Hannah and her aunt through the parlor, with its deep red sofa and matching wing chairs arranged before a brick fireplace with an ornate oak mantelpiece. By the large front window, two other comfortable-looking chairs sat on either side of a well-polished table holding a beaded lamp and a collection of small porcelain dogs. More ceramic animals were displayed on the shelves of the large glassed-in case standing in a corner next to a tall, leafy philodendron.

The large dining room was dominated by a long table draped in white linen beneath the gleaming crystal prisms of a sweeping chandelier. Various soft-hued paintings of flowers hung in gilt frames on the walls, and a huge breakfront all but filled the far wall.

Hannah got a quick glimpse into the white kitchen, enough to note neat shelves and sparkling clean counters. There Lady Evelyn introduced Hannah to the staff. They all smiled politely as their names were mentioned, and Hannah tried to commit each to memory as she followed the countess back to the vestibule.

"As you can see, we've managed to maintain this residence far better than Blackthorne Hall." Lady Evelyn spoke over her shoulder as she led the way up the curving stairway.

"This was not part of some great design." She smiled tightly. "It was just that Quinton's father spent most of his time in London and saw to it that his surroundings here were kept up to snuff. My son enjoyed entertaining very much and so robbed Blackthorne Hall of its best pieces so as to preserve appearances here."

Lady Evelyn turned abruptly and led Hannah and Amelia up the curved stairway, past the tall clock on the landing. The second floor contained a drawing room done in shades of pale green, Quint's study, and the room Lady Evelyn had shared with her husband. It now held a billiard table and several smaller tables meant for playing cards.

Hannah glanced away from the look of pain that crossed the woman's face at this silent reminder of the son who had thrown the family so deep in debt, and her eye fell on her aunt Amelia. She was frowning also, and Hannah noted that she looked paler than usual.

"Aunt Amelia, is something wrong?"

Her aunt glanced sharply at her niece, then smiled wanly. "I'm a bit tired. As Lady Evelyn mentioned earlier, the last days have been rather eventful. I think they're catching up with me."

Lady Evelyn immediately led them to Aunt Amelia's room on the third floor. Decorated in blue and cream, the room was at the far end of a dark-paneled hall. Hannah left her aunt in the competent hands of the maid, Sarah, and followed Lady Evelyn again, noticing that on this floor the draperies were beginning to show the same worn and faded patches she'd seen at Blackthorne Hall.

"This is the Rose Room," Lady Evelyn said as she opened the door. "I hope you will be comfortable in it. Quinton's room adjoins yours, and mine is right across the hall if you need me. Now"—she smiled tightly—"I, too, am fatigued. I plan to rest until dinner, which will be served at six."

With those words she crossed the hallway and entered her room. Hannah gazed around the room that would be hers for the duration of their stay in London. It was not nearly as large as the room at Blackthorne Hall, nor was it as brightly lit. Hannah crossed the deep rose-patterned carpet, with its design of cream-colored flowers and green leaves, to draw back the rose brocade draperies and stare out the window.

She had no view, for a scant four feet away was the outside wall of the brick house next door. If she tilted her head back and looked up, she could just make out a patch of blue sky between the roofs of the two houses.

With a sigh born of weariness and uncertainty, Hannah crossed the room to the wide bed with its mahogany headboard and bent to remove her boots in preparation for a nap. There was little else for her to do, since Lady Evelyn had told her the clothes that had arrived yesterday had already been unpacked. Besides, a sudden weariness had made her eyelids heavy. She let them close as she lay back on the cream-colored bedcover, remembering that Quint had said he would be out late tonight. Perhaps a short rest would help her stay awake until he came home.

Quint did not come home for dinner, and neither had he returned when Hannah once again retired to her bedroom at nine o'clock. She'd requested a bath and found the warm water waiting for her in a hip tub before the fire and little Liza waiting to attend her.

Hours later, sitting by the fire in the small cream-colored chair reading a book she'd borrowed from Quint's study, Hannah heard the clock chime midnight. She blinked, realizing she'd dozed off, and placed the book in her lap to stretch. As she closed the book and stared into the dying fire, she thought of Quint's words earlier that day. What *had* he meant? Had he desired that she wait up for him and been too reticent to ask? Or had that been his polite way of letting her know he wasn't up to a repeat of the night before?

Placing the book on a nearby table, Hannah rose and stepped over to the door that separated her room from Quint's. Hardly breathing, she leaned against the door and listened intently for some sound of motion. Hearing nothing, she straightened and glared at the door a moment. For all she knew, Quint could have entered while she dozed by the fire and might already be snoring in his bed.

Once again Hannah sighed. With a shake of her head, she crossed her soft carpet and drew back the covers on her bed, then went around to the bedside table and pulled out the candles her maid had provided. She fixed one long white taper into the candle holder, lit it, then reached up to turn the key in the lamp, reducing the light in the room to the dancing glow from the candle by her bed.

She removed the silken dressing gown and placed it over the edge of the bed, gazed down at the film of gray fabric that made up her long-sleeved nightdress, and sighed yet again as she slid beneath the covers. When she closed her eyes she reminded herself that she'd been warned that her husband had a busy schedule planned.

Quint entered the nearly dark entry hall and handed his hat and cloak to the waiting butler. "Thank you, Barrows, for waiting up. Has everyone else retired?"

Barrows nodded. Quint lifted his chin. " You are excused for the night. My apologies for the lateness of the hour."

Quint walked up the stairs slowly, a frown creasing his brow. He should not have gone to his club after his business dinner with Williamson. He'd stopped in only to check on a business acquaintance, but the news that the Duke of Ludmore had been found dead, with a bullet in his head, that very morning had kept him longer as he tried to clarify the facts.

Facts were sketchy, but rumor was rife. He heard from several men that the police inspectors suspected suicide. A gun known to have belonged to Ludmore was found beside his body, and several servants reported that the duke had been angry and despondent since returning from St. Albanswood two evenings before.

Quint recalled that Ludmore had attended neither the wedding nor the reception. He was aware that the duke had shown a marked interest in Hannah earlier, but he strongly doubted that a man like Ludmore would take his own life over a thwarted chance with a woman. Gossip had it that the duke had learned of yet another financial setback, and Quint wondered if he'd received this information before or after returning to London.

Quint shook away these thoughts as he reached the third floor. He paused before Hannah's door, staring at the raised panels lit by the gas globe on the wall in the center of the long hall. She had said she would wait up for him, but now it was well after midnight. Logic told him she must have gone to sleep long ago. Still, he couldn't keep his hand from straying to her doorknob, twisting it slowly, and pushing the door open.

Hannah lay curled in the center of the large bed. A small square table between the near wall and the bed held a white candle, and her sleeping face was lit by the flame as it waved and danced in the rush of air. As Quint watched the play of light and shadow on her delicate features, his lips tightened with disappointment. He released a deep sigh, then pulled the door shut with quick impatience and entered his own bedroom.

Jamison, his valet, rose and crossed the dark green carpet to help Quint shrug out of his jacket and waistcoat. He dismissed the servant and began loosening his tie as the grateful man left the room. Quint sat to remove his shoes and had just taken the second one off when he heard a loud crash from Hannah's room.

Quint dashed out of his room and down the short hallway to push her door open. Enough light filtered in from the hallway for him to see Hannah bent over the table that had fallen alongside her bed.

"What happened?" He kept his voice low as he rushed to her side and helped her right the piece of furniture. Hannah straightened with him and looked up through the shadows.

"I woke up to total darkness. My candle must have gone out, and in my panic to get the matches out of the table drawer, I upset the whole thing."

When Quint felt a shiver run through the small form next to him, he placed his arms around her. "I'm sorry. That was my fault."

"Yours?" Hannah's arms stole around his waist as she lifted her head to look at him.

Quint nodded. "I came in to check on you, and when I shut the door the draft must have blown your candle out."

"You just got home?" Hannah's voice was a low whisper.

Quint felt a shock of desire flow through him as he nodded again.

"I tried to wait for you." Hannah's voice was low and husky.

Quint's lips curled in a smile. "Thank you." His voice was just as low as he bent his head to hers and touched her lips with his.

The tender caress and the warmth in Quint's voice lit a hot, sensuous flame in Hannah's belly. Without thinking, she raised her hand to the back of Quint's neck, tunneling her long fingers into his thick hair as she pulled his head down, intensifying the contact of his lips upon hers.

Quint's mouth opened over hers; his tongue urged her

lips to part, then entered the moist warmth of her mouth. His hands moved over her, sliding up and down the gossamer material of her gown, till both of them were filled with longing.

Bunching the sheer material of her gown in his long fingers, Quint inched it upward till he could slip his hand beneath the fabric to cup the satin warmth of her softly molded bottom. Hannah gasped against his mouth and moved her hands to his half-opened shirt and began working at the remaining buttons.

An impatient desire quickened in Quint's veins. With one quick motion he pulled the gown up over Hannah's head, then stood staring down at her body shining pale and lush in the soft light from the door.

Quint frowned and looked up from her enticing form to stare at the open doorway. "Hannah." His voice was low. "Stay here. And don't be afraid."

Chapter 18

Hannah stood very still while Quint walked over to the open door. When it swung shut, leaving her in complete darkness, she blinked and drew a quick breath.

"Hannah." Quint's voice was a soft, warm anchor in the blackness. "Talk to me so I can find my way back to you."

"Quint, why don't I just light the candle?" She hesitated as she felt Quint reach her side. His warm hands bracketed her face and forced her head back slightly as she went on. "Then we could see what we're—"

Her words were cut off when Quint's mouth descended to hers, taking her lips with hungry pressure, sliding one hand down along her cheek to trail the length of her neck and chest, then close gently over her breast.

Hannah swayed against him, felt his clothing rough against her nakedness, and slid her hands up to finish unbuttoning his shirt. When her hands reached the waistband of his trousers, she hesitated a moment, then slowly began opening them with her long slender fingers, smiling as Quint lifted his lips from hers to gasp sharply.

He reached down, took Hannah's hands, and held them away from the throbbing desire that threatened to peak beneath her gentle touch. He stood there, jaw clenched for a moment, then forced a grin to his lips.

"My dear," he whispered, "I think you are doing quite well enough without seeing what you're doing."

Hannah blushed at the gruff chuckle in his voice, and when he released her hands she let them fall to her sides. She listened to the sound of clothes brushing against skin, acutely aware of Quint as he finished removing his shirt and pants, then sighed and smiled when he once more enfolded her in a tight embrace and pulled her to him.

Her arms encircled his neck as her lips searched for and found his, her body glowing with a feverish heat as she pressed herself to Quint's lean-muscled form. Suddenly all the strength seemed to drain from her legs, and she sank gladly onto the mattress when Quint pulled her onto the bed.

There, in the total darkness, she let her slender legs entwine with his. Hands explored, lips met, then met again, and with every moment Hannah felt the need his kisses and caresses awoke grow with frightening speed and intensity. She lay back willingly when Quint positioned himself over her, lifted her hips in anticipation, and whispered his name on a pleading breath.

Quint entered her slowly, filled her, then retreated. Hannah arched up to him, inviting him to repeat this action, and he obliged, moving more and more quickly in response to her whispered urgings and the demands of his raging need.

Hannah closed her eyes against the mingled pleasure and pressure building with each thrust. She bit her lip as the bed began to spin beneath her, strangling back a cry as she felt herself being drawn into a world of blinding physical release, and raised her hips higher to hold Quint deep inside her as the waves of pleasure pulsed through her.

Quint's arms tightened convulsively around Hannah as

the rhythmic throbbing brought his own pleasure to climax. He held her to him, whispering her name over and over as he poured himself into her, then continued to hold her as he relaxed against her, rolling them both to one side as his ragged breathing began to slow to a more even tempo.

Hannah took a deep, shaky breath as she adjusted herself to his embrace, shifting her head so that it rested on his shoulder. She opened her eyes to the blackness once more, but felt no fear. Her lips curved as she felt Quint pull the covers up over them, then let her eyes close again as her sated body drew her into sleep.

Quint was gone again when Hannah woke up. She frowned at the indentation in the pillow next to hers. When she sat up and looked to her right, she smiled slightly, for a lighted candle winked at her from its holder. Hannah shook her head as she gazed at it; it had only burned down an inch or so. A soft smile curved her lips as she realized that Quint must have spent most of the night with her. His grandmother had mentioned that he rose early. Apparently he'd lit the candle when he awoke, probably before dawn, and left it to burn lest she wake to darkness before the sun rose.

Hannah rose and threw her silver dressing gown on as she walked to the window and drew back the rose-colored draperies. Looking up, she saw thin wisps of clouds tinted shades of pale pink and yellow.

Dawn. A new day, a new world for her out there. She and her aunt had spent several days in London after arriving in England, shopping and obtaining a solicitor to correspond with the one handling her father's affairs in Boston, before contacting her uncle. She'd seen a little of the city, and now she knew she would be dealing with the most rarefied element of London society, a world apart from what she was accustomed to.

When her aunt informed Lady Evelyn that Hannah had

been out in society in Boston, Amelia had been telling the truth. What the woman had failed to mention was that these forays had been less than successful, despite Hannah's extensive training and the care she took to walk and speak as properly as any Boston Brahmin. It seemed that no matter how delightful people found Miss Hannah Bradley to be, or how well connected her great aunt was, they continued to believe that Hannah's life on the fair circuit with her father might have tainted her somehow, leaving her a less than desirable friend for their daughters and a major risk to have around their sons.

Hannah's lips twisted wryly as she moved from the window to the large mahogany wardrobe. Some of this was her own fault, for she had taken secret joy in telling stories of her youthful adventures to the younger men and women. She'd delighted in seeing their eyes widen with wonder as she described the excitement of tents being raised in the early morning, the smells of the various foods on sale, the jugglers and acrobats who'd tutored her, and of course the pure joy of free flight in her father's balloon above the kaleidoscopic colors of the fair.

Hannah gazed at her dresses, then reached in for a simple ivory muslin with a demure high collar of matching lace. She would tell no tales of those days here. When asked about her father, she would explain that he had traveled much and that she had spent most of her life quietly with her mother, then her aunt, in Boston. She would do her best to mold herself into an image that would fit her new title of Countess of Chadwick in the same way she would let her body be molded by the heavily boned and starched corset her grandmother-in-law insisted she wear.

The dining room was deserted when Hannah arrived, but tempting smells drew her to the array of silver-domed serving dishes on the large breakfront.

"Good morning, dear."

Aunt Amelia's cheery voice made Hannah turn from spooning food onto her plate to smile at her great-aunt.

"Good morning to you, Aunty. It looks as if the two of us are the early risers this morning. Did you sleep well?"

Her aunt nodded. "And you?"

Hannah nodded also and turned back to finish filling her plate to cover the warm blush she could feel rise to her face.

"I'm happy to hear that both of you find your accommodations satisfactory."

Lady Evelyn's sharp voice echoed from the doorway. Hannah bit her lower lip, aware that now her cheeks must be very pink as she glanced over her shoulder at the woman. She managed a very polite "Good morning, Your Ladyship. I trust you slept well also."

When the three women were seated a serving girl entered with a pot of tea.

When the servant had left, Lady Evelyn cleared her throat and spoke quietly. "Quinton gave me some very distressing news this morning before he went out. The Duke of Ludmore is dead." Hannah lifted her head to stare in shocked silence as the countess went on. "Apparently he killed himself shortly after returning to London. Quint only heard about this last evening, but the body was discovered yesterday morning."

Hannah shook her head in dazed wonder. "Why would he do such a thing?"

Lady Evelyn lifted her teacup. "I have no idea, and no desire to speculate on the matter. I leave that sort of thing to the gossips, who do it so very well."

The dowager countess took a sip of tea, then placed the cup back in the saucer and lifted her fork, putting an effective end to the discussion. Hannah turned her attention back to her own food, finding it suddenly tasteless as she recalled the last time she'd seen the duke, standing next to her uncle Charles and glaring at her with hard black eyes.

"I've given a great deal of thought as to how we should spend our day."

Lady Evelyn's words made Hannah glance up in surprise to find the woman looking at her over the rim of her cup. After taking a small sip of the steaming liquid, she returned the cup to its saucer and went on.

"I considered taking both of you on morning calls, but decided I don't wish to handle this situation in that manner. We shall wait for society to come to us. And it will, you can be sure, if for no other reason than that these people are insatiably curious. You will be introduced to quite a number of them at the Duke of Uxley's soiree tonight, of course, which should get things moving. And, since I have very definite ideas on how I want you to present yourself, we shall go shopping today. Quint mentioned that your wedding ring needs to be made smaller, so we shall see to that as well. Miss Bradley, you are welcome to accompany us, if you wish."

"No, thank you," Aunt Amelia replied.

Hannah turned to her aunt with a look of surprise and dismay. The last thing she wanted to do was spend a whole day alone with a woman who seemed to look upon her as nothing more than an inconvenience.

"I'm still feeling a little weary," Amelia explained. "Besides, as Hannah knows, shopping bores me."

Hannah didn't know anything of the sort. Though her aunt rarely shopped for herself, she'd always seemed to enjoy helping Hannah choose her clothes, and she had wonderful taste. Hannah stared at her aunt a moment, and when Amelia only smiled before turning her attention back to her food, Hannah let the matter lie.

An hour later, the coach carrying Hannah and Lady Evelyn drew to a clattering stop in front of a shop on Regent Street. Hannah let the footman hand her down, then stared at the curving bank of buildings that lined both sides of the avenue. The walks beneath the striped awnings were alive with fashionably dressed men in top hats and derbies and gracefully gowned women wearing wide brimmed hats and moving at a leisurely pace from store to store.

Hannah followed Quint's grandmother into a shop bearing the name of Madame Desjardin. As the door shut behind them, Hannah gazed at the most impressive array of finery she'd ever seen in one shop. She was so awed at the thought of actually buying something there that she forgot to resent the fact that the choice of item was not to be hers.

Quint walked into another building several blocks away. He'd spent much of the morning with the solicitor Aunt Amelia had engaged earlier, going over various forms and handing over Aunt Amelia's signed agreement to the settlement papers. Now it was time to present this to his banker.

Two rows of marble columns marched down the length of the bank. Quint strode along the green carpet running between them, went past the tellers at their windows, then entered the first office on his right. Johnson, the slender, dark-haired secretary, greeted Quint with a smile, then led him to a door inset with frosted glass and inscribed with a name: J. W. Bently, President.

Bently looked up from a neat pile of papers as Quint entered, and smiled as he rose to offer his hand. "Good to see you, Blackthorne. I understand you wish to have some funds transferred today."

"Yes, *into* my account, for once." Quint nodded as his lips twisted into a wry smile, a smile that faded as he shrugged. "It isn't as much as I had expected, of course. I had a change of plans."

Bently lifted one brow questioningly and Quint started to explain. "My betrothal to Cicely Summerfield has been broken, and—"

Quint stopped speaking when the banker held his hand

up. "No need to tell me," Bently said. "Lord Kendrick was in here earlier this morning. We had a long chat."

Quint nodded slowly. The two men sat down while Bently looked over the papers Quint presented him, nodding from time to time. Finally he placed them on the desk in front of him and looked at Quint.

"And you want all of this transferred to your account?"

Quint shook his head. "No, I have decided to keep some out for investment purposes."

"Oh? You've decided to take my advice on that shipping company I told you about?"

"Yes and no." Quint grinned. He and Bently had been doing business for several years, and Bently had more than once recommended a short-term investment that had paid off well. "Squire Summerfield has offered to let me join him in raising Herefords down in West Sussex. We both have fair grazing grounds available, and being neighbors, we can easily share breeding stock."

He paused and shrugged. "The squire seems determined to demonstrate that he harbors no ill will over what has happened, but it also sounds like a good opportunity for me."

Bently's brows dropped into a frown; then he glanced quickly down at the settlement papers, making Quint look at him more closely. "What's wrong, old friend?" Quint asked. "Have you heard something that might make you think this wouldn't be a wise investment?"

Bently lifted his eyes and gazed at Quint from under frowning brows for several moments before speaking slowly. "The squire is a very canny man, Blackthorne. I've never known him to involve himself in anything that isn't profitable. However, his associates in these arrangements are sometimes less than fortunate."

Quint frowned. "What are you saying?"

Bently shook his head and lifted his broad shoulders

slightly. "I'm not *saying* anything," he said. "Neither is the Duke of Ludmore."

Quint blinked in surprise as Bently stood abruptly and offered his hand. Quint stood also. As the men shook hands, Bently looked into Quint's eyes and spoke again. "If you are looking about for a partner, I suggest Lord Kendrick."

Quint was still puzzling over this last remark when he stepped out into the bright sun. Everyone knew Kendrick was indebted to an impossible degree. In fact Quint himself had overheard the earl discussing another loan with Squire Summerfield.

This thought almost caused Quint to stop walking in the middle of the street. Summerfield. The man was well known as a source of quick cash. More than one of Quint's fellow club members had taken advantage of the squire's largess when temporarily short of funds. He'd never heard of any problems there, but these men had borrowed only for short periods, not time after time, like Kendrick and others, including Ludmore.

The thought of Ludmore made Quint shiver. He straightened his shoulders and picked up his pace to keep his appointment with the decorator he'd hired to begin refurbishing Blackthorne Hall. He was going to have to make some changes in the plans the man had outlined, now that he had less money to work with.

As Quint walked down the street he mused over the fact that he did not feel at all upset by this turn of events. Then he smiled. After the last two nights in Hannah's arms, what man *could* be upset? Hannah's brand of warmth was worth far more than the kind provided by new carpets and draperies.

His hand strayed to his right breast pocket. He'd kept out fifty pounds to present to Hannah for pocket money. He'd never approved of wives being forced to beg their husbands for money, and he wanted her to have some to spend as she wished.

Quint's walk down Regent Street took him in the direction opposite to the dress shop, from which Hannah and his grandmother emerged behind a footman carrying several packages. The footman quickly stored the purchases in the boot of the carriage as Lady Evelyn led Hannah across the street to a small coffee house for a light lunch.

Hannah smiled as their tea was served, and glanced over at the woman. "Thank you."

Lady Evelyn looked up sharply. "For the clothes? You mustn't thank me. They are a necessary expense, and I'm quite aware that the styles I chose won't show you off to your best advantage. However, that's not what we are about right now."

Hannah lifted her chin slightly. "Exactly. I am to play the role of a meek and modest young woman, and those clothes will enhance my performance. Do you want me to act shy and reticent at tonight's party as well?"

As the old woman stared across at Hannah, a ghost of a smile teased the corners of her deeply lined mouth. "No," she shook her head slowly. "I don't want to take the charade that far, nor do I wish to strain your acting abilities. I will settle for quiet and reserved. Perhaps with just a touch of hauteur?"

Hannah smiled. "I think I can manage that."

During the meal Lady Evelyn coached Hannah on how to handle introductions and briefed her on the correct titles by which she should address marquesses, dukes, earls, viscounts, and their wives. The woman also filled Hannah in on little bits of gossip, and by the end of the meal both women were smiling.

The coachman had pulled the carriage around, and the footman helped Hannah and the dowager countess ascend.

The vehicle rattled down the street for several moments, then pulled to another stop. Hannah glanced out to see a large shop window full of glittering jewelry. Above the door hung a gilded sign: Messrs. Petrie and Yarrick, Jewelers.

The brass bell tinkled as the door closed, and the three occupants of the store looked up as Hannah and Lady Evelyn entered. Hannah blinked when she recognized her uncle Charles and her cousin Hartley standing at the counter in front of a small mustached man with a fringe of dark hair edging his bald pate.

"Cousin Hannah." Hartley lifted his eyebrows as he called out her name. "And Lady Evelyn. What brings you here today? Out spending Quinton's money?"

Hannah stiffened as she prepared to return a sharp retort, but Lady Evelyn spoke first. "My grandson purchased Hannah's wedding band here a few days past with the understanding that the size could be adjusted, if necessary, at no charge. Are you Mr. Yarrick?"

The small man behind the counter shook his head in a jerky manner. "No. I'm Petrie." He moved toward the door behind him as he spoke. "Let me get my partner. He'll be happy to—"

Mr. Petrie stopped speaking as he ran into a tall, lean man who stepped into the doorway from the back room. Hannah smiled at Petrie's comical reaction as he looked up open-mouthed at the roughly garbed man. Then her own mouth fell open as the stranger turned to stare at her and she found herself looking into a pair of pale, almost white, eyes.

It was the man from the dock in Calais, the one she had seen exchanging something with Pierre Bertrand. Hannah stared into his eyes and saw a look of dawning recognition, before he turned and disappeared into the room behind him. Hannah glanced at Mr. Petrie. He was staring at Hartley and the squire.

"Was that Mr. Yarrick?" Lady Evelyn's impatient question made Petrie twist around and shake his head. "No. He's not. He's . . . a delivery man. I'll be right back with Mr. Yarrick."

Hannah watched Petrie disappear through the door, and frowned as she turned to her uncle and cousin. "I've seen that man before," she said.

Hartley raised one thin eyebrow. "Petrie?"

"No, the other one. When Quint and I were in Calais I saw that man exchange something with a man who was suspected of being a jewel thief."

The squire looked at her quickly. "Are you certain Jarred was the man you saw? He's been working for Petrie and Yarrick for some time and is considered a most trusted employee. If you are going to accuse the man of consorting with thieves, I hope you are very certain of his identity."

Hannah was sure. She remembered that thin, long face perfectly and knew she could never mistake those pale, icy eyes. She started to tell her uncle this, but Lady Evelyn stepped to her side.

"Hannah." The dowager countess's sharp voice drew Hannah's gaze to the older woman. The gray-green eyes behind the silver frames were narrowed. "You *were* quite distracted that day. Besides, I think it best that you not discuss your *visit* to France."

Hannah opened her mouth to reply, but at that moment Mr. Petrie returned with his partner. She stood quietly while Mr. Yarrick held her small hand in his large, heavy one to measure her finger, but she waged an internal battle. She was certain she'd seen this Jarred person in Calais. However, she had no way of knowing what he and Pierre had given each other, and, she reminded herself, it was really none of her business.

After the stocky jeweler assured Lady Evelyn that the

ring would be ready the next afternoon, Hannah turned to follow the older woman to the door.

"Hannah." Her uncle's voice made her swivel back. He bowed slightly, then lifted one brow. "I suppose we shall see you at Uxley's. I trust you will enjoy your debut as the new Countess of Chadwick."

Chapter 19

The soft strains of the evening's first dance drifted up the wide marble stairs to where Squire Summerfield stood with his son.

"She looks very proper tonight," Hartley mused as he watched Hannah, wearing a gown of pale yellow, swirl around the room in the arms of her new husband. Quint, he noticed, held his head low, as if whispering to his bride.

"I was certain she would." The squire straightened his black tie. "She's a very attractive young woman, also a very emotional and strong-willed creature. There's bound to be trouble there sooner or later."

"Do you think the trouble will involve us? Jarred says he's certain Hannah did see him in Calais." Hartley's eyes narrowed as he glanced at his father. The squire shook his head.

"No. She won't see Jarred again, for one thing. Besides, what can she say? She saw two men exchange a couple of items. It could have been anything."

He turned to glare at his son. "Just see to it that Jarred and the two Frenchmen stay out of sight for awhile, and then leave things alone. None of this would have come about if you hadn't to tried interfere in the balloon race.''

Hartley's hands clenched into tight fists at his sides, and his throat tightened in his effort to keep his voice low. ''Before you begin telling me yet again that I can do nothing right, Father, let me remind you that it was *you* who told me I needed to win to keep Lord Kendrick happy.''

''And a sorry mess you've made of that, my boy. His Lordship has been very elusive these last few days. Fortunately he's too deep in debt to me to avoid me for long. Despite your bungling, there's still a chance of securing Lady Anne and the Kendrick title for you, unless her father decides to follow Ludmore's way out.''

Hartley gave his father a quick glance at the mention of the Duke of Ludmore. The squire glanced back with a lift of an eyebrow and a shrug. ''I certainly hope it won't come to that. Now, I have others to speak to. Put your time to good use tonight and woo Lady Anne while I see what I can do about her father.''

Hartley nodded. His father descended the stairs as the dance came to an end, but Hartley stood watching Quint lead his wife over to Lady Evelyn before joining a collection of gentlemen on the opposite side of the room.

Hartley's eyes narrowed as he stared at his cousin. She was a spoiler, just as his sister Carolyn had said. Hannah had been in England just over two weeks, and already the Summerfields' lives were turned upside down. He didn't know how his father managed to keep his temper with the girl. The squire had wanted to gain a hold over Blackthorne Hall ever since Hartley could remember. Now that Hannah had taken Cicely's place in Quinton's home, the chances of gaining that foothold were slim at best.

''Oh, there you are, my friend.''

Hartley jumped at the sound of a jovial voice and turned to see Parker Blackthorne standing on the step beneath him.

Hartley stared into his friend's hazel eyes for a moment before twisting his lips into a smile.

"Yes, here I am. And what are you doing up here with me? I rather expected to see you dancing with my sister, newly liberated as she is."

Parker shook his head, then smiled sheepishly. "I did ask for a dance, but her card was full already. Funny, being thrown over can ruin a girl's social position, but I guess the circumstances surrounding Cicely's situation have brought out the chivalry in our fellow bucks."

Hartley shook his head. "You'll lose her if you don't move soon, Parker. I know she cares for you."

Parker frowned as he watched Cicely move across the dance floor in the arms of yet another titled gentleman. "Perhaps, but she's a dutiful daughter, and knows what her father wants." Parker paused as he turned to Hartley. "As do you, my friend. You should hardly be encouraging me to make a move toward your sister. What would your father say?"

"He'd most likely kill me." Hartley grinned at his friend. "But I find my father's aspirations tedious in the extreme. Besides, Carolyn has already given him a little lord and lady with Summerfield blood, and once Lady Anne and I are married we will oblige him similarly."

He paused as he cast a sidelong look at his friend. "However, neither Carolyn nor I possess a heart. It doesn't matter to either of us whom we marry so long as we are comfortable. Cis is different. She was miserable when she thought she was going to marry Quint. She deserves some happiness."

"She deserves a husband with prospects."

Hartley shot a quick glance at Parker. The young man's habitual smile and easy manner were gone. A deep frown drew his reddish brows together as he stared down at the dance floor. "I'm completely without prospects," he went on, "except for your father's generous offer to buy me a commission in the navy. I suppose I should take it. It would be best for everyone if I were no longer around."

Hartley stared at Parker a moment. He didn't want him to go off to sea. Parker was the one true friend he had, the one person who looked up to him, who didn't find fault with everything as he did.

Hartley stared at the young man a moment as an idea began to take shape. "Forget the navy." Hartley spoke in a low voice. "And forget my father's needs. Think of your own needs. Think of Cicely's. Who knows? Something might come up, a change of luck, perhaps, that will clear the way for you."

Parker shook his head, laughing his cynical laugh. "Yes. Perhaps some relative I've never heard of will leave me a title and fortune."

Hartley's lips curled into a sly smile. "You only need the title. My sister will provide the fortune."

Several dances later, Parker was subjected to the same suggestions regarding Cicely when he danced with his new sister-in-law.

"Parker, I know Cicely cares for you deeply." Hannah looked up into his eyes. "But you must be aware that the squire is pressuring her. You're going to have to move quickly and probably do something drastic, or she will be married to someone else."

Parker shook his head and lifted his brows. "And most likely, very happily."

It was Hannah's turn to shake her head, and she did so vehemently. "No, she won't be happy. Listen, Parker, Cicely is in love with you. She told me so." At his quick look of surprise, Hannah spoke more urgently. "I have every reason to believe that if you were to show her your true feelings she would defy even her father to marry you.

And"—she paused, frowning— "I don't want to hear about money and titles. She doesn't care a fig about either of those things."

Parker glanced to one side just in time to see Cicely dance by in the arms of the recently widowed Viscount Marley, a gray and balding gentleman of some fifty years. Cicely's features looked as if they had been carved into a pleasant expression, one that lacked both life and joy. He frowned. "So what do you suggest we do, elope?"

"Yes." At Parker's sharp glance Hannah smiled and shrugged. "If you feel it is necessary. And it probably is in this situation. You are right in assuming that Uncle Charles isn't likely to give you his blessings."

Parker shook his head. "You don't know what you're suggesting, Hannah. No doubt eloping sounds quite romantic to you, but English society sees it as scandalous."

"So?" Hannah lifted her shoulders. "You won't have money and you won't have a title. A good scandal is better than nothing."

Parker stared at her for a long moment, then began to laugh, shaking his head as the dance came to an end. "Ah, I hope my brother realizes what a jewel he's found in you," he said quietly as he led her across the dance floor. "Quint needs someone to bring light and laughter into his life. I just hope he remembers what happened with Felicia, and gets his nose out of his ledgers long enough to notice the treasure beneath his nose."

Hannah glanced up at him quickly, remembering the story of Quint's first wife. Parker would have been seventeen at the time, with more in common with the young woman than her duty-bound husband.

Parker grinned at Hannah as he walked her over to his grandmother, and Hannah smiled back. No, Parker was not the type to steal another man's wife. Beneath his jovial facade was a man with as strong a sense of honor as his brother possessed. She only hoped that sense of honor didn't prevent him from finding the happiness he deserved.

"You seemed to enjoy your dance with Parker," Lady Evelyn said to Hannah after her grandson had left.

Hannah nodded. "He's a very nice young man."

"I suppose he is." The dowager sniffed. "But then, so was his father."

Hannah turned to the older woman, and after a quick glance to see that no one stood nearby, spoke in a low tone. "Lady Evelyn, it has been my experience that most people behave the way other people expect them to. Obviously you see him as taking after his father, so he obliges you by showing that part of him. I find Parker an honorable, intelligent man, capable of doing great things, should he so choose."

Lady Evelyn's eyes narrowed, and Hannah braced herself for a thorough set-down. She was saved, however, when Aunt Amelia joined them. The next hour and a half passed with torturous slowness for Hannah as she talked with her aunt and Quint's grandmother, danced several more times with various men, and did her best to be pleasant to the women to whom Lady Evelyn introduced her.

There was little doubt that these ladies approached her only out of curiosity, but after Hannah listened politely to their pointless gossip and the endless discussions of fashion, many of them seemed to thaw, and soon she had several invitations to come calling. Hannah noted the silent pleasure dancing in Lady Evelyn's dark eyes at this, but felt no sense of accomplishment or joy herself. She was beginning to feel the strain of watching every word she uttered and acting in a circumspect manner. She'd played the demure, retiring wife past the point of endurance, and she longed for Quint to claim her for one last dance, then take her home.

An hour earlier Quint had been planning to do just that as he watched his wife grin up at his brother while Parker twirled her around the dance floor. Quint had every intention of claiming Hannah's hand for the next set, when the Earl of Kendrick struck up a conversation.

"I want to congratulate you again on that magnificent bit of horseflesh you were riding the other day," Kendrick said. "Have you given any thought to racing him next season?"

Quint shook his head. "You know as well as I what kind of outlay that takes."

"I also know there won't be another three-year-old that will be able to beat Hippocrates at Epson next spring. I might be out of the racing game, but I keep an eye on it, and I think your horse deserves a chance to run." Kendrick stopped speaking as he rubbed the bald spot above his fringe of gray hair. "I'll tell you what," he said at last. "If you keep him in training, I'll pay the entry fees."

The surprise Quint felt at this suggestion must have shown clearly on his features, for Kendrick chuckled dryly. "You're wondering where I'm going to get the money. Well, I'll tell you. Last week I auctioned off a prime piece of land I'd been holding on to and sold the last of my late wife's jewelry. I went to the bank this morning and paid off all my debts."

The man paused to gaze through narrowed eyes across the room. Quint followed his gaze and caught sight of Squire Summerfield as Kendrick continued. "I have a few more markers to pay up tomorrow, and then I'll be in the clear, with a fair amount left to invest, over and above my living expenses. Bently is going to help me out there, but racing is hard to get out of the blood."

The man paused again and smiled up at Quint. "Hippocrates captured my fancy. If I ever saw a horse with the kind of heart it takes to be a winner, it's that horse. I don't know what you've heard about my circumstances, but let me assure you that my troubles had far less to do with the horses I picked to win than with the humans I chose to trust.''

Quint looked at the man for a long moment. "You are suggesting a partnership involving my horse."

Kendrick nodded. "Yes, and more, if things work out. I want to build a stable, but I'm too old to do it alone. If you have indeed inherited your father's knowledge of the animals, we could be very successful together. I'm not suggesting the money will be there immediately, but this is an investment a man can put his heart into."

Kendrick's words conjured up memories Quint had long ago shoved to the back of his mind. He could see the immaculate stalls, smell the mixture of horse and hay, feel the excitement of jockeys before a race.

"You don't need to answer me yet, Blackthorne," Kendrick said quietly. "Think on it. But if your horse is to run at Epson next spring, he needs to start training soon."

Kendrick's words continued to echo in Quint's mind a half-hour later as he handed his grandmother and his wife into the rented carriage. The clopping hooves of the horses drawing the vehicle away from the house teased his imagination.

"You and Kendrick were talking for a long time." His grandmother's sharp voice pierced Quint's reverie, and he looked over to her. Behind the wire frames of her spectacles, her gray-green eyes stared at him as he nodded. "You were discussing horses."

It was a statement, not a question. Quint raised one black eyebrow. "Your hearing is quite remarkable, Grandmother."

"Lady Foxworth overheard you. You aren't seriously thinking of racing that horse on a regular basis, are you?"

"I might be."

"Quinton, you can't have forgotten the state of our finances, or how they got that way."

"No, I haven't," he answered dryly. "I rarely think of anything else. I also haven't forgotten that Father never lost money on a horse he bought and trained. He frittered it away at the gaming tables and on young women."

Quinton frowned and reached across the carriage to take his grandmother's hand. "Believe me, I'm quite aware of our history, and I've no intention of following in my father's footsteps."

He fell silent after that and remained so the rest of the way home. No trace of anger appeared as he walked up the stairs behind the three women. He brushed a kiss on his grandmother's cheek as Aunt Amelia made for her door, then smiled and spoke softly to Hannah as he opened the door to her room.

"I'll be with you in a couple of moments," he whispered. "I have a surprise for you. Dismiss your maid for tonight. I'll perform her duties."

Hannah stood in front of the fire in her room, warming her hands before its dancing flames until Quint, wearing his green dressing gown, stepped through the connecting door and crossed over to stand behind her.

Hannah jumped slightly when his fingers touched her back, then relaxed as they began moving down the yellow silk to unfasten her buttons. "You know," he said in a low voice, "I think I should do this for you on a permanent basis. I figure I could save up to twenty pounds a year if I let Liza go."

Hannah smiled at the teasing words and shook her head. "You wouldn't put a hardworking girl out of a position. Besides, you leave before I get up in the morning. Someone has to tie my corset."

Quint finished with the last button and slowly pushed the gown down over Hannah's shoulders and let it fall to the floor in a crumpled yellow circle. His hands slid up her back until he found the tie to the corset she'd mentioned, and he chuckled. "Well, I must admit that's hardly to my liking. I much prefer removing your clothes."

Hannah felt a shiver of anticipation slip down the center of her. As soon as he untied the corset, she helped him remove it and the rest of her underthings. Finally, completely naked, she turned as Quint took her into his arms and drew her into a breathless kiss.

Several moments later, when he lifted his head, he spoke in a heavy, dusky voice. "Aren't you going to ask about the surprise I mentioned?"

Hannah blinked. "I thought you might be referring to this."

Quint grinned and shook his head as he placed one hand in the pocket of his dressing gown. "No, my dear, I was speaking of this." He drew out ten five-pound notes and held them fanned out like a hand of cards for her inspection. "This is yours, to use as you see fit."

Hannah looked at the money for a long moment. She understood the gesture and what had prompted it, but she didn't want money, especially when she thought of the worn draperies and carpets in both Blackthorne homes. What she wanted from Quint was time, time to talk, to stroll together beneath leafy trees so she could learn more about this man who was her husband.

Hannah lifted her eyes to Quint's. He smiled as he gazed down at her, his expression changing and his eyes darkening in a way that started Hannah's heart racing again. As he began to lower his head to hers she spoke quickly.

"That is very thoughtful of you. But I have no need of money. Your grandmother has spent far too much on me already. I know you need money to restore Blackthorne Hall, and just because my uncle made a sly suggestion about my position in your household is no reason for—"

Quint laid a finger lightly over Hannah's lips, stopping her mid-sentence. In a husky voice he told her, "I don't want to discuss my grandmother or your uncle at this point,'' then brushed his finger to one side as he lowered his head to capture her lips in a kiss that sent a flame of pleasure blazing through her, down to the very soles of her feet.

For Hannah, the next several days passed in a mixed blur of ecstasy and growing concern. Her days and evenings were spent on social calls, teas, and shopping trips in the company of Lady Evelyn. Aunt Amelia usually begged off, claiming she preferred to rest and read. It was Wednesday before Hannah had a chance to speak to her aunt in private, and then Amelia explained that she felt it best for Hannah to develop a relationship with Quint's grandmother.

''I suppose you're right,'' Hannah admitted. ''But at least when you're along, I don't feel that I'm the only woman in the gathering who doesn't find all the gossiping and sipping of tea a shocking waste of time.''

''I hope you aren't including Evelyn in that statement.''

Hannah looked up in surprise at her aunt's familiar use of the countess's given name, and at her defense of the woman. Amelia's wrinkles deepened as she smiled.

''Lady Evelyn and I have reached an understanding, now that she realizes how good you are for her grandson. I believe she's growing to care rather deeply about you, my girl. In fact, she mentioned to me this morning that she's concerned that you seem to be a little distracted.''

Hannah stared out the window as she mulled over these words. She had begun to sense Lady Evelyn's growing affection. She and the woman had spent many long hours together in the last several days, and though they never spoke of it, their mutual love for Quint drew them ever closer. Hannah only wished she'd spent one-tenth as much time with Quint as with his grandmother. Maybe then she would have some idea how he felt about her, other than as a bedmate.

''Quint never talks to me.'' Hannah spoke softly as she

gazed unseeingly through her aunt's window.

"Never? Now, that's a slight exaggeration, isn't it?"

Hannah turned to Aunt Amelia. "No, it isn't. He and I are never alone during the day. Our only daylight outing was a single ride together in Hyde Park. I was hoping I could chat quietly with him, learn a little more about what to expect once we return to Blackthorne Hall, but before we'd ridden a quarter of a mile, Lord Kendrick joined us. For the rest of the ride he and Quint discussed horses, racing, and stables. Then, the moment we got back to the town house, Quint excused himself and disappeared into his study."

"Your husband warned you that he would be very busy here, you know." Aunt Amelia's dark blue eyes rebuked Hannah softly as she looked up at the girl.

Hannah sighed. She knew very well how crowded Quint's schedule was. She had gone to his study more than once, hoping to find him with a free moment, only to be greeted by an empty room and a small red leather book crammed with scribbled appointment times.

"You do go out together each evening," Aunt Amelia said.

Hannah almost laughed. The evenings were even worse. She saw her husband for only a few moments at a time. As soon as they arrived at whatever function they were attending that night, someone would whisk Quint away, leaving Hannah with a group of women she hardly knew and with whom she had to watch her every word and action. She had been forced to bite her tongue so many times it was almost always sore.

Only after they were home and she was alone with Quint in her room did she feel free to express herself. But that expression was of a physical nature only, and as thoroughly wonderful as this was, she was growing frustrated as well as concerned.

"I don't know how to explain how I feel." Hannah paused as her throat tightened. "I can't help but contrast my marriage with that of my parents. They discussed everything when Papa was at home. He valued Mama's insight, and even when they disagreed, he respected her right to hold her own opinion." Hannah shook her head. "Quint has no more idea what I think or who I am than he did the day we met. I'm beginning to believe he still thinks of me as some wood nymph he's captured to fulfill his every fantasy, not a flesh-and-blood person with feelings and ideas."

Amelia looked into her niece's bleak eyes and reached out to take Hannah's hand. "I'm sorry. I didn't realize what a strain all this has been on you. You must love him very much."

Tears filled Hannah's eyes, tears she tried to blink back as she nodded. "I do." Her voice caught in her throat, so she took a deep, shaking breath before speaking again, forcing a smile to her trembling lips. "I guess I'm truly my mother's daughter. She once told me she fell in love with Papa the moment she met him. Of course, Papa fell in love with her just as quickly. I guess it's too much to hope that I would be as lucky as she." Hannah turned to her aunt with a shrug. "I suppose it would help if I'd inherited some of Mama's patience."

Amelia grinned and shook her head. "I'm afraid you are more like your father in that respect. I can remember him tapping his toe in annoyance when he thought the sun was taking too long to rise." She chuckled as she watched Hannah laugh quietly and brush the tears from her eyes, then spoke softly. "Hannah, perhaps you should explain your feelings to your husband."

Hannah's jaw tightened as she shook her head. "I can't. I want to know how he truly feels about me. With Quint's sense of duty, I'm afraid if I come out and ask, he will tell me he cares because he believes it the proper thing to do."

Tears welled up in her eyes again. "That's the last thing I want to be to him."

Amelia took her niece's hand. "You don't have to confide your love for him, but you should explain that you need to be part of his life, more than just an ornament on his arm."

That evening Hannah thought of her aunt's words as she sat in the box next to Quint listening to the first act of Wagner's *Die Meistersinger*. She had hoped to get Quint to talk with her on the ride to the opera house, since his grandmother had accepted another engagement this evening, but she'd been able to accomplish nothing.

The hollow clopping of the horse drawing the hired carriage through London had filled the silence. Quint sat next to her, his shoulder touching hers, but it was obvious that his thoughts were elsewhere. He had greeted her with a perfunctory nod, his eyes barely skimming the low neckline of her mauve silk gown. Hannah had tried to speak with him a few times, but he'd only responded to her conversational gambits with a brief nod or a distracted remark.

Now, glancing at him from time to time, she saw from his blank stare that he was no more interested in what was transpiring on the stage than she was.

At the opera's end, she and Quint descended to mingle briefly with the glittering crowd in their silks and chiffons, nodding to someone here, stopping for a few words there, but always moving toward the door until they stepped out into the thick fog that had descended during the opera, turning the July night cold and damp. Quint signaled for their carriage, and Hannah turned to watch it come into sight. The driver's features were obscured by a black cap and matching muffler worn so high across his face that Hannah was amazed he could see to maneuver the horses down the street.

Quint handed Hannah into the carriage, then joined her. With a jingle of the reins, the vehicle lurched forward.

Hannah felt Quint's hand close over hers and turned to find
him looking at her closely.

"I must apologize," he said.

Hannah tilted her head to one side. "For what?"

"For my boorish behavior this evening. I'm afraid my
mind has been on other things."

Hannah smiled and lifted her brows. "I'd noticed."
When his frown began to deepen, she laughed. "What was
I to say? 'Oh, Your Lordship, it is I who should apologize,
for being such a little chatterbox'?"

Quint's slow smile twisted across his lips and his eyes
narrowed. "Am I in for a wifely scold?"

"Perhaps." Hannah glanced up at him. Her heart was
beating quickly. Maybe her fears had been unfounded,
maybe it was just the press of business that kept him from
her except for the time they spent in her bed. "This is, after
all, the first time we've been out, just the two of us, since
we returned from France," she said.

Quint's smile stiffened. He'd had a very trying day. Not
only had he barely escaped being run over as he crossed
Curzon Street that morning, but this was the third time today
that someone had hinted he was neglecting his bride.

The sun hadn't finished rising when his grandmother appeared in his study and said she was pleased that her in-
vitation to the Bankmores' that evening would give him
some private time with Hannah. Then, later, he'd met Parker
at their club, where his younger brother stayed while in
London. Again Hannah's name had come up, but Parker
wasn't at all subtle. He came right out and warned Quint
not to make the same mistake with Hannah that he'd made
with Felicia.

The carriage took a sharp turn as Quint scowled at Hannah. "We've been alone," he said. "Unless you have someone secreted in your room at night whom you haven't told
me about."

Hannah shook her head gently, determined to keep the conversation light. "Of course not. But we hardly have time to talk then, do we?"

"You would rather talk?"

"No, not then. But at some time during the day I would like to carry on some conversation with my husband."

Despite Hannah's best intentions, a touch of impatience had crept into her voice. She knew Quint had heard it, because he sat up a little straighter before he replied. "Hannah, I thought I had explained to you that I would be very busy while we are here." His voice held barely checked impatience. "As it is, there aren't enough hours to accomplish all I need to."

Hannah's hands tightened in her lap and she spoke quietly, carefully controlling her tone of voice. "I do understand, Quint. But I feel very left out of your life. Perhaps if we talked a little each night before . . ."

Her voice trailed off as Quint turned away from her. She stared at him, gazing out the window into the London blackness, and slowly a deep anger tightened all her muscles.

"Excuse me, Your Lordship." Hannah spoke very quietly, her voice hard. "I didn't mean that you should explain your transactions to a mere woman. Perhaps when we return to Blackthorne Hall, you would prefer to take me back to the woods where you found me and exchange me for a more docile nymph."

Quint twisted back to her. Hannah looked up at him, but could not see his face clearly. "Hannah," he said, "I—"

His words were cut off by a surprised grunt as the carriage jerked to a sudden stop. Both of them were thrown forward. Hannah braced herself on the opposite seat and pushed herself upright, but by the time she'd regained her seat, Quint had already righted himself and thrown the door open.

"What the devil is going on here?" he demanded as he leapt to the ground.

" 'Tis a small matter of larceny," a deep voice replied. "Please hand over all your valuables or I shall be forced to shoot both you and the young lady."

Chapter 20

"Ah, our esteemed driver." Quint's words echoed with a sarcastic chill. "Well, this is an interesting scheme, waylaying unsuspecting opera patrons after a performance. Your ingenuity is to be commended." He paused as he released his hold on the carriage and moved away from it. "However, I'm afraid I must disappoint you this evening. I have but ten pounds on my person, and my wife carries no money at all."

"Who said anything about money? I believe I used the word 'valuables.' Do you perhaps have a watch?"

Hannah felt as if her body were frozen to the leather seat. She hadn't moved a muscle since the voice first called out, but had kept her eyes focused on Quint as she listened to the man's harsh, muffled voice.

"Of course," Quint said, "and a pair of gold cuff links."

"Well, hand them over, then."

There was an undertone of arrogance in the man's voice that seemed out of place for a thief. Hannah's fingers tightened in concentration as she listened intently for his next words.

"And then please see that your lady steps forth. She may

have no money, but I'm certain she has something of value."

These words made Hannah look up quickly. Quint extended his arm and opened his hand to reveal three shining objects, one large and two small. A gloved hand snatched them up.

"Fine, now your wife."

Quint shook his head. "My wife stays in the carriage. She can hand me her jewelry and I'll give it to you."

"No. She gets out. Now."

When Hannah saw Quint open his mouth, she forced her muscles to propel her toward the open door. Before her husband could say a word, she looked out, ignoring Quint as she glanced around quickly for the man with the muffled voice.

The carriage had been pulled into a narrow alleyway. Tall buildings rose on either side, and a brick wall loomed in front of the horse, blocking any chance of escape in that direction. The dim light from the carriage lamps revealed that the muffled figure in black had backed up to stand near the horse's flanks.

He was of medium height, dressed in a black jacket and trousers with a black cap obscuring the color of his hair. The lower part of his face was still hidden by the muffler and his eyes were narrowed as he aimed a shiny black revolver at Hannah.

Her lips curved in a tight smile. "Good evening, sir." She paused as she leapt lightly to the ground, then reached for the clasp of her cape. "As my husband told you, I have no money, and as for jewelry "—she let her gray cape fall open, revealing her mother's single strand of pearls— "this is the extent of it."

"Take it off."

A quick shiver slithered down Hannah's back at the undisguised menace in the man's voice, and just as quickly her jaw stiffened. She saw the glint of satisfaction in the man's eyes and knew he sensed her fear. With deliberate slowness she reached up and back to undo the stiff clasp and take the necklace off, gazing at him levelly the entire time.

"Here." She stretched forth her hand, dangling the string of pearls by the silver clasp. "Take it and be off."

The man stepped forward, and once more his gloved hand shot out. Hannah was left holding nothing more substantial than air as he stepped back and lifted his gun.

"Oh, I'll be off. But first I have some further business—"

"Hey, now, wot's goin' on 'ere?" A husky voice rang down the alley to break into the thief's words. The man's head jerked as he peered past Hannah and the rear of the carriage. The voice echoed again. "I say, who's there?"

No one spoke, but Hannah noticed that the man had taken two steps back, toward the brick wall behind him.

"Hey, now," the voice seemed closer. "This is Officer Bostiwick of the Metropolitan Police. No one's to be in this 'ere alley. Now, answer—"

The rest of his words were lost in the sound of scuffling feet as the robber turned and raced for the wall. As Hannah watched his shadow scramble to the top, a smile formed on her lips, a smile that froze when she saw the man straddle the fence, turn, and raise a straight arm.

"Quint!" she shouted just as a shot rang out. A whistling sound near her left ear made her jump away from Quint; then another shot echoed in the night. Hannah hit the cobblestone pavement with a gasp, then gasped again as she saw Quint stagger and fall backwards.

Heedless of danger, Hannah scrambled to her feet and hurried to where her husband lay on his side, quiet and still. Hannah held her breath as she touched his shoulder and gently rolled him onto his back. His eyes were closed, but she could see no sign of a wound of any kind.

A sharp sound from the wall made Hannah turn in fear, but the light from the carriage lamp revealed that the lean figure had made his escape. A deep moan brought her attention back to Quint. She released a relieved sigh when she saw his eyes flutter open and his right hand cross his body to clutch his shoulder, white against the black of his jacket. Then, as she stared, she saw two dark lines spread down from the spaces between his fingers to form two meandering lines over the back of his hand.

"Oh, Quint, you've been shot."

"Yes, it seems so."

Another wave of relief washed over her at the wry tone of his voice. She leaned closer to him. "Does it hurt badly? Can you sit up?"

When he nodded, she assisted him into a seated position. Still clutching his shoulder, Quint glanced at the wall, then back at Hannah.

"The policeman, is he following the thief?"

Hannah shook her head.

"Well, why the bloody hell not?" Hannah blinked in surprise at his sudden loss of decorum. "My God, the bugger was going to kill us. Where is that fool officer?"

"There is no policeman, Quint. There never was one."

Quint paused in his attempt to get to his feet and glanced sharply at Hannah. "What do you mean? I heard him."

"No." She shook her head. "You heard me."

"You? Don't be ridiculous. It was a man's voice, and it came from the other side of the carriage."

"No," a husky voice answered. Quint glanced at the interior of the carriage where the voice seemed to originate. "It was only me." This time the voice seemed to come from Hannah, but her mouth was closed. "A little trick I learned many years ago from a kindly ventriloquist," she said with a smile.

Quint stared at Hannah a moment. ''Really? It was you?''

Hannah nodded. ''Yes. I'll be glad to tell you how I learned to do this, but I think we need to get you to a doctor first.''

''No.'' Quint shook his head. ''I want to go home.''

When Hannah opened her mouth to protest, he shook his head impatiently. ''The explanation for my decision will have to wait also. But if it will make you worry less, I don't think the bullet lodged in my arm, just grazed it. Now, do my wife's accomplishments include the ability to drive a carriage?''

Hannah smiled and nodded.

Barrows let them in when they arrived at the town house, and kept an admirably implacable countenance when he saw the blood staining the hand Quint held to his shoulder.

''Has my grandmother retired?'' Quint asked as the door was closed behind them.

''Yes, sir.''

''Good. You are to say nothing to her about this.'' Quint began mounting the stairs, with Hannah at his side. He spoke over his shoulder to the butler. ''You may retire yourself now. My wife will see to my needs. Please send a footman to the company we rented the carriage from. Tell them the driver abandoned us and they can retrieve the coach from in front of our residence.''

Hannah didn't say a word as she followed Quint up the stairs, down the hall, and into his room. He gave her a small smile as she entered behind him, then turned to his valet.

''Thank you for waiting up for me, Jamison. However, I will not be needing your services tonight.''

The man blinked in surprise, but Quint's scowl apparently kept the servant from questioning his master. With a small bow and one sharp look at Hannah, Jamison took his leave, closing the door softly behind him.

"Help me get these things off, won't you, love?"

The endearment, spoken in such an offhand manner, somehow touched Hannah deeply and she found herself fighting tears as she gently stripped off Quint's bloody jacket, waistcoat, and shirt. When Quint turned toward her, she clenched her jaw tightly to keep from crying out as she stared at the jagged, bloody line creasing the front of his shoulder and part of his chest.

"I suppose you mean for me to bandage that."

Hannah's voice shook and Quint's scowl deepened. "I would appreciate it, unless you feel it will make you ill. I can ring for Jamison and—"

"No." Hannah interrupted him with a shake of her head. "I can see to it. Lie on the bed, please."

Quint sat on the edge of his large postered bed while Hannah removed several towels from the washstand.

"We need hot water," she said matter-of-factly. "I want you to lie quietly and hold one of these towels tightly to the wound while I go downstairs and heat some."

She turned as she reached the door. "And yes, the list of my talents does include lighting a stove."

An hour later a very pale Quinton Blackthorne lay back against his pillow and sighed softly. Hannah frowned at the thick white bandage as she drew the covers over him, then sat on the edge of the bed and gazed into her husband's heavy-lidded eyes.

"You were lucky, you know. The bullet just gouged your skin a bit as it went by, so you should recover quite nicely, though you can expect a great deal of pain and stiffness for several days. Now, I want to know why we could not call a doctor about this."

Quint's sigh was louder and deeper this time. "Because if we called in a doctor, the story would get out, and we'd once again be the main topic of conversation in London.''

Hannah gazed at him a moment, then shook her head. ''Quint, I must tell you I am weary of all this concern about what these people think about me. As far as I'm concerned—''

''Hannah,'' Quint broke in. There was a weary note to his voice, which increased as he went on. ''My reasons this time have nothing to do with the 'scandal' of our sudden wedding.'' He gazed blankly up at the ceiling. ''I've decided that Summerfield is right: breeding Herefords will be profitable. However, I don't want to borrow money from him to get started, nor will I become his partner. I'm trying to secure backing from Albert Smithers, a man so conservative that any kind of notoriety at this point could make him reconsider lending me the funds.''

Hannah frowned. ''I received the impression the other day that you and Kendrick were planning to join forces to breed and train horses.''

Quint sighed and shook his head. ''I'm afraid I'll have to disappoint the man. Raising horses is a gamble, no matter how much knowledge and experience the two of us bring to it.''

''You didn't seem to feel that way when we were riding in Hyde Park. Don't you think you'd fare better if you invested in something you really cared about?''

Quint narrowed his eyes as he looked into hers. ''Money doesn't have emotions, Hannah.''

''No.'' Hannah shook her head. ''But people do. And I believe that our deepest feelings tell us the right things to do, what choices to make. Not everything in life responds to logic, Quint.''

Quint looked into her eyes a long moment. Then his eyelids drooped wearily. ''Try convincing my grandmother of that.'' His eyes closed completely, then opened with a start. ''Now it's your turn to explain.'' His voice was stronger. "I want to hear how you learned to make your voice come from an empty carriage."

Hannah smiled into his heavy-lidded eyes. "It's a very simple story, really. I've told you before that I accompanied my father on several circuits of fairs and such."

She paused and Quint nodded. Hannah glanced across the nearly dark room, picturing an old man on a chair in the bed of an open wagon set up like a stage, with a black curtain behind him. On his knee sat a doll the size of a three-year-old child.

"We met William Cornblum and Willy in Omaha the summer I was ten. Willy was a dummy." She glanced at Quint. "A large wooden doll with a mouth that can be made to move."

Quint nodded. "I've been to the music halls. I know what you mean. William spoke for Willy."

Hannah shifted her eyes to gaze back into the shadows, smiling slightly. "Right. But William was a master at throwing his voice. I was utterly fascinated by this, and so was my father. The two men struck up a conversation, and before I knew it they'd arranged for William and Willy to travel with us." Hannah's smile widened. "I took turns, riding with my father one day and with William the next. To make the time go faster on the road, William taught me first to change my voice, then to make it seem to come from other places."

A sigh whistled past Hannah's lips after she stopped talking. "Funny, I never thought that particular talent would be of any use."

Hannah glanced down at Quint to gauge his response to her story, then smiled softly. His eyes were closed completely, and beneath the blanket his chest rose and fell in slow, even breaths.

* * *

Hannah rose early the next morning and hurried to Quint's room to check on him. The room was empty, the bloody clothes and towels gone, and his bed remade. Shaking her head, Hannah went back to her chamber to dress, then joined Lady Evelyn and Aunt Amelia for breakfast.

"I was most distressed to hear of Quint's close call."

Lady Evelyn's words made Hannah pause and glance at the woman as she lifted a forkful of ham to her mouth. "He told you about it?"

"No, Lady Wixtrome informed me of it last night at the Bankmores'. She was walking down Curzon Street with her daughter yesterday and had just spied Quint step into the street several yards in front of them when four horses pulling a wagon thundered by. Apparently it just missed running Quint down, before turning down a side street and disappearing."

That evening as Hannah and Quint waited for his grandmother to join them so they could depart for the ballet, Hannah turned to ask him about this, but he shrugged the incident off. "That sort of thing happens all the time. Traffic in London is abominable."

Hannah raised her eyebrows, infuriated by his cool reply. "I suppose everyone who's almost run over in the morning is also a robbery victim that night."

"Hannah, the crime rate in London is worse than the traffic. No more discussion of these matters, please." He spoke softly. "I don't want my grandmother to know about last night's skirmish any more than I wish for word of it to reach Albert Smithers. It's all best forgotten."

But Hannah found it very difficult to forget the events of the evening before, even as she watched the dancers leap and pirouette across the stage. She couldn't control the shiver that shook through her as she remembered the fear gripping her when Quint reeled from the shot. And from time to time when she glanced at him, she could see him wince as he moved his shoulder, and knew he was remembering, too.

When she went downstairs during intermission, she bumped into her cousins. Cicely embraced Hannah warmly, but Hartley turned away stiffly and made for the opposite side of the lobby.

"He's a little upset tonight," Cicely explained as she watched her brother walk away. "He just learned that Lady Anne left for the country yesterday."

"I'm sorry to hear that." Hannah forced the polite lie to her lips. The news was a great relief to her. Lady Anne deserved someone who would marry her for her beautiful brown eyes and her sense of humor rather than for her title. "I gather from the cold look in your brother's eyes that he holds me to blame for this."

Cicely sighed. "Yes. But don't worry; his anger will blow away."

Hannah smiled weakly, then turned back to Cicely and noticed the pink glow in her cousin's cheeks and the bright glint in her blue eyes. "Cicely, are you keeping secrets from me again?"

"What do you mean?" Cicely spoke with an exaggerated air of innocence.

Hannah's eyes narrowed. "I mean the happiness I see fairly radiating from you. Has something happened that I should know about? Something to do with a new relative of mine, perhaps?"

The soft pink glow in Cicely's cheeks deepened to a rose-colored blush, but before she could answer, Lady Winslow stepped up to exclaim over their dresses. By the time the woman left, the ballet was about to resume and Hannah had to return to her box, her curiosity unsatisfied.

Quint didn't come to Hannah's room that night. She lay in the dim flicker of the candle, staring up at the cream-colored ceiling, and told herself this was probably because his shoulder was hurting him. Still, she kept recalling the two aborted arguments she'd led him into in as many days. Men didn't like women who disagreed with them, she'd been told at Madame Lavoisier's.

Last night, in discussing Quint's decision against starting a stable, their basic differences had again become glaringly apparent. Hannah sighed. She wasn't handling this at all well; the situation was going from bad to worse. At least before, she could find comfort in Quint's warm arms at the end of the day.

Hannah hurried out of bed the next morning, donned a simple morning gown, twisted her hair loosely atop her head, and went searching for her husband. She lifted her shoulders in an acquiescent shrug when she found his bedroom empty, then rushed down the stairs to his study, asking herself all the while just what it was she wanted to say to him.

There was no one in the study either. The brown velvet curtains had been drawn to one side and dim light fell on the appointment book in the center of his oak desk. Hannah opened it to see one notation after another under the day's date without any break, another day of frustration mocking Hannah's determination to speak to her husband.

That evening as the carriage was brought around, Hannah stood next to Lady Evelyn gazing dispiritedly at her ice blue dress. It didn't suit her at all. The neckline was a simple wide V trimmed with matching blue lace that also formed the sleeves, which ended just above her long white gloves. When she'd glanced into the mirror earlier, she'd noticed that the fitted bodice nipped in at her waist then curved over her hips nicely before flowing to the floor. But the color and style were more suited to Cicely's pale beauty. Not that it mattered. She doubted Quint would give this dress any more notice than he had any of the others she'd worn in the last week.

"Well, I shouldn't say it," Lady Evelyn remarked as she adjusted the black silk shawl around her shoulders, "but I am more than happy to see this week come to an end. I should be looking forward to the prince's ball, but I'm weary and I'll be very glad to get back to the country."

She gave Hannah a sly smile. "If you were to ask most of the people at the party tonight, many of them would confess to sharing my sentiments. That is, if they were honest, which of course, few are. Everyone seems so very excited to see a new Season start each spring, and equally, if secretly, happy to see it come to an end in July."

Hannah tried to return the countess's smile, but tonight her spirits were at their lowest ebb. Not only had she been frustrated in her attempts to speak with Quint earlier in the day, but she'd just learned that he would be changing at his club and would meet them at the ball.

She told herself she ought to be excited at the prospect of attending a ball at Marlborough House as a guest of Prince Edward, but she saw it as only another occasion where she must stand mute at Lady Evelyn's side, pretending interest in boring conversations, or dancing with partners whose ineptitude on the dance floor was matched only by their incompetence as conversationalists.

This assembly of people was far more impressive than any of the others Hannah had attended. Women wore gowns decorated with seed pearls, and tiaras glittered atop several heads. All the men wore cutaway coats. Diamond studs sparkled on shirtfronts and cuffs, while many a lapel were decorated with the glint of gold.

Quint arrived shortly after his wife and grandmother and did Hannah the honor of claiming the first dance of the evening. Several times as they moved across the floor she observed a quick tightening of his facial muscles. Finally she frowned and asked softly, "Is your wound causing you some pain?"

"A little," he replied through smiling lips, keeping his gaze above her head.

"Have you at least cleaned it again?"

Hannah's voice was a little sharper than she'd intended. Quint glanced down with a frown. "Yes. Jamison saw to changing the dressing. I didn't think you would want to go through that again."

"Oh?" Hannah found that she was suddenly and unaccountably furious with this man who so coolly dismissed any concern she might have for his welfare. "That's a very interesting assumption. I suppose a 'proper' wife, one with the correct sensibilities, would be expected to shrink away from such things. I beg your forgiveness for exposing my lack of sensibilities in my concern for you."

The music came to an end at the same moment as Hannah's speech. She stepped quickly out of Quint's arms and turned to leave. His fingers around her wrist spun her back to face his tight features. His eyes shone with a deep green glint as he leaned toward her to speak in a low voice.

"I have no idea what you're angry about, Hannah, but I have no intention of discussing it here. We'll speak when we get back to Blackthorne Hall."

As Hannah let him escort her to Lady Evelyn's side, she scoffed inwardly. She and Quint wouldn't speak when they returned to Blackthorne Hall, unless he was referring to the urgent, pleading whispers that escaped their lips as their bodies communicated. Between his duties to his tenants and his plans to raise cattle, she'd be lucky if she caught a glimpse of him at meals.

Hannah moved over to the long table at the end of the room searching for a drink of punch. Instead, she found her cousin Cicely standing next to Parker. Hannah's frustration melted away as she embraced them both.

"Parker, where have you been keeping yourself?" she asked. "I thought I could expect you to come by and cheer me up."

Parker gave Hannah a crooked grin. "Has my brother buried himself in his work already? I'll have to have another talk with him about that."

"Well, you'll have to track him down wherever it is he goes when he's at Blackthorne Hall. I'm told we leave tomorrow."

"Oh, really?" Cicely's voice lifted slightly. "Would you do me a favor, then?" Hannah turned to her cousin. Cicely was blushing deeply. "I . . . won't be home for another week. The Reverend Mr. Smythe was expecting me to start teaching a Bible class on Monday. Would you please tell him I'll have to put it off for a few days?"

Hannah nodded as she stared at the bright glint in Cicely's eyes. The young woman's lips quirked into a half-smile, and she excused herself abruptly. "I have to get back to Father. Good-bye, Hannah." Her blue eyes lifted. "Good night, Parker."

"Good night," Hannah murmured. She watched her cousin's pale gold skirt sway as Cicely walked away, then turned to find that Parker had left her as well. When she spied him across the floor talking to Quint, Hannah shrugged and turned to the refreshment table for a cup of punch.

Parker cleared his throat as he reached his brother's side. "Well, Quint. You and Grandmother are quite a pair, you know that?"

Parker's mocking words made Quint turn quickly and stare into his brother's hazel eyes. "Have you been drinking again, Parker?"

"No. I've been talking to your wife. Are you the least bit aware of how unhappy she is?"

''My wife is none of your business.'' Quint's brows lowered to a deep scowl.

Parker stiffened. ''That's what you told me when I warned you that Felicia was miserable.'' When Quint's eyes narrowed, Parker shook his head. ''Look, Quint, I've told you before, Felicia and I were friends. Hannah is my friend, too.''

Parker glanced away for a moment, staring at a group of people all of whom were trying to speak to their host, the prince. When he looked back into Quint's frowning eyes, Parker's features were open, vulnerable. ''I know what it's like to be placed in a pigeonhole and forgotten. I hate to see that happen to someone else.''

Quint's scowl eased as he gazed into his brother's eyes. ''Is that what Grandmother and I have done to you?''

Parker lifted his chin, his lips taut. ''Essentially.''

''I'm sorry. I—''

''Don't apologize. I've had a comfortable life. From time to time I'd like a chance to prove I'm capable of greater accomplishments than playing billiards and racing balloons, but I really can't complain.'' Parker glanced down at his feet, then back up to Quint's eyes. ''Don't worry about me. Worry about Hannah.''

Before Quint could reply, Parker pivoted and walked quickly away, to disappear in the crowded room. Quint stared for a long moment at the spot where he'd last seen his brother, then gazed across the room to watch Hannah approach his grandmother.

After she had given Lady Evelyn her punch, Hannah felt a strange restlessness take root in her soul as she watched the portly, bearded prince circulate among his guests, his hearty laugh booming across the room. The joyous sound echoed in her mind as she faced her next dance partner, and she was barely aware that she'd begun to talk in a more animated fashion and was actually letting herself laugh out loud when the man made a comment that was honestly amusing.

She wasn't even nervous when, after that set, Prince Edward himself stood before her, acknowledging Lady Evelyn's introduction. Hannah didn't hesitate to accept his request for a dance, and when he mentioned he'd heard that her father was a balloonist and began asking questions, Hannah warmed to her receptive audience and told His Highness stories of her adventures in the air and on the ground with Matthew Bradley.

Hannah thoroughly enjoyed the prince's amazed response. At the end of the dance she continued to hold his rapt attention as he drew her into a corner. She never noticed the crowd that gathered around, until a woman gasped when she described what it was like to parachute out of a balloon.

It was then that Hannah turned to see the people encircling her and the Prince of Wales. She stared at their faces a moment until she felt her gaze inexorably drawn to the rear of the crowd where Quint stood, his face a blank mask.

"I'm sorry, Your Highness." Hannah managed a smile as she turned back to the prince. "I didn't mean to go on at such length."

The prince shook his head. "Pray, do not apologize. Your stories are marvelous. Have you met my friend, Miss Ellen Terry? She's an actress, you know, and she loves to hear about people like the ones you've described. She collects characters, as it were. Will you be in London next week?"

Hannah shook her head. "No, we leave for St. Albanswood tomorrow."

"Pity. She would so love meeting you. Perhaps next Season."

Hannah nodded as several women stepped forward, all commenting on her interesting life, all with an eye on the prince, until one caught his interest, leaving Hannah free to slip away.

Neither Quint nor his grandmother spoke on the way back to the town house. Lady Evelyn wore a small frown and looked at Hannah occasionally, but Quint sat stiff and silent, staring out the window. Hannah glanced at him from time to time, searching for some clue to the degree of his anger, but his face was completely still and empty of expression.

Hannah felt an answering emptiness within her breast, and when they reached the house, she walked swiftly up the stairs to her room, where she shut the door without a backward glance, then let the tears stream down her face, heedless of Liza's curious looks as she helped prepare her mistress for bed.

Chapter 21

Hannah's eyes ached from crying. She lay still in her bed, staring at the soft glow of the candle she'd lit, listening to footsteps ascend the staircase, then pause in the hall across from her room. She heard the murmur of two voices, first Quint's, then Lady Evelyn's.

It was the first time since entering her room that Hannah had been completely aware of anything outside her own misery. She had moved with dreamlike numbness while Liza helped her dress for bed, conscious only of the shameful tears burning behind her closed eyelids as she relived the evening, aware that in one night of indiscretion, she'd undone an entire week of playing at being proper and demure.

The moment Liza left the room, Hannah had fallen onto the bed and let her tears fall freely as she sobbed into the pillow. Knowing that she'd failed Quint was a sharp pain in her chest, but the fact that he'd appeared to be so displeased the first time she had acted naturally all week brought an even deeper ache to her breast.

Now, her sorrow spent, Hannah listened to Lady Evelyn's door close with a click, then stiffened as Quint's measured tread moved on down the hall. Her heart beat faster as his footsteps grew louder. When they moved past her room unchecked and his door clicked shut also, new tears filled Hannah's eyes. She had planned to ignore his knock, but his cool dismissal of her opened a fresh wound in her heart, and sent more tears down her cheeks to dampen her pillow.

After a few minutes Hannah brushed the moisture from her cheeks. Rising on one elbow, she leaned over the edge of the bed, to blow out the candle, then lay back to blink up into the dark. She felt no fear of the complete blackness, only a deep sadness. Somehow the total darkness felt right, seemed to be a part of the emptiness she felt inside her, to foreshadow the life devoid of joy she would face if she and Quint could not come to an understanding.

Hannah didn't remember falling asleep. When she heard her door open, her eyes flew open and her heart gave a joyful leap. She stared at the doorway, then blinked at the sight of Liza standing in the pale light of morning, holding a tray of covered dishes.

"Lady Evelyn wishes to leave for Blackthorne Hall as soon as possible, Your Ladyship." The girl placed the tray on a table near the fireplace, then picked up a poker to stir the embers of the fire to life. "She requests that you be ready to leave within two hours. I'll add some coal to the fire to warm you while you eat, then begin packing your things."

Hannah ate very little. She slipped into her warm peri-winkle-blue wrapper and sat by the fire, but still shivered with a coldness that ached bone deep. Finally, in an effort to get her blood moving and warm herself, she pushed the tray aside and helped the maid pack the large trunk sitting on the floor.

"Lady Evelyn said to pack but one trunk today," Liza said. "I'll bundle up whatever we can't fit in here later, and have it sent down to the Hall."

Hannah nodded as she placed the pale blue dress she'd

worn the night before on her bed next to the white shirtwaist and black skirt she would wear for the ride back to the country. "That blue dress can come later. I doubt I'll want to wear it for a while."

Hannah spoke little as the coach swayed from side to side on the road to St. Albanswood. She stared out at the foggy landscape and listened to Lady Evelyn and Aunt Amelia discuss the merits of fish meal as a food for roses. Hannah was pleased that her aunt and the dowager countess had discovered a mutual interest in growing roses, especially since their conversation kept Lady Evelyn from discussing Hannah's behavior of the night before.

Hannah had braced herself to face the countess's scorn when she followed her aunt Amelia downstairs to embark on the trip, but Lady Evelyn had surprised her by smiling brightly and congratulating them on their punctuality before turning to lead them to the carriage.

Then as the vehicle moved through London, the countess had pointed out several points of interest, to which Hannah managed to nod politely as she fought to keep from shivering. Lady Evelyn's obvious attempt at keeping the atmosphere light warmed Hannah somewhat, but the knowledge that Quint had left on Hippocrates without waiting for them made her spirits as gray as the fog outside. She pulled her cape closer around her, but still she felt cold.

They stopped for refreshments at the same inn they had lunched at on the way to London. Hannah forced down almost half of her meat pie, trying not to remember the tender moments she'd spent with Quint in the nearby woods.

Very little was said on the second leg of the trip, as both older ladies fell into a doze shortly after leaving the inn. Hannah, tired of staring at the fog and misty greenery along the roadside, sighed and looked down at her tightly clasped hands.

Her gaze fell upon the dainty golden band on the third finger of her left hand. She couldn't recall the words the minister had muttered at their wedding—she had been too frightened and upset to register them—but she'd heard the traditional vows before. Love, honor, cherish, and obey.

A slow frown began to form over Hannah's eyes as she thought the words over. She'd fulfilled them all, with the exception of one little indiscretion the night before. So why was she was feeling so disheartened?

Hannah's heartbeat picked up as she thought of all the times in the past week that she had tried to mold herself into the person Quint seemed to need. She could think of tens of times that she'd said the exact opposite of what she thought, smiled when she wanted to frown, kept silent when she wanted to laugh with amusement or scream with frustration.

And what had Quint done all this time? He had gone about his precious business affairs with nary a change in his schedule, save to spend an hour or so in her room each night. And when that was no longer novel to him, what then? Would she feel as lonely and invisible at nights as she did during the daytime?

No! Hannah's head snapped up and her eyes burned an icy violet-blue as she stared out into the mist. Quint had taken the same vows as she; he should have to make concessions as well.

By the time the carriage reached Blackthorne Hall, Hannah was thoroughly warm. Anger raced through her veins as furious thoughts tumbled through her mind. As soon as the carriage pulled to a stop in front of the house, a footman handed Hannah down. She glared up at the gray building with the kind of fury a woman might reserve for her husband's mistress. As the footman was helping Lady Evelyn down from the carriage, Hannah turned to Barrows, who stood in the doorway, and asked, "Where is Lord Blackthorne?"

The butler looked surprised. "Why, Your Ladyship, I believe he is in his study."

"Of course." Hannah pivoted, gathering her cape about her as she stepped through the door, then held her skirt high as she stalked up the stairs.

Hannah felt a moment of trepidation as she approached the heavy door that led to Quint's study. She hesitated a moment, her hand on the brass knob, then clenched her jaw and straightened her shoulders as she pushed the door open.

The heavy door swung wide and banged against the wall loud enough to make Hannah blink as she stepped into the room. Shelves filled with books lined the walls. Two armchairs faced each other in front of the large window to her right, and directly in front of her Quint sat bent over a desk covered with papers. He looked up sharply from what he was reading to stare at Hannah in stunned surprise for a moment before lowering his brows over his eyes.

"You're home."

The matter-of-fact tone of Quint's voice and the slight lift of one brow made Hannah want to scream. Instead, she merely grasped the door and swung it shut behind her, never taking her eyes off Quint's.

"Home? I'm assuming that means your home. It's certainly not *my* home."

Quint's frown deepened. "Hannah, of course it's your home. You are my wife. What's mine is yours."

Hannah laughed mirthlessly. "Well, that's fair, I suppose, since I have nothing to call my own now."

Quint rose to lean across the desk. "Hannah, what is the matter? You have money of your own. I gave it to you several days ago, and I mean for you to spend it any way you choose."

"Oh?" Hannah lifted her brows. "Any way at all? I can purchase a circus tent, perhaps, and practice on the trapeze? Or what if I order a new balloon and commence giving rides at Saturday markets?"

Quint's brows moved together as he shook his head. "Hannah, what is this all about?"

"It is about me, the person I am. If this is truly my home, then I should be free to be myself. Perhaps even to be taken into your confidence regarding your plans for this place, so I can feel that some small part of it is mine. To feel that you see me as the wife and partner I want to be, and not some doll to be paraded about."

Quint looked across at Hannah for a long moment, his eyes narrowed so that she could not read their expression. "Hannah—" he began, only to stop with a look of annoyance at the knock at his door.

"Yes?" he called out. The door opened to reveal Barrows standing in the hall next to Hannah's uncle Charles.

"Squire Summerfield to see you, sir."

Hannah glanced from the ill-concealed smile on her uncle's face to the scowl on Quint's. There was no doubt that the squire had heard at least part of her conversation with her husband. Quint glanced at her, his features taking on an apologetic twist. Before he could utter the dismissal she knew was coming, she took a step back.

"I shall take my leave now." She turned away from Quint and walked toward the open doorway.

"Hannah!" Quint's deep voice made her stop and pivot to him once more. "We will talk later. We have several matters to clear up."

Something in his even tone made all the fight drain from her. With a brief nod of her head she turned and walked out the door, ignoring her uncle completely as she crossed in front of him. She descended the staircase slowly, her hand on the smooth banister, then opened the front door and stepped outside.

As the door clicked shut behind her, the carriage pulled away, giving her an unobstructed view of the woods between Blackthorne Hall and Summerfield Manor. Hannah stood still for several moments, staring at the misty green depths, then walked down the stone steps and hurried toward the forest.

The trees took on more definite shapes as Hannah drew closer, and a break between two elms formed a welcoming entrance to the woods. She stepped beneath branches that entwined above her head and found that she was walking on a well-worn path leading into the very heart of the forest.

Hannah drew her cloak more closely about her as she followed the twisting trail around rocks and over protruding tree roots. When she came upon a small, sparkling stream, she turned to her left to walk alongside it, letting its soft song soothe the shaky feeling in the pit of her stomach.

The path seemed to stop at a tall hedge, but the stream trickled through at its base. Hannah stood in front of the wall of intertwined branches for several moments before noticing a small section that was less dense. She parted the branches with her hands and found she could pass through. Limbs and twigs caught her skirt and cape, but she tugged them free with one hand while the other held the upper branches to one side as she forced her way through the tangle of leaves.

Hannah sighed with relief when she pulled free of the grasping hedge. The small stream trickled at her feet and she stood still as she followed its path with her eyes to find that it emptied into a large pool only five feet in front of her.

When Hannah lifted her gaze to examine her surroundings, her eyes widened and she gasped softly as she stared at the pond wrapped in misty gray and the stone bridge arching over it.

Her heart began to pound, and tears sprang to her eyes as a deep ache filled her breast. Through blurred eyes Hannah stared at the bridge, remembering the morning she had sat there and a strange man had mistaken her for a wood nymph.

Hannah shivered when she felt the mists swirl around her as they had that morning, charged with the same magic that had captured her mind and heart. Her tears seemed to dry as quickly as they had formed. She looked down at the gold band around her finger, shining so bright in this world of gray, then looked around her again, feeling the terrible pain in her chest dissolve, to be replaced by the beginning stirrings of hope.

This was where she would bring Quint to talk. Once he felt the enchantment of the forest again, she would be able to explain her deep love for him as well as her need for acceptance and approval. A tiny smile curved Hannah's lips as she made her way toward the bridge. She was tired from her walk. She would dangle her feet above the water until she was ready to go back and find Quint.

"I hate this place," Pierre Bertrand muttered as he followed William Jarred down the forest path. He rubbed at his newly grown blond beard and shivered. "It is cold and damp and dark," he said as he rubbed the sleeves of his white shirt, then pulled the front of his blue vest together.

"It is all those things." Jarred flipped the collar of his tan jacket up as he turned his pale eyes to the Frenchman. "But with luck, we shouldn't have to be here long. They are expected to return today. They may be in the house even as we speak. We have only to watch and wait, and we will have our prey."

"And how long will that be?"

The deep voice made Jarred turn. Antoine leaned against an oak tree, hacking lightly with his large knife at the branch he held in his hand. He also wore a simple shirt and vest. A thick black beard covered the lower part of his face, outlining his large mouth as he glanced up with a scowl.

"Not long, I'm sure. I am told that the young countess has a restless nature. It shouldn't be too long before she takes a walk to visit her cousin or goes out riding alone."

"I hope you're right." Pierre straightened. "Things should have quieted down enough in France for us to return. I want to get back where it's warm."

Jarred stood up and trained his light eyes on the man. "And I want to get back to London. This type of work isn't much to my liking, but since it's paying so well, we'd best not complain too loudly." He shrugged. "Actually, killing pays better than thieving. It should; it's messier." Jarred grinned at Pierre, then glanced at the other Frenchman and said, "Antoine, stand here and watch the house while your brother and I look around."

Antoine shoved himself away from the tree trunk. As he lumbered forward, Pierre frowned into the taller man's eyes. "I thought we would be going back to the cottage."

"Soon. Don't worry. My boy Rufus will see to it that the fire stays lit. While we're out here I want to explore this place thoroughly. I was told this path goes through the woods and leads to the squire's land. This is where we will catch her, so I want to locate a good spot to lie in wait."

Pierre sighed as he shook off a chill, then turned to follow Jarred along the edge of the tiny stream, knowing it took him farther away from the warm fire whose warmth he so craved.

Sitting on the bridge, Hannah shivered and blinked. The cold of the stone bridge beneath her had seeped through the layers of material she sat on as wisps of mist swirled over the leaden surface of the pond. She'd been staring into the clear water beneath her dangling feet, plotting different ways to coax Quint into coming here with her.

The sudden chill made her aware of the deep silence that had fallen over the enclosure. Hannah lifted her head, listening as she glanced around. She heard nothing, no birds singing, no animals scurrying. Suddenly the spot seemed to lose its friendliness.

Hannah got to her feet and carefully crossed the uneven surface to the shore. Her boots sank into the soft earth along the water's edge as she walked toward the break in the hedge and pushed the branches apart.

The twigs seemed more determined to hold her back this time, catching immediately on the hem of her skirt so that she had to keep bending down to tug the captured material free. She was looking behind her as she reached the other side, tugging her trailing cape through. When it caught and held on a large branch, Hannah had to grasp the cape with both hands and tug. The fabric ripped away so suddenly that Hannah lost her balance and began to fall.

Strong hands grasped her from behind. Hannah's heart leapt as she turned her head, expecting to see Quint's green eyes scowling down at her. Instead, her eyes locked with a pair of white-blue eyes. Her breath caught in her throat, but before she could scream, a hand closed over her mouth.

"Where is Hannah?"

Quint burst into the parlor where his grandmother was having tea with Amelia. Both women looked up quickly.

"I thought she was with you." Lady Evelyn put her cup down, frowning.

"No." Quint shook his head impatiently. "She left when the squire came to speak to me."

Aunt Amelia brushed some crumbs from her fingers. "She's probably in her room, then."

Again Quint shook his head. "I looked there." He turned without another word, only to reappear several moments later.

"I've asked the house staff about her. None of them have seen her at all." He stared at his grandmother as he lifted his hand to rake through his hair. "Where could she have gone?"

Amelia gazed at him a moment, her wrinkles deepening with thought. She lifted her head with a sudden gesture that caught Quint's attention immediately, and she smiled at him.

"Cicely," she said.

Quint frowned. "Cicely?"

"Yes." Amelia nodded. "I could see that Hannah was upset today. Cicely has always been her closest confidante, so I'm sure that's where she went."

"Then she's in for a disappointment." Quint frowned as he started for the door.

"Why?"

Lady Evelyn's question stopped him, and he turned to her. "Because Cicely isn't at home. The squire just told me she was supposed to leave London with him this morning, but when the maid went in to wake her, Cicely was gone. Her room was empty and a portmanteau and several dresses were missing as well. I was looking for Hannah to ask if she knew anything about this, but now it appears she must be innocent of any such knowledge—that is, if you're right about where she's gone."

Lady Evelyn looked up at her grandson. "Look for the coachman. If he's gone as well, we'll know Hannah asked him to drive her to the manor. If so, she's probably already learned that her cousin is missing and will be returning any moment."

A few moments later, the coachman stood in the doorway of the carriage house and shook his head at Quint. "Lady

Blackthorne didn't speak to me at all, sir. But I did see her crossing the lawn toward the woods as I rounded the drive toward the stables.''

Quint stared at the man for a long moment. A slow smile parted his lips. The woods, of course. If she'd found the path through the trees, she would have reached the manor house and learned about her cousin's disappearance by now. If not, she was very likely lost, as she had been the day he found her.

Turning on his heel, Quint made quickly for the entrance to the woods. His boot heels dug into the hard dirt as he strode quickly forward, shoving branches out of his way as he hurried. He narrowed his eyes to see more clearly as the light grew dimmer with the advent of late afternoon. As soon as he caught sight of the trickling stream, he began to follow the path to his left.

With each step Quint felt a strange fear clutch his heart. Over and over he told himself that Hannah had only gone to see her cousin. Any minute he would run into her on the narrow path.

By the time he reached the hedge, he'd begun to wonder if Hannah had come this way at all. She knew nothing of the path, and at any point could have taken a wrong turn. He had just decided to reverse his direction when he spied a shredded swatch of gray material dangling from one of the lower branches.

Quint's heart began to pound and his lips to part. She *had* come this way. He bent to remove the slip of gray from the twig, then froze as a slender object gleaming against the dark brown earth caught his eye. He bent to examine it, and his heart came to a thudding stop. There, half buried in the weeds, lay Hannah's silver comb, and in the soft ground in front of it he could clearly see the fresh print of a large boot.

Chapter 22

A twig snapped beneath Hannah's ankle-high boot as Jarred urged her on through the dim, eerie mist. Aware of the heavy steps of the three men accompanying her, she tossed her head to get the tangle of hair out of her face, and tried to remember all the twists and turns she'd taken so far, hoping she would somehow find a way to escape.

She felt as if she'd stepped into a nightmare since coming through the hedge. Jarred's cold eyes had filled her with terror, and she had struggled against his grasp until a long, thin blade appeared in front of her eyes. Slowly she had shifted her gaze, following the slender arm of the man who held the weapon until she met the smiling dark eyes of Pierre Bertrand.

"No tricks today, *madame*," he said softly, moving the blade slightly so that it glinted in the mist. "You must come with us. Now."

No other words passed between them. Hannah followed Pierre, and Jarred walked behind them until they reached Antoine. His broad figure blocked the path. He held a notched branch in one hand, and his wide, pointed blade gleamed in the other. The smile flashing out of the darkness

319

of his bearded face had made her stop so suddenly that Jarred bumped into her with a grunt.

She turned then, tried to rush past him, but Jarred grabbed her arms, twirled her around, and forced her to walk forward again, to follow the Bertrands.

Now Hannah peered around Antoine's broad figure as he slowed down. She could see that they were entering a clearing, but the heavy mist made everything in front of her appear a gray-green blur. As they passed out from beneath the trees into the open air, Hannah's straining eyes made out a well, built of gray rocks and covered with the skeleton of what had once been a pitched roof.

Hannah narrowed her eyes further as she spied a large square shape in the mist ahead, then stumbled as her foot struck a large stone. A tug on her cape kept her from falling and she glanced back to find Jarred's cold eyes staring at her. He dropped the hem of her cloak, and she continued down the flagstone path.

When she looked up from the moss-covered stones, she saw that the square shape was a cottage. Hannah could make out a thatched roof and patches of white walls peaking from behind a thick cloak of ivy. As they moved closer, she could see that the ivy vines had entwined with a climbing rose till they threatened to swallow the small house.

Hannah stared at the cottage, slowing almost to a stop until Jarred shoved her forward. She all but tripped over the threshold, where the silent Antoine stood beside the open door. When she gained her footing, she looked around the room. Directly in front of her a large fireplace with a thick oak beam for a mantel filled much of the wall. Three rough ladderback chairs had been drawn up to the hearth; the only other pieces of furniture were four blanket-covered mattresses on the wooden floor. Several small windows were set in the dingy gray walls around the perimeter of the room, windows so choked with ivy leaves that little light could enter.

The door slammed shut behind her as Jarred shouted, "Rufus!"

Hannah paid little attention to the men as she peered through the dim light at the small fire on the hearth. Then with dawning recognition, she looked to her left and saw exactly what she'd been expecting to see—a narrow open stairway leading along the far wall to a trapdoor in the ceiling. In the floor at the foot of the steps lay the rectangular outline of another door. Hannah knew that a second set of stairs, beneath that door, led to a cellar. She also knew the exact layout of the room below.

"Move, *madame*." Pierre raised his voice. "I don't want to have to say it again."

Hannah stepped forward, staring around the room. "Thomas Higdon's cottage," she breathed.

"What did you say?"

Jarred stepped in front of her. Hannah blinked. "This was my grandfather's cottage. My mother once lived here."

"Interesting," he replied, then lifted his head and shouted again, "Rufus! Where the hell are you?"

"*C'est vrai?*" The amusement in Pierre's voice made Hannah turn to him. He raised one blond brow and smiled tightly. "This is where your mother lived?" When Hannah nodded, his smile widened. "You English have a word— ironic, no? Well, it is very ironic that your mother lived here, *madame*, for it is here that you are to die."

Hannah's heart slowed and she lifted her eyes to meet his dark ones. She saw no trace of amusement there. Her throat felt dry, tight, as she whispered "Why?"

Pierre's brows lifted. "Because we have been hired to kill you. But not yet." His tight smile returned. "You will live for a while. Perhaps I could get you to show me a few more card tricks."

Hannah shivered and backed away from him. "I thought you were just thieves," she said.

"No."

Antoine's deep voice drew Hannah's gaze to the fireplace, where the powerful man stood warming his hands. "We are thieves *extraordinaire*," he said. His small dark eyes held hers. "We are very good at whatever we are paid to do. You will feel no pain."

Hannah shivered and fought the sudden dizziness that made her sway. A loud crash made her jump and turn around. She saw that the cellar door had flown open, and a small boy about ten years old, dressed in the rags of a street urchin, rose from the opening. His light brown hair straggled into the same pale blue eyes his father possessed.

"Is this the one?" he asked.

"Yes, my boy," Jarred replied, "this is the Countess of Chadwick. Your Ladyship, this is my son, Rufus Jarred."

Hannah glanced from Rufus to his father, to find Jarred smiling widely. "You really made things easy for us, Your Ladyship. We should probably hold off informing our employer of your capture, so he feels he's getting his money's worth. But my French friends are anxious to get back to work in their homeland, so we'd best get this over with. Rufus?" He turned to his son. "You go inform our friend that we have his quarry, safe and sound in the cellar."

The boy ran out of the cottage, and Jarred turned his icy eyes to Hannah. "And you go down those steps. There's a bunk and a blanket there. Now."

He had drawn a knife as he spoke. It was neither as long as Pierre's nor as broad as Antoine's, but it gleamed with deadly intent in the glow from the fire. Dim light filtered through the opening as Hannah walked down the wooden steps and made for the small cot. But even before she reached it, the trapdoor closed with a bang, leaving her in total darkness.

Hannah steeled herself to ignore the surrounding blackness as she groped for the blanket she'd seen. Her fingers closed over the rough material and she lowered herself onto the thin mattress. Trying to ignore the way the emptiness closed in around her, she wrapped the blanket around her and lay on her side.

She knew she wouldn't be able to sleep. Her body was too stiff with fear for that. But she no longer had the strength to sit upright, only to curl up in a ball and try to fend off the waves of terror. Someone wanted her dead, had hired men to kill her. Who?

The answer came quickly to her numb mind: her uncle. Hannah bit her lip and drew her knees up to her chest. Uncle Charles was obsessed with seeing that all his children married aristocrats. And he was completely ruthless, of that she was certain. How else would one describe a man who would sacrifice his daughter's happiness at the altar of his own twisted dreams?

Hannah shivered as she contemplated her fate. If her uncle managed to kill her, Quinton would once more be free to marry Cicely. Of course, there would have to be an appropriate mourning period, but then both the squire and Quint would be on their way to fulfilling their dreams.

Hannah shook her head. Quint would not view her death in such a cold-hearted manner. Despite the anger at him that had sent her fleeing to the forest today, she knew he cared for her. If nothing else, he would hold a yearning memory of those nights of pleasure they'd spent together. Hannah sighed. Nights that numbered far too few.

A shiver of remembered ecstasy rippled through Hannah as she recalled Quint's lovemaking. She shook her head at the darkness. She wasn't ready to die. She wasn't about to let her uncle steal away her chance at happiness, or Quint's. Her husband might not realize it yet, but she was good for him. Or she could be, once they had a chance to work into each other's lives. She had to find a way to ensure they would have that chance.

Hannah took several deep breaths and closed her eyes against the darkness and her mind against her fears. She concentrated on picturing every happy moment she'd spent with Quint, seeing a clear picture of him holding her comb as they stood on the bridge that first morning, then visualizing the exhilaration on Quint's handsome face as they cleared the cliffs in France, and finally recalling the tender passion in his eyes as he pulled her to him on their wedding night.

The sound of the cellar door swinging open an hour later made Hannah sit up quickly. Her fears descended upon her again as the memories of happiness started to fade. Now she stared at the opening and watched a pair of black shiny boots begin to descend the wooden steps.

Hannah braced herself to face her uncle. She tried to think of ways she might convince him to spare her, but she could come up with nothing to offer that would compensate for his loss of the titled grandchildren he wanted so desperately.

Hannah took a deep breath, drawing in the distinctive aroma of pipe tobacco. She held that breath as the slender form moved down another step, preparing herself to face her uncle's cold stare, then gasped when Hartley's smiling face came into view.

"Hello, Hannah," he said. "I must thank you for being so obliging. I thought it might be weeks before we got a chance to nab you, especially with Cicely missing."

"Cicely's missing?" Hannah was completely bewildered. She was so totally surprised to see Hartley when she'd expected her uncle that his last words were all that had registered in her mind.

Hartley chuckled dryly. "Well, everyone else thinks

she's missing. I know where she is, of course."

Hannah frowned as she became aware of the meaning of his presence in the cellar. "What are you talking about? Have you kidnapped her, too?"

"Oh, my goodness no. Parker did, in a sense. They eloped last night. I want to thank you for your efforts in that respect, by the way."

Hartley's boot scraped on the dirt floor as he lowered himself to sit on the bottom step and gaze across the cellar at Hannah. Even in the dim light from the room above, she could see his smile.

"In fact, you have been so helpful that I'm actually sorry you will have to die. But you will. You and Quint."

"Quint?" Hannah breathed. "Why Quint?"

"So that Parker will become the Earl of Blackthorne, and my sister his countess. It's a perfect plan. Even my father would have to agree." The wry amusement in Hartley's voice turned to barely suppressed fury at the mention of his father. "Of course, Father will never know of this. He'll just keep on thinking of me as a bumbling fool while I arrange these little pleasant surprises for him."

Hannah shivered. "Surprises?"

"Yes, imagine how pleased he'll be when he learns that you and Quint have been set upon and brutally murdered by a band of thieves here in our very own forest. He'll be shocked, just as he was when Ludmore died. But soon he'll see how well things worked out for him."

Hannah swallowed. "You killed the Duke of Ludmore?"

"Oh, no. I was here in the countryside when that happened. I paid Jarred to do it for me. He's very good at breaking into houses. That's something else my father never gives me credit for: I hire only the best. Jarred is not only an accomplished thief but a crack shot as well."

Hannah shivered again. "Is he going to shoot me?"

"Most likely. I think you deserve to go quickly, since

you've made things so easy on me. Actually, until two days ago, I wasn't going to kill you at all, only Quint.''

''Quint? Why—'' Hannah paused a moment, then widened her eyes. ''You hired that man to rob us and shoot Quint.''

Hartley nodded. ''As well as the driver who almost ran him over on Curzon Street. You see, when Quint is dead, Parker will inherit his brother's title, and my father will be very happy that Cicely has run off with the lad. I didn't think you mattered, until I realized you might already be carrying a young heir. So you shall have to die after all.''

Quinton crossed the red and black carpet in the parlor, something he'd been doing repeatedly ever since it became too dark to continue his search in the forest. He had examined the ground near the comb and found more footprints. He followed them, but the light had grown dimmer by the moment, and soon the tracks had become too faint to see in the growing darkness. He knew it was foolhardy to go on in the growing dark and risk obliterating the trail with his own footsteps. Maddening as it was, his search would have to wait for the next morning.

Now he wasn't even sure those boot tracks were connected with Hannah in any way. He stared at the window in front of him. The diamond-shaped panes broke up a pale reflection on their black surface. He stared blankly at this, then turned to where Aunt Amelia sat on the burgundy settee.

''Hannah wouldn't run away, would she?'' he asked.

The old woman looked up sharply. ''Why should she do a thing like that?''

Quint ran an impatient hand through his hair, for perhaps the dozenth time. ''Because just before the squire arrived, we were having a disagreement. Or rather Hannah was expressing a great deal of anger and frustration. I didn't get to say much.''

Amelia tapped her chin with a long finger. ''Well, Hannah does have a temper. Not a fierce one, mind you. She's the most placid of people until she feels cornered.'' The woman paused and shot him a quick glance from under her eyelids. ''Did she give you any indication what had upset her so?''

Quint lifted his hands in an expression of frustration and shook his head. ''She said something about this not being her home, and something else about having lost everything that was hers. None of it made sense to me.''

''Well, it makes sense to me.''

Lady Evelyn's sharp tone made Quint turn to see his grandmother lean on her cane as she entered the room. He hurried over to pull a chair around for her, and once the countess was settled in it she glanced up at him.

''I'm afraid we've both been to blame for Hannah's discontentment, my boy. I was so worried about smoothing over any scandal, so intent on seeing to it that Hannah presented herself in just the right way in London, that I never really looked at the remarkable woman you had the exceptional good fortune to marry. I'm going to tell her that, too, as soon as we get her back.''

Lady Evelyn stopped speaking as she fixed her grandson with a sharp gaze. ''She has every right to be unhappy with us, you know, after the way we've been acting. Especially last night. I could see she was very upset with herself after those stories she told to the prince.''

''What stories?'' Amelia looked over quickly.

''Oh, I don't remember them all.'' Lady Evelyn waved her hand. ''A great deal about circuses and such. The sort of thing one shouldn't admit knowing about, especially when one bears the title of Countess of Chadwick. But''— Lady Evelyn sighed—''the prince seemed to enjoy the tales.

Hannah obviously won his favor, so there was really no harm done.''

Aunt Amelia stiffened and frowned. ''Does Hannah know that?''

The lenses of Lady Evelyn's spectacles winked in the light from a nearby lamp as she turned to Amelia. ''I would imagine not. The subject never came up. Hannah was very quiet on the way home and didn't seem inclined to talk much.''

''Well, what could she say?'' Amelia asked. ''The poor girl no doubt felt that she had disgraced you both and was too embarrassed to speak.'' Amelia looked from the countess to Quint. ''She wants to please you, she truly does. But all this emphasis on behaving in a manner totally foreign to her nature makes her believe you don't care for her.''

Amelia stood. ''I'm going to bed, and I shall pray that my niece shows up in the morning.''

After she left, Quint sat down and rested his head against the high back of the brocade chair next to the one his grandmother occupied. He stared at the black, empty window. Without Hannah his life would be every bit as empty. She had brought light into his gray, duty-bound world, made him look at possibilities rather than what had always been.

He was in love with her, he realized. Deeply, hopelessly, irrevocably. And he'd never once told her. Instead he'd let his body communicate for him, hoping that would be sufficient, that he wouldn't have to face the terror of giving his heart away, of trusting that Hannah wouldn't take it and abandon him.

''Quinton?''

At the sound of his grandmother's voice he turned. She was getting to her feet, but when he started to rise to help her, she lifted a restraining hand. ''Don't get up. I can make my way upstairs just fine. I just wanted to tell you, I think you are a good boy.''

Quint blinked, and his grandmother smiled. "You've listened well to me, perhaps too well. I want to see you happy. That's far more important than seeing you wealthy. Now, good night."

Quint watched her leave, then turned to gaze at the window, thinking about what the two women had said, and aching to have Hannah back in his arms where she belonged. He closed his eyes, felt the room begin to rotate, and recalled feeling a similar sensation the day he took off in *Skylark* with Hannah. Once again he floated over Blackthorne Hall and saw how small and insignificant it appeared when compared to the vibrant golden-haired woman at his side.

Quint was sitting in the same chair when dawn lightened the sky, filtering through the same deep fog that had lain over the treetops the day before. He opened his eyes and gingerly stretched muscles cramped from his awkward position in the chair. Slowly he got to his feet and tried to blink the sleep out of his eyes.

A knock on the door made him jump, then rise quickly. He crossed the carpet in five long strides and almost collided with Barrows in the entry hall as they both reached for the doorknob. The butler gave Quint a startled glance, then stepped back to let his master pull the door open.

A young boy stood on the step, cap in hand. His brown hair was tousled and his vest and knickers had a worn look to them. He looked Quint up and down before he spoke.

"I need to see the Earl of Chadwick."

"I am the earl. What do you want?" Quint spoke quickly, then stood waiting impatiently for a reply as the boy stared at him a long moment, a frown forming over his pale blue eyes.

"*You* are Lord Blackthorne?"

An angry response leapt to Quint's lips, until it struck him that after sleeping in his clothes he must not cut a very aristocratic figure. He knew his hair must be in complete disarray, and no doubt a dark shadow shaded his unshaven face.

"Yes, I am Lord Blackthorne." Quint controlled his impatience. "What do you want?" he asked again.

The boy's frown disappeared. "I've come about your wife, sir. The lady fell, sir, in the woods late yesterday evening. My father found her and took her to our cottage, since she'd hurt her leg badly and couldn't walk."

Quint narrowed his eyes at the boy. "Why didn't he bring her here?"

The boy stared directly up at Quint and shook his head. "She weren't awake, sir. She was senseless as a sleeping babe until after suppertime. When she finally woke up and told us who she was, t'were too late to come through the woods. My father sent me here at first light."

Quint stared at the boy a moment, then turned to Barrows. "Send someone for Hippocrates. If Hannah's hurt her leg she'll need to ride back." He paused and looked back at the boy. "Come in here and wait. You can ride with me and point out the way."

"It's down this path, sir."

The boy pointed to the right as the horse stepped beneath the covering of trees at the forest's entrance. Quint nodded and urged Hippocrates down the path.

"What's your name, son?" Quint asked over his shoulder.

"Rufus Jarred, sir."

Quint nodded. "I don't remember seeing you about before."

"We just came here, Your Lordship." The boy spoke in a quick, excited clip. "My father worked for Squire Summerfield in London, but we wasn't happy in the city, so he told us we could have work here, and the cottage as well. Me mum likes that, she does."

Quint nodded slowly as he watched the path in front of them. "What kind of work does your father do?"

"Oh, me dad does odd jobs in some o' the big houses. Masonry work, mostly. He just finished repairing the brick wall around the squire's house."

"I see." Quint's brows dropped to a frown as the path narrowed. "Are you sure we're going the right way? I don't remember a house back here."

"It's just a cottage, sir. Small and cramped. Been abandoned for a long time."

Quint straightened slightly in the saddle. "Ah, yes. I think I know the place you're talking about. If I remember, the forest gets very dense through here. I think it's best we dismount and continue on foot. That way you can lead."

"Fine, sir." Rufus slid to the ground. His pale eyes glimmered as he smiled up at Quint. "We aren't too far away from the place. Me dad will be right glad to see you."

Chapter 23

Hannah shifted in the straight-backed chair as she glanced to her right, where Hartley stood by the fireplace. He took the pipe out of his mouth and blew three perfectly formed smoke rings while his other hand, resting on the mantelpiece, lay loosely closed over a black pistol.

Hannah stared at the weapon a moment, then glanced at the other men. Jarred and Pierre sat cross-legged on a mattress beneath the front window, each staring into a hand of cards while Antoine crouched in a corner scraping his broad blade along a piece of wood, sending long, pale curls to the floor to join the circle of shavings surrounding him.

After shaking a stray lock of hair out of her eyes Hannah glanced at her own hands, which were tied tightly together and resting against her rumpled black skirt. A shiver skittered over her arms beneath the thin cotton of her shirtwaist. A morbid anticipation filled the air. She glanced at her cousin. He looked so certain of himself, as confident as he'd been last night in the cellar when he'd laughed at her and bragged of his plan.

Hartley's complacency filled Hannah with impotent rage. She wanted to hit him, kick him, do anything that would

cause him pain, that might prevent him from killing her and
Quint. Words were the only weapon she had, but the strip
of silk tied around her mouth deprived her of even that.

And what could she say that she hadn't said the night
before in the cellar? Then, too, anger and frustration had
made her lash out at her cousin in the only way she knew
how.

"Your plan will never work, Hartley," she had said, then
stared through the dim light to see him lift an eyebrow in
amusement.

"Oh, and why not?"

"You are counting on Quint to be blinded by his concern
for me, to come rushing here heedlessly on the word of a
child he's never seen before. He's too level-headed to do
that."

"Too dispassionate, you mean?" Hartley's mocking
smile gleamed in the dark. "Yes, Quint has always been a
spiritless sort, but full of honor. You are his wife. He'll
come," he assured her. "And don't think he'll be suspicious
of Rufus. The boy is a very convincing little actor, I assure
you. Your husband will walk through that door completely
off guard, the perfect prey. Then all we have to do is dispose
of your bodies and go about our lives."

Hartley's offhand attitude had only fueled Hannah's anger
further. "You know what, Hartley?" she had asked. "Your
father is right. You *are* a fool if you think you can do this
without getting caught. Someone from Blackthorne Hall
will have to let the boy in. Do you think that person won't
remember the boy's eyes? After our bodies are discovered,
the servants will report everything they know about the boy
to the authorities, and when Rufus is caught he'll tell everything he knows about you. I don't think you'll be able to
count on his loyalty when he's faced with prison."

Hartley's answering chuckle made the hair on her forearms rise. "You're just like my esteemed father," he said.

"You underestimate me shamelessly. Did anyone suspect foul play when Ludmore died? And what about Felicia?"

Hannah's heart thudded to a stop. "Felicia?"

"Yes, Quint's lovely first wife."

"I know who she was, and I know how she died. She fell from her horse and struck her head on a rock."

Hartley shook his head and smiled. "No, dear cousin. I struck her on the head as she sat by the roadside waiting for me. Then I loosened her saddle to make her death look like an accident."

"Why?"

"Because the poor girl completely misinterpreted the depth of my interest in her. She was determined to ask Quint for a divorce." He paused and sighed. "I can just imagine how my father would have reacted to *that* scandal."

Hartley had stared into the darkness for several moments before shaking his head and smiling once more at Hannah. "So you see, I am far more resourceful than anyone gives me credit for. Your death and that of your husband will appear to be the work of a band of poachers who have taken over this abandoned cottage. I shall convince our old game-keeper that he has seen the murderers; I understand they are very fierce-looking. They resemble our friends the Bertrands somewhat, but by the time the authorities begin seeking them, Pierre and Antoine will be back in France. As for the boy, he and his father will disappear into the anonymity that is London, never to be connected to me."

Hartley's laughter now echoed in Hannah's ear as she shifted in her chair and watched him take another deep draw on his pipe. Three more smoke rings curled above his head as he reached into his waistcoat pocket for his watch. A second later he snapped it shut and turned to Jarred.

"The boy's been gone quite some time now."

Jarred lifted his pale eyes from the cards in his hand and shrugged. "Rufus knows what he's doing. He won't hurry the earl, lest Lord Blackthorne become suspicious. I've trained the lad well, you know.''

"I hope so. We've—'' Hartley stopped speaking. He straightened away from the fireplace, staring at the ceiling. "What was that?''

Jarred shrugged. "Some birds roost in the thatching; others come to take the dead grass for their nests. We heard them rustling up there all night long.''

Hartley continued to frown at the ceiling, then lowered his gaze to Pierre as the Frenchman spoke.

"I for one do not like just sitting here, waiting. Perhaps we should take up positions in the forest and surprise him there''

"No, *mon frère*.'' Antoine spoke quietly, keeping his eyes on his ever moving knife. "There are too many ways to escape in woods this man knows so well. With the four of us in here, there's no way he can escape once he enters.''

"There had better not be,'' Hartley muttered. "We've come out in the open now. There's no mask—''

Again Hartley stopped speaking and looked up. Hannah had also heard an unmistakable creaking sound above her. She watched her cousin glance over to Jarred and Pierre. They still held their cards, but were staring intently at Hartley. When he gestured for them to move to the foot of the stairs, they silently obeyed. Hartley tightened his hand over the handle of the pistol, raised it, and aimed it toward the trapdoor leading down from the attic. Then he resumed speaking.

"Hannah here can identify us. This has to be carried out with thoroughness so that the rest of us can get on with our lives.''

Hannah was barely listening to him. All her attention was directed toward the stairway. Antoine, grasping his sharp knife in his hand, had begun to mount the wooden steps. Pierre followed, his stiletto held at readiness also. When

Hannah heard a scraping sound behind her and to her left, she glanced out of the corner of her eye to see Jarred move to the front door.

The third step creaked as Antoine placed his considerable weight on it, and the Frenchman smiled. The next two steps creaked also, but he never took his eyes off the trapdoor above him. As his dark head neared the ceiling, he stretched his free hand forward, preparing to shove on the door, only to jump and gasp when it suddenly opened inward.

Antoine regained his composure in an instant and started to mount the next step, but before he could lift his leg, a pair of booted feet swung down from the opening, hitting him square in the chest. Antoine's knife flew into the air as he flung his arms wide in an attempt to keep from falling, but the blow threw him backward into his brother, and they both toppled to the foot of the stairs.

Pierre lay sprawled beneath the weight of his brother, motionless, his eyes closed. Antoine, however, was conscious. He lifted his head, and Hannah held her breath, waiting for him to rise. Instead, a look of surprise blended with pain crossed his face. His dark eyes gazed into Hannah's a moment, then rolled upward as his head fell to one side. Hannah stared in horror as he rolled off his brother to lie face down, with the hilt of Pierre's knife protruding from his back.

Hannah's eyes widened at the sight, but a loud thud drew her attention back to the stairs to see that the booted man had landed on the center step. Her heart began to race as he took two steps down, then turned, grasping the slanting rail and staring into the room.

Hannah stared into Quint's green eyes for a moment, then lifted her hands to the handkerchief tied around her mouth, jerked it free, and choked out, "Quint, Hartley has a gun."

Quint placed his hands on the rail and vaulted over it as she spoke. He winced as he touched the floor, and remem-

bering his shoulder wound, Hannah gasped. His eyes met
hers for just one second, then lifted to gaze beyond her,
and Hannah turned. Hartley's pistol was pointing directly
at her husband. She stood, planning to throw herself at her
cousin, when she saw Hartley frown and lower the gun.

The scuffling of feet behind her made her turn as Jarred
charged toward Quint, brandishing his knife.

"What have you done to my son, you bastard?" Jarred's
words were a low growl as he thrust his knife toward Quint's
stomach. Hannah's heart leapt again, this time with fear,
but Quint deflected the blade with a quick uppercut to the
man's extended arm.

"Your lad is safe," Quint bit out. "He's tied up in the
forest."

Quint's words had no affect on Jarred. The man swung
his blade back in a murderous arc. Once more Quint escaped
the deadly blade, but as he stepped back he was forced
against the stairway. Jarred moved in just as Hartley
shouted, "Stand to one side, Jarred."

Hartley's voice echoed across the room. Hannah turned
to see that he had moved toward the two men and that the
hand holding the gun moved jerkily from side to side. Hannah glanced over to see Jarred begin to back away from
Quint, leaving her husband a clear target for Hartley's bullet.
Hannah turned toward Hartley again and without a second
thought forced her stiff legs to move and ran into him as
hard as she could.

Hartley fell to one side, crashing to the wooden floor with
Hannah on top of him. Above his enraged curse, she heard
something fall with a heavy clunk, then slide across the oak
floor. As Hannah placed her bound hands on the floor in
front of Hartley to push herself to her feet, she saw that the
pistol had come to rest about four feet from the fallen Bertrand brothers.

"Damn you!" Hartley's vicious words hissed in Hannah's ears as he threw one arm around her waist and pulled her to her feet as he stood. "You are *not* going to escape me."

Even as she struggled against his grasp, the sound of scuffling feet and heavy breathing drew Hannah's attention to Quint and Jarred. The taller man had Quint pinned against the stairway. Quint's hand clenched Jarred's wrist as the blade of his knife inched downward. Hannah jerked forward, broke Hartley's hold on her, and stumbled toward the struggling men, trying to get close enough to help her husband.

"Get back here, bitch." Hartley's fingers closed over her upper arm with bruising force. Hannah tried to pull away, but he spun her around to face him, then bent forward and tossed her over his shoulder like a sack of grain.

Hartley's shoulder drove into Hannah's stomach with such force that she cried out in pain. She blinked back the tears that had sprung to her eyes, then lifted her head. A motion near the bottom of the steps caught her eye, and she watched in horror as Pierre rose from beside his brother's lifeless body. His black eyes glinted with hate as he staggered to his feet and glared at the two men struggling at the foot of the stairway.

Hannah tried to follow Pierre's gaze as Hartley began to walk across the room. Her stomach continuously pounded into his shoulder and the room seemed to bounce before her eyes. Then the jostling stopped, and a creaking sound announced the opening of the front door.

The bouncing motion halted, and Hannah wondered if Hartley had turned his head, as she had to watch Quint break Jarred's hold and flip the man off his feet with a force that sent his knife skimming along the floor to the wall behind them.

A moment of elation made her forget the pain in her stomach and ribs when Quint slammed his fist into Jarred's face, and the man's pale eyes rolled back in his head. All sense of triumph faded in a flash when a slight movement caught her eye and she turned her head to see Pierre limping toward Hartley's gun.

Hannah felt her cousin jerk beneath her as he pulled the door open. Pale light washed into the room as he stepped over the threshold. She could hardly breathe as her stomach rose and fell on Hartley's shoulder, but she forced out a cry of warning: "Quint. Watch out for Pierre."

The fog engulfed Hannah as Hartley's boot heels echoed on the flagstone path. The door swung shut behind them, and Hannah began kicking and pummeling her cousin, but Hartley just continued to stride forward with quick, jerky steps that nearly jolted the breath from Hannah's lungs.

She managed to lift her head to see the cottage fading into the mist. As Hartley moved past the stone well, she twisted around so that her mouth was near his ear.

"Your plan isn't going to work, Hartley," she gasped.

Hartley's hands tightened around her legs as he replied, "Cousin Hannah, you are the fool. Quint is as good as dead, but if by chance he escapes Pierre's fury, I have you to draw him to me. My plan *will* work, one way or another."

Hannah turned her head to speak to him once more, but a branch whipped across her face. A second later she heard a horse snorting softly farther down the path leading into the woods. Hartley came to an abrupt stop, then spoke in a low tone. "Ah, our friend Hippocrates, if I'm not mistaken."

Hartley stepped forward, only to halt again after about ten paces. A whinny and a louder snort, followed by the sound of a hoof pounding the dirt told Hannah of the horse's instinctive distrust of the man approaching him, and for the first time in two days, Hannah smiled. She was still smiling when Hartley placed her on her feet, grabbed her bound hands, and started to drag her toward the horse.

She pulled back as she caught sight of a figure lying on the ground to one side of the path. "Rufus," she said. Two large pale eyes gazed up at her from the only part of the boy's face that wasn't tightly wrapped in a gray silk cravat.

"So?" Hartley shrugged.

"You aren't going to leave him here, are you?"

Hartley glanced at the boy as he deftly unwound the reins holding Hippocrates to a tree trunk, then pulled Hannah to him roughly, catching her around the waist with his arm and glaring into her eyes.

"He can lie there and rot, for all I care. It's most likely his bumbling that's responsible for ruining my plans. Now get up on this horse and sit still, or I swear I'll have the animal trample the boy to death."

Hartley's eyes blazed with pure hate for one moment before he placed his hands on Hannah's waist and hoisted her up in front of the saddle. He mounted behind her immediately and brought his arm forcibly around her ribs again as he struggled to control the suddenly prancing horse.

Hartley's free hand jerked on the reins. The stallion's head came up, and Hannah gasped out a warning: "Rufus, roll out of the way, quickly." A moment later, the horse reared and jumped to one side. Hartley rose in the stirrups while pulling back on the reins, forcing Hippocrates to drop forward. When his front hooves touched the ground, Hartley tapped the horse's flanks with his boots, urging the animal forward, and Hippocrates began to take slow, jerky steps.

The horse stopped with a jolt when the loud report of a gun split the air. Hannah gasped, and behind her Hartley chuckled as he urged the horse to move toward the cottage in the clearing.

The sound of the shot echoed within the gray walls of the structure. A piece of ceiling crashed to the floor, barely missing Quint and Pierre as they struggled for possession of the gun. Quint grunted as shards of pain knifed through his injured shoulder. His eyes narrowed as he tightened his hand over Pierre's, feeling the fingers beneath his close over the metal handle. Then he clenched his teeth as he drew on his last reserves of strength.

Pierre sent a tight, sneering smile up to Quint, as the man tried to jerk his hand sideways. Quint's grasp relaxed for just a moment allowing Pierre's arm to jerk downward without control. He took advantage of the Frenchman's surprise to pull him around, then ram his knee into Pierre's groin. The outlaw gasped, his eyes opening wide, and Quint repeated the move.

The gun clattered to the floor as Pierre bent forward and clutched his crotch with both hands. Quint bent to retrieve the pistol, then dashed for the door. He threw it open and ran outside, reaching the well in the center of the clearing just as Hippocrates stepped out of the forest. Quint stopped in his tracks, lifted and aimed the pistol, only to freeze when he saw that Hartley's body was shielded by Hannah's.

Hartley's features twisted into a nasty grin. "Give it up, Blackthorne. You aren't going to shoot."

Hannah held her breath as Quint's eyes met hers. She gazed across the short space, her eyes wide, her heart racing as Quint shifted the pistol and pulled the trigger.

The shot whizzed far above her head. As Hippocrates reared, Hartley gave a short laugh and released his hold on Hannah as he used both hands to gain control over the horse, leaving Hannah with no way to keep her seat on the prancing animal.

As soon as Hippocrates ceased fighting, Hartley dug his boots into the horse's heaving sides to urge him into a murderous charge. Hannah felt herself begin to slide to one side as the horse approached its master, but she could only stare in horror as the huge animal raced toward Quint.

A scream tore at Hannah's throat as she saw Quint drop

to the ground at the same time the horse stopped and reared, forelegs flailing in the air. The sudden motion sent her tumbling off the saddle, head over heels, to land on her feet and stumble backward. As she fell, Hannah heard an anguished scream rend the air, a scream that was cut off suddenly when her head struck the ground and a burst of light flashed before her eyes, followed by complete blackness and utter silence.

"She will be fine."

Aunt Amelia's voice rang with conviction, though her white eyebrows were lowered in a concerned frown as she stared down at the still form in the bed.

"I'm sure she will. She's a strong young woman." Lady Evelyn spoke softly from her chair on the other side of the bed. "Dr. Brockton seems satisfied that she will recover nicely. He's a good man, for a country physician. I trust him."

Aunt Amelia nodded slowly, then lifted her dark blue eyes to gaze across at the other woman. "Then why has she been unconscious for over twenty-four hours?"

Lady Evelyn met Amelia's bleak look with one of her own, then shook her head slowly. "The doctor's been checking on her hourly. He says her heartbeat and breathing rate are perfectly normal, and he did say that sleep will bring about the quickest healing."

"Was he referring to Hannah or himself?" Aunt Amelia's voice rose sharply as she glanced back at her niece's pale features. Almost as soon as she spoke, she shook her head. "That was an unkind remark. The man went without sleep all night. I shouldn't begrudge him a short nap." She paused, then went on in a soft voice. "I just feel so helpless. Hannah's never been ill a day in her life."

Tears of frustration and fear welled up in Amelia's eyes

as she gazed at her grand-niece, and as she watched through her blurred vision, the golden head on the pillow seemed to move slightly. Blinking away her tears, Amelia watched as Hannah's brows formed a slight frown beneath a puckered forehead. Aunt Amelia held her breath as the young woman's thick lashes fluttered slightly, then smiled as Hannah's eyes opened slowly.

Hannah stared up at the mahogany ceiling, studying the pattern of raised medallions. They seemed wrong somehow, out of place. She gazed at them, ignoring the dull throbbing pain at the back of her head, as she tried to remember climbing into her bed. All that came to mind was a dark and dank room beneath a wooden floor.

The cottage! Memories flooded Hannah's mind with lightning speed, and without thinking she sat straight up and called, "Quint!"

"Hush, hush." Aunt Amelia's soothing voice came from Hannah's left. Hannah felt herself sway as pain shot through her head. She turned from the waist to look at her aunt, who peered deeply into her eyes. "Take it easy, my girl. Everything is all right. Lie back against these pillows."

Hannah shook her head again, wincing at the pain that clouded her vision. "Where's Quint?" she demanded. "Is he hurt? Did Hartley kill him?"

"He certainly did not."

Quint spoke from the door. Hannah turned to see him standing just inside her room. His hair was a tangle of black curls, two full days' growth of beard darkened the lower half of his face, and his right arm rested in a white sling. Hannah thought he had never looked better. Her eyes rose to meet his, and she spoke softly. "I heard someone scream just as I hit my head. I wasn't sure who it was."

As Quint crossed the room to Hannah's bed, Aunt Amelia and Lady Evelyn moved quietly toward the door. Hannah kept her eyes on Quint's, noting the small frown over his dark eyes as he perched on the edge of her bed and took her hand in his.

"The scream was Hartley's. He's dead."

"Dead? How?"

"He tried to run me down." Quint shrugged. "Hippocrates reared at the last moment, throwing Hartley off his back. He fell into the old well head first. The doctor thinks the fall probably broke his neck, although he could have drowned in the well. He didn't respond when I called down to him, and he'd fallen too far for me to reach him. Besides, I was more concerned about you."

Quint's voice deepened to a husky whisper as he said these last words. Hannah felt suddenly warm and light as he sat on the edge of her bed, holding her gaze as he raised a gentle hand to her cheek. She stared up at him, noticing the deep lines around his eyes, which underscored the concern in his voice. He looked so tired, so worn. She glanced at his arm, then remembered the shot she'd heard and sent him a frightened look. "Were you shot again?"

Quint shook his head. "No, but the wound from the other night was reopened in my struggles. The doctor wants me to keep my shoulder still until it heals."

Hannah nodded slowly. "You are all right, then?" Hannah's voice faltered the words as she gazed up at the face so near hers. Quint nodded slowly, then began to lean toward her, his gaze moving from her eyes to rest on her lips. Hannah tilted her head back as her lips parted with anticipation and longing.

"Well, I hear my patient is awa—"

The masculine voice made Hannah and Quint both jump, and turn toward the door. They turned to see the speaker's face take on a color just slightly lighter than his bright red hair. Quint smiled tightly as he stood.

"Yes, she is, Doctor. She seems quite well, but I would appreciate your expert opinion."

Hannah watched warily as the slender red-haired man came around to stand on the other side of the bed.

"I really do feel just fine," she said.

"Your head doesn't hurt?"

"Well, yes." Hannah gingerly touched the back of her head. Her fingers encountered a large, tender lump that throbbed at her touch.

"Look at me, please."

The doctor's voice was soft but firm. Hannah shifted her gaze to meet a pair of honey-brown eyes that peered into hers for several long moments. Trying not to blink, Hannah asked Quint, "What made you enter the cottage through the attic?"

"Rufus."

Hannah blinked at that. "The boy told you that Hartley and the others were in there waiting for you?"

"Not voluntarily. But I became suspicious when the lad mentioned that his father had done some work on the brick wall surrounding Squire Summerfield's London town house. The place is enclosed by a wrought-iron fence."

Quint paused as the doctor took Hannah's wrist and stared at the pocket watch he held in his hand. "Rufus is quite an accomplished liar," Quint continued. "I never did get a straight answer from him. So I felt it best to leave him in the woods and approach the cottage with caution."

The doctor looked up as Quint stopped speaking and nodded. "Amazing. Even better than I'd hoped. There's no sign of concussion and her pulse is normal. Apart from that nasty lump at the back of her head, I would say she is fine."

Dr. Brockton paused and turned to Hannah. "I would recommend you stay in bed a day or so, however. You may find yourself becoming giddy from time to time, and it wouldn't do for you to fall and hit your head again."

"No, we can't have that." Quint spoke before Hannah had a chance to reply. As she turned her head to look at him, a sharp pain flashed through her skull, increasing her anger and frustration. Again Quint was assuming he knew what was best for her, ordering her to bed like a small child, incapable of judging her strength for herself.

"Quint." Hannah spoke firmly. He turned his attention from the doctor to her and lifted his eyebrows inquiringly as she started to go on, "I refuse to—"

"Excuse me, Your Lordship."

A deep voice cut off Hannah's budding protest. She halted in mid-sentence and turned to glare at the butler. Barrows blinked once, then spoke to his master. "I apologize for interrupting, sir, but Squire Summerfield has arrived. He is waiting in the study, as you instructed."

Quint nodded to the butler, then turned to Hannah. "I'm sorry. We'll talk more later. I have to see the squire as soon as possible."

"So do I." Hannah swept the bedclothes to one side and began to swing her legs over the edge of the bed.

Quint placed his hand on her knee and frowned. "What do you think you're doing? You heard the doctor. You are to stay in bed."

"Not now, I won't. I have several questions to ask my uncle." Hannah tried to rise from the bed, but Quint's hand prevented her from moving. She looked up into his eyes and spoke more firmly. "Quint, the man's son almost killed us. For all I know, Uncle Charles knew all about the plan, possibly even instigated it. You heard the doctor." Her voice deepened as she mimicked Quint's own words. "I am fine. I promise not to fall. But I *will* speak with my uncle."

Several moments later, wearing her periwinkle dressing gown over her white nightdress, Hannah arrived in the study to find her uncle seated in the dark green chair in front of Quint's desk. As Hannah held her husband's good arm, he escorted her to the opposite side of the desk and let her sink into the comfortable leather chair.

"I appreciate you taking the time to come speak with me." Quint's voice was level as he turned to the squire. "We have several matters to discuss."

"If you are referring to my son's death, you can save your words." The squire's small eyes narrowed as he looked up at Quint. "I have talked with the constable investigating this, and he has advised me that until he has determined how and why my son was killed, I should not speak of the matter with anyone, least of all you."

"Least of all me?"

"Yes. After all, it was your horse that *supposedly* threw my son into that well. There are no witnesses, of course, so we have only your word that such an unlikely thing did happen."

"Only Quint's word?" Hannah started to stand, but the pounding in her head made her sit back down as she went on. "What about the others—the Frenchmen and that Jarred person and his son?"

Her uncle's lips curled slightly as he turned to her. "The body of a dark-haired man was found in the cottage. All we know about him is that he was stabbed in the back. We have no idea who he was or what his nationality might be. As far as I'm concerned, this story of Hartley kidnapping you is just that, a tale you made up to cover the fact that your husband killed my son."

Hannah stared at him in disbelief. "What reason would either of us have for doing that?"

"I have no idea." Her uncle shrugged. "I did not come here to discuss your reasons. I came to inform you that I have learned that Cicely and Parker have eloped, and to tell you that I have no intention of accepting them in my house when they return. I've no doubt they will come to you for shelter, and I want you to know that they will arrive empty-handed. I am disinheriting Cicely. Now''—he rose as he spoke—''I have funeral arrangements to see to.''

The squire started toward the door, but before he could reach the knob Quint crossed the room in four long strides and stepped in front of the man. ''Our conversation is not over, Summerfield.''

Chapter 24

Quint narrowed his eyes at the squire, then smiled tightly as he went on, "Please take your seat so we can finish."

"I told you, I have nothing else to say."

Quint lifted his brows a notch. "But I do. Now, please, sit down."

Hannah watched the squire stare into Quint's eyes for a moment, saw the muscle tighten in Quint's jaw, then lifted her brows in surprise when her uncle resumed his seat.

"Now." Quint moved to the opposite side of the desk, leaned forward, and gazed at the older man. "You aren't the only one who has been in contact with the authorities. As soon as I got Hannah safely back to the Hall yesterday and was assured that she would recover, I sent word to a friend of mine at Scotland Yard. I urged him to watch for a tall man with very distinctive light eyes, in the company of a ragged boy and possibly a blond Frenchman."

Squire Summerfield raised unconcerned eyes to Quint's. "I suppose you have a reason for telling me this? I certainly know nothing of any such people."

"You do, too." Hannah leaned forward and had the satisfaction of seeing her uncle turn a startled look toward her as fear crept into his gray eyes. "You certainly know Mr. Jarred. You and he were both at Petrie and Yarrick the day I took my wedding band in."

The squire's eyes narrowed; then he lifted one shoulder and smiled. "Two men can be in the same store without being intimate acquaintances."

"But that isn't the case here, is it?" Quint glanced from his wife to her uncle as he went on. "Shall I tell you my theories regarding you, Summerfield?"

Again the squire shrugged. "If you insist."

"I do." Quint paused as he straightened. "You are a parasite. A very clever man, undoubtedly, but a parasite. You were born without a title, but were determined to raise the name Summerfield into the peerage. To this end you used your intelligence to amass a sizable fortune, taking what little capital your holdings yielded and investing it wisely. Am I correct so far?"

The squire fixed a level gaze on Quint. "In saying that I manage money well? Of course."

Quint crossed his arm over the one in the sling and began to pace alongside his desk. "But you weren't satisfied with mere money; you hungered after position. More than that, you hated those who were born to a higher station. You wanted to see them tumble to a position lower than yours."

Quint stopped and leaned toward the squire. "Tell me, Summerfield, was my father the first victim of your little schemes? You must have derived great pleasure from lending him money again and again, especially after he'd signed the forest over to you. You enjoyed offering him chance after chance to join in your investments—ventures from which only you gained and which left him even deeper in debt."

Quint straightened. "You know, I used to think my mother took all the jewelry my father had bought for her, but after talking to Kendrick, I'm beginning to suspect I was wrong. Did you offer my father the same deal you offered Lord Kendrick, to hand the jewelry over to Petrie and Yarrick in return for paste copies and a few pounds? Tell me, was it your idea to set up an arrangement with the Bertrand brothers to sell the jewels in France where they wouldn't be recognized by anyone, or did Petrie and Yarrick suggest that?''

The squire lifted his chin and looked directly into Quint's eyes. ''I don't know what you're talking about.''

''Yes, you do,'' Quint replied. ''You and your son have been systematically ruining titled men for years, taking advantage of their weaknesses and counting on their need to protect their names to keep them silent. I can't prove that you helped my father bankrupt my family, but Lord Kendrick has kept some very incriminating records of his transactions with you, and he is no longer willing to keep silent. Although Ludmore apparently preferred death to dishonor, Kendrick wants restitution, no matter what it does to his name.''

''Lord Kendrick is a fool, and everyone knows it.'' The squire stood and glared at Quint. ''He can prove nothing. And I assure you if he tries to blacken my name or the memory of my son he will be—''

''*Your son*,'' Hannah broke in, getting to her feet, ''hired Jarred to kill the Duke of Ludmore.''

''No.'' The squire then glared into her eyes as he shook his head.

''Yes,'' Hannah answered firmly. ''Hartley told me all about it. He said he wished he could tell you about it so that you'd know he could carry out a plan so smoothly.''

The squire shook his head again, then slowly sank back into the chair and stared blankly at the desk. When he lifted his eyes, they were once more cold and narrowed. ''I don't believe you and neither will anyone else.''

''Will you believe William Jarred?'' Quint asked softly

as he leaned across the desk. When Summerfield looked at him, Quint spoke again. "I received a telegram from my friend in London. They caught Jarred and his son in the alley behind the shop owned by Petrie and Yarrick."

At this bit of information, all the color drained from the squire's face and he slumped back in his chair as if the energy had been drawn from his body. Quint glanced at Hannah, then back at the squire. "Look, Summerfield, I know you've ruined many men's lives, but I don't think you've taken any. If I thought for one moment you had anything to do with the attempt on Hannah's life—"

"I didn't." The squire straightened and glared at Hannah. "I may hate you for coming here and ruining all my plans, but I wouldn't have arranged your death. Hartley wasn't a killer either." He stopped as he choked on his words, then went on softly, "I don't know what happened to him. He must have gone insane."

Hannah thought about her cousin's boasts, how he was going to make his father proud by killing her and Quint, leaving Parker to inherit the title now that he was safely married to Cicely. She also remembered all the times her uncle had spoken to Hartley in a tone that said he thought his son was worse than a fool. She knew exactly what had happened to her cousin, but she couldn't tell his father. Her uncle was a despicable man, but his life was crumbling around him, and Hannah could not bring herself to add to his destruction.

"Something obviously twisted Hartley's mind." Quint spoke softly, then straightened and raised his voice slightly. "But whatever was behind his actions, he has already paid for his crimes. I can see no point in blackening your family name by revealing all that happened at that cottage."

Hannah looked up sharply, to see Quint lean forward, resting his hand on the edge of the desk again as he went on. "If you agree to certain stipulations, I'm willing to let a very different story be told, one in which your son is painted as a hero who died trying to save Hannah and me from thieves who were hiding in our woods."

"What stipulations?" The squire bit the question out with obvious reluctance.

Quint's brows quirked up. "First you are to reimburse Kendrick for all the money you tricked him out of. In return he will keep silent about what you've done. Second, you are to cease all similar 'lending' and end your relationship with the firm of Petrie and Yarrick."

The earl stepped around the desk. "This is in the way of a word to the wise, by the way, for that jewelry business will be under the heavy scrutiny of the criminal investigators if I'm not mistaken."

Quint paused again. His face was grim when he went on. "Third, you will give Cicely the exact dowry she was to receive upon her marriage to me. And finally, you are to return to the Blackthorne family the deed for the forest that lies between our lands."

Summerfield stood abruptly, a stony look hardening his eyes. "That is blackmail. I won't agree to it."

Quint shrugged. "Then the real story will come out about Hartley. And with it, I imagine, rumors about your unscrupulous dealings with Mr. Jarred."

"It wouldn't work anyway." The squire shook his head. "Word would leak out and I'd still be ruined."

"The only people who know the whole story are members of my family and my friend at Scotland Yard. Oh, and Jarred, of course. But I have a feeling he could be easily silenced with a little bribe. As far as my servants go, they know only that Hannah was kidnapped and that Hartley and one other man were found dead at the cottage, nothing more. Kendrick will be more than happy to keep silent if he has his money back. Think about it, Summerfield."

Hannah watched her uncle. He sat tall in his chair, glaring at Quint for several moments, then stood. "We'll do it your

way, but this is to be the last of the discussion. As I mentioned, I have a funeral to arrange.''

He opened the door, and stepped out into the hallway,
slamming the door behind him. Hannah rose to stand next
to her husband as Quint stared at the closed door. Her head
was pounding, her eyes hurt, but she had him all to herself
now. She wanted to talk to him, explain what she'd been
trying to tell him before she went into the forest.

''Quint?'' She reached out and laid a timid hand on his
bandaged arm. He turned and looked down into her eyes.
''I need to talk to you.'' She paused as a sudden attack of
dizziness made her close her eyes. When she opened them
again, Quint was frowning. ''I have been very upset the
last several days,'' she began. ''And—''

Her words were cut off by a gentle finger placed over
her lips. ''Hannah.'' Quint's voice was firm. ''You have
to go back to bed. We will talk when you feel better, perhaps
tomorrow.''

With those words he put a strong arm around her and led
her to her room. Hannah frowned, but her head hurt too
much to argue and she barely had enough strength to place
one foot in front of the other. By the time he helped her
back into bed and she lay against her pillows, she could
hardly bear to open her eyes, but she managed to open them
slightly as Quint asked, ''Do you want me to send for the
doctor?''

Hannah shook her head slightly. ''No.'' She let her eyes
close again. ''I just want to sleep.''

''We'll talk soon.'' Quint's whisper could barely be
heard. ''We need to straighten several matters out.''

Hannah slept most of that day, awakening finally at din-
nertime to accept a tray of food. Aunt Amelia sat in the
chair next to her, reading, while Hannah attempted to fill
her empty stomach without bolting her food. Finally her
aunt looked up from her book.

"I'm glad to see you have such an appetite. How is your head feeling?"

Hannah took a sip of water to wash down a bite of rare roast beef. "Better. The bump still hurts when it touches anything, but my head doesn't ache as it did earlier. Where's Quint?"

"At the squire's. Some man arrived from London this afternoon, and the two of them took off for the manor. Your husband told me to tell you he would probably be there late. He also left word that we were to send a messenger if you slept longer than we thought proper. He's been quite concerned about you."

Hannah glanced at Aunt Amelia. "Oh? Well, I suppose be has."

"My dear, the man is madly in love with you."

"Is he?" Hannah's voice quavered. "Oh, I've no doubt he's concerned. He's a responsible person. And I am under his charge. But how can he be in love with me? He hardly knows me."

"Hannah, you've known each other barely three weeks. Give him some time to know his mind."

"Why? I know my mind. *And* my heart." Hannah stopped, placed her napkin on the tray, and sighed. "I sound like a petulant child, don't I?"

Her aunt nodded.

"Well, perhaps it's because I *feel* like a child, cosseted and protected, told where to go and what to do."

"I think you need to tell these things to your husband."

"I would love to. But something always prevents us from talking."

Amelia stood to take the tray. "Well, tonight I'm going to do the cosseting and tell you to get some more sleep. Perhaps tomorrow you will get a chance to speak with Quint."

The next day Hannah spent barely half an hour with her

husband. She had just finished her bath and had come around the screen tying the belt of a blue dressing gown around her waist when Quint walked into the room. Hannah watched his brows lower in his familiar frown as he gazed at her. Her face grew warmer, and she saw the hunger in his eyes as they focused on her hands.

Quint looked at Hannah, her hair drawn up in a loose knot atop her head, tendrils curling around her flushed face. His gaze dropped to her hands, still on the belt of her robe, and memories of loosening a similar belt and letting the misty gray silk dressing gown slip down to reveal her soft nakedness filled his mind. His body remembered, too. His blood pounded in his ears and his loins tightened as he stared at his wife, trying to recall what it was he had been about to say.

Hannah's knees grew suddenly weak as she gazed at her husband. With her left hand she grabbed the edge of the screen behind her and closed her fingers around the smooth wood as she fought the strange weakness. This intense desire, as wonderful as it was, was just one of the things that always seemed to interfere when she had a chance to speak to her husband. As much as she longed to walk into his arms and lift her mouth to his, she had to talk first.

"Quint?" She managed to speak calmly. "Do you have a few moments? I need to talk to you."

Quint blinked, then shook his head. "No, actually. I came to tell you that I'm off to Hartley's funeral."

"Shouldn't I go, too?"

"No. You should rest some more. Besides, I don't want you near your uncle. My friend Roberts came down from Scotland Yard last night and we went to see the squire. Summerfield has agreed to everything we spoke of yesterday, but at one point in the conversation he became quite irrational, blaming all this on you. Cicely and Parker had just arrived, and from what I gathered, Cicely gave her father the idea that you had some small hand in encouraging her and my brother to run off together.''

Hannah's cheeks grew warm. ''I did suggest that once to Parker, but I didn't really expect him to take me seriously. I just wanted them to admit their feelings for each other.'' Her voice trailed off as she finished; then she frowned. ''If Cicely is home, I really should attend the funeral with you. She must be very distraught over her brother's death. Does she know the real story?''

''No. I told Parker, of course. He's also very upset, since they were such good friends, but we agreed that Cicely doesn't need to know all the details.''

Hannah stared at Quint for a moment. Her hands tightened into fists as she shook her head slowly. ''That is ridiculous. Cicely is no baby. She loved Hartley, true, and I'll have to admit he was a good brother to her. But Cicely deserves to know the truth, just as I deserve to decide whether I am well enough to attend this funeral.''

Hannah saw Quint's jaw tighten again. Her hand tightened on the screen behind her as the room swayed slightly.

''All right,'' he said at last. ''Do you feel well enough to go?''

''No.'' Hannah paused and watched Quint's eyes widen slightly. Her words surprised her every bit as much, but she knew she'd only appear a headstrong fool if she insisted on going and then disgraced herself by fainting. ''I'm still a little dizzy, so I will go back to my bed. But I would appreciate it if you would find time to speak with me when the funeral is over.''

As soon as Hannah mentioned that she was dizzy, Quint had begun walking over to her. By the time she was finished speaking he stood in front of her, gazing intently into her eyes. ''I told you we would talk. But for now, let me help you back to your bed.''

When Hannah was once more lying beneath the covers,

Quint touched her cheek as he gazed down at her. "Tomorrow we shall talk. If you feel strong enough, come to my study after breakfast."

Hannah stared at the ornate knob on the door of Quint's study as she straightened the skirt of her simple ivory gown. She placed a trembling hand on the high lace collar and swallowed twice to ease the tightness in her throat. Now that the moment had come to speak to her husband, she wasn't certain she could find the words to express her feelings.

She loved him. Her body craved his touch. She found him fascinating, frustrating, and wonderful. But she didn't want to be someone's duty, and she feared that was all she was to him. Even if she could make him understand that, she wasn't sure she could trust his reaction.

Hannah took a deep breath as she reached for the doorknob. She had to try to make him understand without making him angry, as she had in the carriage the night he was shot. She turned the knob slowly and pushed the door open.

Quint looked up from his papers to meet her gaze, then placed his pen in its holder and stood. He was dressed in a gray waistcoat and pants, and Hannah noticed he no longer wore his sling. Before she could question him about that, he spoke.

"Good morning. How are you feeling today?"

"Fine, thank you."

"No more dizziness?"

Hannah shook her head.

"Well, then, do you feel well enough for a little walk around the grounds while we talk? I have a few things that need looking into."

Hannah felt her fears of the moment before melt into a feeling of futility. It seemed there was always something important to pull this man's attention from her. She nodded numbly, then followed Quint down the curving stairway and out the front door. Once they'd descended the stone steps Quint guided her down the path that led to the stables at the rear of the house.

"The funeral went well." Quint spoke quietly as he walked along next to her, his hands clasped behind his back. "I heard some of the villagers talking, and they are all agog over what a hero Hartley turned out to be. They seemed a little surprised, but willing enough to believe the story they were told."

"I'm glad, for Cicely's sake," Hannah said.

"Oh, speaking of your cousin." Quint turned to look at Hannah. "Cicely and Parker will be moving in here tomorrow. I was going to ask you if you'd speak with the housekeeper about arranging quarters for them."

Hannah looked up, and smiled slightly. "I'd be glad to, but I really don't know the Hall well enough to make any suggestions. I'll ask your grandmother."

"That's a good idea. She'll know which rooms are in the best repair." Quint shrugged. "With Cicely's dowry, they'll be able to afford to refurnish their rooms however they choose."

Hannah glanced over with a small smile. "You know, Quint, perhaps we could just move them around Blackthorne Hall, from one section to another, until it's all redone."

Hannah watched Quint closely and thought she saw his lips twitch, but when he turned to her his eyes were serious. "My grandmother tells me I have failed to make you feel needed, feel that you are truly my wife. Is that so?"

Hannah's heart sank as she stopped walking. She hadn't wanted anyone else to speak for her, but at least now her feelings were out in the open. "In some ways, yes," she said, "but—"

Quint held up his hand to stop her. "I'm sorry, Hannah." He took her hand in his. "After we were married I just assumed my life could go on as before. I never gave much consideration to what you would do. However, I've thought of little else since Grandmother spoke to me.'' He tugged on her hand and they started to walk toward the corner of the stable as he went on. ''Grandmother would probably prefer to continue overseeing the housekeeping for a while, of course. But there are other things to keep you busy, such as the village school. And of course the church has several functions, which I understand are normally organized by the ladies hereabouts.''

Hannah stared up at him. She could almost see her name on an appointment book in his study—Hannah to the vicarage for tea . . . Hannah to organize the herb garden . . . Hannah to visit the tenants. A slight breeze slipped around the corner of the stable. Hannah shivered as she stared at the gravel path beneath her feet.

''Of course,'' Quint went on, ''there will be times when you might prefer simply to get away from this little village.'' As he finished speaking Hannah felt his hand cup her chin and lift her head so that her gaze swept across the grass to a large wicker basket. Her eyes widened, and she lifted her head farther and saw *Skylark* swaying against the bright blue sky.

Hannah stared at it in disbelief for a moment, then turned her wide eyes to Quint to find him smiling broadly. ''You look surprised,'' he said. ''I promised I'd send someone to Émile and Madeleine's to bring it back for you.''

''And you are a man of your word,'' Hannah spoke in a voice husky with suppressed emotion.

''Sometimes a man of not enough words.'' Quint's smile faded as he looked down into Hannah's eyes. ''I love you, Hannah Blackthorne. I fell in love with a wood nymph, full of life and laughter, and if it seemed that I wanted you to become something else, I'm sorry. I want you just the way you are, impractical and wise at the same time.''

Hannah blinked away the tears welling up in her eyes, and shook her head. "I'm sorry, too. I've been too impatient, wanting to hurry what can't be hurried."

"Perhaps that's what has been missing from my life," Quint lifted his head to look at the silver balloon, "a sense of urgency that has nothing to do with restoring the past and everything to do with dreams for the future." Quint looked into Hannah's eyes, then smiled. "Are you up to taking a ride? I thought we'd scout out the best place to build my training track."

"You're going to raise horses?"

Quint lifted his brow. "Yes. You and Lord Kendrick have persuaded me to put my money where my heart is. Parker is going into partnership with us, too. It's time I gave him a chance to participate in the Blackthorne fortunes, or losses, whichever the case may be." Quint gave her a wry grin, then tugged on her hand again. "Come, let's go up while the air is calm."

Quint led Hannah to the new basket and lifted her in. She felt the bottom of the basket give beneath her feet and looked down to see she was standing on a thick mattress. She looked up at Quint, who smiled and spoke softly as he stepped in. "Don't say anything in front of the men."

"What men?"

Quint lifted his eyes and nodded. Hannah turned and watched six men approach. Once they reached the basket, four of them grabbed the edge, while the other two released the ropes holding the balloon to the ground.

Quint's voice rang out, "Hands off."

The men stepped back and the balloon slowly began to rise. Hannah watched the earth fall away and felt the familiar lightness and joy fill her, then turned to Quint to find him gazing around with a similar sense of wonder. Her eyes filled with tears of joy. Here was the Quint she had fallen in love with, a man sensitive enough to be caught up in the wonder of fantasy and strong enough to free himself from the prison of his responsibilities without relinquishing any of them.

And in freeing himself, he had freed her. Hannah glanced down at Blackthorne Hall becoming smaller by the moment. It no longer looked like a prison. It was home. Her heart swelled with pride and love, for the man and for the place she would enjoy helping him restore—now that she knew it wasn't a rival for Quint's affections.

"Hannah."

Quint's voice was deep and husky. She looked up to find his green eyes gazing darkly down at her. "Do you think you can find a gentle air current, little pilot?" he asked. "One we can hover safely in, say for an hour or so?"

A foretaste of pleasure twisted down through Hannah as she nodded and watched Quint's head bend to hers. Her lips parted softly as his mouth closed over hers with gentle pressure, and she arched against him as his hands slid around to cup her buttocks and pull her closer. She felt his desire as strongly as she felt her own and opened her mouth wider to admit his probing tongue.

Hannah was breathless and weak when the kiss ended, her body glowing with combined passion and emotion. She felt as if the world were swirling around and around, then remembered where they were.

"Quint," she gasped. "The balloon. If we're not careful we'll be swept away again."

Quint lifted his head. His lips were twisted into the lopsided grin that always brought a smile to Hannah's lips, and his eyes gazed into hers with the hunger that had the power to turn her warm and weak. "I've already been swept away, my dear," he said. "And I don't expect to ever truly have my feet on the ground again."